Praise for *The Summer We Lost Her*

"How much stress can a marriage take? Tish Cohen answers this question with skill and artistry, capturing subtle shifts in mood and feeling as she escalates the pressure on her characters. They're forced to face their own foibles and weaknesses as well as each other's as they confront the mystery at the heart of this story."
—CHRISTINA BAKER KLINE, #1 *New York Times*-bestselling author of *Orphan Train*

"Cohen writes with command of a strained marriage facing unfathomable challenge, knowing precisely when to reveal and when to withhold. . . . Impossible to put down."
—CATHY MARIE BUCHANAN, *New York Times*-bestselling author of *The Painted Girls*

"Dazzlingly unfolds the complexities of a fracturing marriage, the secrets we build our dreams on, and the fierce yearning to be someone other than who we really are. Compassionate, startling, and so full of life, the pages breathe."
—CAROLINE LEAVITT, *New York Times*-bestselling author of *Pictures of You*

"A compelling and complex portrait of a marriage and regret. Cohen spins a moving story with a high-stakes plot that won't let you go until you know the family's fate."
—HEIDI W. DURROW, *New York Times*-bestselling author of *The Girl Who Fell from the Sky*

The Summer We Lost Her

The Summer We Lost Her

A Novel

Tish Cohen

HARPER
PERENNIAL

First published under the title *Little Green* by
HarperCollins Publishers Ltd in an original trade paperback edition: 2018
This Harper Perennial trade paperback edition: 2019

HarperCollins books may be purchased for educational, business,
or sales promotional use through our Special Markets Department.

HarperCollins Publishers Ltd
Bay Adelaide Centre, East Tower
22 Adelaide Street West, 41st Floor
Toronto, Ontario, Canada
M5H 4E3

www.harpercollins.ca

Library and Archives Canada Cataloguing in Publication
information is available upon request.

ISBN 978-1-4434-1086-1

Printed and bound in the United States
LSC/H 9 8 7 6 5 4 3

For Lucas and Max

I wondered if that was how forgiveness budded;
not with the fanfare of epiphany, but with pain gathering
its things, packing up, and slipping away unannounced
in the middle of the night.
—KHALED HOSSEINI, *THE KITE RUNNER*

New Jersey

....

2006

I t was one of those things that never should have happened—the kind you turn over, splay open with pins, and examine at intervals for the rest of your life because it will never, ever cease to matter. Any little interruption could have changed the timing: a slice of bread in the toaster too long, a stalled van on the 287, a song on the radio you just had to hear to the end.

Elise Sorenson stepped outside to a frosty October morning. The frenzied weekday choreography of grave-faced commuters marching to the train and parents stuffing schoolchildren turtled by backpacks into SUVs had finally given way to quiet. The odd yellow leaf spiraled softly earthward. She could see her breath as she climbed into the car.

No riding in the third trimester had been her husband's only request. Her obstetrician's advice was straightforward: any sport you are already proficient at is safe to continue, especially at Elise's level of experience. Dressage riders competed at the Olympics while pregnant, for God's sake. The doctor had left it up to Elise to determine when to stop, and when she reached twenty-eight weeks—her belly the size of a domed screen that keeps flies off a picnic ham—it felt right to stay on the ground.

Anyway, her horse was young. It wasn't a bad idea to have her coach train him for a few months.

It had been three weeks since she'd stopped riding, and having nowhere to go every morning still felt strange. Lonely. You couldn't spend five days a week debating cloth diapers versus disposables. More often than not, habit drew her back to the stable. The place was more than just a barn for Elise; it had been her home for the last part of high school.

She arrived that day to find Ronnie Goodrich schooling her horse in the arena and slipped behind the low, dust-covered wall of the viewing area to watch. Steam puffed from the animal's nostrils as he cantered around the far end. The only sound was the powdery thud of hooves and the familiar waxy squeak of good saddle leather.

It was still pretty outside. The arena doors and windows were flung open to the quivering riot of scarlet, mulberry, and gold in the woods beyond. Another month or two and the place would be sealed up tight, heaters on the ceiling glowing like embers.

A somersault in her abdomen and Elise's hand instinctively went to her stomach. This baby was an acrobat. Over three pounds now, a recent ultrasound showed. And already sucking its thumb. *Her* thumb. The baby's position had finally allowed for a peek.

Soon Ronnie's working students filed in—three moon-eyed, flat-bellied girls who floated along the barn aisles like cult follow-ers, armfuls of freshly laundered saddle pads and flakes of sweet hay offered up in exchange for lessons and board from the great man. Elise had done the same at their age. Lara, Amy, and Kirsten. Amy waved excitedly, gestured toward Elise's stomach, whispered, "So cute!"

Too soon, the ride was over. Elise wasn't ready to leave this haven yet, she thought, as she stepped into the soft give of the arena footing. Indie hadn't had a thorough brushing in days. His hooves needed polishing. Besides that, she'd give his silver bit and the fit-tings on his bridle a good scrub with a toothbrush. Lanolin balm over the stirrup leathers with a damp sponge, reach farther under the saddle flaps than usual.

As Ronnie loosened the girth, he raved about the horse's unusual combination of enthusiasm and absolute calm. The animal was kinder and more tranquil than most humans. As if embarrassed, Indie gently tugged on Elise's sweater with his lips. It made the students laugh. Swoon, even—teenage girls are always horse-sick. Elise had started to lead the gelding back to the barn when Amy asked if anyone had taken a photo of Elise atop her horse the day she'd stopped riding.

"Seriously, how darling would that be with your baby bump?"

Very, was the squealed consensus.

Still, Elise hesitated. But Indie was so gentle and trustworthy, Ronnie's preschool-age nieces and nephews had been led around the arena on his back. Ronnie had given a rider with autism from Colorado a lesson on the horse that summer. He was, as they say, bomb-proof. Besides, it would be just for a second.

Kirsten held the reins while Elise stepped up onto the mounting block and, with some difficulty balancing, swung her leg over the saddle.

The little gray dog came out of nowhere.

CHAPTER 1

Greenville, North Carolina

....

June 2015

Even with the flight's fifteen-minute delay and the half-hour drive from Newark to Montclair, she'd still make it to the school on time, Elise thought as she tightened her seat belt and forced herself to slow down and breathe. She checked her watch—1:15 p.m. There wasn't a lot of wiggle room.

A striking woman with flippy black hair and a breezy linen shirt over white jeans paused in the aisle, her destination clearly the window seat. "Sorry. That's me over there."

Elise shifted to allow her seatmate to pass in a moneyed jingle of bracelets and the faintest waft of perfume. Once the scent dissipated, Elise realized that, in the confined space of the 747, in her breeches and sweatshirt, she smelled vaguely organic. Bestial, even, covered as she was in sweat, sunscreen, and show-ring silt.

After three weeks in North Carolina and, ten weeks prior to that, three months in Florida, Elise Sorenson was finally on her way home. She'd been at the Tryon horse show in Mill Spring that morning with a very late test time—9:45—for a woman who needed to be in another state by afternoon. After her ride, without taking the time to change, she raced back to the house she'd shared with six other international riders, most of whom she didn't know; one of whom (the one who did jump squats after midnight and, she was nearly certain, helped himself to her protein powder) she wished she'd never met; and all of whom were fighting for the same thing: better scores than they'd earned in Florida so they could be long-listed for the U.S. equestrian team in Rio next year.

She'd thrown her bags into the back of her coach's rented Land Rover, left Ronnie to accompany the horses back to Newark, cleared security in record time considering it was the first real weekend of the summer, and made it, breathless and glowing with anticipation, to seat 19C.

She checked her watch again. 1:25. *I'll be there*, she'd promised her daughter last night on the phone.

Thumps came from beneath the floor as luggage was heaved into the belly of the plane. Then the breathless *pong* of the flight attendant call button. She reached up to blast the overhead vent in case her seatmate noticed the *eau de cheval*, then glanced around at the other passengers. Some of them must be horse people, she thought. Anyway, she was probably being paranoid.

With a mother who worked part-time as a doctor's receptionist and a father whose John Deere salesman-of-the-year dreams never materialized, Elise Bleeker had grown up in a depressed neighborhood. It lay along the western border of Lower Vailsburg in Newark, New Jersey, and was not-so-lovingly dubbed "the Coop" because it wasn't uncommon for people to keep a backyard chicken or two. The Trumbulls, who lived directly behind the Bleekers, kept hens in a converted shed along the property line. On a hot day, the caustic smell of excrement drifted through Elise's window, permeating every soft surface. You couldn't get it out of your nose. She was certain it attached itself to the clothes her mother hung out to dry. It might have even clung to her hair. Her suspicions were confirmed on the bus one day when a young boy held his nose and told his father something stunk. Elise slipped off at the next stop. That shame never fully leaves a person.

Now, movement beside her caught Elise's attention. With every click of an overhead bin being pushed shut and every thump of a passenger rushing past, Elise's seatmate braced for impact. The woman pulled the safety card from the pouch at her knees and stared at it, hands shaking.

Elise leaned close. "If it helps at all, I'm on my way to a very important event back in Montclair, something I—one hundred per-cent—must attend. And if I arrive safely, you arrive safely."

The woman's fingers went to her necklace; she was clearly embarrassed. "Ridiculous to be such a baby. I'm forty-five years old."

"Nothing ridiculous about being afraid of something and going ahead and doing it." Elise realized her paddock boots were smeared with barn dirt and tucked them beneath her seat. "Maybe more ridiculous to board a plane covered in mud."

"You're Elise Sorenson. You can be forgiven."

Elise searched her memory. Was this someone she was sup-posed to know?

"I'm not a stalker." The woman held out a manicured hand for Elise to shake. "Laurel Sabados. Getting my girls to and from barns and horse shows and tack shops has been my full-time job since they were old enough to talk. My eldest, Jessa, had a photo of you on her corkboard. From *Dressage Today* magazine, I think?" When Elise didn't correct her, Laurel continued. "You were her idol."

Were.

Admittedly, Elise had taken a risk that morning. Dressage is all white gloves and tails, top hat and hair twisted into a netted bun. The one event set to music, the Grand Prix Freestyle, is typically done to Bach, or Gershwin, or "A New Argentina" from *Evita*, per-haps. But Tamara Berlo-Chang had just scored 73.39. Elise needed to make a statement and switched her music to something decidedly more edgy at the last minute: Lil' Kim singing an expletive-spackled song called "Lighters Up." The judges were in such a fluster, they'd held off scoring. "Sounds like you saw my test."

"I loved it." Laurel paused, then added, "I don't care what anyone said."

Wait. "What did they say?"

"Oh, you know how people are." Laurel raised the window shade with the tip of a finger, peering at the ground traffic, then snapped it all the way down. "Doesn't bear repeating."

"Don't tell me. Tamara Berlo-Chang is your daughter's new idol?" Elise sighed nervously. "Deservedly, without a doubt."

"No. You remained her heroine to the end. Jessa died last year."

Elise's stomach dropped. For all the guilt she lived with, things could have turned out far, far worse. "Oh . . . god. I'm so sorry."

"Drunk driver—another teenager, actually. Home from Pepperdine for the summer. Out there on a baseball scholarship." Laurel held a deep, bolstering breath. "He lived. Jessa didn't."

"God." Elise sat with the weight of this woman's tragedy. "That's . . . I don't know what to say. How on earth do you go forward?"

Laurel pulled a folded tissue from her sleeve cuff and refolded it. "Minute by minute."

"And the driver?"

"He's in prison. Two young lives destroyed."

A passenger leaned over Elise to stuff his bag into the overhead bin with enough force that it rocked her seat. His tie swung into her space and she leaned away.

"I've wondered many times since whether I am supposed to forgive him," Laurel said.

"And do you?"

"Jessa deserved more." Her eyes searched the chair back in front of her for answers that weren't there. Then Laurel made a deliberate shift in body language: she pushed her fists into her lap, fixed her gaze on Elise, and smiled through eyes now tinged with pink. The moment had passed. "Enough about my life. What takes you to New Jersey on such an important mission that you're going to keep the plane up in the air for it?"

It was like coming out of a darkened movie theater, surprised anything exists beyond the story you were engrossed in. Elise blinked hard. "Gracie, my eight-year-old, is in her first play tonight."

"How lovely."

"I've been home less than three months total this year. This will be my longest stretch back with her and my husband. So it's a bit of a reunion."

For a Grand Prix dressage rider with Olympic dreams who lived in the snow-covered tundra that was the northeastern United States, it simply was what it was. Elise shipped down to Wellington, Florida, in late December with her Hanoverian gelding, which meant the family spent many Christmases beneath palm trees. She flew home for family time as her competition and training schedule allowed, and Matt and Gracie drove down for the odd long weekend. This season, however, Elise's scores had been all over the place— concerning with Rio only one year away: the 2016 games were the reason they'd bought Indie all those years ago. And for Tokyo in 2020, Indie would be nineteen. There was no way to know if the horse would be up to it. Maybe with the sale of Matt's family cabin there would be money to buy a youngster, but to have another horse ready? Possible, but only if everything went smoothly.

Once the shows in Florida ended, after a couple of well-earned months at home, she and Ronnie had trekked down to North Carolina. Trouble was, her scores there were up and down as well. It had gotten to the point where, Elise could tell, Matt was afraid to ask during their bedtime phone calls. He asked about the weather. Her workout schedule. How she slept.

All the money Elise had spent this past season, all the time away, may have been for nothing.

"Tough on a family, this lifestyle, I suppose," said Laurel. "Lots of Skyping."

"Every day, if we can. And Matt is a rock. But, believe me, I face a whole lot of judgment from the moms in the schoolyard."

Laurel *tsked*. "The choices mothers make are so under the microscope, aren't they?"

After the accident, Elise didn't allow herself to ride again for nearly three years. It took Matt and Ronnie sitting her down for an intervention at the Tiny Rhino Café in town to get her back on a horse. "Sometimes deservedly."

"And sometimes not."

Flight attendants and stray passengers busied themselves with overhead compartments and seat belts that needed fastening.

"It's not the traditional way to parent, but you have to believe your child will learn by example, right? How to really go for it," Elise said.

As for her own drive, she certainly hadn't learned from example. While her father, Warren, with his twinkling green eyes and his politician's smile, had always taught her she could accomplish whatever she set her mind to, his own methods were sorely lacking. "What you have to do is believe, princess," he used to say. "Because if you don't believe, they don't believe." And there her large-framed mother, Rosamunde, would sit beside him, ever hopeful that the big-talking man who'd swept into her life to woo her away from finishing her college degree had been the right choice.

Elise had had many a long, lonely flight to think about what drove her to fight this hard. It didn't come from Warren's encouragement at all. Her fire came much later, from the shock of his betrayal—an act that cost her mother her life. But Elise couldn't think about that now. Sorrow was an indulgence she didn't have time for.

Laurel was staring at her. "You're one of the most talented riders in the country, Elise. Being traditional is never really going to be an option. Nor should it be."

Elise glanced down at the Summerhill Prep program in her lap. *The Blossom King* was the end-of-school-year play and Gracie had been selected to draw the cover illustration: a frowning cherry tree next to a vain monarch. He had in his possession three things:

the desire for a robe made of petals, a newly sharpened axe, and a henchman willing to use it. What he didn't see was the morality lesson charging at him like an invisible freight train.

The curtain would go up at five. Hopefully, Matt would score two front-row-center seats so their daughter could feel her parents' adoration from the stage, where she was to play a baby koala waiting for a breakfast of ripe cherries. That the freckle-faced joey had been born in Branch Brook Park, New Jersey, hadn't struck the drama teacher as remotely improbable. Nor had it worried her that said marsupial insisted upon wearing a tiara. It was, after all, as Gracie had pointed out the previous evening on the phone, in the froggy voice that had earned her the nickname "Little Green," her stage debut.

Awkward for Elise's reunion with her husband to happen in front of every parent and teacher in the school, but after a self-conscious embrace, Matt would pull her hand onto his lap, fold her fingers into a ball, and cover it with his own. It was the hot little stone of their love. From this pip sprang their life together.

Two hours and five minutes, then this plane would land. Another fifty minutes or so, if traffic was kind to her, and she'd be with her family. It was always a bit of a strained dance when the three of them reunited. With Gracie because she'd have forgotten that Elise had any authority, and with Matt . . . well, with Matt because he'd been running the show for an extended period and his wife's return always tilted the parenting balance.

First thing in the morning they'd bundle into the car and drive to Matt's old family cabin in Lake Placid. The thought of it—four and a half hours together in the same vehicle—was nothing short of heaven. Elise had popped into Target the night before to stock up on coloring books and markers, juice boxes, and a mini Rubik's Cube for the road, and crammed it all into her carry-on bag. Matt and Elise would have chocolate croissants and steaming dark roast coffee from the little French bakery in Montclair.

Her phone lit up. Matt. The sound of paper shuffling, then the deep growl of his voice. "I smell jet fuel and oversalted cashews."

She tucked her chin into the phone. "I smell the frustration of clients who don't pay on time and mounting desperation to have your wife in your arms."

"Got me on both."

"We're late to take off." The *pong* of another call button. "Should be any minute, though."

"Meet me inside the school, then. I'll be the devastatingly sexy man, front-row center, who's had way too many cold showers lately."

"Tell Lil' G I can't wait to squish her to bits."

"Aaand we'll give the cheeseburgers and shakes a pass."

"You're so not funny. Like, you shouldn't even try."

"Love you madly, E."

In their early months of dating, he'd sent her roses on her birthday, ordering them over the phone. The florist had transcribed "I love you madly" as "I love you badly." It had become a running joke. "Love you badly," she said now before hanging up.

Beside her, Laurel had pulled out a library book and settled in to read.

"Excuse me, Ms. Sorenson?" A tap on her shoulder. The flight attendant who'd welcomed them while boarding, a young woman with a silky ponytail, tidy tortoiseshell glasses, and plum-glossed lips. "We've just had a call in the cockpit. You're wanted over on Equine Air. The pilots have had to delay takeoff for a horse that's become upset."

No. No, no, no. Elise leaned forward. "*My* horse?"

"He won't load, according to the transport team."

"He has a companion animal, a donkey. He'll follow Poppins."

"Apparently, the donkey's been led on and off several times, but the horse won't budge."

Indie had had a bad flight when Ronnie brought him over from Germany as a four-year-old in the spring of 2005. Bad weather tossed the 737 like a leaf for hours, and a stallion on the plane panicked, tried to make a break for it halfway over the Atlantic. The vet on board successfully sedated him, but not before Indie learned that travel is a menacing, six-headed beast to be avoided at any cost. It was nearly six months before he would willingly board a trailer in New Jersey, and he only did so with the help of a donkey Elise bought for $250 on their honeymoon that September after watching the overburdened jenny being forced to carry bulging tourists with bulging luggage up a six-hundred-foot cliff in the searing heat in Santorini.

The lop-eared donkey had the look of a beloved teddy bear that had been through the wash too many times. She immediately took on the horse, nearly twice her size, as a child she'd been hired to mind, earning herself the name Poppins. She mollycoddled the gelding, protecting him from rambunctious horses in the paddocks and always allowing him the last mouthful of hay. Like a good governess, Poppins taught Indie how to load by trotting up the ramp of the trailer and back. *See how simple? You can do it!*

Clearly, a plane was a different experience.

"They asked for your permission to take the horse to the cargo area until alternative arrangements are made."

"The cargo area . . . with the donkey?"

"I don't think so. The donkey would continue to Newark."

The amount of money Matt and Elise had spent to purchase such a talented horse was astronomical and, to them, the investment of a lifetime: $250,000. They'd used Matt's inheritance from his parents, and then some, and later took on a massive mortgage to buy the house in Montclair before Gracie came along. Indie was a coddled, sensitive horse trained to CDI—Concours de Dressage International—the level required for Olympic consideration. He had that magic combination of exquisite cadence and big, bouncy movements, without a flighty temperament. To leave him with airport ground crew in a clanging, banging, overheated cargo bay would be irresponsible and cruel. And dangerous. If he injured himself trying to escape, or, god forbid, colicked, the results could be tragic. Horses are herd animals. You don't leave one alone in a strange place.

Not to mention, a single stall on Equine Air ran $5,000. Matt and Elise didn't have anywhere near that kind of cash to pay for another flight, whenever that would be. This wasn't exactly American Airlines. The only reason Indie was traveling with thirteen other dressage horses, hunter jumpers, and polo ponies—and one hee-hawing au pair—was that Ronnie had sold his treasured Wunderkind, the now retired Dutch Warmblood he'd won a bronze medal with at the 2012 games in London, to a wealthy beginner looking for a schoolmaster, leaving an empty double stall on the plane.

"Is it possible I could run over there and get back before take-off?" Elise asked the flight attendant.

"Do you have checked luggage?"

She'd hauled her luggage onto the horse trailer earlier. If she had checked her bags onto the flight, it might have bought her some time—at least long enough for the baggage to be removed by ground crew in case Elise didn't make it back. In a post-9/11 world, airlines were rightly squeamish about bags left behind by passengers who deplane. "No."

"Then the pilot can't wait. I recommend you remain in your seat. The horse will be stowed securely. It's very safe—"

Stowed. "Like a set of golf clubs."

"I know it's not ideal." The flight attendant frowned in understanding, but looked up toward the galley, where one of her colleagues was gesturing for her to hurry. She stepped back. "But the staff in the cargo area are terrific with animals. Arrangements for another flight will be made for the horse. And you can be in direct contact with the staff when we land."

The thought of her daughter stepping out onto that stage, looking out to see an empty seat beside her father, turquoise crutches hidden behind the curtain until she had no choice but to pull them out . . . Elise couldn't breathe from the agony. It was what had kept her going these last three weeks—playing that moment of Gracie coming on stage through her mind on a never-ending loop. She'd planned (to hell with what the other parents thought) to stand up and cheer. Blow two-handed kisses to Gracie from the audience and embarrass her funny, freckled, ribbit-voiced girl with the enormity of her love.

And Matt. Sweet, patient, kind, long-suffering-in-*so*-much-silence Matt.

But she couldn't take such a chance with Indie. She couldn't risk the animal's life because he was left behind like a vintage Studebaker awaiting shipment to a faraway collector.

There was no other choice. Elise unbuckled, forced her body out of the seat. After wishing Laurel a beautiful, smooth trip, Elise gathered her bags from the overhead bin, followed the trip attendant up the aisle, and stepped off the aircraft that would have taken her to the only place in the world she wanted to be.

CHAPTER 2

New Jersey

....

Matt prickled with impatience to get out of the suburbs and up to the lake, groaning and striking his palm against the steering wheel of his old BMW when traffic on the Watchung overpass came to another exasperating halt, red tail-lights blurred by rain. Six thirty on a Friday night was, of course, a terrible time to head north. A four-and-a-half-hour road trip could turn into six hours, bumper-to-bumper. They'd meant to set out Saturday morning, all three of them. A family. Then Elise didn't turn up for the play. And when Matt and Gracie returned to the house, they saw four of Gracie's classmates file up the neighbor girl's front steps for a sleepover Gracie wasn't invited to but was able to observe through the kitchen window. The car had already been packed for the morning. What else was a father to do but insist they pile in and hit the road?

"Dad," Gracie asked from the back seat. "What's a motherless 'tard?"

Matt Sorenson spun around to look at her. Funducational—Summerhill Prep School's after-school care program, which Gracie called Stunneducational—had been canceled that afternoon, so

Matt had left work early to bring his daughter home and get her ready, then drop her off for dress rehearsal looking reasonably well-cared-for.

Now, after drama feigned and real, after a pre-road trip spin through McDonald's drive-through for a burger, she had ketchup on her cheek, her hair was a knotted mess, she wore a tiara tipped at an angle that looked more drunken than darling, and I MAY BE WRONG BUT I DOUBT IT was markered along her forearm in fine-tipped purple. From the moment Matt had found her backstage after the final curtain, her expression had been that of a recently exiled royal: exalted and misanthropic, wearied and replete.

The life of an actress.

He'd been trying, without much luck, to settle his outrage. Elise had been on the plane. *On the plane*. Who, after having been away so much of the year, when headed home for their only child's first stage performance, all buckled up on a flight set to take off in minutes—no high winds or ranting passenger or malfunctioning electrical system to justify a big delay—gets off the flight?

The text came in when he'd still been at the office. Actually, typing his out-of-office reply, as they'd be in Lake Placid for two weeks. The reason? They had to sell the cabin his grandfather had built in 1947. The reason for that?

Dressage.

Having to tell Gracie her mother couldn't make the play was, of course, devastating. Matt almost couldn't bear her disappointment. That he would be there was no consolation whatsoever. He was the parent she could count on. He was the don't-forget-your-lunch guy. The dispenser of the daily vitamin. The remover of grape juice stains. It made him dispensable, because that's how kids think. Harkens way back to Romeo and Juliet. You want most what you can't have. And too many days of the year, Gracie couldn't have her mother.

Matt would have done anything to get Elise to the school in time. He'd have missed the play himself. Flown to Greenville and set up a sleeping bag right there in the cargo bay. He'd have sung lullabies, fed the horse carrots he'd julienned to prevent choking, pressed his lips to the gelding's hairy forehead to check for fever. He was good at this stuff. It had been such a perfect day until then, could he not make this one simple thing happen? Surely a father's will, *this* father's will, had that much force.

"Where did you hear that?" he asked his daughter.

"Hear what?"

"That 'motherless . . . ' I'm not going to repeat it."

Gracie picked up the remains of her burger from the seat beside her and used it to point out the drizzled window. "Look."

A van had squeezed up onto the shoulder beside them. The hopeful female driver waved and pointed at the freeway as if her need to get moving was greater than his. She mouthed, "Please."

No way—he'd fought hard to get this close to the freeway proper. He had only three car-lengths to go. At this point, Matt felt his on-ramp position *defined* him. He adjusted the mirror to look into the back seat. "You didn't answer me."

"From Petra. During intermission."

"Who was she talking about?"

"Duh." Her gray eyes still had a Gerber baby–like purity.

"Petra. She's the understudy?"

An emphatic nod.

"Yeah . . . the understudy is always jealous of the lead. Everyone knows that."

"She knew my lines so good."

"'Well.' It's 'so well.'"

Gracie's feet thumped against the seat Elise should have been sitting in. "You didn't make me practice."

Matt raked his fingers through once-black curls that were now more a tarnished silver. Pewter, at best. "I did *so* make you practice."

A deep sigh. "You needed to yell it."

....

The marriage was at its breaking point. There, he'd said it. Or at least thought it. All this living apart, Matt playing single father most of every winter . . . He understood Elise's goals. He wasn't a Neanderthal. Her passion for horses, for riding, for her sport, was the sexiest thing about her. The look on her face when atop Indie, even just to school him in Ronnie's arena, was almost indescribable. Fire and water. Earth and air. Absolute peace and furious determination. From the start, Elise had been one of those people who made you feel like reaching farther. Like anything was possible. She wasn't like anyone. She wasn't normal.

Trouble was, after—what?—twelve years of living this way, normal wasn't looking like such a bad gig. Was it so wrong at fifty to think it might be time to re-evaluate? He'd been flipping through *Sports Illustrated* that week on the train and had stopped on a story about a gymnast from Uzbekistan who, at forty, was shooting for Rio in 2016. Think about it—the average age of a gymnast on the U.S. team in 2012 was sixteen. Nadia Comăneci won a handful of golds at fourteen, retired at nineteen. This forty-year-old wasn't just considered unusual to shoot for Rio, she was being touted as a miracle.

As the train pulled into Penn Station and people stuffed paperbacks and iPads into briefcases, tucked newspapers beneath elbows, moved crisply to the doors, Matt didn't budge. Was it terrible to be jealous of this Oksana Chusovitina's lucky bastard of a husband because his wife would be washed up after Rio?

At this point, it didn't look like Elise was even going to get there. Her scores had zigzagged this year, and for what? A seriously disappointed daughter and the K2-sized mountain of debt that comes from any of the horse sports. Bonus: every year the horse aged beyond his early teens, he dropped in value. Matt thought about the cost of a gymnastics leotard, even throwing in a hair ribbon. Hell, make it a hair ribbon made of platinum and rose-gold threads delicately braided and tasseled with diamonds and the sperm of one of those Tibetan mastiffs they inject with lion's blood in China. It still didn't come close to the expense of buying, then supporting a decade of boarding, feeding, and training a fancy horse from Germany.

Tonight was the last straw—wait, strike that. Straw is for horses that don't cost as much as a down payment on a house. It was the last fluffy cedar shaving.

One of their neighbors in Montclair, Jason Hyndeman, a hedge-fund manager with, Gracie once joyfully pointed out, the junkiest-looking actual hedge on the block, had offered this advice to Matt on the sidewalk: "Follow the three Fs of investment. Never buy anything that flies, floats, or fucks."

Elise's horse might as well have wings and a rudder.

In his rear-view mirror, Matt saw that Gracie had dozens of tiny stuffed animals pushed down into the seat crack so only their heads were showing. "What's with all the animals?"

"I'm bringing them with me. To teach them things."

"Like what?"

"Like they have to behave. Each one will get a hug, but only if they wait. Because there's a rule."

"What rule?"

"They could get stepped on by me because they're so small. Or they could get hugged. They just have to wait and see."

Jesus. Another reason they had to normalize life. Elise's absence was starting to wear on Gracie as much as it was on him.

The woman in the van waved frantically, encroaching on Matt's lane now. Her hair was coiled atop her head, and with her long neck and drapey sweater, she looked like a ballerina fresh from the barre. He could feel his resolve waning. Who was he kidding? He wasn't proud of it, but he'd never been able to resist an even remotely attractive woman.

There was a permanent sense of inferiority bestowed upon a male who had to grow into his looks. Matt had been born with an odd face: chin too small for his pale, wide-set eyes and arched brows that winged outward at the apex, giving him a look that was vaguely evil, or Vulcan. His classmates would describe him as like-able enough, but unpredictable. As if he might flick a match into the school Dumpster or drown a cat at any minute. With eyes like that, you kept your distance.

It didn't help any that his grandfather—who raised him after his parents died—had been born handsome and assumed Matt attracted girls just as he had. Nate, who'd divided their time between a Manhattan apartment when school was in and the cabin Matt was about to unload when it wasn't, had gotten it into his head that his grandson was a ladies' man.

"Whatever you do, don't get her pregnant," Nate would say with a wink, whether Matt was headed out to fill a tin can with worms in the Adirondacks or pop down to the lobby to check for mail in the city. In his elementary school years, the joke had mystified Matt. But later, once the urges of puberty hit and an aggressive growth spurt left his body gangly and his face gaunt, Nate's words shone an embarrassing spotlight on Matt's reality: he was failing at what mattered most—the possibility of one day having sex. And there was little certainty things would ever change.

Miraculously, when his bones stopped aching from long winter nights spent growing, Matt began to put on weight. His body muscled up. His face filled out. He still looked faintly dangerous, but in a way that was less indictable and more, as the Lake Placid girl who took his virginity would breathlessly whisper, "intoxi-cating." The females at Stuyvesant had long since written him off—in high school, you remain who you've always been—but girls at parties, girls up at the lake, girls at Tower Records began to take notice. Matt's social life changed in what seemed like an instant.

Still, that kind of insecurity, coupled with the very real worry that you might remain a virgin forever, never quite leaves a man.

Matt slowed to allow the ballerina in the van to slip in front of him.

Gracie's foot bounced against the back of the passenger seat. "Petra said her mother wouldn't have missed the play for anything in the world."

"The flights out of Greenville were grounded from the rain." Matt couldn't tell his daughter the truth—that her mother had chosen to deplane. "What was Mom going to do? Walk?"

"I know. She can't control the weather." Gracie swiped ketchup off her freckled cheek with a finger and licked it off. "She's not God."

"So, what did you say to Petra?"

His daughter turned to the window, her elfin face so like Elise's it made his heart swell. The girl reached out to run a finger across the fog on the glass. "That her mom's a husbandless ho-bag."

"Gracie!"

"What?"

"You weren't raised to talk like that." Even if it was kind of true.

"All kids talk like that. It's not against the law."

"You don't have to break the law to be wrong. What we say and do in this world matters."

Traffic inched forward, exhaust puffing between vehicles like dragon's breath. These long separations from her mother were damaging Gracie at a core level.

"Can I call Mom?"

Matt passed his phone into the back seat. "She may not have landed yet."

"How long are we going to stay at the cabin?" Gracie asked as she scrolled through Matt's phone for her mother's number.

"Long enough to get it ready to sell. About two weeks."

"I never get to go there since Great-Grandpa died."

Matt sighed. They were in danger of losing their home in Montclair. The cost of Elise's horse and training had overtaken their ability to keep up. They had no way to pay the first installment of school fees for September, and even with Matt's health-care plan at work, there were extra costs for Gracie's physiotherapy and specialists. And, since Nate had died two years back, maintaining seventy acres in Lake Placid, much of it waterfront, had brought enormous expenses they weren't prepared for. There were staggering tax, insurance, and security payments. Every time a branch fell across a power line or a squirrel tripped the alarm, Matt got a phone call. The dock was sagging into the water, and the septic system needed to be replaced.

Besides, that afternoon had changed Matt's own game plan. He'd *finally* been offered a partnership with his law firm. Nothing had come easy to Matt. He'd had to take the bar exam three times before passing. He'd been a sole practitioner like his father and grandfather but, unlike them, he'd struggled to bring in clients. He'd joined Barrans, Opel, and Gopnick as an associate eleven years back, but with Elise's winters in Florida, once Gracie came along, he'd been unable to throw down the hours of the other lawyers.

As he was rushing out to get Gracie to her play, Lyndon Barrans had called Matt into his office, with its tufted, butterscotch leather sofa and chairs, and crystal decanters of whisky tucked between legal books, poured each of them a finger of Balvenie DoubleWood, and made the offer. At age fifty, Matt was finally being invited to become a permanent part of the team. A hugely gratifying and long-overdue moment. The investment would be heavy, $150,000, but he'd be able to participate in profits. The sale of the cabin would provide the money. But Barrans made it very clear: Matt would have to step up his billable hours in a big way. Which meant he could no longer be both mother and father.

Elise had to get real. Plus, Matt wanted another baby. It was never his intention to have just one. He'd grown up an only child. He didn't wish it on Gracie.

"We'll be able to travel and do lots of fun things. You'll see."

With the phone on speaker, they both listened to two rings and then Elise's message clicking on. "Hey, it's Elise. Do it at the beep." Gracie ended the call.

"Probably still in the air."

Gracie slid the phone onto the center console. "Are you going to miss the cabin, Dad?"

He'd spent every childhood summer and holiday at the cabin; the two generations before him had lived there year-round and, once Matt was out of school, Nate had moved back there full-time. All those memories of rock and moss and towering evergreens, lazy roads edged with sand, and cold lake water so deep and dark you couldn't see your feet. His mother's Thanksgiving turkeys, slow-cooked in the Aga range. His father's upside-down fires made of birch logs. Christmases that twinkled with colored lights and snow falling like sifted sugar. And, always, one of Nate's German shepherds lying in front of the fire.

"Dad?"

The rain had softened to a misty drizzle. Traffic moved and at last they pulled onto the freeway. Matt inched his way over to the fast lane and settled in for the long drive north. It would take about two weeks to spiff the place up, get it listed. And that would be that. Someone would buy it and, hopefully, love it the way he had.

That part of his life would be over. Done. Kaput.

"Only a little." Two lies in one day. Terrific. "But the Sorenson family is ready for a new chapter."

Satisfied, Gracie pulled on her headphones, trapping a fall of hair against her face, and directed her attention out the window. She pulled her shirt collar to her chin to hide that she was sucking her thumb—a habit Elise had worked hard, and thus far failed, to break.

Matt waved a hand at the back seat to get her attention. "Hey, Little Green?"

With a wet thumb, she twisted the headphones away from one ear.

"Mom's coming for sure. You'll see her tomorrow."

Headphones slid back into place. Her gaze settled once again on the window. A few moments later, the thumb found its place again.

It was time. He was going to tell his ambitious, to-the-moon-and-back wife that he and Gracie needed her at home.

....

CHAPTER 3

The pilots of Equine Air—dubbed Air Horse One by the horsey set—minimize positive or negative g-force with extraordinarily gradual takeoffs and landings. When an animal feels weightless, it may fight to find the floor, and too much movement can cause a million-dollar horse to slip and fall. As a result, pilots also take great care to avoid even moderately unstable air.

Elise hadn't made it back to her (comparatively luxurious) flight full of humans. She'd had to make the trip beside Ronnie in the tiny, bare-bones human compartment of Air Horse One.

But all that really mattered was that she'd missed her daughter's play.

"I don't think you understand," Elise said over the pointed hiss of the engines as the aircraft finally made its descent into Newark. A low-pressure system from the upper Great Lakes had delayed takeoff until nearly five p.m., and rain in Newark had them circle overhead for nearly fifty minutes. Elise had tried to call Matt before takeoff but he hadn't picked up, likely in the audience with his phone on silent. They'd be halfway to the cabin by now, which meant she'd

25

have to drive up alone. "He left *without* me. I understand he's upset, but to just pack her in the car tonight and head north?"

"Exactly why I never got married." Ronnie's bulk was no match for the tiny seats, and he leaned against the wall, where a window would have been on a regular plane. The passenger area of Equine Air had no such luxury. It comprised twelve seats filled by vets, grooms, owners, and assistants, all partitioned off at the back of the plane—essentially a gutted, windowless Boeing 727 lined with rubber matting and cedar shavings, with moveable stall dividers. No in-flight entertainment, no in-flight meals. Not for humans, anyway.

Ronnie's silver horse trailer had been backed up to a high-sided ramp that led straight into the plane. Elise had run across the tarmac and boarded the trailer to find Indie white-eyed and dancing, tossing his nose in the air with a jangle of metal fittings and hammering of hooves, as if the ramp at his feet led directly to hell. But he calmed immediately when Elise took his sheepskin-wrapped travel halter in hand and murmured to him softly, running calming hands over his crest, along his topline, then down his legs, wrapped from the knee down in padded shipping boots. She pressed her face to his warm cheek, feeling his lashes tickle her forehead. His breathing slowed and a contented nicker rumbled from his center as he slid his velvet muzzle over her shoulder.

A clatter from above and Poppins appeared, almost rearing in excitement when she saw Elise. Finally, the fuzzy governess had backup. Long, black-tipped ears pricked, she hopped like a rabbit down the ramp, spun, and rocketed back up again. *There are hay nets on this plane! And carrots! We will travel like royalty!*

Elise took the side of Indie's woolly noseband, clucking softly, and that was that. Indie nickered and pawed the ramp before following his loved ones up and into the aircraft, where he allowed himself to be led into the double stall next to Ronnie's youngster, a bratty gray Oldenburg named Hellchild. At Indie's side, Poppins let out a long sigh of relief.

Now, the plane touched ground and roared to a stop so smoothly they might never have been in the air in the first place.

"Marriage is like a horse's anatomy. The entire setup is fucked from the start." Ronnie looked at Elise. "Excuse my French."

"You practically raised me. I'm used to your French."

"You've got this massive weight and muscular force coming down on tiny little sesamoid bones at the fetlock that can fracture with just the right pressure in just the right spot. And once that happens, it's never the same. I watched my parents go through it. A few disagreements about money, someone says something unforgivable, and the rest of their lives they're all, 'Thank you, dear' this and 'Don't you look nice tonight, darling' that. Then he goes off to sleep in the guest bedroom with a glass of bourbon and she takes up with her astrologist." Ronnie pulled out his phone and turned it on in hopes of a signal. "Anyway, let's give your husband a pass on this one. Matt's a good guy. Something about his eyes has always reminded me of your dad. I ever tell you that?"

Elise stared at him. "Sometimes it's as if you go off on these tangents just so you can give Warren a plug at the end."

"The man's paid one hell of a price for what happened."

"Can we change the subject?"

"I blame that ridiculously fancy high school they sent you to." He tried holding his phone in the air, shaking it like an Etch A Sketch. "Course, McInnis Hall was what brought you to my stable."

"Ronnie."

"Fine." He gave up on his phone and slid it back into his pocket. "At least you have your career." As the plane taxied to the cargo bay, Ronnie offered her what remained of a roll of mints. When she waved them away, he popped them all into his mouth. "Or you had one until today."

Elise winced, remembering. "That's . . . thank you. Helpful."

She did trot transitions around the outside of the ring, focused on the soft thud of Indie's footfalls in the sand, the rhythmic squeak of saddle leather, the tinkling of the bridle's curb chain.

What she'd planned to ride to was a lyric-free medley of songs from *The Sound of Music*. That was the safe choice. But it had been a bad year and she'd been unable to decide whether safe was the right move. She had a deal with the sound technician, and this moment was her last chance to make the switch to music that was decidedly more . . . brazen.

Just then, a garbled faraway voice on the loudspeaker announced, "Tamara Berlo-Chang on Mademoiselle Secretary, seventy-three point three nine."

Anything over 73 was a dream score. Elise kept her eyes straight ahead as a roar of approval rose from Tamara's camp, in the stands and in the aisle where her barn was stabled. Elise needed at least a 72 to get long-listed.

A crackle from the loudspeaker announced, "Next rider in the ring: Elise Sorenson on Independent Spirit."

She squinted up at the sound booth and held up two fingers.

Safe wasn't going to get her there.

A tidy cadenced trot took them to the center, where they stopped. Elise saluted the judges and waited for her music. Dark, thundering hip-hop filled the stadium. Indie exploded into the passage, a big, majestic trot so elevated the ground could be a trampoline.

The beat, the lyrics—the word "fuck"— polarized the crowd. Some were on their feet, cheering. Others were slack-mouthed and aghast. It wasn't until she'd saluted the judges again and started out of the ring that Elise caught a flash of Ronnie, one hand clamped over his forehead, having pushed back his Grange Road Farms cap in horror. As they exited, he fell in line beside the horse, hand on the bridle to lead them out. "What. The living hell. Was that," was all he'd said.

Now, he coughed, choking on his mouthful of mints. "If you'd run it past me beforehand, I'd have told you Elaine Ehrenworth was on the panel."

"No way could she make out the lyrics."

"I don't think I've ever seen them withhold a score before." When the coughing abated, he crumpled the wrapper. "The good news is you won't be beleaguered by parents wanting to pay you to coach their children. Or speak at any pony club events. You'll be safe from annoying sponsors who want to fund your career."

The plane came to a gentle stop and the high-pitched whine of the engines cut to silence. Muffled snorts and stomps indicated the horses were aware this part of the journey was over. A perky member of the flight crew opened the door dividing man from beast, and the grooms mobilized. The bustle of dismantling hay nets and water buckets began in seconds.

"They can't disqualify me." Elise unbuckled herself. "Can they?"

"Judges are the gods we pray to; you know that." Ronnie stood and stretched, his hands pressed against the ceiling, the letters on his ancient Rolling Stones T-shirt peeling and distorted. "They'll do their thing—which is whatever the fuck they want. And we'll do ours—suffer and survive it." With that reassuring nugget, he disappeared into the business of humans moving horses.

Elise pulled out her phone and turned it on. She needed to connect with Gracie and Matt before they entered the Adirondacks, land of the spotty cell signal. She'd already decided she couldn't wait until morning to see her family. She'd drive up that night. Shower, pack, and go. All around her, other phones started to ding and buzz to life.

She looked at her own and realized it had gone dead.

When did life get so complicated—or, more to the point—when did *she*? She used to be so relaxed and sure about her relationship. There wasn't the constant measuring of each other like there was today. You just knew in those first few years. Matt was a sole practitioner struggling to land clients and Elise was down to weekends and a few evenings in her admin job because riding was eating up more and more time. They were saving every spare cent, still hopeful that one dream client could fund the horse Elise needed. Recently, yet another horse owner had pulled her ride out from under her because he was moving or had a niece who'd decided to stop playing cello and ride.

But they were happy.

The walk-up they shared in Hoboken had hallways smelling of overcooked broccoli, windows leaking icy winter air, radiators drying the place so much they had to set out saucepans full of hot water or they'd get nosebleeds in the middle of the night. In July's humidity, nothing was dry. Not the plaster ceilings, not the dish-cloth hanging over the tap, not the Ivory bar in the soap dish. Even the remote control was greasy and slick.

They'd never bothered to buy a television—they were burst-ing with love and lust for each other, so who the hell needed one? Besides, the androgynous hetero couple in the apartment to their left was just so fascinating. The two of them in their dark jeans and matching man shirts buttoned to the chin. Their tiny glasses and power strides. Their hipster magazine, *Popeye*, written in Japanese, which forever landed in Elise and Matt's mailbox, was addressed to Jan van den Bas, and they couldn't figure out which one was Jan.

Then childbirth brought out Is-Jan and Isn't-Jan's previously well-hidden and remarkably feral sexual personas. The baby may have been sporting tiny glasses of its own—Elise and Matt were never quick enough to catch a glimpse inside the stroller (a sleek chrome and black leather contraption). The infant couldn't have been home two weeks when its parents launched into highly vocal, never-before-heard, early morning lovemaking. It became an event, one of the cornerstones of Elise and Matt's week. They took to pour-ing themselves cups of coffee, sitting on the floor on their side of the wall, and taking bets on whether Isn't-Jan or Is-Jan was in the lead. And then—after what turned out to be the last sexcapade—Matt made the mistake of cheering out loud when the sighs and groans went silent. Is-Jan and Isn't-Jan had the last word: they switched rooms and put the newborn next to Matt and Elise. It would be months before either slept a full night again.

But even with the lack of rest . . . Elise had a little potted violet plant on the windowsill in the kitchen, and a trough of pale geraniums on the fire escape. She picked up mismatched vintage chairs for their table, painted them all the same sprightly turquoise for unity. They took an art class together at MoMA and hung their utterly devoid-of-talent paintings on the walls. Matt was thirty-eight—giddy that he'd finally found love. Elise was twenty-six. Damn it, they were happy. What it was about those days—she'd analyzed it many times—was that they were even. Money hadn't factored into their lives that much yet, except that they were saving it. It was just the two of them sitting on the fire escape, eating takeout curry, and talking about their dreams, assuring each other that, together, everything was possible.

Now, the plane bobbed with horses being led down the ramp. Several whinnies from impatient animals anxious for their turn. She gathered up the sweatshirt she'd removed on the flight and the magazine that had fallen beneath her seat and started toward the front of the aircraft.

If only she could restart this day. Play the music she'd originally chosen for her program, will her flight to take off before she could get the news about Indie's refusal to board. Having to drive north by herself, get to the cabin, and tell Matt that (a) she'd officially blown the entire year and (b) she'd possibly destroyed her reputation in the sport . . . She couldn't bear to think what his reaction would be.

Ronnie appeared from the mouth of the plane to stare at her, phone in hand. His head shook from side to side as if he was trying to clear an annoying song.

"What?" she said. "The judges? What'd they say?"

A pair of polo ponies being led toward the ramp rushed the aisle and got into a tussle for the lead. Ronnie and Elise moved out of the way as, nearby, another horse kicked a stall divider in excitement. The grooms shouted, the ponies were separated, and order was restored.

Ronnie took her shoulders and searched the plane's walls and ceiling before focusing on Elise's face. His words came out slowly. "Seventy-five point nine."

"Wait. What?"

"You heard me."

She blinked stupidly. "But . . . I thought they hated—"

"You've just become a contender for Rio, kid." He pulled her into his peeling T-shirt and squeezed.

Her face mashed into his chest, she let this sink in. Over the years, she'd done all the things one did when trying to achieve the barely achievable. She'd begged the universe. She'd drawn the Olympic rings on a scrap of paper and slept with it beneath her pillow. She'd imagined getting the phone call. It had been her dream ever since her mother died. Over twenty years to get to this moment, to have her name in any way connected to the Olympics.

He kissed her forehead and pushed her away. "Go see your family. Tell them it's all been worth it. This is the news you've been waiting for."

CHAPTER 4

Lake Placid, New York

....

The black velvet slither of Highway 86 morphed into Main Street, and there they were. Matt lowered his window and drank in the heady, gnashing scent of clean air and pine that once defined his summers. He rolled slowly past the bowling alley, neon sign still flashing NORTH COUNTRY OWL. The "B" in "Bowl" had gone dark decades ago, and locals had called it "the Owl" ever since. Then the gas stations and the nostalgic alpine signs of postwar motels for urban folks who couldn't afford the rustic splendor of Lake Placid Lodge or Whiteface but still wanted to vacate sticky, airless cities. He loved that the best nod to modern times these places had going was a boast about color TV and free Wi-Fi.

He passed the skating oval and the timber-framed architectural majesty of the Olympic Center, flanked as it was by world flags hanging in the dark like sleeping bats. Then the village proper, which, ironically, sat on bustling Mirror Lake, not Lake Placid, a quarter mile to the north. The once-important post office and the old stone church on the water, the tiny white library with its Norman Rockwell front porch. Then the shops with their cheery awnings and window displays. And Starbucks, of course. The coffee chain had moved into the old video store a few years back, replaced the seedy, peeling white paint with river rock cladding.

Every hundred feet or so, wooden benches invited tourists to sit long enough to unwrap a block of fudge for a wide-eyed child. He slowed to a crawl as he passed the last bench on the strip. It was dedicated to Nate—Matt had arranged for the brass plaque himself. It seemed the least he could do to commemorate a man who had done so much for the area.

Headlights flashed from behind and Matt started to pull over to let a rusted pickup truck roar by. Before he was even halfway out of the lane, the driver—a heavily freckled girl in a plaid shirt—whooshed past, swerving dangerously close to Gracie's head, pressed against the window as she slept. He drew in a sharp breath, reminded of his parents. Reminded that everything you hold dear can disappear in a flash. Not until his heart stopped hammering did he drive on.

Lake Placid peaked early—way back in 1932, when it hosted the Winter Olympics the first time. That kind of global recognition had set the expectations of the village on a certain course. Trouble was, nothing really came next, not for decades. A local council—headed by Matt's grandfather until about ten years back—worked on bids for many Winter Games, but wasn't successful again until landing the 1980 games.

Now, often considered the venue of the last small-town Winter Olympics, it seemed to Matt that Lake Placid had settled into a place content to live in its glory days.

The car started the slow, narrow climb up Mirror Lake Drive. Past the enormous, and storied, white clapboard Interlaken Inn. Then the sprawling cottages and pines lining the winding road, until, finally, up on the left, blackened stone gates and a brown-and-ocher sign announcing SELDOM SEEN ROAD, aptly named because you don't see roads this breathtaking every day. And didn't the Lake Placid tourism folks know it—and feature it heavily in their promotions.

Densely forested, this unfurling ribbon of packed earth and gravel wasn't a road to navigate with any speed at night if you didn't know it like Matt did. There were a few open stretches where you could pick up speed, but many of the bends were so narrow you reversed if a car came from the other direction, and a few of the homes sat so tight to the road you could almost reach an arm out the window and touch them. Seldom Seen boasted a pleasing lakeside mix of humble cabins, as well as some of the most breath-stopping multimillion-dollar homes, or "great camps," in the Adirondacks. The families that lived here, be they locals or weekenders, differed enormously in wealth. But they had this in common: they were lucky to share a tiny piece of heaven and they knew it.

The Sorenson cabin, about a third of the way up the east side of Lake Placid, sat tucked behind a screen of pines, nearly out of view from the road. It was one of the last homes before the road pulled away from the water's edge and curled inland. Matt pulled the car onto the cabin's crunchy stone driveway, weeds and grasses now blurring its edges.

It had been two years since they'd been here. They drove up that spring to help Nate turn over the gardens and found him fetal and lifeless in the grass. Not a vision that was simple to erase. It had taken this long for Matt to steel himself enough to return, and even so the visit was propelled by necessity.

It had seemed Nate would never die. It couldn't possibly happen. The man avoided doctors and made it to ninety-six. Matt was fairly sure his grandfather died only because he'd had to put down his beloved German shepherd at the almost unheard-of age of twenty-one. Gunner never left the old man's side, even accompanying him to the office.

As the car's headlights slid across the face of the big house, the wear and tear was hard to miss. One shutter had torn loose and hung upside down from its lower hinge. The chinking between the logs was starting to crumble, and one of the cedar posts that supported the porch had begun to split. Dead center between the windows on the second floor, however, the Sorenson family crest endured: a large, blocky "S" constructed of peeling birch logs, mounted on a slate shield—a badge on the face of the cabin for generations.

Between house and garage was his grandfather's Range Rover. For the briefest of moments, he imagined the old man would be waiting inside. Ridiculous—of course the car would still be here. It had been Matt's job to sell it and he hadn't been able to contemplate the task. Anyway, it might bring in a decent buck. He made a mental note to get the word out. It was inanimate, after all.

Rubber, glass, and metal.

When his parents had announced they were going to the Dominican Republic for their fifteen-year anniversary and Nate was coming to stay, the only thing eleven-year-old Matt worried about was whether or not they'd bring him back any sharks' teeth. But he would look up from a *M*A*S*H* rerun one afternoon in their Upper East Side apartment to learn that his entire world had imploded.

On the screen behind Nate, Hot Lips Houlihan strode through the camp toward the shower tent in her robe, a sight that would usually have Matt sitting up taller and hoping for a gust of wind. But Major Houlihan ceased to exist the moment Nate started to speak. He explained that the roads in the Dominican were narrow and precarious, that it had been raining and his dad had had a bit of champagne, that it happened quickly, and even though forty is far too young to die, you had to be thankful for the instantaneousness of a car meeting a speeding farm truck head-on.

Rubber, glass, and metal. And, in this case, blood.

When Matt's grandfather moved his suits and his electric shaver and his shoe-shining kit into the apartment on East 74th, between

First and Second, Matt realized the man was far more eccentric than he'd once believed. Nate scrubbed his white hair with Ajax to ward off a jaundiced cigar halo. Once a week he soaked his feet in apple cider vinegar to prevent fungus. But Matt knew he'd gotten lucky with Nate, who'd always doted on him and that spring became father, mother, grandfather, and grandmother in one. He'd taught his grandson invaluable life lessons.

In seventh grade, Matt partnered with Howie Stueck on a geography project worth 20 percent of the term mark. Matt's talents lay squarely in writing, while Howie was a gifted artist. The deadline for the project was fast approaching and, for some reason, Howie refused to do drawings after school or on weekends. Matt was livid—his end of the project was not only the tougher part, but he'd spent at least a dozen hours researching the gold rush, California's political history, earthquakes and water shortages, and the Pacific coastline.

Two nights before it was due, Matt complained to Nate over spaghetti and meatballs at the kitchen table. "All he's done so far is the geographical map and a drawing of the state flag. We're going to fail."

Nate twirled pasta around his fork and popped it into his mouth. He chewed for a long time before he spoke. "Why'd you pick him, then?"

"I didn't know he was lazy."

"You've been in school with him for years. How did you miss it?"

"Because he's a really good artist. And he gets all A's."

"Uh-huh." Nate took another mouthful. "And you think this Howie wants to keep all the A's for himself, is that it? He doesn't want to share them with you, even if it means he gets an F?"

Matt put down his fork, pushed his plate away. Nate's meatballs were always pink and wet in the middle. He was starting to feel sick. "No."

"Then what gives?"

"I have no idea."

"Where does this Howie Stueck live?"

"The Bronx."

"These works of art Howie makes—does he usually do them in school or at home?"

Matt thought about this. Howie was always drawing at school. Even at recess. And if he wasn't drawing on school paper or bristol board, he was drawing on a ratty little pad he kept in his pocket. "School, I guess."

Nate wiped his mouth with a napkin and stood up. Without a word, he motioned for Matt to put on his shoes and grab his coat.

This was how observant and caring his grandfather was. He'd figured out that the Stuecks were short on cash. That on the family's hierarchy of needs, art supplies came in far lower than basic life necessities like housing, heat, and food. So Nate and Matt went to the drugstore to purchase a forty-eight-pack of colored pencils with the plan that Matt would get to school early the next day and sneak them into Howie's desk. Whether or not he left a note was up to Matt.

When the morning bell rang, Matt watched Howie slide into his seat, open his desk to search for a pencil stub, and freeze. The kid picked up the colored pencils and looked around, confused. When he could find no obvious gift-giver, he pulled open the flap and ran a finger along the crisp, sharpened tips. He selected what might have been his favorite color—bright orange—and started to doodle in his scruffy little pad.

Howie brought the remaining seven California drawings to school the next morning, and they turned the project in on time. They got an A.

Matt switched off the engine and climbed out to stretch his arms over his head, shake out his legs after the long drive. They'd made good time, considering the traffic. It was just past eleven o'clock. A barely there new moon allowed the stars to shine brighter, sharpening the serrated topline of the mountains, some still snow-covered. A pair of bats cut across the sky overhead and darted back up to the trees. He stood there a moment and allowed the soft, downy memories of childhood to pad him once again. Make him feel the way he used to—sure of who he was. Confident the slightest weight wouldn't sink him. This visit would be good. They would reconnect as a family, and the cabin sale would set the three of them on solid ground.

He opened the rear door and reached down to unbuckle his daughter's seat belt. "Wake up, princess. We're here."

CHAPTER 5

·········

Matt switched on a lamp made of deer antlers, and the amber glow brought his entire childhood to life. Thick log walls, bulging stone fireplace, plank ceiling, the head of a lifeless buck Nate found at the side of Highway 86 some thirty years back. Heavy paisley curtains edged with navy velvet cloaked the windows and a threadbare rug stretched across floorboards worn down by generations of Sorenson triumphs and heartaches, worries and joy.

The same puzzles and games lined the built-in shelves of the dining room. The same ashy fireplace tongs. Same basket of logs. Same stack of creamy wool blankets with multicolored stripes his parents used to buy on weekend trips to Quebec City before he was born. "Iconically Canadian," his mother used to say. The Hudson Bay Company's point blankets were prized by fur traders, miners, and First Nations people, and were traded for beaver pelts, buffalo robes, and moccasins.

"You coming?" Matt called back to Gracie on the front porch. She made her careful, clickety-swish way inside with the crutches she'd attempted to camouflage last summer with stickers that were now gauzy, grayed, and torn. It was something he and his wife battled over—whether or not to push her to walk without them. It was Matt's belief that they should allow Gracie to take the lead. Her ability to walk unaided was precarious. She could sustain a serious injury from a fall.

As he tugged sheets off sofas and armchairs, he inhaled decades of dust, old birch logs, fireplace ashes, and the smell of wet dogs that had been invited to sleep on the sofas and beds.

Gracie was on the hearth now, comparing her height to the firebox. "I can almost walk into the fireplace."

"Remember the rules here."

She sighed. "No grown-ups around means no lake, no forest, no road. No fun."

"Boom." Matt stopped at the kitchen, its deep ceramic farmhouse sink and banged-up camping kettle as familiar as the fine hairs on the back of his hand. He loved that nothing had ever changed in the house. The linen tea towels his grandmother had monogrammed with the Sorenson "S." The dancing mice salt and pepper shakers on the shelf—the pepper mouse still boasting a jagged raised scar from Elise having accidentally knocked it to the floor. She'd panicked that Nate would hate her for it. Which he had.

The first time Matt brought Elise up to the cabin to meet his grandfather, the old man, wearing a deep green Christmas sweater over shirt and tie, had waved Matt into his office while Elise was upstairs getting ready for bed.

"She's a beautiful girl," he said, as Vince Guaraldi's "Christmastime Is Here" wafted in from the other room. "Striking. She's smart and driven. That ambition—it's admirable. Aspirational, even. If someone figured out how to liquefy it, pour it into our coffees every morning, we'd all be drunk on it and running the world. But I'll tell you and I want you to listen. Really listen. She's from a very different world. That girl is not like us."

"Come on, lots of couples come from different ends of the social spectrum. It's not a big deal." Matt was well aware of who Elise was, where she came from. It didn't bother him in the slightest. His girlfriend, with her platinum bob and intoxicating smile and natural effervescence, was shiny and new. He adored her passion and focus. He'd even go so far as to say it inspired him to reach further himself. Muster up the confidence to apply to a big firm, rather than plod along in his own practice. Certainly, that was where the big money was—at least for a guy like Matt, who was uncomfortable pushing people for business. Elise didn't let anything stop her. Which was what it took to get to the top of any field, right? For the first time in as long as Matt could remember, he was truly happy. He'd found love.

"That hunger—you can smell it a mile away. And it's going to make your life miserable."

"So I'm better off attached to someone without direction?"

"That's not what I said. This one is grasping. She's always going to put herself first. It's going to be trouble." Nate wrapped his lips around the cigar and held the smoke in his mouth. When he exhaled, he pointed the cigar at Matt. "Listen to your grandfather. Don't marry Elise. And if you're stubborn enough to do it in spite of what I say, don't have kids. I've practiced family law my entire life. Do not have children with a woman who sees you as a stepping stone." A creak from the landing caused Nate to stand. He licked his fingers and extinguished the tip of his cigar. "You lost your parents far too young. I wouldn't wish that on anyone. But look at you. You're handsome. Smart. A lawyer. I didn't do such a bad job raising you, huh?" He chuckled to himself and reached out to squeeze his grandson's shoulder. His tone grew somber. "You found your way. But you're the exception, Matthew. Believe me when I say that an absent mother can destroy a family."

Even then a tiny spark of truth, of recognition, had charged the air with clarity.

Matt did want what he himself hadn't had for nearly long enough. A real mother for his children. Someone who valued family like he did. Elise was completely disconnected from what remained of her family. Her interest in her own blood relatives was almost recreational. As if they were something she'd heard about, like green apple pilsner, and might be game to try one day when she wasn't in training.

Matt stood in the doorway of his grandfather's office and let the room soothe him. The big wooden desk. The creased leather chair Matt used to spin in until he couldn't walk a straight line. The legal books and thrillers on the bookshelves. And the smell! Ancient books, lemony furniture polish, and the spicy sweetness of a half century of cigar smoke. Jesus, it brought him back.

And there, on the wall. Framed newspaper photos and articles about his grandfather's legendary kindness.

Nate's love for the area was as widely known as his generosity. When cash-strapped local farmers or business owners were turned down by the bank, they knew to come to Nate for loans. He worked tirelessly on the Olympic bids. And, because of his love of dogs, he willed a quarter million to the North Country Animal Shelter to completely rebuild their facilities. Not that that choice hadn't given Matt pause—what a difference it would have made to his life with Elise if they'd had that cash these past couple of years.

If there was a king of Lake Placid, Nate had been it. By association, Matt grew up feeling respected, special. A cashier in the village had once joked to young Matt that the Sorensons were the First Family of the Adirondacks. Right away he'd thought, *Yes. That's how it feels.*

"Hey!" Gracie's face was deep inside a bureau drawer in the living room. "Mouse poop."

"Don't inhale that!"

"I want to know if it smells the same as a llama's."

Was it worth asking where on earth she'd ever smelled llama excrement? "You can get a disease called hantavirus from mouse feces."

She slammed the drawer shut.

Matt moved to the wall of framed photos behind the desk to examine a black-and-white shot from the local paper. It was 1966 and Nate stood proud in suit and tie with an arm around the shoulders of one of his farmers. Matt's father, George, still stringy as a young father, was at Nate's side. Behind them, the grainy outline of a barn and the sweet spoon faces of the dairy cows. Matt had always loved these pictures. Loved imagining George and Nate walking around the barns, offering advice with gentle lowing in the background. It seemed a satisfying, peaceful existence. A good life.

From the other room, a piercing, needle-in-the-eardrum scream. Then, "A dead dog!"

Matt raced out of the office to find Gracie holding a big white sheet that she must have taken off a huge, lumpy, furred—and yes, dead—dog.

Jesus Christ. It was Gunner, Nate's ancient German shepherd. Nate had had the old boy stuffed? Matt and his family had all been there the week after Nate died, but they'd been too preoccupied to poke around the place much, so this was the first Matt knew of it. He stared a moment, then knelt to inspect withered and leathery black nostrils. Gunner's once gleaming black head was now grizzled, dry, and scurfy, oddly solid and cool to the touch.

As far back as Matt could remember, his grandparents had bred Alsatians. His grandmother kept them in the big kitchen, in a caged area to the side of the enamel Aga, a cobalt-blue beast of a range that helped heat the main floor during the cold months. With every litter of what looked like tiny black bear cubs, the family sold off all but one. Until Matt married Elise, who was allergic to dogs, he'd never been without a German shepherd in his life.

Of all of them, Gunner had been a standout. He was so protective he'd slow Gracie's descent on a slide by holding the back of her T-shirt in his teeth. He was known to trot into town Saturday mornings before anyone was up to wait for a cheese scone from Torte Reform, the bakery owned by the second wife of the town court judge. The dog's one vice was his daily marking at the base of the front steps. Nate considered it a sign of devotion. This most glorious of animals now sat glassy-eyed and stilled for eternity, his aged front legs forced into a widened stance that looked vaguely painful, his head cocked so far to one side it almost appeared detachable.

Matt tipped the dog sideways to read a label stitched into the animal's belly: PETS IN PERPETUITY: NEVER SAY GOODBYE. PATENTED FREEZE-DRY TECHNOLOGY.

"What's wrong with him, Daddy?"

"Well, he's dead, for one."

Knowledge of Nate's eccentricity wasn't contained within the family—it had always been something of a local legend. The man issued loans only on a Saturday. He swam across the lake every morning it wasn't frozen. Pulled on his fitted black swimsuit and bathing cap, dove off the dock, and settled into the clean, sharp rhythm of a front crawl so precise his strokes barely disturbed the water's surface. In the years since the 9/11 terror attacks, he'd become a survivalist, digging out a root cellar beneath the back porch and having it wired for electricity. It was supposed to be a "safe haven," and Nate had stocked it with seed, fertilizer, canned food, medicine, clothes, a shovel, and tools.

"And freeze-dried, for another."

Still. There was something about the dog's presence that brought his grandfather right there into the room. He could almost feel the deep timbre of Nate's voice in the floorboards. See his shoe reaching into the fire to nudge a log farther into the embers. Taste the man's watery spaghetti sauce.

Gracie tapped Gunner's great horned toenails and looked at her father, eyes wide. "Are we going to go to jail?"

"Reasonable question, Little Green. But stuffing your dog is as legal as it is gruesome." Matt pulled the last sheet off his grandfather's old leather chair by the front window and looked at it a moment. "However, your great-grandpa thought it was important to preserve him. So I think we have to live with it."

"Me too." Gracie removed her tiara and climbed onto the chair to place it on the dog's head, where it tipped over an ear, then kissed his lifeless snout.

"Done." Matt bundled the dusty sheets and headed through the kitchen. "We need to get you right up to bed. It's nearly eleven thirty. Almost time to get up and make breakfast."

"I'm not even one bit tired."

Right. The downside of allowing his daughter to sleep the entire way up.

The four-season porch was his favorite part of the house. His mother, Lynn, calling him in from the water to eat dinner at the long, battered table. Rainy days playing Monopoly with his father. Hot summer nights doing puzzles with his grandfather. Such promise life had back then. Consistency. Every autumn morning, you could count on a mirror-calm lake and a gauzy mist hanging over the mountains. The old birch tree that leaned out over the water's edge, always threatening but never tipping over. Every night you waited for the surround-sound scritch-scratch of crickets.

He took the linens through the screen door and onto the stone path to shake out the dust. There, the starlight made the lake shimmer.

For the first time since before the play, Matt allowed himself to relax. He would let go of his anger at his wife, he decided. They'd been apart so much this year. No sense in making things ugly, not while they were all here on vacation reconnecting as a family.

The sound of a fire crackling and snapping next door caught his attention. He watched as a woman in ripped jeans and a dark red tank top handed a stick to a boy—another kid up insanely late—in the firelight. She helped the child push a marshmallow onto the end, then held her own marshmallow over the fire. Her nose was short, her heart-shaped face had an ever-charmed, always-mischievous expression that said "Convince me." He knew that face almost as well as his own.

The woman looked up. "Matty Sorenson? No. Freaking. Way."

CHAPTER 6

·········

After a few wrong turns, with the drizzle finally having stopped, Elise pulled off Seldom Seen Road and onto the long, heavily treed driveway just after two a.m. The day had been brutal—well over twelve hours of travel. After sorting out Indie and Poppins on the tarmac, she'd taken a cab to the house. While charging her phone, she took a twenty-second shower, pulled on the long, silky cobalt skirt Matt adored her in, and sprayed herself with his Hermès Eau d'Orange Verte so she could smell him the whole way up. She filled the car with water bottles, almonds, and fruit, as well as clothes she'd need for two weeks at the cabin, and hit the road to face rain on and off the entire way up.

She pulled up next to Matt's car and paused, fingers still curled around the keys. As excited as she was, she half dreaded going in. Matt hadn't picked up when she'd called—back where she still had a cell signal that lasted more than a couple of minutes. She had no idea if her husband was too angry to speak to her or if their respective positions on the drive up had simply meant either one phone or the other was in a dead zone.

Also . . . was he really going to be thrilled about her news on the night she missed their daughter's play? Part of her wanted to wait until morning to tell him about her score, because shooting for Rio meant a whole host of extra competitions over the next twelve months. Then again, given her erratic scores this season, it might be better to let him know the year hadn't been for nothing after all.

She looked up at the house—set so far back it was barely visible from the road. In the harsh glare of her high beams, it looked tragic. Spent. An upstairs shutter dangled like a false eyelash after a long night spent crying, tears still drip-dripping from the eaves.

Everyone at the barn knew Elise's code name for the cabin: Alcatraz. That ominous "S" shield looking down on her. From the moment she first saw the family crest, it had felt like a KEEP OUT sign on a clubhouse. This was the last place on earth she wanted their little family reunion to take place. The readjustment of being back together was tough enough without the disapproving omnipresence of Matt's late grandfather.

She turned off the car and a puffy silence filled the interior.

The only thing more intimidating than the quiet was the dark. You couldn't pick a place more terrifying. On a light pollution map she'd found online while helping Gracie with a school project, there was a massive gap at the top of New York State, between Albany and Montreal. That black hole was the six-million-acre Adirondack Park, full of bears, wolves, coyotes, and cougars—not to mention an infinitesimal number of blackflies ready to burrow into your hairline and leave your neck swollen and bleeding and on fire with itch. And somewhere in the upper quadrant of that dark hole sat the Sorenson cabin.

With all the costs of keeping the place after Nate died, and with all of Matt's memories there, she'd always felt guilty that she never encouraged a visit. But how could she, with the way things had been?

She'd never met Matt's parents, obviously, but it was pretty clear the Sorensons were people who came into the world ready-made.

Whatever they accomplished was secondary to who they were in the first place. Elise had come out of the womb fists clenched and ready to hustle—to Nate, she was a being from another planet. All he could see was that she was from less. To him, that meant she *must* be using Matt to climb higher in the horse world, grasping at Sorenson family money to make a name for herself in a sport she couldn't otherwise afford.

What bothered her more was how transparent her background had been.

The summer between seventh and eighth grades, Elise had taken a part-time job that paid her under the counter: assistant custodian at the outdoor community pool. Her responsibilities—while the other teenagers flirted with each other in the shallow end or gossiped on lounge chairs, their tanned bodies slick with coconut-scented Hawaiian Tropic oil—included keeping the pool deck and women's change room swept, and towel- and litter-free, as well as watering hedges scorched by chlorine, and, yes, scrubbing the restrooms. One evening at the end of her shift, as she made her way through the empty lobby, the open lid of the overflowing lost-and-found box caught her eye. The temptation was too strong to pass up; she dug through the jumble inside. It was staggering to see what wealthier kids lost and never bothered to look for. She pulled out a pale pink Polo shirt with green horse and rider embroidered on the left breast, looked around to make sure no one was watching, and stuffed it into her backpack. She'd never had a designer anything.

The junior high Elise attended drew students from shabby clapboard houses with sagging sofas on the porches, intimidating mansions with flickering gas lanterns and circular driveways, and everything in between. But still, on the first day of school Elise wore the shirt like a new skin. In a Ralph Lauren top, she didn't feel like her family's poverty defined her. The days she wore it were always the best of the week.

A few months later, wearing the collar flipped up, hair in a ponytail, Elise strode through the cafeteria with her bagged lunch, looking for a safe place to eat, and felt Jillian Lucado, Franca Poole, and Carey Jubert staring at her. Her first thought was that the shirt belonged to one of them and they were about to call her out on her theft. It would be mortifying. Or maybe she'd worn it too often.

But then Carey sang, "Hey, Bleeker. How bleak is your life?"

You can put as many bandages as you like over the scab on your elbow, certain you've protected your wound. But all the while, your chipped molar is exposed, announcing to everyone around that you haven't been to the dentist. Carey and Jillian and Franca saw right through her.

Movement on the roof caught Elise's eye and she leaned closer to the windshield for a better look. There was a dark huddled mass, some kind of animal, atop the porch overhang. She waited a moment and the creature started to creep along the front of the house. A raccoon would make the most sense, but a raccoon would be grayish, with a striped tail. This animal was completely black and she couldn't tell if there was any kind of tail.

God almighty. Was that a small bear?

She watched as the animal rose up on hind legs to inspect a window frame. How was she going to get into the house with a bear ready to pounce? It was too dark to see anything beyond the car's headlights—there was no way she could get out. Chances were ridiculously high that a ferocious mama was out there in the blackness someplace, ready to rip apart anything or anyone who came between her and her offspring.

"A mother's protectiveness is genetically programmed," Rosamunde used to say when she came home from the obstetrics office where she worked as a receptionist twice a week. "Nature does nothing without reason. Baby relies on mother for survival."

It had been their routine ever since she could remember. Elise would finish her homework at the kitchen table—Warren would be in the garage making lures, or watching fishing videos on the old TV in the basement—and her mother would get her ready for bed and then cuddle her daughter so close she could almost reabsorb her. Together, they would lie in the crush of pillows and stare out the window at the night sky. "From the moment of conception"—Rosamunde would pause to kiss the top of Elise's head—"you and I became a perfect little world. A tiny planet."

How Elise loved those nights. Rosamunde would fill her daughter in on the women who came into the doctor's office, bellies swollen with promise. "Mrs. T. was in this morning with cramping. Turns out she'd been helping her sister move—five flights of stairs. Can you imagine? A bit of bed rest should set her straight . . . That poor librarian had another miscarriage, but she's determined to keep trying . . . And would you believe Mrs. Stiletto Heels is pregnant again? I swear, that woman gets pregnant from the sound of her husband's car in the driveway."

It was no surprise that Rosamunde chose to work for an obstetrician, given her past; her own mother had died delivering twin boys before Rosamunde turned two. Her brothers, Owen and Jonah, lived. The three children were largely raised by their grandmother. Their father had no choice but to work two jobs to keep them all in winter boots and Band-Aids and peanut butter sandwiches.

The tragedy created in Rosamunde an utter fascination with mothers and their infants—even before birth. College was easy for her to drop out of when Warren came along and promised her a house so big it would have an indoor waterfall, cars so fancy they'd have seats made of butter, and so many babies they'd be tripping over them. She swallowed his dreams whole—no questions asked about how he planned to get there when he spent more time in a tinny rowboat, pulling lures off his hat and tying them to the end of his fishing line, than making sales calls to local farmers.

The trouble started when, in the years after Elise was born, no more babies materialized. Eventually, Dr. Nadal ran a few tests; Rosamunde had stopped ovulating. There wouldn't be another child.

Elise looked out into the dark again. Ridiculous to be trapped in a car after the long drive. Pretty soon, her bladder would demand relief. She leaned back in her seat and tried to distract herself by stretching her legs.

It had been Nate who calculated the cost of competing at the international level, which was her ultimate goal in the early days. Seventy thousand a year, minimum. Nate believed if it weren't for Matt, Elise wouldn't be competing at all.

Matt pointed out that there are people who own extraordinary horses who aren't themselves talented enough to show them, so they pair up with a top rider. Without Sorenson money, Elise would have continued on that path. It was what she'd been doing all along.

In Nate's eyes, she'd trapped his treasured grandson, but he couldn't have been more off base. It was Matt who'd pursued her.

It was 2002, in the midst of a record heat wave that had showed no sign of breaking. Elise was twenty-five, Matt was nearing thirty-eight. She'd been stuck in her tall boots because Ronnie's staff had left the showgrounds early with the boot jack. Dark clouds had begun to gather at the sky's edge, and the air hung heavy with rain that desperately wanted to fall. It didn't help that Elise's ancient Corolla had no air-conditioning and her legs had swelled on the long drive back to Jersey City, where she'd been renting a studio apartment in a particularly run-down part of town. But her passenger seat was scattered with red ribbons. She'd just had her best show ever, competing at second level for the first time. She'd placed first in every class on Ronnie's excellent Dutch Warmblood, a silver-white gelding that would suffer a tendon tear in the back paddock six months later and be gifted with retirement.

The rain started just as Elise pulled up to her building at Baldwin and High. She crossed to the coffee shop on the other—nicer—side of the street in search of a kind stranger with strong hands and a sense of adventure.

Seated by the window had been an athletic woman whose Teva sandals and baggy tie-dyed tank made her seem approachable. The woman thought Elise's predicament rather funny, but had trouble tugging the stiff leather off swollen flesh.

Matt Sorenson had been nearby working on a laptop. Wearing a Brooks Brothers shirt and stainless-steel watch with a racy black face, he was clearly not from the area. Elise would later learn he was waiting for his car at a repair shop down the street. He became interested in her predicament and wandered over to have a go at her boots. He put all his focus on freeing her heel, with little success. "Jesus. Maybe you should go up a size." Finally, the boot came off, leaving dried mud and flecks of straw on his palms. He glanced outside at the rain as he tugged off the second one. "How are you going to get home in socks?"

She gestured, with some embarrassment, across the road to a squat, pus-yellow building between a U-Haul depot and A-1 Self Storage with a six-foot-high barbed-wire fence. One of the front-facing windows was covered in tin foil. Another in a faded American flag. "It's not far."

"I can't let you run across the road with no shoes on." He leaned over his knees, motioned toward his back. "Hop on."

She shook her head no and, boots in hand, thanked him, then went out into the rain. Waited for a break in traffic and ran back to her life on the shabby side of the street. The fellow with the dirty hands was free to return to his. She never expected to see him again.

A week later, she found a brown paper bag in her foyer. Written on the front of the sack was: *To the dressauge rider with the punishingly tight boots.*

Inside was a wooden boot jack. Elise pulled it out and replaced it with a twenty-dollar bill. Wrote on the bag's other side:

Sorry, I don't accept gifts from men with straw on their hands.

P.S. My name is Elise.
P.P.S. You misspelled dressage.

She left it in the foyer, hoping none of her neighbors would abscond with it. A day later, the now rumpled bag was back. Inside was a receipt from a tack shop for $29.50 and a note:

It all makes sense now—you've clearly never bought a boot jack in your life. You owe me $9.50. Which I am prepared to accept in the form of insincere flattery—but I expect my money's worth. Meet me at E. 76th and Fifth on Monday at 7. You may or may not see Woody Allen heading into his jazz gig as we pass the Carlyle en route to our more modestly priced eatery, so maybe go lighter on the manure. A little spit and polish goes a long way with him, from what I hear. Yours, etc., Matt Sorenson

And so it would go.

Elise glanced up at the roof once more: no sign of the bear. Taking her eyes off the animal had been a mistake. She scanned the gables, then the garden. It had to have shimmied down the trellis. Could it be lurking in the yard now? Or worse—on the porch?

She pulled out her phone to wake Matt, only to find she still had no signal. He would be lying in his childhood bedroom, snoring softly, in his usual white T-shirt and boxers. And Gracie. Their daughter would be lying on her back, arms and legs flung to the far corners of her twin bed, duvet kicked to the floor because "It suffocates." Gracie would forgive her for missing the play. She would; Elise was nearly certain. That was the sweetness of children: they would forgive their parents for almost anything.

Whether that parent forgave herself was another story.

What Matt thought about the accident, how much he thought about it, *if* he thought about it—Elise didn't know. What had happened had taken the shape of a big, bloated silence between them.

The urge to hold her daughter, to tuck herself softly beneath her husband's arm, now overtook all sense and caution. Elise gathered her bags to her chest and raced through the blackness to the door.

She could smell her daughter before she could see her. That intoxicating mix of sugary perspiration and baby shampoo seeped out onto the landing. Elise quietly opened Gracie's door. Slipped into the bedroom. A small nightlight beside the dresser offered just enough of a glow to reveal the tiny mound of sweetness, that shiny dark blond hair on the pillow, plump, sweaty limbs having pushed off the covers. Crutches lay in wait on the floor.

On the nightstand, one of her favorite photos of Gracie sat in a fat wooden frame. It was taken right here in the cabin on Christmas morning three and a half years ago. Double-A Christmas, they called it. Gracie had been asking for AA batteries for ages, because some of her favorite toys had stopped working. Matt had had a huge divorce case that bled from fall into winter, and Elise had been preparing to ship to Florida a bit late that year because Indie had had a minor injury. Batteries had become a running joke almost. Gracie asking, Matt and Elise looking at each other, praying the other had remembered. Weeks passed this way until Christmas morning, when Gracie pulled a jumbo pack of Duracell batteries from her stocking. She stood there, so adorable in her sweet red footie pajamas, crazy bedhead. Her smile was so joyous it could have lifted the house from the ground. Even later, back in school, when the kids were asked to describe their winter breaks, all Gracie had written about were the batteries.

Elise wrapped herself around her daughter now and kissed her. "Hey, sleepy one. Wake up. Mommy's home."

"Mom." Her voice was a low scrape.

"How's my little sweetheart?"

Flushed, Gracie stretched and fumbled behind her head for one of the dozens of stuffed animals she had fanned out around her pillow.

Elise buried her face in her daughter's hot neck as Gracie pulled down a giraffe with an upturned snout that gave the distinct impression he wasn't buying whatever you were selling. She squeezed the tiny creature.

"What about *my* hug?"

"Giraffey needs it more. I haven't hugged him in, um . . . " She paused to calculate. "Thirteen days."

"Thirteen, huh? How do you know that?"

Gracie held up her giraffe. "I know because there are twenty-five and I take turns. So no one gets hurt feelings."

"Do you know how much I missed you?" Elise tried to blow a horsey kiss on Gracie's belly, but her daughter pulled her top down to block the kiss. "How was the play? I'm so, so sorry and sad I missed it."

Gracie's thumb found her mouth and she spoke through it. "If your plane crashed, I told Dad we should have an open casket. Because you're pretty."

"What?" Elise stared at her, incredulous, then gently pulled thumb from upper palate and held it. "Why would you think such a thing? Sweetie, were you worried my plane was going to crash?"

"No." The child's eyelids fluttered and she rolled onto her side. Again, the thumb went into her mouth. Again, Elise worked it out and dried it off. "But he said then we could get a German shepherd."

Really? Was Matt that angry? She leaned down to kiss her daughter's forehead. Thumb reinserted itself. Thumb-sucking had certainly been Gracie's self-soothing remedy of choice. But that spring, with Elise's concentrated remedial plan of fabric Band-Aids, pickle juice, cayenne pepper, pretty manicures, online photos of upper palate and bite consequences, and, finally, a sock pulled over the hand at night, she'd really cut down on "Thumb," as Gracie had always called it. Elise had assumed the habit would be gone altogether by the time she returned. "Honey, you know Mommy loves you very much."

An ardent nod. "Duh."

"I'm just wondering about Thumb again. She seems determined to thwart our efforts, doesn't she? Do you want a sock for your hand? Maybe then she'll sleep through the night and stop disturbing you."

"'Kay." Children are open to self-improvement—tiny sponges ready to grow into their very best selves. Gracie wanted to be a big girl and abolish babyish behaviors. Elise took a long, polka-dotted sock from the dresser drawer and slid it over the girl's wet fist, then tucked Thumb deep under the covers and kissed her daughter's forehead. "You get back to dreamland and we'll have fun in the morning." She noticed now that Gracie's pajamas smelled like smoke. "Did you and Daddy make a fire?"

Another nod.

Elise got up to close the curtains so the morning sun wouldn't wake Gracie too early. When she turned back, the child was asleep with Thumb parked in her mouth. Next to her on the mattress, the spotted sock.

....

Elise tiptoed to the end of the hall to Matt's bedroom. They'd made minor changes over the years to accommodate their visits, however infrequent: his brass twin-sized bed had been replaced with a queen. A second dresser and a nightstand for Elise's side of the bed. Two hooks for robes inside the closet. She opened the door and blinked stupidly. Matt wasn't in the bed.

There was only one other place he could be. She opened the door to Nate's room and waited for her eyes to adjust. Sure enough, the hulking swell beneath the sheets turned into her husband. Above him, centered with the headboard, hung Nate and Sarah's wedding photo. Terrific. Her reunion with her husband, a period always steeped in tension the first few days, made much more prickly this time because of a missed play, would now take place beneath the disapproving eye of her dead grandfather-in-law.

Matt snored softly. Elise padded across the bare floor, pulled back the duvet, and worked her body beneath it until she could wrap herself around him, until she could put her head on his chest and hear the beat of his heart. He smelled of smoke and soap and red wine. She tapped his jawline until he stirred, stretched, and groaned. He rolled over and found her warmth. Pressed his rough, stubbly mouth to hers to kiss her sleepily.

His eyes still closed, he mumbled, "I smell four and a half hours of Dr. Laura on satellite radio."

"I smell a man with a bear on his roof who slept right through having a bear on his roof."

He sat up and glanced at the clock radio—2:34 a.m. glowing green—and blinked in confusion. "Wait . . . you came straight up?"

"You missed the part about the bear." She let him pull her close, melted into his warmth and bulk, and kissed him. "Hello."

"I remember you." He rolled her over and lay half on top of her, grinning and nuzzling his jaw against her face. "You're the one who thinks bears parachute in from the sky, and I humor you because you're cute when you're wrong."

What a relief. He was being adorable; everything was going to be fine. Better than fine. Wonderful. She ran her hands up to his shoulders. "It was real. A small black bear."

"Why didn't you call from the road?"

"I tried. It was like one of those nightmares where you try to use a phone but your fingers don't work. Unbelievable how bad the signals are around here."

"It's the reason bears catapult up onto roofs in the first place. To mess up the cell signals."

She glanced toward the blowing curtains. "We should keep the windows closed. What if it got in the house?"

He moved on top of her and rested his weight on his elbows. "Shut up and kiss me, E."

She loved it when he called her "E." Their kiss was just what she'd imagined on those nights back in Tryon—so tender and sweet it was drunk-making. She sank into it, then pulled back. "Hey, did you tell Gracie if I died in a plane crash she could get a dog?"

"Not out of the blue."

"*Matt.*"

"What? She asked."

"And you said yes?"

"Sure."

"Why?"

"Because we would totally get a dog. Also, FYI, it doesn't have to be a plane crash. Meteor, quicksand, aneurysm. Whatever. Just have to figure out which breeder. And time it so I can get a few days off work."

She started to laugh. "You're such an ass."

"Can we skip all this romantic talk and get busy?" He grabbed her ass and squeezed. "Seems like forever since I've felt a woman's thighs."

"Yeah, that's a little generic, buddy." Something shiny on the floor caught her eye. She wiggled out from beneath him and sat up. It was a pot of water.

He answered her unspoken question. "Roof was leaking."

She lay back down again and he slid his hands up and down her thighs. Maybe she shouldn't tell him her news here, in Nate's room, with a wild animal at the window. With her husband half-asleep and the other half ripping off her underpants. "Why are we sleeping in here, anyway?"

"Mattress is a DUX." He pulled off her panties and yawned into his hand. "It's got give. Like sleeping on a slice of angel food cake." He pounced from the side, tickling her until she squealed and pulled back. "Let's play naughty baker."

"How is naughty baker sexy?"

"I don't know. You be the hot inspector person who gives him an F. *Unless . . .*"

She raised herself up on one elbow. "I'm *so* sorry about today. I never should have said yes to Air Horse One in the first place. I should've sent them both on the trailer."

"Shh. Stop it. It's done. There will be other plays. One messed-up schedule isn't going to destroy us." He kissed her. "We're good."

"Promise?"

"Promise."

"Has it been tough—being here now that Nate's gone?"

He rolled onto his back and groaned. "Aaand, there goes his manhood." He crawled out of bed and, in his wrinkled yellow-and-navy-plaid boxers, walked to the bathroom to pee with the door open. "Like a break and enter, actually. And totally not what he envisioned, right? Us unloading it to strangers." He leaned over to flush, then turned on the tap.

"I feel bad, babe."

"Don't." He walked back into the room and kissed her. "It's the right thing to do. The only thing. Gracie's school fees alone."

As he sat on the bed beside her, she studied the dark smudges of sleeplessness beneath his eyes, his stubble coming in gray. What if it were the other way around? What if she had to be the single parent for so much of the year, and every extra dollar she made went toward Matt's dream? What if she had to sell the lake house she'd practically grown up in? She'd like to think she wouldn't resent her partner, but would she? Was she as great a person as Matt? "So, you're not going to believe it—I have huge news. As in, colossal."

"Good. So do I. Let's see whose news wins."

"What's your news?"

"No way. You go first so my news can warm up. Pop a few steroids. Get into fighting form."

Her progression hit her: all the years of training, all the shows she did and didn't make, watching four sets of Olympic games pass her by. Not just pass her by, even; she'd come close to being shortlisted but just missed. She'd been thinking earlier this year that she might wind up as one of those almost-stars local papers print articles about. She could see the headline a few years down the road: "Elise Sorenson—What Went Wrong?" And then, today. The freestyle, the music, the delayed decision. And, finally, the score. "I've just become a contender for Rio."

His expression didn't change as he took a moment to process this.

"It means a more intense winter, as in, insane, and they announce the short list in May. If—it's kind of scary to say this out loud, because I don't want to jinx myself, or Indie—but if somehow, by some crazy miracle, we make it onto the short list—that will be eight horse-and-rider combinations—we go to two trials out of three in Compiègne, Roosendaal, Rotterdam. Then the Olympic team gets announced in July. And then, maybe, maybe, maybe, right?" She paused to breathe. "How crazy is this?"

"Seriously. Wow. Like, just wow . . ."

"I know. I'm afraid to even imagine it."

"Your score today must've been off the charts."

"Gift from the gods, for sure."

"Holy shit."

She looked at him, so open and joyful. She might have been mistaken, but it seemed like his eyes were moist. She reached a hand up to cup his stubbled cheek. "And you—what's your news?"

"Mine?" He shook his head, leaned down to kiss her. "It wasn't about me—just that I got her entire play on video. So we can all watch it together in the morning. Breakfast and movie in bed."

"Most." She pressed tiny kisses to his jawline. "Perfect." Let her lips travel up to his ear. "Husband." Flicked his earlobe with her tongue. "In the history of husbands."

"Can we make a deal?" he said. "We book time after Rio."

"Book time for . . . ?"

"Another baby."

She didn't have the same urge Matt had to expand the family. The three of them seemed so right. And with Gracie getting older, life was sure to get easier. "Definitely something we should discuss."

He smiled and moved on top of her again. The blissful familiarity of his warmth, his weight. His mouth searching hers. His hardness pressing against her hip. His stubble scraping against her cheek. All the months of getting up at dawn, of running and lifting weights, of riding the same complicated moves over and over until sweat blurred her vision and her legs turned to rubber, of holding an effortless-looking position in the saddle no matter what muscle she'd strained, of missing her loved ones—all of it began to fade and Elise gave in to the sweetness of being home.

CHAPTER 7

·········

Matt woke overheated and sweating before dawn. With
Elise's back pressed to his, he'd become a furnace. He
shifted to the cool promise of the mattress edge, waited
a few moments to make sure she hadn't woken, then, careful not to
squeak the iron bed frame, pushed back the covers and made his
way to the bathroom.

After splashing cold water on his face, he examined his grainy
reflection in the mirror, mouth slack, chin dripping. He pressed a
towel to his stubbled jaw. Elise's news couldn't have had worse timing. They'd be able to fund it—and more—with the sale of the cabin,
but Matt was going to have to call Lyndon Barrans and refuse the
partnership. The hours of Funducational weren't going to allow it:
final pickup was six thirty p.m., but Matt tried to get there around
six so Gracie would never be the last one to go. They could certainly
hire a nanny so that Gracie could be in her own home if Matt's hours
increased dramatically, but what kind of life would that be for a child?

A soft breeze brought in the smell of the lake and the sweet musk
of the wet forest floor. He glanced outside. The stars had re-claimed

the night sky. It was just bright enough now to see that the rain had reduced Cass's bonfire to a pulpy, sodden mess.

He'd thought he'd never see Cass again. Decades ago, she'd gone off to see the world and her parents had sold the place to their best friends and moved to the city. Last night, with Gracie on his back, Matt had picked his way through the cedars into her yard, a bottle of red from Nate's cellar and two good wineglasses in his hands. After hugs and introductions, he'd left his daughter by the fire to make s'mores with Cass's son, nine-year-old River, a polite little character who gave Gracie a deep bow, then offered his hand and said, in a fake British accent, "The pleasure is mine."

Matt followed the boy's mother into the house.

Cass had been the girl next door who took his virginity.

The summer he was seventeen, he returned to Lake Placid with his new, beefed-up physicality. Cass had changed as well, all leggy and sensual. She'd circled around him like a lioness one night, before curling her finger and sashaying down to her boathouse to light a joint, pull off his shirt, and change his world. He couldn't believe it. This was a girl about to be homecoming queen at Lake Placid High. As far back as Matt could remember, there'd been a succession of boys on dirt bikes and in pickup trucks pulling into the Urquhart driveway, hoping to bask in her glow. And now she wanted him.

If that wasn't enough, she was also Nate-approved. "Think about Cass," Nate would say. "Now there's a girl who's even a little wild. They don't have a lot of money, the Urquharts, but they're our kind of people. They're from the lake. Cassidy doesn't have to spend her time reinventing herself. She knows who she is. More to the point, she *likes* who she is."

They passed through the den at the back of the house, a room that had clearly been renovated. The back wall was now all windows and a sliding glass door. Gone was the woodstove that used to sit in the corner; now a two-sided fireplace divided the television room from the dining room. On another wall was a haunting black-and-white portrait of River at about four, shirtless, hair freshly cropped, huge eyes. "You take that?"

"Guilty."

"Jesus. You've got talent."

The den was open to the kitchen, where Matt set the glasses on the counter, then glanced back to satisfy himself that Gracie was keeping a safe distance from the heat and that River wasn't a demon child waiting for the right moment to push her into the flames. All was well. The kids seemed to be chatting shyly in the firelight.

"I brought glasses just in case you tried to serve my grandfather's Caymus from a mug," he said. It was as though no time had passed. As ever, her kitchen smelled of bourbon and patchouli and wet dog. The appliances were new—stainless and hulking—but the cupboards were still the Southern yellow pine he remembered. "Wine like this deserves a proper glass."

"Snob." She handed him a corkscrew as he tried to ignore the slice of tanned belly showing between her tank top and jeans, the long curls knotted at the nape of her neck, that same unapologetic gap between the whitest teeth he'd ever seen. He couldn't believe they were back in the same room together. "You think I don't have wineglasses?"

Matt opened the cupboard that had always held the Urquhart dishes and mugs. Nothing matched, and any glassware consisted of chipped juice cups and mugs. "The prosecution rests." He filled the wineglasses to the widest point. They clinked crystal and he sat at the table, still nestled beneath the front window. "I figured I'd never see you again after you left for your 'degree in life.'"

She trapped her tongue between her teeth with a teasing smile. Then, "Hey, somewhere between hand-rolling tea leaves in Kyoto and mopping up vomit in a bar in Haight-Ashbury, I wound up with a doctorate, baby."

He laughed. "Happy to be back?"

"For sure. I think the place you grew up, no matter how shitty or how stunning, it's just in your blood. You've absorbed it. The minuscule toxins from every spider bite, the mouthfuls of lake water, the dirt embedded when you skinned your knee—it's all part of your DNA. So you can go live elsewhere and love it. But no place is going to make you come alive in the same way." Her voice was raspier than he remembered. She reached down to rub the side of a foot with an etched silver ring on one toe. "Anyway, whatever. My brilliant new theory."

He tipped his head to one side and said nothing. She'd rounded out more as well. Gone were the concave belly and narrow hips he'd known by heart when he was young. Now, her hips had a comfortable curve, her stomach a sexy swell. She smelled like cilantro and still had that smoky indifference that used to drive him crazy.

"What?"

"Come on, Urquhart. You were never that poetic . . ."

"You're such a prick. I bare my soul . . ." Grinning, she grabbed the washcloth hanging on the tap and threw it at him. The rag splatted on the floor, leaving a wet mark on his shirt. "Anyway. Look at you all grown up." Cass glanced at his wedding band. "Married and everything."

"You're not?"

"*So* not."

"A little emphatic."

"Yeah, well. Long, ugly story with a beautiful child at the end." She pushed a strand of curls off her face. "Trust me, you don't want to hear it."

"I've got time."

"I'll give you the short version. I'd been living between New York and San Francisco. Met this guy from Sonoma one night, seemed pretty cool at first. Charles Coyne. He was launching his own vineyard. Bit of a trust fund baby, but whatever. We had a good thing for a while. Then I got pregnant and Charles wasn't as thrilled as I was about the 'accident' that is our son and pretty much went

AWOL. Never gave us a dime—every excuse under the sky. So I bolted for my parents' place in Hoboken. Didn't really like the city vibe for Riv, so when Mom's friend Jeannie put this place back on the market to open a summer camp . . . here I am." She grew quiet. "You remember my mom?"

Of course he remembered Ruth, mannish feet forever in ancient Birkenstocks. She'd always been baking. The Urquharts' old black Lab mix, Garcia, and Matt's childhood shepherd, Elsa, fur slick and spiked from the lake, would wait patiently—tails thwacking against the kitchen cupboards—to lick the bowls. As tweens, Matt and Cass would sit at the bar in bathing suits, arms and legs cold and pimply from having just climbed out of the lake. Her father, Edward, would be strumming his guitar in the family room. And when the buzzer went off, he'd join them in the kitchen. Ruth would pull zucchini bread from the oven, slice it up, and set it on their plates like it was double-chocolate birthday cake loaded with candles. Tasted terrible—like she'd pulled it out of the compost heap, pressed it into a metal pan, and left it in the oven to dry out for a few days, but that didn't matter. Matt wolfed it down just to watch Ruth beam, to hear her say, "See? Now that is what real food tastes like."

Cass's parents were card-carrying Deadheads. They ran a business called Castle Care, a property management company offering first-class service for the grand Adirondack chalets, cabins, and lake houses: everything from mail pickup to snowplowing before homeowners made the trek out from the city. The business was somewhat seasonal, so in the shoulder months Ruth and Ed were free to follow the Grateful Dead, young daughter in tow.

"You had the greatest mother on earth."

"Not sure she was much of a mother. I never knew where my shoes were, and she'd get stoned out of her mind and spend all weekend swiveling her hips, topless, on the road. I would literally wander barefoot around Soldier Field, an orphan of LSD." Cass grinned. "Thank god for Jeannie. She was the one who'd take me back to the camper and put me to bed. You know she and Brice never even watched the concerts? They went from show to show selling tie-dyed shirts and vegetarian burritos in the parking lot."

"I still see the photo sometimes," Matt said. He conjured the famous image: in a field in Bethel, New York, surrounded by glassy-eyed concertgoers, with one shirtless teenage boy dancing behind her, was a three-year-old girl with wild, tawny hair, barefoot, eyes closed, face up-tilted, in a flowered dress, ropes of beads tied around her neck, lost in the music. No parents in sight. The picture had appeared on the cover of *Life* magazine with the credit "Anonymous." The accompanying article described it as emblematic of "the final labor pains of the American Dream as the baby boomers redefined it." Whoever took the photo never went public.

"Me too. Saw it in a diner in Chicago about five years ago," she said. "Hanging on the wall beside the cash register, just above a sign that said, 'World's Best Pie.'"

"How was it?"

"The photo?"

"The pie."

"Worst goddamned pie I've ever tasted." Cass had aged in a way that made it hard to look away from her. Fine wrinkles fanned out from her eyes when she smiled. The only jewelry she wore was a braided string around her neck, likely made by her son. "Always the way with world's best anything. I told the waitress I knew who the girl was. She said, 'Yeah? You and everyone I've ever met.' So I kept quiet."

Matt laughed. "And where are your parents nowadays?"

"You didn't hear? Dad died about ten years ago."

"Oh no. I'm sorry."

"Yeah. Mom's alive and kicking. Mostly kicking, actually. Remember Pat and Lulu Geary across the street—in that little stone place?" Matt nodded, and she continued. "They were selling, so I bought it for Mom with Dad's insurance money. This place too, actually. I needed to keep an eye on her. She's not all there any-more. Dementia. Not that shocking, I guess." Cass hoisted herself onto the counter and bounced her heels against the cupboard doors.

"They were all so damned sure they were going to change the world."

"No joke. They thought it all mattered—the length of their hair, the fringed shirts, the free love. Like each little statement was tak-ing us all somewhere. Every time they had sex with a stranger or called a cop a pig, it was going to make a difference."

Matt glanced outside to see the kids holding long sticks over the fire now, roasting marshmallows. They'd graduated from nervous chitchat to full-on laughter.

"So . . . " Cass moved to the table, tucked herself close to the window, and lit a cigarette. She blew smoke rings through the screen and watched them fade to nothing outside. "Why are you not talking about wifey?"

"Elise. And I'm not 'not talking about' her."

"Give me her best quality. Then her worst."

To discuss Elise behind her back struck him as disloyal. Come to think of it, there wasn't really anyone he shared details about his marriage with. Of course, Cass wasn't just anybody. She was his oldest friend. Someone who'd known him before his parents died.

"Come on . . ."

Best quality. Had to be her bizarre ability to deal with any sort of emergency, especially if it involved a total stranger. Matt had planned their first date to the tiniest detail. She was a beautiful girl with elegance and boots that didn't fit and a funny little dimple next to her mouth. This date mattered. He'd booked a cozy Italian place near the Carlyle Hotel and splurged on a new cologne—Hermès Eau d'Orange Verte—because the saleswoman at Bloomingdales said, along with citrus and patchouli and soap, it hinted of leather. Matt hoped a rider might be subliminally entranced. Anyway, his MasterCard wasn't quite at its limit.

There she was, sitting on the low wall at the park's edge at East 76th. Wind billowed her dress around her knees and she fought to keep it down.

A shy hello, a double-cheek kiss as he greeted her, and they turned to the street, waited to cross Fifth Avenue. A helmetless couple on Segways came bumping along the brick sidewalk, their vehicles unwieldy as they navigated tree roots that swelled the sidewalk in places. As the pair drew close, the woman, wiry russet braids lying on her shoulders like fox pelts, pitched forward and struck her head on the bricks with enough force you could hear the fleshy *thunk*.

By the time Matt realized what had happened, Elise was down on her knees, helping the woman. She had one person calling 911. Another giving up his blazer, which Elise laid over the woman as if she were tucking in a treasured child.

Never, in all his years, had Matt seen a more sweetly generous or more nurturing gesture—to a total stranger. This horseback rider with the too-tight boots was one of a kind. When the ambulance arrived and they left for the restaurant, Matt curled an arm around Elise's neck and kissed the top of her head. He was never going to let this superhero go.

"She has this insane ability to handle emergencies. Like once we were in a hotel room in Chicago and someone tried to get into our room in the middle of the night. I had my hand on the phone, dialing the front desk like a good coward does. She was at the door, banging on the inside of it, scaring the guy off. She says she doesn't even decide to jump into action. Her body just takes over."

Cass nodded. "She's tough when it counts."

"Pretty much."

"Worst?"

His gaze moved away from Cass, settling on her battered red leather sandals on the fraying mat by the door. The obvious. "Elise is a rider. Big-time, as in she could be headed for the Olympics. So she's not around enough. And that makes for a life that's never quite right, if you know what I mean. Today there was a whole kerfuffle with the horse not boarding onto a plane, and Elise missed Gracie's first play. So that was kind of brutal."

"I'll bet." An uncomfortable moment passed, then Cass's face warmed. "Hey, do you remember Saturday nights at the airport? We used to score beer from Fenton's brother and lie at the end of the runway."

Jesus, those nights had been perfect. "We'd stare at the stars. Solve the world's problems."

She nudged his calf with her toes. "And other stuff."

"You never could keep your hands off me, Urquhart. Admit it."

"You're so deluded. Hey, remember that time Nate climbed to the top of the big oak out front?"

"He was going to cut it down, one dead branch at a time."

"I thought he'd be the one dead when he fell—what was it, like, forty feet? He hit every goddamned branch as he dropped."

"Right? Then limped into the house to change into a suit before calling nine-one-one."

"And insisted the paramedics take him to Elizabethtown because the nurses are cuter there."

Laughing, Matt refilled their glasses, glanced outside to see River launch a burning stick at the shoreline and jump for joy when it hit the water. Gracie watched from the big log by the fire.

Cass stood to rinse her cigarette butt under tap water and push it into an empty Coke can. "So, what's the plan? You guys staying the summer?"

"Just here to sell."

"You've gotta be shitting me."

"Two weeks to prep the place and then we list."

"Your grandfather might climb out of his grave. Your father, too."

"Yeah, well."

"This town is going to freak out when they hear, that's all I'm gonna say. Some developer will want the land to slap up another Lake Placid Lodge. But if you're serious, my boyfriend, Garth, is with Alpine Realty. Number one, three years running. And you can trust him, which is something rare in that business."

"I'd thought Sotheby's. But sure."

Outside, Gracie's marshmallow fell from her hand and rolled a few feet down the slope toward the lake. As River launched another stick, she threw a quick, self-conscious glance toward her crutches, then crawled toward the marshmallow.

"She's a doll. I've always wanted a little girl. Did she injure herself?"

"Mild cerebral palsy from an accident when Elise was pregnant." Doctors had been batting around the possibility from the moment Gracie drew her first terrifyingly belated breath. Before that night in the maternity ward, Matt had thought cerebral palsy was a genetic defect—something like Down syndrome or a hole in the heart. But cerebral palsy is caused by a brain injury or malformation during pregnancy or birth. Every case is unique. Damage might impact anything from a child's posture and reflexes to muscle tone and control to motor skills—you didn't necessarily know for years. In Gracie's case, Elise's accident had caused something called hypoxic ischemic encephalopathy: acute brain injury due to asphyxia. Asphyxia due to placental abruption. "Her case is considered quite mild, and she will improve, but cerebral palsy doesn't exactly go into remission."

"What kind of accident?"

"She got on a horse. Just for a second, but it didn't go well." Before Cass could respond, he added, "At that level, it's normal to ride pregnant. Even the doctors are cool with it until the third trimester. You do what you've always done if the pregnancy is healthy, right?"

Cass ignored the question. "And what about operating?"

"The doctor we're seeing has suggested a series of possible surgeries to straighten the bones in her legs."

"And what do you think?"

Gracie's doctor was a marathon runner who bounced on his toes. He couldn't keep still and spoke so fast Matt felt he missed a lot of what he told them. "Elise is all for it. But I . . ." One thing his grandfather taught him was, if you want to stay healthy, you stay far away from doctors. You don't interfere. "Surgery is an option for down the road. She has a lot of growing to do."

Cass was silent a moment. Then, "Are you pissed?"

He knew she wasn't referring to the doctor. Their daughter hadn't been due for nine more weeks. He'd been in a rush to get to court that day. Straightening his tie, he'd flicked off the bulb in the walk-in closet and stepped into the inky thickness of the bedroom, where Elise lay asleep, hardly daring to breathe lest he wake her. The narcoleptic surrender that slammed other pregnant women had skipped his bride. From the moment she'd found out, she was predatory in her edginess, her inability to sit still, pacing the perimeter of every room in the house, as if looking for a way out of her own body.

He'd left the bedroom. At the next doorway, he stopped: the early morning light was hitting the bars of the waiting crib.

Downstairs, looking for his black brogues, he dug through the coat closet, beneath Elise's winter riding boots, everyday riding boots, and sneakers. He banged residual barn dirt from his shoes. It wasn't until he was about to leave, keys in hand, that he noticed Elise's paddock boots by the front door. She'd continued to go to the barn, of course. Her coach was training the horse. Still, he debated going back upstairs. Waking her to reassure himself that, when she did go, it wouldn't be to ride. But he was late and traffic would be a nightmare. He grabbed his keys and left.

What good would anger do now? It was what it was. Matt watched a housefly travel along the bottom of the window screen, then stop and rub its forelegs together. He pried the screen loose and set the insect free. "You go forward," he told Cass.

Cass accepted this without comment. Then pointed. Gracie had wiggled closer to River on the log. After a few moments of watching, she said, "They put that little bundle in your arms, and boom. Game over."

There had been no bundle placed in Elise's arms. Gracie was pulled from her mother's unzipped belly a deep purplish blue. Elise was anesthetized, so only Matt saw their daughter's tiny legs, little bird hands and feet with fingers and toes spread, flailing in the air as one person passed her to the next. Then wires sprouted from her torso. She was put into an Isolette. The primal moment where mother meets baby got mangled.

She weighed three pounds five ounces.

"Yeah." Suddenly he needed to touch his daughter's hair. He stood with a scrape of his chair. "Let's go out and join them."

Wineglasses in hand, he and Cass went through the den again. This time, a stack of large books—all the same—caught his eye and he picked one up. *American Dreamer.* The cover was the Woodstock photo, with CASSIDY URQUHART emblazoned across the bottom. "This is yours?"

"Comes out next week." She watched him flip through the pages. Photograph after photograph of children in motion. "I'm with an art house press. Small publisher, but you get a lot of attention."

"These are stunning."

She shrugged.

"You're a serious talent. And how smart to use that photo on the front."

"My editor thought it would help sell books—'photos by the Woodstock Girl!'"

"Ever find out who took it?"

"The publisher tried to track him down, but no luck. So they figured what the hell? Let's use it. He never came forward to sue *Life* for publishing it. Anyway, I kind of love that we don't know, that he's this flickering memory of a scraggly red beard and a crazy name. Patch. Or Badge."

"Probably the only one at Woodstock besides your parents and the musicians who could afford a camera. Which means he had a job. There's one clue."

"Don't spoil the mystery."

On the back cover was a quote by someone named Val Reiser. "Urquhart's work stands up to Leibovitz in her early days . . ."

Matt stared at Cass. That explained, beyond her dad's life insurance, the improvements she'd made to the house and the ability to raise River on her own without a full-time job. "Do you sell most of your work?"

"Don't get me started on selling. Everyone makes money except the artist. My agent makes money, the gallery owners make money, the resale dealers make money. Even the buyers make money. Collectors who bought into my work in the early days—they paid next to nothing. And now they're selling my stuff to third parties for tens of thousands of dollars. They make a mint, while I get screwed. I don't profit from it at all."

Matt disliked talking money. It was the way he was raised. But Cass was likely starved to discuss her predicament with someone. "More often than not it goes the other way, though, right?" he asked her. "Buyers who gamble on new artists lose money. Artists like you are anomalies—and the reason the resale market exists."

"Yeah, well. Somehow the really big money ends up flying around me, without ever landing in my hands. I've been considering moving back to California. They have this Resale Royalty Act. Artists can claim royalties in resales. Or they could, anyway. Not sure if it still exists. But New York State—hello, we're ground zero of art, right? We've never had any such thing." She shrugged. "Whatever. I love taking pictures. All these little moments. They matter more and more to me as time passes, because you can't get them back. Good or bad, you can't undo them. There's something beautiful about that."

A blush crept up Cass's neck to bloom on her cheeks. He had a flash of her as a teen—a few months younger than he was. She was sitting alone in her parents' orange Volkswagen Beetle in the driveway, smoking a joint, blasting the Police's "Every Little Thing She Does Is Magic"—the anthem of every adolescent boy who pined for a girl he didn't have the balls to ask out.

"They're having a launch party for me at the Bookworm in town next week," she said. "I have this fear it'll be only my mom and Garth in the audience, so if you guys are around . . ."

"I doubt that'll happen, but we'll be there."

"You hear about the bears this year?"

"No."

"One walked into Pharma World at noon last week. Strolled right on through the automatic doors and headed for the deli counter like he was picking up a platter for a party. It's pretty crazy. Someone said the cold spring we had meant the plants came up wa-ay late. Then I heard it's the females, they're all amorous this year for some reason." She started outside with a chuckle. "They're club hopping."

"You could've mentioned that before we left the kids outside, Urquhart." Matt stepped out the back door behind her and down the steps toward the fire. A heavy cloud cover had rolled across the sky. Maybe the rain had followed them.

"We haven't seen any around here. Yet. Hey!" she called out. "Who wants to play I Spy with My Little Eye?"

"Ten minutes, Cass," Matt said. "It's after midnight."

He watched her get the kids settled in chairs. If he'd been asked back then how Cass Urquhart would turn out—hell, if you'd asked anyone alive in the sixties how the Woodstock Girl would turn out, everyone would have described her exactly as she was: laid-back and insanely talented, living in Lake Placid, barefoot around a bonfire. Priorities in order—cupboards full of chipped mugs, but walls covered with portraits of her son.

....

Back in Nate's pillowy bed, Matt glanced at his sleeping wife. He had no choice but to decline the partnership. There was no telling an athlete who's hoped and prayed and trained and sacrificed, who's dared to attempt something almost no one on earth will ever accomplish—now that her dream might actually come true—that the timing was a little off. This wasn't a job to Elise. It was her life.

Chapter 8

....

She'd forgotten how chilly an Adirondack morning in June could be. With her husband and daughter still asleep, Elise pulled a heavy sweater of Matt's over T-shirt and shorts, pushed her feet into moccasin slippers, and started downstairs, blowing on cold hands.

She'd woken up from a terrible dream.

There she was, standing outside a church, trying to pull open a door that had locked after Matt and Gracie went in. When she peered through the window, Gracie had become a young woman in a wedding gown. Tall and slender, with no crutches, she moved with refinement and fluidity. She was getting married. But Elise could see her only through a window. It was freezing outside. Snow started to fall. Elise raced from window to window and banged on the glass with an open palm. No one turned. She couldn't see Gracie's face. She could see now that there was a coffin in front of the altar. It was also a funeral, but whose? There was Matt, in the first pew on the right. He was holding hands with a woman. She turned enough so that Elise could see her face. It was her father's second wife. And the person in the coffin was Elise.

Most certainly inspired by Gracie's plane crash question. And a waste of mental energy to think about for even one more second.

On the paneled wall going down the stairs, the same familiar family photos: Sorensons on the lake, Sorensons on the ski hill, Sorensons at weddings, Sorenson Christmases. Matt's cap-and-gown grad photos from high school, undergrad, law school at Rutgers. Photos of Gracie as a baby, a toddler; one when she was five and Nate was teaching her to steer his antique boat. Finally, at the bottom of the stairs, a few photos of the three of them that Matt had hung to make his wife feel less like an outsider.

As Elise crossed through the living room, she caught sight of an animal in her periphery. A dead German shepherd on the hearth—stuffed? As she caught her breath, she realized it wasn't just any German shepherd; it was Gunner. Nate had had his own dog taxidermied. Clearly Gracie had seen it: her tiara sat drunkenly over his ears.

This was right out of a John Irving novel. Which was it—*The Hotel New Hampshire*? A taxidermied Labrador. Like Sorrow, this animal was thoroughly capable of scaring someone to death.

She'd have to talk to Matt. They were *not* going to have Nate's dead dog staring at them for the next two weeks.

In the kitchen, that vintage Ski New York poster she'd always loved. A woman in a snowflake sweater and red ski pants swishing down a slope on Splitkein wooden skis against a deep cobalt sky. Above the poster, Matt's late grandmother's old hickory Flexible Flyers were nailed to the log wall.

She opened the door to the cool, moist air of the screened back porch, long ago winterized with electric baseboard heaters and thick storm windows. The battered antique table had to stretch twenty feet across the room—the top made from one long slab of pine. Neither the benches along the sides nor the mismatched wooden armchairs at the ends had cushions. Maybe Elise's behind was bonier than the Sorensons', because the hard wood never seemed to bother them.

Tweed-covered chairs and sofa, and a coffee table groaning with board games, sat on a trampled rag rug in front of the fireplace. And lurking in every nook, every cranny . . . spiders.

In one corner leaned a group of canoe paddles. Above the fireplace, crisscrossed wooden snowshoes. Along the strip of wall above the windows, a series of paint-by-numbers, all done by various Sorensons over the years, including Gracie.

Ralph Lauren himself couldn't have conjured up a decor more quintessentially Adirondack.

Outside, silvery-gray mist obliterated everything but the softened outline of the shed, the mass of blackish-green trees just beyond that, and the smooth surface of the lake. There was movement down by the water, not at their beachfront, but next door. A gorgeous woman in a big sweatshirt and bikini bottoms, darkish red-brown hair pulled back in a curly knot, sipped coffee at the end of the dock.

Elise felt the tiniest bubbly sensation deep in her belly—a sip of San Pellegrino. It had happened more than once in the past few days, and she had been wondering if she'd eaten something slightly off or was fighting a stomach bug.

Her phone vibrated in her pocket. Ronnie.

"So here's what it's like the day of the opening ceremonies," he said when she picked up. "They keep all the athletes in a huge room for hours. You're in there with the best of the best, right? In the downtime, you start to play games with the other members of the U.S. team. 'Why is that Russian athlete so small?' Then you realize: gymnast. 'Why is that runner smoking a cigarette?' Right—he's French. They hand you a brown paper bag. It's your lunch: a peanut butter sandwich, milk, and an apple. It gets that fancy. Then you change into whatever your team's designer has decided you'll wear."

"Go on."

"Later, you start to hear the dull roar of the stands filling up. Because countries are called out in alphabetical order, you'll have a good long time to watch the other teams step out. You'll see the thrill on their faces from the monitors where you wait. There'll be lights and music. Any number of weird effects. Finally, it's time for the U.S. team. You file out of the dark and into the razzle-dazzle of camera flashes from the media stations all around you. You look out at all these athletes from all over the world, each of them thinking, 'Holy hell, I made it,' just like you. The only thing that feels better than that moment is when they hang a medal around your neck and play 'The Star-Spangled Banner.'"

"And you're telling me this right now because . . . ?"

"Mademoiselle Secretary has a high suspensory tear. Tamara's pulling out of the Pan Ams in Toronto. Games open July tenth. Dressage on the eleventh, twelfth, and fourteenth."

Elise sank down into a creaky wicker chair, tucking cold toes beneath her. The implications of Tamara's misfortune, and the reason Ronnie had called so early, began to sink in.

She tilted her head back to stare at the plank ceiling. "And she's traveling reserve."

"Was. Now you're traveling reserve."

"I'm going to the Pan Ams?"

"And I want you back early, before they convene at Gladstone."

She stood in the kitchen, dazed. Life was changing so fast. But she didn't have to return right away—she could take a few days up here. Still. How to tell Matt? How to tell Gracie?

She thought, stupidly, for a moment, *What if Gracie comes home with me?* She could hang out at the stable while Elise rode, as she'd done so many summer days in the past. No. Gracie was far better off here at the lake with Matt's full attention.

Breakfast. Get breakfast going. She'd stopped for groceries on the way out of Montclair to surprise her husband and daughter with

French toast and fresh-squeezed orange juice. She set the old cast-iron pan on the stovetop, watched a dollop of butter spit and sizzle in the heat, then cracked four eggs into a large bowl.

As she started to beat the eggs with a fork, glasses in the old porcelain sink caught her eye and she froze. Two stemmed glasses, each with a tiny puddle of red wine inside. She picked one up. It had lipstick on the rim.

She glanced outside. The woman was gone.

The familiar hammering inside her rib cage. Every time she was away, she convinced herself she'd beaten it. The distance padded her somehow, made her feel independent and strong. But when she returned, the fear that Matt might abandon her wrapped itself around her neck once again and squeezed.

It was September 7th, 2004, the last time they'd celebrate the anniversary of their first date before the wedding day came along a year later to eclipse it. Elise wanted to go to the River Café, an old floating barge permanently moored beneath the Brooklyn Bridge. The food was widely known to be mediocre, but the atmosphere was iconic New York City. There they were, Annie Hall and Alvy Singer, basking in the golden interior, looking out at the watery purples of the East River, the jewel-box Manhattan skyline, the ominous underside of the bridge, while Gershwin wafted in from another room. It was a bridge and tunnel crowd for sure, but a big rush of pride came with that view.

"It was right in front of you," Elise said, shaking out her napkin and refolding it on her lap. They were headed to the cabin the next morning, for Nate's birthday. Matt had bought his grandfather new binoculars and had searched the entire apartment for Scotch tape so he could wrap the gift. Elise arrived home to pull the tape out of a drawer he'd looked in three times. Matt had been certain she'd planted it there.

"Your plan is showing, E, and it's not pretty." He dipped a piece of bread in olive oil and popped it in his mouth. "You want to slowly drive me mad by hiding things and magically finding them."

"And what would my end goal be?"

He considered this. "The heady intoxication of superiority. Winning at all cost. I wind up in a straitjacket and you get the bed to yourself. No more toilet seats up . . . that's a bonus."

"Actually . . . " She ran her fingertip along the mouth of her wineglass. "This isn't sounding half bad. Plus, way less laundry."

"Matt Sorenson. Can I never be free of you?" A woman with long black hair and a killer smile stopped at their table.

Matt got up to give her a quick hug. "They don't like to advertise it," he said, "but my job is to make sure the newbies have zero life outside the office." He held out a hand to the towering bald man beside her—her husband, Brent—then gestured toward Elise. "Finally you get to meet the beautiful woman I'm seeing. Elise, Harriet and Brent. Harriet came to us from Gerhart Lewison Carter. She's on the Maaske case with me."

"And the Sincero case, and the Langton-Wan case, and the Levin case." Like every woman who worked with Matt, Harriet wore heels Elise could never walk in.

"Nice kid," Matt said when they'd gone. "But she makes this weird clicking sound when she's focused." Matt mimicked it by inhaling saliva pooled in his cheeks. "Gets annoying."

Elise stared out the window, lost in thought.

"What?" he said. "What'd I do?"

"*The woman you're seeing?* We live together. 'The woman I'm seeing' is what you say on the third or fourth date. We blew past 'the woman I'm seeing' ages ago."

"That's ridiculous. Harriet knows we live together."

Elise was quiet. She put her fork down and set her hands in her lap.

"Elise, come on. Don't overanalyze this. It means nothing."

"It doesn't mean nothing. It shows you're not fully committed. It's like the name thing."

"What name thing?"

"You don't want me to take your last name if we get married."

"We're not even engaged yet."

"Still!"

"All I said was, why take a longer name than you already have? And what about for riding? You have a name that's already established."

"But you should *want* me to take your name. See? Then I make the choice. All these mixed messages add up. They make me feel like . . . where did the floor go? It doesn't feel solid."

"Babe. You and I both know this isn't about me."

She looked at him, feeling her cheeks flush. "Don't start with my father."

"Okay." Matt stood. Walked around the table, got down on one knee, and took her hand. "Elise Bleeker, when I ask you to marry me one day, will you take my name?"

She swatted him away, softening. "Jerk."

"If you loved me, you'd call me 'stupid jerk.' I find 'jerk' impersonal and, thusly, offensive."

They were engaged five weeks later. Married the following September. He'd been right. She'd overreacted.

"Boo!"

Elise spun around now to see her beautiful daughter in the doorway. She set down the glass and opened her arms to hug the child, still in her hippopotamus pajamas. "Look who's up! Come here. I need my Gracie fix."

"Watch this." Gracie wriggled out of reach. She planted her crutches two feet ahead and propelled herself into the sofa cushions in a yellow ball of triumph.

Elise clapped. "Spectacular. Perfect ten."

"Is that an Olympic sport?"

"Long jumping *is* an Olympic sport," said Elise. "You'll have to start practicing without crutches." She placed more sopping bread in the pan. "And I still haven't gotten my hug."

"But I can go farther with crutches."

"You could start practicing smaller jumps first. Teensy ones in a safe spot." Gracie needed to build and strengthen her leg muscles. Nate had insisted that she would learn to walk unassisted in her own time, though, so Matt's mind was set. His esteemed grandfather's word trumped the advice of any medical doctor; it was up to Gracie to decide when to let go of her crutches. No nudging.

"Dad says I can get a wheelchair on his insurance. It would be free."

"What?"

"It would be fun. I could pretend I'm paralyzed."

What was Matt thinking? "You should not be thinking about wheelchairs, sweetness."

Gracie knelt on a kitchen chair, reached into her mother's big red vintage handbag, and pulled out a sunglasses case.

"Honey, you know how I am about that purse."

Her daughter sat back on her heels. "Crazy."

"Pretty much. But I have another one upstairs that you can play with."

"Can I go see River today? He's going to feed a mouse to his snake."

"Sure. Where does he live?"

Her daughter pointed next door. Interesting. Elise made her tone deliberately casual. "Did you meet River's family last night?"

"We went there. His family is Cass. Her picture was on the cover of a *magazine*."

This must be the Woodstock Girl—Matt's first girlfriend. There were photos around the cabin of her. "I thought she didn't live there anymore. She moved back?"

Gracie groaned and rolled her eyes. "I'm eight years old." She slumped over the table as if she'd been beheaded. "How do I know?"

Great. Elise would go home Wednesday to train while her husband and daughter hung for another ten days with the goddess on the dock, with whom Matt shared memories bathed in the golden light of childhood nostalgia, the *actual* girl next door, and her son—who has snakes. How could that possibly mess with Elise's focus?

"Come over here. I'm going to teach you how to make French toast."

Gracie made her way across the kitchen and let her mother lift her up onto the counter. Elise put the spatula in her daughter's hand. "So, you slither this under the bread. Detach it from the pan, then, with a quick twist of the wrist, you flip it over."

They flipped it together and the bread sizzled and crackled in the hot pan.

"Very impressive," said Elise.

"Did you win at your horse show, Mom?"

"Actually, by some miracle, I did."

"Are you going to the Olympics?"

"It's looking better than it did a week ago."

Gracie opened and closed the drawer behind her knees, pulled out a spoon that she tried to hang from her nose. "What would happen if a coyote wanted to be an Olympic figure skater?"

"I'd say he'd have to work *really* hard. He'd have to listen to his coyote coach and take in every bit of advice." Elise dunked another slice of bread. "If he does that, maybe he can win a gold medal."

"But what if someone leaves the door open where they keep the gold medals?" Gracie giggled. "Then he could just take one."

"But his medal won't mean anything. He'll have accomplished nothing."

Gracie's freckled nose crinkled. "But he'll have a *really* shiny necklace. And—hello!—he's pretty good at skating."

Elise flipped the bread. Even considering Gracie's limitations, was it enough for her to aspire to being "pretty good" at whatever she chose to pursue?

When Elise's fourth-grade public school teacher, Mrs. Ramirez, encouraged her to take part in the winter talent contest, Elise chose to sing "It's the Hard-Knock Life," from the musical *Annie*. Every night, she practiced in the den, to her parents' joy and delight.

"You are my treasure," said her mother. "I can see your soul when you sing."

"You're going to be a star. Famous and rich." Her father's eyes danced. "Don't let anyone say you won't, princess. We make our own opportunities. That's how life works."

No one could ever accuse her parents of parroting each other.

Elise was to follow Alexa Batali, a fifth grader with a strawberry birthmark over one eye, who sang "Candle in the Wind" with a voice so clear and strong, Elton himself would have wept.

Backstage, Elise watched the crowd. Gone was the shifting, the coughing, the whispering that had accompanied Benjie Verlander's drum solo. Alexa's golden voice had the entire audience—even Elise's parents—enraptured. Right then, Elise understood excellence. She pushed through the stage door before Alexa's standing ovation hit its peak. By the time she reached the trampled snow on the playground, tiny clouds of her own breath blurring her vision, she understood. "Pretty good" was an utter waste of time. Anyone could be pretty good at something; not everyone could be excellent. And anything less wasn't worth striving for.

Now, Elise turned to her daughter and cupped her chin. "Your job in life is to discover where your greatness lies. Because *everyone* has the potential to be excellent at something. You need to find your excellence and then go for it."

The moment was too serious for Gracie. "That makes me want to quit everything."

"Maybe it's swimming."

"Why do you always talk about swimming? It's so boring."

"Swimming is not boring."

"You talking about it is."

What Elise didn't say was that, in the water, Gracie would be weightless. Once she learned the basics, the different strokes, treading water, floating, she would be fluid and free in a way she obviously wasn't on land. Riding specially trained horses was another fabulous sport for anyone less than fully mobile. But Gracie refused this as well. "You've got to learn one of these days. Face your fear."

Still on the counter, Gracie leaned sideways to flip another piece of egg-soaked bread and sent it sailing to the floor. She squealed with laughter as Elise scooped up the mess.

"Hon, can you grab a tea towel from the cupboard?" Elise motioned to an upper cupboard next to her daughter and Gracie twisted around.

"Hey, hey, hey." Matt trotted across the kitchen to scoop Gracie off the counter and onto his hip, where he bounced her playfully. "We don't sit on counters, princess. You know that. It isn't safe." He leaned over to kiss Elise's cheek. "Good morning, my lovely."

"I was right beside her."

"No worries. You've been away for a while, is all."

Don't say a word. Elise smiled.

Still in her dad's arms, Gracie pulled the cupboard door open, sending tea towels tumbling out onto the counter. There, on the center shelf, lay a large pile of feces—worryingly fresh.

Shrieks. Groans. The patter of running feet. In five seconds, Elise and Gracie were out of the cabin and in the car, with Matt sauntering out to reassure them that those were not bear droppings. Possum, maybe, or raccoon, but *definitely* not bear.

The sign looked exactly as it had since Matt's childhood: EAGLE GAS AND VARIETY hand-painted in a loopy, hesitant white script on a piece of faded evergreen plywood. As ever, a bell clanged every time a car drove over the rubber hose at the pumps, and signs on the windows boasted LIVE BAIT! AND FUDGE!

Elise and Gracie had gone straight inside. Matt made his way around back to the restrooms with a key attached to a greasy stick, still wondering why Elise wasn't disturbed in the slightest when Gracie, on the way over, said she was trying to think of injuries to inflict on her stuffed animals. His wife's words were: "Why don't we research different kinds of accidents? Come up with some really creative misfortunes for them."

What the hell? Matt had looked at Elise and, in an effort to get his point of view across without stirring up a fight, said, "Or, here's a crazy idea . . . Why don't you be nice to them? Pretend you're their teacher and enlighten them about your summer."

"Have them spend one night in the cupboard with the bear," Elise said, winking at Gracie. "Then all you'll have left will be dozens of shredded limbs and tiny eyeballs. Maybe we could gather them up to make one really monstrous creature."

"Yeah!"

Matt drove on, stunned. When he next glanced at Elise, she was digging for something in her purse. "How about we ixnay the iolence-vay?"

His wife glanced up. "Excuse me?"

"He said 'nix the violence' in pig latin, Mom."

Elise pulled out her phone to check for messages and slid it back into the bag.

Now, Matt watched a pair of crisply clean gulls peck at crushed Doritos on the asphalt as he unlocked the restroom door. A great ugly monster gull swooped down out of nowhere to drive them off in a macho display of flapping and squawking and strutting. He pushed the door open.

It was almost like walking into his childhood home, he knew this bathroom so well. The floor had been replaced. It used to be ratty brown linoleum; now they'd done it up in gray tile, the grout of which had gone black with grime. Hard to tell with the toilet—the enamel bowl was rust-stained back then, when he used to throw up in it, and it was rust-stained now. The walls—cheap white tiles—were covered in crude drawings of breasts and penises, as well as unchecked teenage wisdom, from the ill-advised *Vote for Satan!* to the far more practical *Never stop pooping.* Below the toilet paper dispenser, vital instructions: *Pull for Arts Degree.* And below the condom machine change slot: *Insert baby here for full refund.*

It didn't seem possible that the place had gotten worse with time.

His eyes rested on the fake marble counter and he was hit hard by a sudden memory of Cass sneaking in here with him, horny and drunk enough that last summer to make love against the grimy sink.

Opera music wafted from ceiling speakers at the entry—not what you'd expect from a place that sold deer licks and chocolate-covered raisins branded as "Moose Droppings." Eagle Gas and Variety housed an eclectic mix of wares meant to cover the needs of moneyed weekenders, practical locals, and tourists looking to bring a bag of chips back to the hotel room so they didn't have to crack open the minibar. They carried chipotle chicken panini and salted caramel gelato, had a live-worm dispensing machine, stocked beach towels depicting black bears sunbathing that read I'M BEARY FOND OF THE ADIRONDACKS. They sold expensive evergreen-scented soaps and the odd relic from simpler times: an antique butter churn, a vintage football helmet. Plus, all the brand-new nostalgia you could stomach, for the low, low price of—he picked up a Lake Placid snow globe—$8.95. Ironic that most of these bits of Americana were, in fact, made in China.

Tourists loved the painted tin ceiling, the dirty old black-and-white floor tiles, the long pine counter worn thin at the cash register from nearly a century of toddlers and purses set down while someone dug for change. On hot days, big fans whirred overhead, fluttering the pages of magazines on racks and community flyers on the bulletin board by the open door.

Matt found Elise and Gracie in the dry goods aisle, near the buzzing coolers filled with Popsicles and ice cream. Seeing his wife in slippers and his daughter in pajamas made him realize he was still in the T-shirt he'd slept in. Elise was peering around the end aisle at a middle-aged female golfer dressed in white and gold. She nudged Matt. "I swear to god, that woman made a face at me. Bumped into my arm and then sneered like I spat on her."

"You always think that when we're here—that people are against you."

"Because it always happens up here."

Gracie held up a four-pack of tapioca pudding. "What's ta-ci-op-a?"

Matt didn't hesitate. "It's the most tragic dessert there is. Your grandpa Nate was a terrible cook. After my parents died, he used to take me to Grocery Mart just before Thanksgiving and Christmas to fill our shopping cart with tapioca pudding and frozen turkey TV dinners so the neighbors would feel sorry for us. Invite us over to their family feasts."

"Did it work?" Elise asked.

"Every time." He ruffled Gracie's hair. "I think it's high time you and tapioca get acquainted, what do you say?"

A package of red licorice had stolen her attention. "Nah."

Matt dropped the pudding pack onto the shelves. You really couldn't ever go back.

"Hey, wow. Aren't you Matthew Sorenson?" Matt looked up to see a youngish man behind the snack counter looking at him with something resembling hero worship. Late twenties, fuzzy beard, gentle, open expression, hair tied back in a man bun. His skin was deep olive, his eyes such a pale green they almost glowed. Matt was willing to bet he had half the town's females looking for excuses to drop into the store. He was starting to reply when the guy came forward to shake his hand vigorously, face breaking into a huge smile. "I'm Paulie Gupta. I've seen you around, but always from afar. Your dad helped my folks in a big way."

"Gupta." Matt thought a second. "Your parents are Prasad and ...?"

"Vanya."

"Yes, Vanya. It was my grandfather who helped." Matt remembered the story. The store sat on a forty-five-degree angle to the gas pumps, and it was a tricky intersection, 86 and Grafton. The only direction from which you could pull into the station was heading into town, but most folks wanted to fill up on the way out of town, en route to the interstate. Eagle Gas was failing.

Back then, the variety store wasn't much more than a place to pick up a pack of smokes and a pepperoni stick while you paid for your gas. The only foot traffic was from kids racing in to pull a Fudgsicle out of the freezer. Vanya tried to encourage tourists by selling her "Bengali fudge"—not fudge at all, but delicious, sugary cubes made from milk turned into some sort of cheese with cardamom—along with the windshield washer fluid and scented car fresheners.

Like so many in Lake Placid back then, after being turned away from the bank, Prasad had come to Nate Sorenson for a loan. Nate pointed out that their problem wasn't cash flow; it was access. Even if the Guptas were to cut their prices in half, cars were still going to glide on past and pull into the Chevron station across the street, to avoid the hassle of turning around. You need to change the curbs, he said. Prasad explained that he'd asked for approval from the village, but his request had been denied.

Nate organized a crew to jackhammer all the curbs. Eagle Gas and Variety became the most accessible fill-up spot in town, swarmed from morning to night.

One day, Prasad came to Nate in a panic: people from the highway department were coming—the superintendent himself. It had been illegal to remove the curbs. Nate assured Prasad he'd sit in on the meeting, which was arranged for the second Thursday in July. Nate told Vanya to stop the ceiling fans and jack up the heat. By three thirty p.m., when the superintendent and his team arrived, the temperature in Prasad's office was 104 degrees, according to an enamel thermometer. Within eleven minutes, the people from the highway department signed off on the curbs.

Two weeks later, Prasad permanently changed his pricing strategy: one cent per gallon more than the Chevron station across the street, where cars could only pull in from the north. At Eagle Gas and Variety, you could come from Illinois, Florida, Maine, or the southernmost point of Quebec in Canada. And leave with the best Indian dessert in the Adirondacks.

Paulie was still staring at Matt, grinning. "I'm excited to finally meet you."

The swell Matt felt took him by surprise. Was he that emasculated as a fifty-year-old associate at the firm, a guppy in the pool of successful Manhattan attorneys, that the awe of a kid at a small-town gas station made him feel like a VIP? He'd actually forgotten the last time he felt like someone other than a struggling lawyer, Gracie's dad, or Mr. Elise Sorenson. "Thanks. That's, uh . . ."

"You're a total legend around here. Any Sorenson is a rock star in Lake Placid."

The woman who had—or likely hadn't—snubbed Elise was now watching Matt from the aisle of household bleach and ant traps. His first groupie.

Then Gracie pressed her forehead to the glass display of ice cream tubs, asked for a milkshake for breakfast. Elise started suggesting healthy smoothies, and his groupie reached for a roll of paper towels. Even Paulie's attention turned to Matt's wife and daughter.

His superstar moment was over.

"Do you have protein powders, that kind of thing?" Elise asked.

"Totally. Fat burners too. We've got you covered."

"No. I can't risk those so close . . . no. I'll stick to protein."

Matt looked at her. The USADA—the anti-doping agency—had never chosen Elise for a random drug test this far away from home.

More often, it happened at shows. And she didn't have a show booked anytime soon. "So close to what?" he asked.

Her face blanched for just long enough to reveal that bad news was coming, then she cast him a polite smile. "Let's talk about it later." She turned to Paulie. "I'll try the Green Submarine with protein. And please don't give me the live bait by accident."

"I'd pegged you as more adventurous." Paulie winked. "But you're the customer."

Hmm, Matt thought. Flirting with his wife.

From where he was dropping Green Submarine ingredients into the blender, Paulie turned to Gracie, "What about you, captain? A Vanilla Monkey smoothie? Banana and yogurt. If you like, I can make it with extra monkey. But don't tell anyone. I'm only doing it for you." The blender whirred.

Gracie nodded, then, suddenly shy, whispered to Matt, "I want it with pea-nut but-ter."

Elise's fingers were nervously strumming the counter. "Paulie can't hear you unless you speak up, sweetness."

The child slid her thumb into her mouth and hid her face in her father's T-shirt.

Elise bent down, face-to-face. "Gracie, honey, I want you to clearly enunciate what you want. No baby talk, no thumb. You're a brave girl, right?"

This was what drove him crazy. Elise was happy for Matt to make almost all decisions when she was away, but lifted his authority upon her return. It made him feel like a mid-level manager whose carefully considered decisions are overturned when the CEO drops in. "She's tired," he said to Elise. "And we're in a new place—"

Gracie repeated through her thumb, "I'm tired and we're in a new place."

"She'll have a Vanilla Monkey smoothie with extra peanut butter." Matt slapped a twenty on the counter.

"Really?" His wife stared at him, mouth slack in disbelief, then her gaze locked onto Paulie's for a split second. If Matt had blinked, sneezed, checked his watch, he would have missed it. In that abbreviated moment, this Paulie character mentally joined Team Elise. Hopefully with his clothes on.

The moment passed. Team Elise immediately disbanded— Paulie to scoop peanut butter into the blender and Elise to usher Gracie outside.

So close to what? Matt still wanted to know.

Once he got his change, and poked a straw into his daughter's smoothie, Matt sauntered over to the reason he'd driven straight here in the first place: the fluttering bulletin board. Summer camps. Art lessons. Yoga collectives where you could pay as you plank. Labradoodle puppies coming soon. An event at abolitionist John Brown's farm: a human rights award was being presented to the living descendent of a local family. Matt had spent many a rainy camp morning at that historic farmhouse re-enacting tense pre–Civil War scenes in which John Brown and his wife risked their lives hiding former slaves in their cellar and enabling their escape to Canada. Might be good to take Gracie to the award ceremony.

A local attorney, Christopher Lund, had posted a small notice. Wills/estates, family, real estate, commercial. Sole practitioner with an address right in town. Once upon a time, Matt had thought that would be his life. Low cost of living. Zero commute—there was no rush hour in the Adirondacks. Not unless you included the rush to get to your dock with a nice New Zealand Sauvignon Blanc. You could come home after work to your family, breathe in the cleanest air anywhere. Wake up early enough for a swim before heading to the office. Or a quick loop around the frozen lake on cross-country skis in winter.

The appeal was easy to see.

The big-city version of that had been Matt's original vision. Small practice with loyal clients. Make his own hours, eventually buy the brownstone he'd been leasing space from in those early years—maybe even live up above it. See the name SORENSON on a brass plaque on the door, like his grandfather had in Lake Placid years ago. He couldn't help thinking he might have been able to make a go of his private practice if only he could have given it a few more years. Anyway. If wishes were horses. Or, more apt, if horses were wishes . . .

He looked up now to see Gracie and Elise getting into the BMW, and quickly unpinned a card for Skedaddle Humane Animal Removal, as well as Kostick & Sons Roofing. Not only did they have the leak upstairs, but he'd scanned the back of the house and found a gable where the soffits had been ripped away. Likely the point of entry for the intruder.

On his way to join his family, Matt caught sight of the water through the trees that edged the library. The sun had burned off the morning mist and a spray of crystal fire stretched all the way across the lake.

It wasn't until he reached the car that he realized Elise was in the back seat with Gracie. Terrific. They'd set a new record. Seven hours into their reunion and they already needed distance.

Chapter 9

....

Mom, that's River." Gracie had nudged Elise as they pulled into the driveway. On the porch steps was a dusty, bare-chested forest creature of a child. The boy looked up from picking at the sole of one dirty bare foot, long ropes of sun-faded hair hanging over cheeks smeared with dried mud. He stood when Gracie climbed out of the car and solemnly invited her to witness "the fattening of the serpent," a weekly ritual involving a sacrificial thawed mouse, sold by the pet store in bulk, like a sack of frozen pierogis. Off they went, with Gracie insisting that River come to the cabin afterward to meet her dead dog.

With the Skedaddle Animal Removal people not due until one thirty and Matt chasing down a roofer, Elise had a choice: clean up the aborted breakfast or lace up her sneakers and pound the roads and trails in and around the village for an hour.

Sweaty and exhausted, Elise slowed to a walk as she turned onto Seldom Seen from Mirror Lake Road. An athletic woman looked up from her garden, hair wound up in a bun atop her head and a wet bathing suit darkening her bright terry cover-up, feet pushed into short rubber boots. Behind a wooden fence was the hum of a pool filter. The swimmer shielded her eyes from the sun. "Oh, hello." She took off her gardening gloves and held them in one hand. Behind her was a pristine garage, walls lined with cabinets, shelving, and hooks with spades and rakes and hoes arranged from largest to smallest. "Wonderful to see you two are back together."

Did she have Elise confused with someone else? "I'm Nate Sorenson's daughter-in-law. Or was. I'm Matt's wife."

The swimmer wiped her forehead with the back of one hand and said nothing.

"We were never not together. We're together."

"My mistake." The woman smiled her apology and picked up a spade, pointed to the sky. "Enjoy the sun while we have it. I hear we're in for more rain this week."

Elise waved, told the swimmer to have a nice day, then strode along the weedy road's edge beneath a low, cool canopy of pines. Was she being paranoid? It could mean nothing. For sure it *did* mean nothing. It didn't signify that Matt had a secret mission to end the marriage and had shared it with a woman who loved her garden so much she couldn't be bothered to dry off before climbing into it.

Elise broke into a sprint.

The first work trip Matt had taken once they were married had been to DC with Harriet and an articling student named Timothy. It was early April and happened to be the peak of cherry blossom season. The streets would be a riot of frothy pink romantic loveliness. Matt left on a Tuesday morning, to return Thursday evening. Up until then, Elise had never had a moment of serious distrust of or worry about her husband.

She'd been heavily into spring show season, practically living at the barn. On top of it all, while trimming her horse's tail, she'd sliced into the flesh between the pinkie and ring finger of her left hand. It was sickening how the new scissors cut into her skin like butter. She'd had five stitches, and keeping her hand clean and dry, slathered in antibiotic cream, and fully bandaged had kept her preoccupied. Besides, Matt kept in touch, called each night with anecdotes about Timothy's girlfriend woes and Harriet's bad cold, which he hoped he wouldn't catch.

It was Wednesday—or, rather, the early hours of Thursday morning—when Elise was abruptly awakened by this thought: the condoms beneath the bathroom sink were missing. She climbed out of bed and padded into the master bath to dig through the cabinet, a jumble of aspirin, Band-Aids, old shampoo bottles, tampon boxes, and makeup. Because of her hand, she'd been riffling through the contents of this cupboard several times each day. The condom box was gone.

When Matt got home that night, Elise opened a bottle of wine and tentatively mentioned the missing box. He got up and marched into the master bedroom and bath, returning to the kitchen with the box and insisting it had been in the cupboard the whole time. Was it possible? Could she have missed it in her panic? She supposed so. But Matt was the one notorious for being unable to find anything. A tube of Krazy Glue, a Rolling Stones CD, his car keys—they could be right under his nose and he wouldn't see them. And there was his suitcase, splayed open on the bed.

Which place he'd taken them from, she'd never know.

Before the next bend in the road, Elise slowed to a stop, turned around. Maybe the smart woman just comes right out and asks. Saves herself the anguish, the second-guessing, the sudden urge to peek at her husband's phone. She walked back.

"I'm sorry." Elise put on her best I-don't-really-care-what-the-answer-is-I'm-just-super-friendly smile. "Just out of curiosity, what had you thinking we'd split?"

The swimmer-gardener looked around, either for someone to jump out of her bushes with an answer or because she needed a way to dodge Elise's paranoia. She shook her head, a confused smile keeping things just barely polite rather than judgmental. "I don't know. One of those things that doesn't matter."

A dusty black Honda Civic with a mismatched red hood and Vermont plates came creeping around the corner. Elise willed it to pass quickly so she could take her humiliation by the hand and march it away.

She returned to the cabin, sweaty and annoyed with herself, to see a blue van with aluminum ladders on the roof and KOSTICK & SONS ROOFING on the side parked out front. Two men were ripping shingles and rotted wood from the roof above the master bedroom. One was a puffy-faced man in his mid-sixties, sunburned head shaved to the scalp and a body so squarely packed into its skin that if he lost his balance, he'd likely just lie there, immobile. A human cinder block.

The other man was younger and appeared completely unsuited to manual labor. Handsome and slender, he had long, thick, graying dreads, round tortoiseshell glasses, and a rumpled white button-down shirt with sleeves rolled to the elbows. To Elise, he looked every bit the well-traveled intellectual that people like to gather around at a party to be regaled with stories about his latest research trip to Amsterdam or Istanbul. Both men wore work boots, but the Cinder Block wore boots so battered it was impossible to tell what color they'd started out. The Intellectual wore boots he might have purchased that morning.

She'd caught them mid-conversation as they ran supplies up and rubbish down the ladder.

"Shouldn't think it'll bother anyone if you're a couple minutes late," said the Cinder Block from the ground as he passed up a brown paper–wrapped batch of shingles.

"She can't get her own meals anymore. Not since her fall." The Intellectual had a load of shingles up onto the roof in seconds. "And

I'm sure as hell not going to let her go hungry," he said on his way back down.

"You're gonna take over my business, you're gonna have to work something out." Another batch transferred up the squeaky ladder.

"I'll stay as late as I can."

"I mean, I hear ya. But—"

"As I said. As late as I can."

A cord of firewood on the front porch lined the entire face of the cabin, tidily stacked to the window ledges. Elise dropped down onto the old cotton doormat to stretch over tired legs, pulling face to knees, inhaling the smell of pine and dust and sunscreen. She took her heels in her hands to intensify the stretch in her hamstrings, forcing herself lower, until her chest rested on her thighs. Her nipples stung, she noticed. It was the running bra; it chafed. She made a mental note to throw it away.

She rolled onto her back, bent one knee and pulled her toes back beneath her buttocks to loosen up her quad. Lay there a bit, rolling slightly side to side to increase the stretch, and debated the best time to tell Matt about Toronto. This two-week period had meant so much to them both. All that delicious time to reconnect as a couple. Time they desperately needed as a family. It made her nauseous to think about his reaction. He'd be crushed, but would understand.

Or, this time, maybe he wouldn't. At a certain point he might decide her ambitions were too detrimental to the family. What would she do if the situation were reversed? If Matt traveled all the time and, when he finally came home, announced he had to take off again? Stupid question. She'd assume the worst.

If nothing else, at least she was predictable.

Before heading out for her run, using her cellphone, Elise had poked around online and found short-term rentals in Caledon, the horse country north of Toronto where the dressage trials would be held. Because the cabin wouldn't have sold by then—or, if it had sold, the deal would still be in escrow—she'd hunted down an affordable one-room cottage in the corner of a farmer's field. A nearby town called Hockley Valley looked pretty, with rolling hills and a gorgeous country store that sold everything from champagne and Hunter rain boots to Drano and ant traps. They could drive up to Canada together. Matt and Gracie could be there for the show, and they could all take a bit of time to explore after.

Family Togetherness, the International Sequel.

Her new plan was this: she'd wouldn't leave until Friday. Ronnie could work her horse in the meantime. Certainly, Matt and Elise could get the bulk of the house cleaning done by then, as well as a fair bit of painting.

Maybe they'd go out to the little pizza restaurant in town tonight. Have a quiet dinner overlooking Mirror Lake. The place always stocked coloring books for children. They'd have a ball with Gracie, come back to the cabin, and, after Gracie went to bed, have a glass of wine on the porch. She'd explain . . . They still had five days before she left.

Still on her back, she tucked both knees into her chest and rocked forward and back on her spine, then hopped to her feet without touching palms to ground—a maneuver she'd learned in a power yoga class. A figure on the steps startled her, and Elise gasped.

"You must be Elise." It was the barefoot beauty from the dock, all wild hair and gold eyes drowsy with lashes. She had big, bossy breasts like the front grille of a futuristic high-speed train. Cass opened the screen door, rattling the cellophane wrapping of a large bouquet of flowers in her arms. She came forward and stretched out a hand. Her voice was smoky and deep. "I'm Cass. Matty told me all about you last night."

Matty?

"So nice to finally meet," Elise said. When they shook hands, Cass's chest sloshed like a waterbed mattress, and Elise realized she might be staring at the undulating reason her husband hadn't called her back last night.

"Sorry to keep your husband up so late." Cass's nails were bare, bitten to the skin. "It was like zero time had passed. So amazing to catch up."

"I bet."

"I'm sorry to hear you're selling." Cass glanced toward her driveway, where a modern-day yellow Volkswagen Beetle sat with the doors open. "I have to run and pick up my little boy, but let's all get together later for a swim."

"Yes, let's." *Over my dead body*, Elise thought.

Cass stopped halfway down the steps and ran back to hand the bouquet to Elise. "I forgot . . . These flowers were dropped off at my place by mistake. They're for you." She smiled. Flashed her fingers in goodbye.

Her lips were glossed deep red, like the stained wineglass.

Inside, Elise tore the cellophane from spray lilies and yellow roses and ferns, looking around for Matt, assuming he'd sent them from town and they'd been misdirected. She was thrilled their argument was over.

She tore open the tiny envelope and read the card. The flowers weren't from her husband at all.

Lisey,

Biggest congratulations on earth to my girl. What a score!
Look out, Rio, here she comes!
xoxo Dad

P.S. Would love to hear your voice. My number's the same
as ever.

Phone pressed to her ear, Elise listened to Ronnie's line ring as she marched the flowers through the back porch and down the steps to the stone path. Now, of course, the lilies made sense. They were showy and full of pomp and perfume and promises her father couldn't keep.

Finally, Ronnie picked up. "Don't be angry. He stopped by the barn hoping to see you."

At this, Elise slowed, incredulous. "Warren stopped by the barn? How often does he do that?"

"Hardly ever. Once, twice a year."

"And you let him?"

"Elise . . ."

"I have a right to decide who I want in my life and who I don't." Elise continued down toward the shed.

"Yes, you do. But he's been pretty respectful of you. Not every father would agree to let his sixteen-year-old daughter live at her crusty old riding coach's farm."

"He had no choice. I wasn't going to move in with him and his . . . " Her voice trailed off.

"He totally had a choice. You were a minor, and he could have had you legally removed and brought to his place."

"I'd have run away."

"Exactly. And you'd have been placed in foster care. He loved you way too much to make things any worse for you. I feel bad for him, Elise. You're his daughter."

"Was. I was his daughter."

"I'm *not* entirely sure that's a changeable designation."

She leaned down to pick up a fallen branch and tossed it onto the covered woodpile at the forest's edge. "I don't think Warren would agree with you there. Everything is changeable to that man."

The Coop lay next to Roxborough, a leafy neighborhood in South Orange with curved sidewalks and gaslit streetlamps. Their house sat right on the boundary between two school districts: the run-down Camperdown High School and the elite but public vine-covered McInnis Hall, its brand-new running track and all-glass library proof that public schools could benefit hugely from a moneyed parents' association. McInnis was populated by kids whose Roxborough houses had indoor pools, housekeepers, and matched sets of thick, plush towels.

Elise was about to start ninth grade. They had a decision to make.

Rosamunde had been against McInnis from the start—how would their daughter fit in? Besides that, McInnis was farther away. Elise could no longer come home for lunch. "Our daughter doesn't need to be hanging out with her mother at lunch," Warren said. "She needs to be building a life for herself."

Warren was determined for Elise to attend the more illustrious school. With every passing year, her peers would matter more. If she was stuck with blue-collar folks her entire scholastic life, that's where she'd feel most comfortable. But if she was surrounded by privilege and wealth, she would gravitate toward success. "She's our only child, for Christ's sake. Shouldn't we do the best we can for her?"

The timing was perfect. He'd been given a promotion at work. They'd redecorated the living room. Replaced the kitchen cabinets with white melamine and ripped out the old linoleum floor to sand and stain the hardwood. Warren had leased himself a year-old, dark red Honda Accord. Rosamunde had to keep her Tuesdays and Thursdays at the "baby factory," as Warren called Dr. Nadal's office, but the Bleekers were upwardly mobile. And Warren wasn't about to let his wife's fears hold them back.

It was late August when they were to have their McInnis tour. The kind of sticky, airless day that Rosamunde complained made her hair frizz. She changed her outfit countless times before settling on a brightly patterned wrap dress she'd had as long as Elise could remember, with her trusty mid-heel sandals. No matter what Rosamunde did to her curls, they chose exuberance over compliance. She poodled the top section in a clip, lined her eyes in navy kohl, and spun around for her fourteen-year-old daughter.

"How do I look?" She adjusted her dress, her face damp and flushed. "I want to make you proud."

There was simply too much of Rosamunde—too much pattern, too much hair, too much makeup. She would do exactly what Elise didn't want her to do: stand out.

"You only ever make me proud." Elise reached up to kiss her mother's cheek, smoothed her pink Polo shirt, and followed her parents out the door, praying none of them smelled like a henhouse.

In the car, Warren kept glancing at his wife's outfit. "What happened to that navy skirt you used to have?"

"What's wrong with this?"

"People don't dress so flashy anymore. They dress more classic. 'Business casual' is what they call it."

"I'm not in business."

Warren tilted the rear-view mirror to look at the back seat. "How's it going back there, princess? You ready to take on the world?"

Fairly certain after her singing non-debut that she wasn't up to the task, Elise gave him a half-hearted nod.

They pulled onto a maple-lined driveway and parked at the front of the school. At the top of the stairs was an attractive woman in jeans and a loose white button-down, with dark glossy hair and a compact frame. The vice principal looked classy and understated—so different from Rosamunde. She waved and introduced herself as Briony Lagasse.

"We're extremely proud of our extracurricular activities," Briony said as she led the Bleeker family into the echoing foyer. "We offer tennis, fencing, lacrosse. We also have an after-school equestrian program at a stable over on Grange Road, at the edge of South Mountain Reservation." She turned to Elise. "Have you ever heard of dressage?"

Still on the phone with her coach, Elise opened the shed door and stuffed the flowers into the dusty trash can, then leaned against the doorway, phone still pressed to her ear. "I'm sorry, Ronnie. I should not be lacing into you." She pushed stray hairs off her forehead and looked skyward. "Matt and I are fighting. There's this woman next door . . ."

"Don't apologize. We can talk tomorrow."

"Wait . . . before you go. If I'm going to keep this marriage intact, I can't leave Wednesday. I'll be home Friday."

As she climbed the mossy slope back to the cabin, she passed Cass's wash line, boys' T-shirts, socks, and striped briefs fluttering in the breeze. The only item not belonging to River was a pale tan bikini made of suede—the top of which had, to Elise's mind, cups so roomy a small barn cat could curl up in each. Use it as a hammock.

Sorry to keep your husband up so late.

"Friday?" Ronnie did not sound thrilled.

"I gotta go."

After looking around to make sure no one was watching, Elise unclipped the bikini and took it inside.

CHAPTER 10

....

Matt walked across the yard, dead grass pricking his bare feet, ice-cold bottles of Heineken already sweating in his hands. The roofers he'd hired, Andy Kostick and Lyman Williams, had been working for hours and the thermometer said ninety-five degrees—and that was on the ground. Up on the black shingles, it had to feel like sitting on the roof of hell.

The bushes beneath Kostick's ladder, Matt noticed, were bowed down with debris—decomposed shingles, splintered planks of rotted wood. Matt moved closer to see rusted nails scattered throughout the garden bed, the grass. Weren't roofers supposed to tarp the working areas? Was that not standard?

He found the guys sitting in the back end of the van, legs swinging as they ate sandwiches wrapped in foil and drank from Coke cans beaded with sweat. Andy had a wet towel draped over sunburned shoulders, his face so red it might explode. Lyman's shirtsleeves were now rolled way above the elbows, his dreads tied neatly at the base of his neck.

"Hey," Matt said. "Thought you both might appreciate a little hydration."

"Hot as hell up there." Andy leaned forward to accept a bottle and twist off the lid. "Don't mind if I do."

When Lyman waved his away, Matt set it next to Andy with a wink. "More for you, then. Just don't lose your balance up there." Matt glanced back toward the house. "So, yeah. I was wondering . . . Would you mind tarping the bushes and the grass below where you're working? I don't want my wife or daughter coming across any nails if they come out in bare feet."

Andy looked toward the debris and took a long, sorrowful swig. "Don't have any tarps with me."

"Is there any way to go grab a few?"

"Afraid not."

Matt stared at him. "I'm sorry—why's that?"

"We lose half a day easy by the time I stop everything, go get tarps, plus to clean up midday. I squeezed you in on a Saturday, like I told you. Suddenly, you want us to go running around town, things could get expensive. I'd have to charge you overtime."

This was how the Kosticks of the world—or at least the world outside the city, where there are fewer tradespeople to choose from—got you by the balls. You need them more than they need you, and they know it. Then there was "great camp pricing," over-billing for weekenders. No way was Matt willing to put up with that. The Sorensons went back a century around here. They should be charged like locals.

"So you're a big Manhattan lawyer, I hear," Andy said.

"Well, I'm a lawyer. In Manhattan . . ."

"Isn't that the same thing?"

Not even close, Matt didn't say, glancing at his battered shrubbery.

Lyman had started reading a well-worn copy of Cormac McCarthy's *Child of God*, as if Andy and Matt weren't there at all.

"Last time I drove down to Manhattan had to be a dozen years ago. Couldn't pay me to go back—all that traffic and noise and people everywhere. Cabbies honking all night long. Had a film on my skin that took forever to wash off." Andy slid the towel off his shoulders, pulled hard on his bottle, and wiped his lips with the back of his hand. "Not for me."

"Believe me. There are days I feel the—"

"Give me my little slice of heaven, is all."

"Right." Matt turned to go. "Anyway, appreciate you guys coming on so little notice. Animals crawling through the house isn't exactly something we can live with."

"I hear you. Had a few squatters in the fishing lodge I opened just up the lake. Pulled out an old bathtub and found a possum family living right there beneath the floorboards."

Lyman looked up from his book and smiled, shook his head. "Better than snakes, I suppose."

Matt couldn't hide his surprise. "You opened a fishing lodge?"

"Reopened, I guess you'd say. Place had been left to rot about five years. Nothing fancy. Main office and a handful of cabins on a few acres. Fixed it up a bit, then opened for walleye and pike in May." Andy reached into a box behind him and tossed over a brown T-shirt. Matt held it up against his chest. The logo was classic vintage Adirondacks: a curved pike with KOSTICK & SONS FISHING LODGE in block letters above, and EST. 2015 below.

"This looks great," said Matt, handing it back.

"Nah." Andy waved the shirt away. "Keep it. Wear it around town. Having a Sorenson walking around advertising can't be a bad thing."

"Thanks. I will."

Andy slid off the end of the van and stood. "Always been my dream. Cabins are small but have flush toilets, a cold-water sink, and a single bed. Your oven is your fire pit. Figure next year, I'll put in a small tackle shop, sell lures and bait. Snack foods."

Matt found himself with twinges of jealousy. To have a business out here, the wind carrying the smell of the water and the pines through your office window all day. "Sounds idyllic."

Lyman gave what sounded like a snort. Andy shrugged. "Just a place where guys can come up and forget work, forget the mortgage, forget the wife. Just have a few beers, shoot the shit on the water, that kind of thing. I'll be moving into the biggest cabin this week. Been waiting too long to spend my time anyplace else."

Matt pointed to the company name on the side of the van: KOSTICK & SONS ROOFING. "Guess you've got your sons to carry on."

"Nah. There aren't any sons. Or daughters. I don't have kids. That's . . . whatever. Marketing hook."

Matt nodded. "And what does your wife think of moving to man paradise?"

"Never wanted a wife and too old to start now." Andy looked sideways at Lyman. "This guy could use one, though. I keep saying you'll never find a wife if you spend all your time with your nose in a book."

Lyman barely looked up. It was clear the man's white buttondown had started out the day nicely ironed.

"You two work together a long time?" Matt asked.

Lyman put down his book, finished the last of his lunch, and balled the foil. Bagged it. Shot it into an open trash bag at the road's edge. "Nope."

"Lyman moved into his sister's apartment right next door to mine. Store-top in town," Andy explained. "He grew up here, then came back home after a few years in Albany. I needed an assistant while I got the lodge set up, and Lyman needed the work."

"What'd you do down there?" Matt asked.

"Prof at UAlbany." He opened his book and started to read. "English Lit."

This was getting stranger by the minute. Lyman had a story that he wasn't the least bit interested in telling.

"Lyman's family's been here longer than yours." Andy looked at his assistant. "Mid-1800s, isn't that right?"

"We don't have a fancy sign, but we go way back." He turned the page.

"Anyway. Local, is my point," said Andy.

Ah. Here we go. "Remember," Matt said with a grin, "I'm local, too. So none of that 'great camp pricing' you give to city people."

"Shit." Andy leaned back against the van, shaking his head. "You're about as local as Prince Charles."

"What are you talking about? My family's been part of this place for nearly a century."

"That doesn't make you people locals." Andy held his bottle up to the sun, then finished it off. "I hear you don't come up much anymore. Can't really call that being local, no matter what your grandpa was up to."

Up to? Matt searched Andy's face for subtext.

"All right." Lyman stuffed his book into his back pocket and started toward the house. "Better get back to it."

"If you have any other jobs need doing over the summer"— Andy pulled on a greasy Rangers hat—"give Lyman a call. He's had a rough go of it. Parents thrown out of their own home. Homeless one winter, and his baby sister suffered terribly—lost a leg from the knee down, to frostbite. She worked at the bank just fine all these years, then had a bad fall last spring. Now she's laid up, so Lyman came back to care for her. Guy's working like hell to sock away his money. You have a sister like that, you want to make sure she's okay if anything happens to you."

"We're not actually here for long. Just doing up a few things before we list."

"Huh." Andy looked along the tree line toward the lake and pushed his hat back. "You severing or selling as one piece?"

"Selling it all. Seventy acres, give or take."

Andy contemplated this. "Not often a big piece of land like this goes on the market. Not on this lake, anyway. You'll get one of the big resort chains interested."

"We'll see. Not all of it's on the water."

In the distance, they heard the warbling call of a loon and both waited, silent, for another call. None came.

"It's a nice quiet lake, this. Always has been. Folks around here are going to hate to see that change." Andy reached for his tool belt and buckled it beneath his belly. "All right, Mr. Manhattan. Break time over." He slammed the back doors of the van shut. "Let's get this job done."

"I was wondering . . . How long do you think this'll take?"

"Quick as we can. Two days tops."

Two days for a repair to a bit of roof above the kitchen and another in the rear. In New Jersey, you could get your whole roof replaced in twenty-four hours. With tarping.

"We've got our daughter here—makes things a bit more complicated. We need to get this place listed before we get too far into summer and people's heads get wrapped up in back-to-school stuff."

"I hear you. We've got another job Monday morning anyway." Andy sauntered back toward the house, hammer bouncing against his thigh as he walked. "Local family needs a repair around a skylight, and we're in for a whole lot of rain next week. Decent people." He grabbed the ladder's edge and started up, the ladder bowing with each step. "Unlike some."

Matt stood staring after him. He'd caved in every way a homeowner could. What did Kostick have against him?

"Hey!" From the roof's edge, Andy called back, "Don't forget to wear the T-shirt."

....

CHAPTER 11

The pipes shuddered overhead as Elise turned off the shower, which continued its *drip, drip, drip* into the rust-stained tub. She pushed aside the curtains with a squeak and stepped onto the mat. Grabbed a towel to pat herself dry.

Cass's suede bikini top lay on the counter. Imagine spending money on a bikini made of suede. You'd never be able to get it wet, even. Or sweat in it.

This time, when Elise picked it up, she held it to her chest and looked in the mirror, fascinated that a person could have breasts of such magnitude they could fill these cups. Elise was almost staunchly small-chested. She wore bras, but had always been proud of the fact that she'd never really needed one. Large breasts were matronly at best, vaguely bovine at worst.

She'd always thought eternally girlish was the better way to be.

Equal parts curious and ashamed, she slipped on the bikini bottom, then the top. She set the cups in place and tied the suede strings in back. Inspected herself in the mirror.

That she was disturbed was disturbing. Elise Sorenson was an athlete. She and her body had an agreement—they served each other well. To be disappointed in her physicality now felt traitorous.

She looked like a prepubescent boy in this bikini.

Cass's cups weren't just tents collapsed in the rain, they were empty tents collapsed in the rain. In tragic proof that at thirty-eight Elise was a failure as a modern woman, she folded two washcloths, stuffed one into each cup, and turned sideways to assess herself in the mirror, squinting until her silhouette appeared real. Realish.

If her primary goal was sex, then sure. This shape might rocket her to the top. But her primary goal wasn't sex—not to malign the pastime in the slightest! How would she ride a horse built like Cass? How would she run? Then again, maybe that was what bothered her most. Cass wasn't built to run. She was built to stay.

Elise untied the strings and let the washcloths fall to the floor.

The pop and crackle of a vehicle pulling into the gravel driveway made her glance out the window from behind the curtains. A pickup truck sat in front of the garage, bright orange paint glinting in the sun. SKEDADDLE HUMANE ANIMAL REMOVAL was pasted in individual letters on the side, along with a decal depicting three silhouettes that ascended in size: a snake, a raccoon, and a bear. It looked like the evolution of a species gone terribly wrong.

The man climbing out of the truck was Paulie Gupta from Eagle Gas. She heard Matt ask, as he crossed the lawn in the hot sun, "You also the mayor of this town?"

"Sometimes I think I should be."

She closed the curtains, pulled off the bathing suit, and continued to dry off. While rubbing her legs, she noticed a streak of pink on the towel and stopped. There was a faint smear of blood on her inner thigh.

"Elise! Trap's here . . ."

She pulled on cargo shorts and a T-shirt and hurried downstairs with the bikini top in one pocket, bottoms in the other.

Cass Urquhart could have her body back.

....

Elise watched Paulie pull a long wire trap from the back of the truck and tuck a plastic box under his arm. His shirt had a SKE-DADDLE patch on the breast pocket. "I'm a bit of a Paulie-of-all-trades," he said sheepishly as he followed Matt toward the house. His teal-green eyes dazzled in the sunlight. As he passed, Paulie threw Elise an apologetic look, as if he *knew* the effect he had on women and wanted to assure her what she was feeling was normal. Unavoidable, even. "But this is my real gig. I'm helping my parents out while my business gets going." He grinned. "Then I can move out of my bedroom."

Her hands went to the balled suede in her pockets and she considered what she might do. Cass's driveway was empty, Matt was inside, and Elise needed to lose the evidence of her stagger-ingly pathetic midlife crisis brought on by the hottie next door. She ducked beneath the trees dividing the properties and draped the bikini back over Cass's clothesline.

Matt and Paulie were peering inside the cupboard when she returned.

"Yup, you've got yourselves a raccoon," Paulie said. He turned to the tackle box and popped open a can of tuna, then surveyed the room. "Here's how we'll do this. We'll bag up any food in and around the kitchen. We want to make our trap the only game in town, so to speak. And the traps are totally safe. Spring-loaded door only slams down once the animal is fully inside. So no one's gonna get harmed in the process." He reached into the cage and set the tuna on a platform at the end.

"Could there be babies?" asked Matt.

"If we trap their mama, we're gonna know pretty quick. They'll be climbing over the cage to get to her."

"And what about us—being in the house and all that?" said Elise.

"Huge hassle, and I totally get how inconvenient it is, but we need you guys to stay out so we have a nice quiet cabin, the perfect meal, everything but candlelight and poetry to woo him. Or her."

"And assuming we're successful," Matt said. "Where do you take raccoons? Do you have a sanctuary?"

"That's where things get a bit tricky. The state requires a permit for raccoon removal. I can take him out of your house, but I can't take him away . . ."

Elise's eyes traveled to the sink as Paulie chattered on. The mess of dried egg was still there, but the wineglasses were gone. She wandered over to the glasses cupboard to find them washed and put away. Somehow that was more damning than their presence in the first place.

"What do you do with him, then?" Matt said.

"Take him for a ride. Drop him off somewhere nearby."

"How nearby?" asked Elise.

"You don't want to know."

"Someplace closer to town, maybe? Lots of trash cans behind the restaurants, no need to break into anyone's cabin," Matt pointed out.

"You guys are smart. Your roof is being repaired already, so you'll be locked up nice and tight. He'll go off in search of somewhere simpler to break in." Paulie took a container of baby powder and sprinkled all the counters. "This is so we can watch for footprints. There's a good chance he's long gone now. If not, hopefully we'll catch him tonight. But it could take a week. Depends how hungry he is."

"What's the average?" Elise asked. "I mean, if you had to guess."

"We're probably looking at a few days."

Elise looked at Matt. "Where are we going to stay?"

"Cass's place has an apartment above the boathouse. I'll ask." When Elise said nothing, Matt added, "She won't mind at all."

Precisely what had Elise worried—especially now that she had to leave her husband and daughter up here alone.

"We don't have much of a choice, babe." He waited while Paulie packed up his toolbox and started for the door.

"Like I said, if he's still inside, our best chance for a speedy capture is a quiet house."

Their voices faded as they stepped outside and through the front porch. Elise reached for one of the glasses again. The rim was still ghosted with vermilion.

The Woodstock Girl's lips had staying power.

Later, after Elise had settled Gracie and River on the back porch with pencils and paper so they could sketch the stuffed dog, she stood in the office doorway and watched Matt sort through the contents of Nate's desk. Sunlight bathed the entire scene in a certain honeyed nostalgia too serene to interrupt. Her husband hadn't noticed her yet, busy as he was stacking some files in a Rubbermaid container and sending others sailing like Frisbees into a trash can. She examined him as if seeing him for the first time—that wide jawline and strong brow, cheekbones so sharp they might cut through his flesh. Funny: his look was so unique, but what she loved most about him, what turned her on, was his forearms. They had a might to them that always caught her off guard. Reminded her he was male.

He looked up when she came in. "This Kostick guy is going to hit us with a hefty New York City premium, I can tell. We're going to get totally soaked." He flipped through a blue file folder and tossed it in the garbage.

Elise went around behind his chair and hung her arms around his neck. He smelled of Hermès.

"You won't believe how well he's doing," Matt continued. "Bought himself a chunk of land just up the lake. Started a fishing lodge. Which makes me think—why the hell did I take the LSAT three times? I should've bought myself some steel-toed boots and a pallet of shingles." He stopped, held her arm when she rested her chin on his shoulder. Then guided her around to the front of the chair and onto his lap. "What's going on? You're so quiet."

"I don't know . . ."

He pulled her into the curve of his neck. "If you're thinking of leaving me for Kostick now, forget it. He doesn't want a wife. No kin of any kind. I asked for you."

She sat up, the corner of her mouth twitching. "What about his assistant? Did you ask him? Because he's pretty hot."

"Lyman? I can't compete with that guy. He looks like someone you'd see on the cover of *Vanity Fair*. And he's well read."

"Good to know . . ."

"If he even looks your way, I'm done. Throwing in the towel."

"I made a to-do list, babe."

"Ugh, I hate lists."

"Empty closets and cupboards. Quick sweep out—no real need to scrub because no one's buying this place to move in as is . . ."

"Why not?"

"Because. People are fancy these days."

"This place is fancy."

"It's old."

"It's nostalgic."

"It's falling down."

"Falling down with *love*."

She grimaced at him. "Seriously. We take everything into the garage and make three piles like they do on these hoarder shows."

"What hoarder shows? Who's a hoarder?"

"A keep pile, a toss pile, and a sell or donate pile."

His arms tightened around her. "What say maybe next weekend we could take a day off from making useless piles and take Gracie over to Saranac or someplace we haven't been. Find a nice public beach. Or we drive up one of the mountains. Have a picnic lunch at the top." He spun the chair side to side, sunlight sliding over their knees then dropping to the floor.

"This is the part you're not going to like."

The rocking stopped.

"I feel so awful, I can't even be happy about it—but it really is a big deal."

They'd all be home on July 5th—five days before the Pan Ams started. That was the plan as it stood. But, she'd realized, the team would ship to Toronto days before that to get the horses used to the grounds. "I'm going to the Pan Ams. Mademoiselle Secretary pulled a tendon. Tamara had to drop from the team. I'm the new traveling reserve." She watched as his face went from neutral to pained. "And the games are in—"

"Toronto," he said.

She nodded.

"And you have to not only go, but go early."

"To acclimatize him, yes. Games start the tenth."

"Got it." He rubbed his eyes with thumb and forefinger, then pushed his hand through his hair as he realized the larger implication. "Which means you can't stay up here like we planned. You need to go back early to train."

"Ronnie wanted me back in New Jersey on Wednesday to get us ready. I've pushed him to Friday."

Matt dropped his head back as he absorbed the weight of this news. "And . . . will you be bringing Lyman?"

She looked at him a moment, confused, then understood. They were back to teasing each other. The tension had passed. She stood. Grinned. "Doesn't sound like you're going to kick up a fuss anyway, so I might as well ask him."

He got up to hoist a container brimming with files onto Nate's sofa and forced the lid to click into place. "Don't worry, okay? Gracie and I, we get it. We get you. It's the Pan Ams—how many people get there in their lives?"

"I was thinking—let's go for dinner in town, the three of us."

"I forgot to tell you. Cass invited us all over for a barbecue. I figured we couldn't say no if she's putting us up in the boathouse. A few other people are going as well." He tied up a garbage bag and tossed it into the hall. "Sound good?"

No. It really didn't. Life was changing fast, and she just wanted time with her daughter and husband. The last place she wanted to go was Cass's backyard party.

She forced a smile. "Yes. Of course. Sounds perfect."

....

CHAPTER 12

The screen door closed with a bang as Elise stepped down onto the stone path carrying a huge wooden bowl, plastic tongs resting atop the quickie salad she'd thrown together as a gesture of goodwill. If Cass Urquhart was willing to feed them and put them up for a few nights, at least they weren't coming empty-handed.

She ducked beneath ragged pine boughs to follow the sound of voices and a crackling bonfire, pausing to watch Matt and his ex-girlfriend move around the patio area as River and Gracie giggled on a mossy log. To anyone passing by, they could be a family. The handsome father stood at the barbecue, long spatula in hand, wearing a spattered apron that didn't belong to him. Then the voluptuous goddess of a mother in a long khaki tank dress. She could be Aphrodite herself, with that sprig of ivy tucked into untamable russet curls.

Another woman—late sixties maybe, with fluffy gray hair and a no-nonsense expression on her face—sat in a lounge chair. A local most likely. Dressed in Patagonia and navy Crocs, she was the woodsy Adirondack grandma.

A man somewhere in his mid- to late forties tipped back a beer bottle. Flashy, with his bright pink linen shirt and oversized watch. Overdressed. From the way his focus rested just over people's shoulders, it seemed like he knew about a better party somewhere else. Elise tried to sort out where he'd fit in with this make-believe family. The grandma's feckless son, maybe. The one who sneaks into her wallet whenever she's napping.

Elise's reverie was brought to a halt when her New York City–lawyer husband threw his head back and howled like a coyote, adding in three quick yelps at the end. A moment of silence, then what sounded like actual coyotes yipped back from across the water.

Elise stepped out of the trees with her salad. "Holy coyote, Gracie. Who knew Daddy had mad animal-calling skills?"

"The rest of us have always known Matty's half-werewolf." Cass headed straight toward her. "Good to see you again." The hug that followed was awkward, complicated by the salad bowl that tipped against Elise's top and nudged Cass's shoulder strap down her arm. Now one of the Woodstock Girl's breasts was threatening to shake off its confines and join the party. This woman's body just did its own thing. Cass stood there oozing sex, while Elise stood oozing Trader Joe's balsamic vinegar.

"Let's fix you up." Elise reached out to adjust the wayward strap. "By the way, being half-werewolf is a minimum requirement in the city. You want to get hired at one of the big firms, you need an aggressive wolf call."

Chuckles around the fire, and Cass invited Elise to pour herself a glass of red wine. The woman in Patagonia was introduced not as Cass's mother, Ruth—who hadn't been feeling well and had gone home—but as Jeannie Robbins, Ruth's lifelong friend who ran the local day camp River attended. The man with better things to do wasn't feckless at all. He was Cass's boyfriend, Garth Zima, a hotshot Realtor in the area.

"Your salad looks gorgeous, Elise. So colorful." Cass took the bowl from her and set it on the gingham-covered picnic table loaded with stacks of plastic plates, condiments, and jaunty striped napkins.

"Yeah, Cass's salads are more the ripped-open-bag-of-iceberg-lettuce-and-bottle-of-expired-dressing variety," said Garth, ducking when Cass balled up a napkin and threw it.

"Gracie." Elise waved to her daughter, playing army guys with River closer to the fire. "Come sit with me. I've barely seen you all day."

With hair stuck to her flushed cheeks, Gracie came to sit next to her mother. Only now could Elise see that the child had a sprig of ivy to match Cass's tucked into her tangled ponytail.

Gracie grimaced. "You smell of bug spray."

"You know me. I'll be a swollen mess of histamines by night's end."

"Nothing wrong with being juicy to blackflies. It's a sign you're brimming with health." Jeannie rose to help set the table.

"Hey, are you part of that horse show in town?" Garth asked Elise. "Every year, I forget it exists and then all the trailers start pulling in."

"Such a pain, that," Cass said. "The days before it starts and when it ends, traffic's a nightmare. Good for businesses, though, I suppose."

The Lake Placid Horse Show took place at the North Elba Show Grounds just on the edge of town and ran for about three weeks, beginning in late June, each year. Almost a thousand horses had been trailered in from all over the state; a city of striped tents had already been erected to shelter the temporary loose boxes for horses and tack rooms that would be home to hopeful contenders. It wasn't a place Elise had ever competed, as the showgrounds were strictly hunter jumper, but during an Olympic year, the names that would have competed here were some of the biggest around.

"I ride dressage," Elise said. "That show is for jumpers."

"And Matt tells us you're Olympic-bound," said Jeannie.

"Well," Elise said. "We'll see."

"Elise is being modest. No one works harder, believe me." As Matt moved buns from grill to platter, Cass passed behind and patted his shoulder in thanks.

"I have a superstar husband." *And he's mine, all mine*, she would have loved to say out loud.

Garth had grown interested in Matt now. He tilted forward in his chair, elbows on knees, as if he just might decide to stay. "So, you do all the kid stuff when your wife's away?"

As Matt detailed his routine of getting Gracie to Funducational, then hopping on the train into the city, then reversing the pattern in the evening—all to Garth's impressed exclamations—Jeannie leaned in to Elise to murmur, "If he were a woman, would we even be having this conversation?"

They shared a private smile.

"I couldn't do it," was Garth's eventual declaration. He got up to help Matt ferry charred burgers and hot dogs from grill to table. "But at least the marriage doesn't get boring."

"And you're leaving again?" Jeannie asked Elise.

"Friday."

"All that time apart." Cass bent down to the grass to pick up a broken cracker. As she stood to flick it into the fire, she said, under her breath but loud enough for Elise to hear, "Kiss. Of. Death."

Elise froze, watched Cass sashay back to the table.

"Come everyone," she called. "Eat. Drink. Be merry." The last to sit down, Cass lowered herself into the space between the kids and kissed each on the cheek. "Two little angels to fuss over tonight. I love it."

Elise tried not to wither as Gracie basked in Cass's glow. It was what little girls did. They heroine-worshipped attractive women. Elise could remember once when Gracie was five, she refused to come out of her room when the babysitter arrived, because she wasn't "pretty enough."

Matt held a scoop of lettuce over her plate. "Earth to Elise?"

"Yes, thanks." Her fixation with Cass was ridiculous. Elise turned to Jeannie. "So, your camp. Is it sleepover or day camp?"

"Bit of both," the woman said, smoothing her napkin on her lap. "I get city kids from far-off places: Montreal, Boston, LA—Beijing, even."

"I want to go to camp," Gracie said.

Matt doled out burgers to the adults and said, "Jeannie, you were part of the team who secured the eighties bid, am I right? With my grandfather?"

"I was. Nate worked unbelievably hard. To win was truly gratifying." She pierced a cherry tomato with her plastic fork. "I'd love to see us secure a third Winter Games."

"How did you come to start a camp?" Elise asked.

"Years ago, my husband and I started to wonder, with all the families flocking to the resorts, if someone shouldn't offer a drop-off day camp program so the parents could catch a bit of a break. The hotels have kid programs—some of them, anyway. But not where kids get that real summer camp experience. It's more glorified child-minding. I thought, these parents go online to check out a resort. They see the beautiful photos promising luscious beds, lazy-morning coffees over a misty lake where they reconnect as a couple. But the reality is, their kids wake up and want to go for a swim, and the parents never really get to be that relaxed couple who pad out to the end of their dock in robes, lattes in hand. And then, when Brice died last year, I sold the house back to Cass, renovated a little cabin on the campgrounds, and bought a camp bus to expand our enrollment. Had the staff go to town painting it."

"Brice died?" Matt said. "He was such a nice guy."

The best." Jeannie nodded.

"You should see how cute the bus is." Cass pushed a strand of hair off her face. "Covered in flowers and smiley faces. Total hippie-mobile."

"It means the parents really *do* get to be the couple in the brochure; they don't even have to drop the kids off. We come to them. And we're flexible. Kids might come three days in a row, then hang with their parents. Families can strike whatever balance feels right."

Gracie took a bite of hot dog, leaving a smear of ketchup on her lip that Elise reached across to dab with a napkin. "Can I go, Dad? Please?"

Cass answered for him. "You'd love it. River goes every year, right, Riv?"

The boy nodded, mouth full.

"We're here to be together for the next two weeks, Little Green," Matt said to Gracie. "That's the whole point."

"Little Green after Joni's daughter?" Cass was staring at Matt. "I love it."

"Cass is obsessed with Joni Mitchell," said Garth.

"It was my fiftieth a few weeks back," said Cass. "Garth's gift to me was borrowing the Camp Imagine bus and parking it over at Tupper Lake, where we had a picnic with a bunch of friends and played Joni Mitchell. I introduced him to Joni's best album. Her most personal."

"*Blue*," Matt and Cass said in unison.

Matt had always been appalled that, because of their twelve-year age gap, Elise didn't really "get" Joni. Or Dylan. Or Leonard Cohen. He'd made fun of her being raised on a steady diet of Paula Abdul and Billy Idol.

Risking a further demonstration of her ignorance, Elise said, "Joni Mitchell named her daughter Little Green?"

"Kelly, actually," said Jeannie. "She gave the girl up for adoption and wrote a beautiful song about her. 'Little Green.' Hauntingly beautiful. Like a love letter to her only child."

Cass added, "A lifetime's worth of advice in one song." She ruffled Gracie's hair. "Little Green. Beyond cool nickname you have."

Elise stared at Matt—why had he never once mentioned this?

Humiliating that she was finding this out in front of strangers. In front of Cass. "I always thought it was Gracie's froggy voice . . ."

Matt shrugged, bit into his burger. "It's both. No big deal."

River looked at Gracie and said, "Ribbit," collapsing the two of them in giggles.

Later, the table a battle zone of balled napkins, felled pop cans, ends of burgers, and half-empty glasses, they all sat around the fire, lazy and satiated. Cass got up to rearrange the charred logs, sending sparks scattering skyward, then took a sweating wine bottle, held it up to see what was left, and circled, topping up a few glasses. "Elise, did you hear about the bears this year?"

"My buddy and I saw one on the putting green at Whiteface yesterday," Garth said. "Took the flag right out of the hole. Last week, someone said, a pair of cubs came bouncing out of the woods to play with a golf ball."

"I saw one on the roof last night," Elise said. "Creeping along like he wanted in."

"Probably wanted to get in on that pile-making we're about to do." Matt turned to the others. "We have master pile plans for the detritus of Nate's life. Piles have become the big thing. Apparently they have TV shows about piles."

"I love those shows," Cass said. "Are you going to make those little signs?"

Matt turned to Elise, who nodded, said, "Of course we're making the signs."

"We are all over those signs," Matt confirmed.

"Why are there so many bears?" Gracie asked from the other side of the fire, where she was using the uncoiled end of a hanger to draw a smiley face in the cooled ash.

"We had a late start to spring," Garth said. "Bears woke up hungry and stayed that way."

"People have been seeing bears in their garbage, bears in their yards." Jeannie waved a mosquito away and pulled her chair closer to the fire. "One wandered right out onto a public beach on Mirror Lake two days ago. Middle of the day."

"I don't want to see a bear," Gracie said.

"As long as your mother's around, we're all safe," Matt said. "Everything will bite her first."

"Who wants to hear a ghost story?" Garth rubbed his hands together as Cass returned to her seat. "Nothing better than a little Lake Placid lore." He glanced at the kids. "You guys okay with it?"

"Yes!" in unison.

"You're going to wind up with nightmares, princess," Matt said.

Elise looked at her husband. "Drives me nuts when you call her that. It sends a fairy-tale, wait-for-a-prince-to-save-you message." And it struck too close to her own childhood, to her runaway father's endearment for her when she was young. She stretched her legs out toward the fire.

"She's right, Matt," Cass said. "That's so archaic."

Elise looked at Cass with fresh eyes. "I think I like you."

"Oh, we'll get him in line." Cass winked. "Don't you worry."

The thing was, Matt had had decades to pursue Cass before he met Elise. If he'd wanted to be with the girl next door, wouldn't he have hunted her down? It was ridiculous to worry. Elise left Matt for months every year. Surely she could trust her husband to stay next to his childhood friend—who had a boyfriend right here in town—for one week without Elise.

"Please, Dad?" said Gracie.

"The story's told around our campfire at least once every summer," Jeannie said. "Honestly, parents today deprive kids of so much fun."

"All right." Matt held his hands up. "I give."

"Mabel Douglass was her name," Garth said. "It was September, nineteen thirty-three. Mabel was the first dean of a women's college down in New Jersey, and she was having guests over that night."

Gracie and River scooted closer to the adults.

"Mabel went out for one quick paddle around Lake Placid to gather pretty leaves and *never came back*. All sorts of rumors flew. She'd run off with a dashing salesman passing through town. She'd paddled to the other side of the lake and climbed up into the mountains to live out her years as a recluse. Then, in nineteen sixty-three, thirty *years* later, scuba divers found an old boat way down in the deepest part of the lake, a hundred and five feet down, over by Pulpit Rock. They saw what they thought was a mannequin. It wasn't until one of the divers tugged it by the arm that it happened."

"What happened?" said Gracie, eyes wide.

"It wasn't a mannequin. It was Mabel. She was so well preserved by the cold water, her body appeared to be made of plastic. But when the diver touched Mabel, her arm came right off in his hands! In fact, as they brought her closer and closer to the lake's surface, as the water started to grow less frigid, Mabel's limbs all started falling off."

Gracie gasped, clapped her hands over her mouth in horror and delight. She and River grabbed each other, groaning and laughing.

Garth said, "She's called the Lady of the Lake. Her entire body started to break apart. And just before they surfaced, her face disappeared! Bits of flesh—her nose, then her cheekbones and eyeballs—"

River let out a scream for his new friend's benefit and ran into the house. Gracie grabbed her crutches and gamboled after him, the screen door slamming behind her. An echo bounced back from across the lake.

"Characters," Matt said.

Cass brought a bowl of cherries over to the fire pit and offered it to Garth, who took a handful and set it on a flat rock between Matt and Elise.

"Any plans to move in together?" Elise asked Garth.

The lengthy silence that followed answered the question.

"We don't want to rush it. Right, Cassidy?"

"That's right." Cass rolled her eyes. "It's only been a year and a half. Moving in would be *crazy* . . ."

"Why ruin a good thing, is the way I see it."

"Exactly. God forbid we commit while we still have our teeth."

"My funny, funny girl." Garth reached out and squeezed her knee, then stretched back in his chair and focused on his cherries. After flicking a bruised one into the trees, he turned to Matt. "Hey, I don't want this to be awkward or anything, but if you guys are selling, I'm happy to help. I've sold most of the larger parcels left on these lakes. Saranac. Flower Lake, too. The serious buyers know to come to me."

"Would a single family buy a lot our size for a vacation home?" asked Elise. "Seems awfully big for that."

"Not likely. I mean, the area is known for these large, multi-generational family compounds. You know, the quintessential great camps. But they've sort of been here forever. And with land having gone up so much in value, a plot this size isn't a realistic single-family purchase." He flicked another cherry.

Elise looked at Matt. "Maybe severing the land is a better option?"

"Had a client who tried a few years back. Neighbors put the brakes on it, signed a petition to block the severance." Garth shook his head. "He appealed the decision twice and got shot down every time. It's damn near impossible these days. Plus, a good chunk of what you've got doesn't have road access."

"What do you recommend we do?" asked Matt.

"I've got a guy right now really hot on the area. Texas-owned resort chain just dying to get their hands on the right piece of land. You give me the go-ahead, I can set things in motion."

"What kind of money are we talking?"

"Nearly a quarter mile of prime waterfront on Lake Placid?" Garth spit a seed into a napkin. "You'll never have to work another day in your life."

"If this is a land sale, then"—Elise sat forward—"can we leave the cabin as is?"

"I would say so. It's classic Adirondack nostalgia—no one's going to demolish it. It'll be kept as a satellite outbuilding or superior room if the resort builds individual cabins." He sat back and rested an ankle on one knee. "I mean, there's no downside to fluffing it up a bit. Just don't sweat too much over it."

"And you're fairly certain this will be tempting to a resort?" Matt said.

"Almost a hundred percent. It's next to impossible to secure a prime piece of land that size. So much is under conservation protection."

"I hate the idea of a resort next door," said Cass. "The road will become a nightmare. And we'd be living next to a place crawling with entitled little shits. They'd be partying at all hours. Then there's the boat traffic. Just pull your price down, doll it up, and sell it as the beautiful lake house it is. The land becomes a lovely bonus. Would be great if whoever bought it had that length of shoreline protected through the conservancy, too."

Garth reached out to poke Cass with his foot. "Cass here is a bit of an idealist, if you haven't noticed. But Cass's dream buyer could turn around and do the same thing. Sell to a resort. Ultimately, you have no control. Makes total sense you feel a bit of sentimentality, attachment to it. But once people let go, you'd be amazed at how quickly they move on. If I were you, I'd be prepared for all scenarios. Fix it up and list. But be quick about it. Whatever happens, you want a sign on your lawn yesterday, because the summer market really dies off in July."

"We also have a vintage boat, a Chris-Craft, that can go with the place, if you want to have a look," Matt said to Garth. "A 2012 Range Rover to unload as well. About twenty-five thousand miles on it."

Drinks in hand, sandals flapping against bare heels, the two men walked down to the Sorenson waterfront, leaving the women in front of the fire.

Just as Elise started to say something about getting her daughter settled in the boathouse, the door swung open to bang against the back of the house. "Mom!" Wild and slightly out of breath, Gracie rushed down the back steps: crutches, hop, crutches, hop. "River says they have tuck at camp! That's where you get candy."

"You can also get fruit and nuts. And healthy juices." Jeannie was clearly amused. "And you can borrow books to take home at night."

"It's a great place," Cass said. "I hung around all day when River first started, and I went home feeling he was better off at Camp Imagine than with me. The counselors are sweethearts. It builds such independence."

"We encourage children to find their voices," said Jeannie. "And she can attend for as long or as short a time as you like. A few days, a week. Whatever works."

Surely they could let Gracie go to camp for a few days. It would free up Matt and Elise to get the cabin ready and still enable Elise to have solid Gracie time before leaving on Friday. And it solved the problem of keeping Gracie out of the cabin until the raccoon was caught. Elise turned to Cass. "Are you sending River this year?"

"Not for a few weeks. "

"We have plenty of space," said Jeannie. "And my staff is trained for kids of all needs."

"Can I, Mom? Dad doesn't let me do anything."

As a mother, was she not entitled to make a decision about three days at camp? Matt made all sorts of unilateral parenting choices while Elise was gone.

"I always say to Jeannie that Riv comes home a better person every night," said Cass.

Exactly what Gracie needed.

"Please can I go, Mom?"

"Do you have swimming lessons?" Elise asked Jeannie.

"All levels. We can even do private if she's a beginner."

"She's definitely a beginner." Elise looked at her daughter. "Would you be willing to take lessons?"

"No."

Elise took her daughter's hands. "Swimming is a very important life skill, honey."

Gracie's face twisted up tight as she debated the no-swimming stance she'd held all her life. "Fine. I will swim, but I won't like it."

"Come." Elise held out her arms. For the first time since Elise had been back, Gracie accepted her affection. The child let her crutches drop and wrapped feather-light arms around her mother's neck. The flickering light of the fire, the scritch-scratch of crickets, the hum of conversation between Jeannie and Cass, all faded. "I think three days at summer camp is a terrific idea. Let's do it."

Gracie's face lit up. "Can I start tomorrow?"

"Tomorrow's Sunday."

"That's fine," said Jeannie. "We service the tourists, so she can start any day of the week. I'll tell my assistant to put her on the bus schedule and the attendance sheet. Consider it all taken care of and we can settle up payment at the week's end. Ken will pick her up at eight forty."

"Okay, then. We're all set. You, my girl, are starting camp tomorrow."

Gracie grew an inch. She flashed a big, lopsided grin, then scrambled back to the house and called, "River, guess what!"

The crackling logs and wavering hum of the flames had given way now to the calming hiss of red-hot embers. Scattered around the ash lay fallen marshmallows, a few balled-up napkins, and the melted remains of several unfortunate plastic army men.

"I hope Matt won't hit the roof." Elise twirled her wine in the fire's glow.

Cass slid to the front edge of her chair and kicked off her sandals. She plunked her feet on the rocks that ringed the fire pit and coiled her hair into a messy knot on top of her head. When she lowered her arms, the shoulder strap fell again, dropping the front of her dress even lower.

Was that a smirk on Cass's face as she leveled her gaze on Elise?

"Put me on the case," Cass said. "I can convince that boy of anything."

"Thanks for the offer," Elise said with a measured smile. She reached out once again to readjust Cass's strap. "I've got this one."

....

CHAPTER 13

S wimming to Blueberry Island and back in the early morning mist had always made Matt feel alive. He kept his focus on a perfect front crawl: body streamlined and flat, legs kicking from the hips rather than the knees, each arm rising from the cold water bent, then reaching far beneath the surface with a gentle hourglass pull beneath his torso, a barely there turn of his head to breathe every three strokes—alternating left and right for balance.

Jesus, it was good to be in the lake again.

Sleeping with Gracie between them in Cass's airless and rickety boathouse had made for a sweaty, wakeful night and given him way too much time to think about the partnership—and what to say to Barrans on Monday. What lawyer in his right mind says no to partnership? Even if the buy-in is a problem, the firm guarantees a loan. Beyond highlighting cases that offer particularly big wins or some sort of personal satisfaction, a lawyer has one of two goals: sole proprietorship or partnership.

Matt had already bombed out on the former.

Partnership and a good marriage, two or three kids—these goals might seem amateurish and "picket fence" lined up next to his wife's, but there you have it. By age fifty, you've been a partner for ten, twelve years. It wasn't too much to hope for.

Everyone in the firm would understand, given Elise's success. They'd all give him the high fives, the pats on the back. They'd all go home to rave to their own spouses. But would even one of them trade places?

Anyway. This choice was not about Elise. Nor was it about himself. It was about Gracie.

He supposed he could speak to Barrans, talk about delaying the offer. But there would always be another competition. Elise was never going to change. Even if they never had another child, it would be years before Gracie could stay alone after school.

Elise was at the end of the dock with a big towel when he returned. With a mighty kick, he pulled himself out of the water, dripping all over the weathered boards. She wrapped it around his shoulders. "Happy Father's Day."

"Oh, hey. Right. Forgot all about it."

"Best father on earth." She kissed his wet cheek. "You're up early. It's not even six thirty."

Was it called being up early if you really hadn't slept? The partnership hadn't been the only trigger for his wakefulness. The bed they'd all shared was the same one upon which Matt had lost his virginity to Cass. And after watching the way her body undulated beneath that dress last night, definitely without a bra and possibly without panties . . . was it crazy to think she wanted him to notice? A few times he'd caught her giving him the same look of teasing invitation he remembered from years past.

Stop it. You're happily married.

Pretty happily.

"I love the lake at this hour. So calm and still." He scrubbed his hair with the towel, then patted his face dry. Movement up by the house caught his eye. Lyman had arrived early and was setting up tarps in the bushes below his ladder. Matt waved his thanks—to, not surprisingly, very little response on Lyman's end.

"Gracie up yet?" Matt asked his wife.

"Still asleep. Curled up like a little shrimp. So . . . I have an idea about the rest of our time here. A way I don't have to leave early. Or at least I can leave less early."

He sat on the arm of an ancient wooden chair, put an ankle on one knee, and dried his foot. Wiggled a finger in his ear to shake out the water. "I'm listening."

"We ship Indie and Poppins here. The showgrounds will be out of the question right now, but we could maybe board them at a local barn. I can Skype with Ronnie—maybe the odd time you or Gracie film my rides and I share with him. It buys the three of us time together. It alleviates my guilt. Then, as we already discussed, you guys come up to Toronto."

"That'll cost a fortune. Shipping Indie—and the donkey—all the way up here, plus board for the two of them. Not to mention Camp Imagine. Where's all this money coming from?"

Elise looked at him as if he were slow. She waved around the property. "This place, obviously. You heard what Garth said. We're going to be fine."

"You're counting chickens here. And we won't have our hands on any real cash until closing."

"So we use a credit card in the meantime. We know everything's going to be good."

He slid his feet into leather flip-flops and started along the rocky beachfront for Cass's boathouse, with Elise following. "I don't understand," he said. "We had a plan for this holiday, and you come back and flip it all on its head. I understand the Pan Ams; go back Friday and train without guilt. But sending Gracie to camp was never part of the deal. We haven't even seen the place."

"Cass adores it. You think she'd send her son anywhere that wasn't terrific?"

It was true. That and the fact that he'd known Jeannie for

most of his life were the only reasons Matt hadn't put the brakes on the whole idea. "If she wakes up today and still wants to go, fine. She can go till Tuesday. But if she doesn't, we wave the bus driver on."

"Guys!" a female voice called out from the house. In a short black robe, Cass stood on her back deck. "I've got breakfast up here. And coffee. Bring Grace up, we'll get her fed before the bus arrives."

"On our way," Matt called as they stepped up to the wooden deck that wrapped around the boathouse. Cass gave him a thumbs-up and disappeared inside. He turned to Elise. "I don't want to bring the horse here. Let this holiday be about Gracie, not about dressage. Please?"

She stared at him in silence. Then started up the creaky plank stairs. "Fine. I'll go back Friday on my own."

Matt had never seen a raccoon like this one.

They stood on their back porch after breakfast, a steady, rhyth-mic *bang, bang, bang* overhead, and peered through the kitchen door. There, on the counter, fur sprouting from between the wires of the trap, crouched one very large, very black raccoon. It watched them, dark eyes peering through the bandit mask, twitching a nose covered in flakes of tuna.

Matt held Gracie close as she pointed. "Look, he has no tail."

"It's why I thought he was a bear," said Elise, clearly thrilled to have been right. Or at least less wrong.

"Just like there can be albino raccoons, there are melanistic ones." Paulie pulled on thick, elbow-length gloves and picked up the cage. "Born with more melanin. Funny thing is, these black animals are more adaptive. They tend to live longer and reproduce more because they're less conspicuous at night."

"Why can't we keep him?" Gracie whined.

"Wouldn't be fair," said Paulie. He held the cage to his face and addressed the animal. "You like to roam free, don't you? You don't know how to walk on a leash or beg for treats. And forget pooping outside only. That's just never gonna happen."

Gracie put a finger to the cage around the animal's hind end and stroked the protruding fur. The trap was too tight for the raccoon to turn around, but still. Matt pulled her back. "That's a wild animal."

"Can't he stay for the day at least?"

"You're not even going to be here," said Elise. "The camp bus comes in forty-five minutes."

"How about this?" said Paulie, setting the cage on the table. "You stand beside him and your dad can take a picture. That way you'll always remember him."

"Yes!" Gracie said. "No one will believe a black raccoon."

Matt pulled out his phone. "Okay, but keep a safe distance, please."

Gracie sidled over to the cage, nervous but exhilarated. Paulie came around to stand behind her and grin, one hand on her shoulder, like they were going to prom. All that was missing was the wrist corsage and a fake palm tree backdrop. "How about we just, you know, give Gracie a little space?" Matt said.

"No, Dad. I want Paulie in the picture."

"It's okay, Matt," Elise said, poking him. "It's fun."

Matt snapped a few quick photos, then filled out a check and handed it over. "Thanks again for squeezing us in."

"No worries. I'm glad to help the family who helped mine. It's how the world should work."

Outside, Gracie followed the raccoon trap and Paulie out to his truck, doing a happy little twist every time she planted her crutches. "Where are you going now?"

He swung the cage up into the back of the truck and set it gently on a quilted blanket. "I'm going to release this fellow down the road and then pick up another trespasser: a six-inch red-eared turtle in a laundry room."

"Who on earth calls about a turtle?" Elise asked.

"That little guy's a rescue project. He's got a bum front leg, which is not a good thing for a turtle," said Paulie. "Probably had a scrap with a cat or a raccoon. He needs to strengthen himself by walking around, then swimming in very shallow water. We don't want him going back into the lake until his strength's built up."

Andy came around the front of the house with an industrial garbage bag, and Matt repositioned himself. It was day two of the roofing job, which meant Kostick would be writing up his bill. Matt had thought ahead, pulled on the Kostick & Sons Fishing Lodge T-shirt. Couldn't hurt to keep the marketing angle top of mind as the man made his decision about local or weekender pricing. Matt stepped out from behind Paulie's truck.

"Excuse me, folks." Andy shimmied between Matt and Paulie's open door without so much as a glance at the shirt. "Coming through."

"I love turtles," Gracie said.

Andy's bag split open on the driveway, and he swore quietly as he stooped to gather up the pile of bent nails, paper towels, scraps of wood and shingles, and the heavy-duty plastic wrap the shingles came in.

"What will you do with him?" Gracie asked.

"What I do with every rescue. Post a notice on the wall at the gas station. And until someone adopts him, I'll keep him in my room. Hidden from my mom and dad."

Gracie turned to her parents. "Can I please have the turtle? I would take such good care of him."

"No," said Matt.

Elise nudged Matt. "It's not a bad idea. She's dying for a pet. Besides . . ." She shifted closer, softened her voice. "The injured leg. Learning to strengthen himself. Kind of parallel, don't you think?"

"Turtles are covered in salmonella," Matt said. "Totally unhealthy. People have died, I've heard. I don't think keeping turtles is even legal anymore."

"Ugh," Gracie groaned, slumping over her crutches like a rag doll. "Why does everything have to be legal?"

"Gracie, aquariums are a pain in the neck. They get murky, they smell—"

"But Mom will help clean when she visits."

Matt stared at his daughter. This was how Gracie perceived their lives together? That her mother didn't even live with them? That he was a single father and she had a drop-in mother? He felt his blood pressure rise.

Elise cupped the back of Gracie's head. "Honey, I'm not *visiting* you when I come back. I'm home."

"*Please*. Paulie's going to leave."

"Daddy and I will talk about it, okay?" Elise turned to Paulie. "Can we get back to you? Sorry. I promise we're not always deadlocked like this."

"Absolutely." Paulie shot them both an apologetic grin. "Sorry. Didn't mean to open a can of trouble." He climbed into the cabin and started the engine, began to back out of the driveway, tipping a hand out the window in goodbye. "You get in touch when you figure it out."

Gracie watched him go, toeing the gravel with one sneaker.

Matt pulled his wife back a few steps, out of Gracie's earshot. "Why do we have to go through this every time? All I ask is for a subtler power shift when you come back into the fold. Like, give me some credit for all the weeks and months I've handled on my own. I do know what's good for her. Yesterday at Eagle Gas, then camp. Come on. Kick it back a notch."

"There's a danger to coddling her too much, Matt. She has to make mistakes, fail, discover . . . It's how she'll get strong. If we hold an umbrella over her head every time it storms, she's never going to know how it feels to have rain fall on her face."

Somewhere across the lake, a motorboat fired up. Matt's gaze traveled from his wife's pleading eyes to her set chin. She was so resolute and driven in every way. Even her ponytail couldn't just be. It took the sunlight from behind her head and shattered it into a million pieces.

"No turtle," he said and turned away, Gracie's crumpled face behind him.

CHAPTER 14

....

Fifteen minutes later, Elise was on hands and knees, digging up a few prickly weeds from a garden at the base of an ancient oak, aware she should be wearing gloves. At the road's edge, Gracie—in denim shorts and sunhat, a T-shirt that read DON'T WORRY, NOTHING IS UNDER CONTROL—waited for the camp bus in Matt's old shelter. It wasn't much bigger than a phone booth, a weathered and mossy wooden A-frame that resembled an upended half canoe. Tucked inside was a cracked vinyl bus seat.

"Did you know it was Father's Day, Gracie?" Elise said. "When you get home, you can make Daddy a card."

A vintage pickup bounced along the road, kicking up a cloud of dust. On the driver's door were stick-on letters: LAKE PLACID GOODS AND PROVISIONS, with a phone number. Under that, in italics, *WE DELIVER*. The old man driving gave them both a relaxed two-fingered salute as he passed.

Gracie waved. Her skin shimmered with a generous application of sunscreen, and her fingers and toes had been freshly done the night before in navy polish, to match her mother's. It was Elise's latest offense against Thumb's obvious need for domination.

And subsequent failure, as her daughter's thumb was already in her mouth.

Elise had sought advice from doctors, naturopaths, dentists, parents in chat rooms, and former thumb-suckers. There was no deterrent that was going to break this relationship.

Then again, maybe it wasn't about prevention at all. Elise stood up as a couple pedaled past on matching rented bikes. "What about a fifty-dollar bill if you stop sucking your thumb for a month?"

Gracie regarded her thumb with new interest, the way you might suddenly look at your dog if he was offered a starring role on Broadway.

"Think about it." Elise tugged on a dandelion, but the upper plant broke off in her hand, leaving the root spike deep in the grass. She went at a few more, digging with her trowel to free the roots, experiencing a vague sense of nausea.

"I'm not the kind of person who's motivated by money."

"Okay. Interesting. What kind of thing motivates—"

"Mom?"

Bang, bang, bang went the hammers on the roof. A small black car cruised past. "Yes?"

"You know I love you, right?"

Elise sat back on her heels, completely overwhelmed. Never, ever had her daughter just blurted out an "I love you."

"Sweetness, that makes me unbelievably happy. And you know I love y—"

"Can you go inside? I don't want the kids on the bus to see you."

Reality check. Elise looked at her watch. It was only eight fifteen. The bus was due at 8:40. She moved closer to the split rail fence behind the bus shelter. Pale pink ambling roses used to cover the old wood, but they had been choked out by invasive English ivy and very few roses were in bloom. Elise started to carefully separate vines from delicate stems. "You've got nearly half an hour before you risk any sort of public ridicule."

....

From the first of Elise's Thursday afternoon riding lessons at Grange Road Farms, Rosamunde had arranged her lunch break so she could stand at the end of Ronnie's indoor arena or sit on the bench alongside his outdoor ring and watch her daughter, the same frozen smile always on her face.

Elise didn't want to crack open her life to these rich kids. It was enough that Ronnie was plucking her out of the group to have her demonstrate a sitting trot or a transition from walk to canter. She didn't need her mother squeezing her fists and holding them up in silent cheer. Rosamunde's constant attention on her had become embarrassing.

About five or six weeks into the lessons, while they were driving home together in Rosamunde's old green Tercel, Elise blurted out a cruel lie, telling her mother that Ronnie had laid down a new rule: no spectators during lessons. Rosamunde nodded in silence.

But the very next Thursday, there she was again.

"How I adored, when you were born, knowing how much you needed me. It gave me such purpose. Such reason for being," Rosamunde explained to her solemn daughter that night as they gazed at the stars. This ritual, too, was getting old. Elise was a teenager. She no longer wanted to be tucked into bed by her mother. "It still does."

"Mom, you should go back to school for something. Nursing, maybe. Or ask Dr. Nadal if you could work full-time. It would give you more of a purpose."

Rosamunde gave her daughter's arm a squeeze, smiled through moist eyes. "You, precious, are my purpose."

Matt came around from the backyard, his face grizzled from not shaving all weekend. His right hand gripped the neck of a long axe. "Blade's dull." He pressed his thumb to the edge, as if to offer proof. "I'm going into town, get this thing sharpened. Oh, and Garth was just here—I signed with him."

Elise had never seen her husband with an axe in his life. "What do you need a sharpened axe for?"

"Chopping down the dead birch in the backyard."

"But that's a big tree."

"You do it from the top down. Climb up there and take out one branch at a time as I move down. Then back up to take out the trunk in two-foot pieces."

"Why not rent a chain saw? Even better, a guy with a chain saw."

"Yeah, 'cause that guy-with-a-chain-saw scenario's never gone wrong." He glanced at the roses on the fence. "You shouldn't be working without gloves. You'll shred your hands; go get the leather pair from the shed."

"I'm fine."

Gracie folded her arms in front of her chest. "You people are ruining my reputation."

A stronger wave of nausea made Elise move into a patch of shade and sit on her backside. It was the spicy dandelion smell, she realized. It clung to her hands and threatened to bring up the scrambled eggs Cass had served. "Matt," she called as he headed for his car. "Can you hang on a sec? Just watch her till I'm back."

In the upstairs bathroom, Elise scrubbed her hands quickly and leaned over the toilet bowl, forearms on cold porcelain. A feeling of dread pounded in her chest as realization sunk in. Was it even possible? Could she be pregnant? A baby did *not* fit into her plan right now. She and Matt had barely had sex all year, and the last time shouldn't even count. It was just before North Carolina, and they were half-heartedly fooling around. He'd been so exhausted, he fell asleep on top of her before they even reached for a condom. She didn't even think he'd ejaculated. But her breasts had been aching. The bubbly feeling. The spotting the day before. It was exactly the same as when she learned she was pregnant with Gracie.

Only it would be the worst timing imaginable.

When her stomach quieted, she moved away from the toilet to dig through the cupboard below the sink. She had a vague memory of a pregnancy test she'd bought a couple of years ago when her period was late. It had been a two-pack. One was still there, she was nearly sure.

It could be she was in for a heavy period. Married adults don't wind up pregnant from somnolent half sex. That only happened to teenagers. And she was thirty-eight. Thirty-eight! The odds of an accidental pregnancy were low, weren't they? Low-ish.

There, beneath a mound of toilet paper rolls, hair brushes, and near-empty bags of sports bath salts, lay a long pink box with one foil-wrapped test stick. She ripped it open and sat on the toilet, positioning the stick for maximum contact. The plastic stick bobbed in the urine stream beneath her, and Elise pulled it out and bound it in toilet tissue. Took it to the sink and waited.

The stick started out with one bright pink control line. The second pink line was the one she was desperate not to see. Somewhere far away, on someone's dock perhaps, the Clash's "Lost in the Supermarket" was playing, the distance giving it an eerie echo. She held her breath and counted backward from twenty to calm herself.

It seemed like an hour. It was likely two minutes. A hairline appeared, so faint at first she might have imagined it.

"Elise, I gotta get going!"

Maybe the stick was faulty, because the thread wasn't even pink.

Until it was. The line grew more and more definite, its color morphing from pale blush to deep fuschia, not content to stop intensifying until it had completely changed the course of Elise's life.

She dropped the stick in the sink and leaned over the counter's edge. It couldn't be real. All the years, all the sacrifice. Indie's training at its peak. Everything lined up just right for the first time. This was the closest she'd ever gotten.

"Elise!"

She wrapped the test in toilet paper and buried it deep beneath the empty shampoo bottles and Band-Aid wrappers and threads of dental floss in the waste basket.

Matt couldn't know. Not until she knew what to think of it herself.

Matt was out on the road, chatting to a frail woman well into her seventies, dyed black hair in a wispy bun, feet swaddled in wool socks and slippers. The look on her face was equal parts pleased and quizzical as Matt waved Elise over and introduced her to Cass's mother, Ruth Urquhart. "We *never* thought we'd see you back again, Matthew. And now with your lovely family."

Elise tried to smile. She did a quick calculation of where nine months would take her. Sometime in mid-February? She could ride until the third trimester—most professional riders did. But to take, what? Four months off, the year she was on track for the Olympic Games? Fully stagnant while other riders were rocketing forward? A huge disadvantage.

Bang, bang, bang.

Ruth shielded her eyes and looked up at the activity on the roof. Her fingers were heavy with clunky rings, one made of wood. "My, but you've got a whole lot of work happening over here."

Andy stopped hammering and stood, one foot wedged against the chimney stack for stability. He pulled off his cap, wiped his brow with a meaty forearm, then noticed Ruth watching him and held up a hand.

"Morning, Mrs. U!"

She waved back, looked at Matt. "Andrew Kostick. He was such a diligent boy. Worked at the theater and lectured the movie-goers about not spilling their popcorn or drinks. And if they did, he refused to sell them a new one. Told them to take better care. I always liked that about him." She turned to Gracie, still in the shelter. "That bus stop was where your father waited to be picked up for camp when he was a boy."

Gracie looked up the road for the bus.

"And some days your father would come over for a gingerbread cookie after," Ruth said. "Maybe you'll do the same. Would you like that?"

Gracie nodded.

Elise stopped her hand from going to her belly. Maybe she was overthinking the whole thing. She could just carry on. Confirm with her ob-gyn that she was healthy and strong, and get his okay to compete. It was what everyone at her level did—they carried on.

Matt was staring at her. "What's wrong?"

But everyone didn't have Gracie.

"Earth to Elise?" Then there was Matt. He'd been talking about giving their daughter a sister or brother ever since Elise failed to qualify for the London Games and doubt started to erode his faith in her ability to make it internationally.

"Hon?"

"I'm good. Great."

"You don't look great."

He would be over the moon if he knew. "Just a little tired, is all."

Matt accepted her reason and leaned over to give their daughter a big hug. "You have a great day at camp, Lil' G. And if you're nervous, if you don't like it, whatever, you have them call us." He climbed into his car and lowered the window. "Don't come home with a boyfriend. Or, worse, married." To Elise, he said, "I have to drop by the bank as well. And grab some trash bags."

Elise waved goodbye.

Ruth watched Matt's car drive away, then started back to her place. "I'd better go dig up my recipe. It's been a long time since I've made gingerbread." She turned. "My husband, Edward, will love to meet you, Gracie. Come over as soon as you're back."

Gracie nodded. "I will."

Elise whispered to Gracie, "I will. *Thank you.*"

"I will. Thank you."

After giving her daughter the thumbs-up, Elise returned to her vine-choked roses. In the shadow of the tree, she could think. To tell Matt right now would be the gift of a lifetime. The man's dreams were so attainable it was painful: happy marriage, a few kids, a solid legal career. With anyone else but Elise, wouldn't he have that by now?

The cicadas launched their amorous buzz and a lawnmower droned from someone's backyard. Arcing over it all, the constant banging on the roof. A headache started to take root behind her eyebrows.

"Mom, what's taking the bus so long?"

She checked her watch. At least eight minutes until it showed. "You've got a bit of time yet." Elise tugged hard on a tangled rope of vine and exclaimed when a rose thorn punctured her thumb. She watched the tiny white perforation fill with blood and slipped her thumb into her mouth. Matt had been right. She stood. "Honey, I have to grab a pair of gloves. I'll be two seconds. Don't move."

"Don't hurry back!" Gracie called out.

Elise jogged along the side of the cabin and back porch to yank open the shed door. In the span of a second, she took in decades of dirt and gasoline, the shelves lined with old wine crates full of mud-caked garden tools, tangled wire and balls of twine, leaf bags, fertilizers, and weed killer. She snatched up a pair of dirty leather gloves and spun around. As she raced back out, she caught a flash of Gracie's old wooden high chair.

Passing Lyman on the roof, she trotted back along the side of the cabin, her head spinning with the memory of coming downstairs one morning between Christmas and New Year's to find Gracie in the high chair as a long-limbed and slender-cheeked five-year-old. She was far too big for it, but had convinced Matt they should recreate a photo from when she was a baby—one where she proudly held up hands covered in yogurt and Cheerios. The baby shot was framed, with the more recent photo tucked beneath the frame's edge. It was somewhere in the cabin. In Nate's office, most likely—his grinning face was beside hers in the newer photo.

Elise would look for it while Gracie was at camp. Might even be funny to recreate it now.

As she hurried toward the canoe, Elise was certain of this: for her, a baby interfering with her own aspirations would never justify ending a pregnancy. The choice lay between competing as planned or calling Ronnie to tell him she was out. And she had to decide fast.

Matt wouldn't *want* her to ride, she was nearly certain. But he would agree to it if the doctor said she was healthy. Of course, if Elise hadn't done the pregnancy test, she might not even have known. Her cycle had never been all that regular. It wasn't unusual to miss a month or two. Still—was she going to lie to her husband?

No.

"Gracie, you're not going to believe what I saw in the shed—"

But Gracie was gone. The shelter was empty. Dust on the road swirled as if a big vehicle had just passed. Elise broke into a jog to the roadside to see the flower-and-happy-face-covered tail of the bus vanish around the corner.

She hadn't been gone more than a couple of minutes.

"She climbed inside all by herself," Ruth called from her garden hedge across the road. She was wearing a straw hat now and holding a set of pruning shears.

"She got on the bus?"

"I watched her. Such a wonderful and brave girl. You should be very proud."

Of course, then there was Gracie. When Elise was home in April, she'd taken her daughter to Walmart over in Garfield one Saturday morning to find an inexpensive blackout blind for Gracie's window. She'd been waking too early and Elise was certain the morning light was interfering with her circadian rhythm.

As Elise had pushed the cart—Gracie riding inside it—past the girls' clothing section, Gracie had begged Elise to stop. Pointed at a rack of printed T-shirts and asked her mother to buy her one.

It said BIG SISTER on the chest.

·········

CHAPTER 15

Matt slowed the car as he passed Pinehurst Golf and Tennis, with the same brown clapboard clubhouse, weedy brick path to the pool, paint peeling off the tennis court fencing. Some of his greatest childhood memories were the summer mornings Nate would get him up early to golf at the modest club the Sorensons had belonged to for generations. Nate might have amassed wealth, but he wasn't fancy. He had no interest in being paired up with the high-rolling "corporate yahoos," as he called them, who populated the more exclusive clubs. What Nate wanted from a morning on the links was simple: lungs full of clean air and the camaraderie of his grandson as they carried their own clubs over the hilly terrain.

Nate had been careful never to praise Matt's swing—which the pro at Pinedale had called loose and natural. It had been Nate's firm belief that flattery led to overthinking. And overthinking ruined your game. So the two fell into a comfortable rhythm of silence on the green and idle chatter between holes.

Northwoods Hardware wasn't far beyond Pinehurst. After inquiring at the cash register, Matt was directed to the sharpening station at the back and handed his axe over to the teenage girl behind the counter. He eyeballed her lower lip stud, a tiny ruby that could be a drop of blood from afar, as she informed him it would be a ten-minute wait, but he was free to help himself to coffee and donuts at the complimentary refreshments table next to Lighting.

He found the table, poured a cup of burned coffee, and helped himself to a donut hole from the Dunkin' Donuts box. He then settled down on a vinyl chair and stretched his neck side to side, wiggled his shoulders, hoping to ward off a growing stiffness from his early morning swim.

"I heard from Andy Kostick you're selling your grandfather's land?"

Matt looked up to see Clive Promislow, who owned the only market in town that made deliveries, and who had taken part in Nate's poker games as far back as Matt could remember. Matt recalled Clive as a man with an almost deliberately rigid posture. Now, his back was so stooped, he was nearly facing the ground. What little hair he combed over his liver-spotted scalp was wispy and yellow-white. In one frail hand, a jar of fish food.

"News travels fast." Matt stood to shake Clive's other hand.

"We'll be sorry to see you go. Nate was as much a part of this place as the mountains."

Matt started to say yes. He felt the same way—sorry to go. But Clive spoke first.

"My wife, Phyllis, is with Sotheby's. Has been for forty years. You know, your grandfather always said if he ever sold, he'd give the listing to Phyllis. She'd be more than happy to come talk with you."

Recognition slowly flooded Matt. Yes. It was why he'd been thinking Sotheby's before they even got here. Nate had spoken about Phyllis. "Oh Jesus, yeah. No, I just met an agent, Garth, at my neighbor's place last night, and we're in a bit of a hurry . . ."

"Garth Zima?" Clive paused, rolled his tongue around his mouth as if savoring a candy. "The Ukrainian fellow?"

"Yes. I think so."

"I see him around town in his convertible." Brown irises clouded with a filmy blue-gray fixed on Matt. "Your grandfather wouldn't have trusted him to sell the shed in the back garden."

Matt didn't even like Garth. The guy was self-important. Gave Cass the runaround about moving in together in front of people he barely knew. "I'm sorry. I've already signed with him."

With a dismissive wave, Clive was already shuffling to the register. The Promislows were good people. Church-on-Sunday, volunteering-at-library-fund-raisers kind of folks. They'd had a daughter years back, a little girl who had died, at eleven or twelve years old, of leukemia. They likely needed the money more than Garth Zima. Matt drained his bad coffee, crumpled the cup, and threw it in the trash.

He'd messed up big-time.

By the time Matt returned, some two hours later, a dark green MOUNTAIN VIEW REALTY sign swung in the breeze at the edge of the driveway. *Garth works fast*, he thought. He'd left the contract in Nate's office; he'd go inside and give it a thorough read. Maybe there was a cool-off clause. Twenty-four hours during which he could unsign. Switch to Phyllis Promislow.

But then he realized: Cass. Even if it was legal, he couldn't very well fire her boyfriend.

Andy stood on the rear bumper of his van, securing ladders to the roof, while Lyman loaded unused shingles through the side door. Andy waved and hopped to the ground when he saw Matt. He nodded to the FOR SALE sign as he passed it. "Not wasting a minute here, eh?"

"You know agents. Sign goes up quick as a hare, comes down slower than a tortoise."

"Shirt looks good."

Matt looked down at his chest. Puffed out Andy's logo.

"We were able to finish ahead of time. Took the wood right down to the rafters where it had rotted or animals had chewed through." Andy paused, then handed Matt an invoice with greasy fingers. "Replaced the plywood. Sealed that up tight. Laid down the shingles and waterproofed all the seams where new bleeds into old."

"Eleven hundred dollars?" Matt said, scanning the bill. "It was only about a tenth of the roof."

"You're looking at overtime, seeing as we worked through the weekend. Getting you back into your house as soon as possible was our goal. I think we achieved that."

Overtime. Of course that was coming. "Seriously, Andy. This is pricing for city people."

"My pricing is my pricing. It's the same for everybody. You cut me down, Lyman doesn't pay his rent." He narrowed his eyes as if Matt himself were Lyman's enterprising landlord. "Up to you."

The check should clear, Matt told himself as he wrote it out. Insurance came out of the account at the end of the month. Mortgage payment had already gone through. He handed over the check with a forced smile.

"You shouldn't have any trouble, but if you do, give Lyman a call. He does general handyman work as well." Andy glanced over to watch his successor stack the last of the unused shingles in the van and slide the door shut. "Like I said, his family had a rough go. An eye for an eye is what happens eventually, though. It's how life works."

Matt wasn't sure about that. "I'll definitely keep him in mind if we need anything." He shook Andy's hand, then Lyman's. "You guys did a great job. Much appreciated. I'm sure I'll see you around town."

"Not likely to happen." Lyman swung himself into the passenger seat. Unrolled his sleeves and buttoned the cuffs. "I think we both know that."

Jesus. Upstate folks were direct.

....

All spotting seemed to have stopped—again, exactly like with Gracie. It wasn't until Elise had finished cleaning out the kitchen and bathrooms, and she'd peeled off filthy clothes and turned on the shower, waited for the spray to warm up and clear of rust, that she made a decision. She would do what so many Olympians before her had done. If her doctor confirmed it was safe to ride, she would continue to train through the second trimester. Indie was fourteen now. There was no impulsiveness in his character. He hadn't bucked, reared, shied, or bolted with anyone on his back in almost nine years.

The last time was the day of the accident.

Ronnie could train Indie while Elise was off, and the moment she felt able to ride again, she would. Other women had had babies with similar timing during an Olympic year. Dutch Olympic gold medalist Anky van Grunsven competed in Athens four months pregnant. And if Elise made it onto the short list in the spring, the baby would travel with her. It wouldn't be hard to get one of the female working students to cuddle an infant during the times Elise had to be on a horse.

She'd tell Matt and Gracie at dinner. It was Father's Day, after all.

Just as she wrapped herself in a towel, Matt came into the bathroom, still in his Kostick & Sons T-shirt, and started. "Oh god. You scared me. Thought you were outside."

"Babe." She pulled him to her. "Hold me."

He wrapped his arms around her and breathed into her hair. "You smell perfect."

Her fingertips slid along the swell of his bicep and inside his shirt sleeve to cup his shoulder. "You feel perfect."

He took her face in his hands and kissed her deeply. "I say we take a break from making piles."

"If you insist . . ." It hadn't been her intention to fool around, but she found herself as eager as he was and slid her fingers inside his jean pocket. She pulled him toward the open window behind them so she could lean against the thick sill, unbuttoned his jeans, and worked her hand down the front of his boxers, felt him grow hard. He groaned, pulled away the towel she'd wrapped herself in and dropped it to the floor.

He flicked her shoulders and her breasts with his tongue, and she lost herself in the joy of her husband's desire. So much emotion had hung, for her, on this return. Missing Gracie's play had never been her plan. Nor had arguing over Vanilla Monkey smoothies or day camps or turtles.

Who knew—a baby might even reset their relationship. So much had chipped away; this little one could have the power to make the family solid again.

She pulled Matt's mouth to hers and kissed him.

He kicked off his pants, boxers, clearly intent on making love to her.

Not with the spotting. Soon, but not yet. Elise knelt on the floor and took him in her mouth. Slowly, she stroked the length of him, teased him with her tongue and pulled back, making him wait for more. Finally, with her mouth and one hand, she moved into a steady rhythm. Holding the window frame, leaning into one arm, he came in an instant. She wasn't expecting it and looked up, about to make a joke, prepared for him to be gazing down at her, sheepish and ready with a self-effacing comeback. But his focus wasn't on her at all. His eyes rested on something outside. She looked through the window. It wasn't something he was staring at. It was some*one*.

Cass.

Matt kissed Elise's forehead, pulled off his T-shirt, and stepped into the shower.

By the end of Elise's ninth-grade year at McInnis Hall, they'd moved out of the Coop and onto what might have been the shabbiest street in Roxborough. Still, infinitely more agreeable than living with the smell of chicken excrement wafting in the windows. Sackville Court was dotted with tired homes with classic bones. A lick of paint was needed here, a driveway wanted repaving there. The Bleekers' home needed both, but the move had strained their finances even further than the old kitchen renovation and they continued to live for payday.

Like their old den, the paneled walls of the new family room were covered in mounted fish trophies, one of which was Big-Mouth Billy Bass, who turned his head and sang "Take Me to the River" when you pushed a button. But the big-screen television was new. Birthday gifts were no longer wrapped in Saturday's comics, but dollar store wrapping paper. Indulgences were largely for the sake of appearances. The shampoo bottle might be all but empty, but there was a floral wreath on the front door. The kitchen tap might drip all night long, but the powder room was loaded with soaps shaped like seashells and guest towels with lace trim.

Warren began to run four times a week and do pushups in the backyard. He still loved fishing, but had bought himself a set of used golf clubs and took the odd afternoon off to hit balls at a public course nearby. He wore his hair shorter and ironed his shirts.

Dressage had almost fully taken over Elise's world. She'd become another horse-mad teen girl, but with one exception: she was winning every schooling show her coach signed her up for. Being the best was a heady new sensation, and Elise was already hooked on it. She rode one of Ronnie's own horses and had managed to wrangle hand-me-down breeches and boots, and Ronnie's barn had an assortment of black velvet hunt caps. Rosamunde had a dark blazer her daughter could wear to shows. For now, the shows were cheap—most took place at Grange Road Farms. But once school was out, Ronnie had already made clear, she'd be ready for shows in other parts of the state. With these other shows would come more of a financial commitment. Elise had been doing barn chores in exchange for private lessons all year and would certainly work at the local pool again that summer. By then she would be old enough to hold a job at the registration desk, far preferable to scrubbing toilets, and her hourly wage would be higher. But her paychecks wouldn't come close to covering her competition expenses.

Warren's answer? If Elise had talent, they would do whatever it took. Their daughter was on track to be something special, *someone* special.

Rosamunde, however, was losing her rudder. She didn't look like the women in Roxborough, with their fit little bodies and pert noses and sleek bobbed hair. Her husband was far more comfortable in the new neighborhood than she was. He looked moneyed, somehow, with a straighter nose, more even teeth. Elise fit in better as well—all blond locks and glowing skin, and always in a hurry to go someplace else.

This new world was stealing Rosamunde's family.

At her husband's urging, she organized a bridge group. This new crowd thrilled Warren and intimidated Rosamunde. One of the wives was a paralegal. Another sold real estate. Career women. Plus, there was Briony from McInnis Hall, who brought along whatever man she happened to be dating at the time.

Rosamunde would tidy and retidy all day until, around five, she showered, set her hair, rouged up, and came clicking downstairs in kitten heels far too dainty for her frame. She would start everyone off with martinis. Dining room chairs scraping across the floor let Elise know the game was about to begin. This was when she would sneak down the stairs to watch.

The Briony at Elise's house was different from the vice principal at school. She would usually wear something slinkier. Nothing really overt, but a bit more leg showed. All of the couples knew her from McInnis, and inevitably one of the husbands would make a sexual innuendo, the rest of the men would chide the guy, and the wives would swat their men good-naturedly. Rosamunde's husband was the only one who didn't joke like that. But he insisted Briony sit next to him. Every time.

Rosamunde would be quiet and efficient as she went to the kitchen to prepare another tray of drinks. From the stairs, Elise could see a sliver of her mother moving between the freezer for ice cubes and the fridge for mixers. Before she emerged with the tray, she would drop a few ice cubes in a coffee mug, dump in a heavy splash of Dewar's, and down it. She would stare into space a moment, unaware her daughter was watching. Then she would pinch her cheeks, smooth down her hair, and shake herself into the role of charming hostess as she backed through the swinging door to the dining room with her tray.

Briony's dating stories had become intoxicating to Elise, who listened from halfway up the stairs. Briony's life was big. She got her nails done at a salon every week and had been to Paris that past January.

Rosamunde did what she could to keep up her end of the conversation and once asked if anyone had heard about the Nile crocodile found crawling around in the sewers of Paris back in 1984. "Just imagine. Slithered out of the ocean and into the sewer system of one of the biggest cities in the world."

The table went quiet.

Later, when they were alone, Warren growled to his wife to stay quiet about things she obviously knew nothing about.

"I know more about Paris than you do. You'd never even heard of this crocodile story," Rosamunde snapped.

"Paris is on the Seine. It's on a river, not an ocean!"

A terrible silence blanketed the room. The house. The street. From the stair landing, Elise felt sick for her mother.

Warren's voice was low. "You're showing your roots, Rosamunde." His chair scraped as he stood and went upstairs, closing the bedroom door behind him.

Elise promised herself that year she would never be naive enough to think that what she didn't know about her marriage couldn't hurt her. And yet. Here she was now. Staring out the bathroom window while her husband whistled in the shower.

....

Matt had come downstairs first, wearing leather flip-flops, shorts, and a plain white tee, and started to mix mojitos they could take out to the road while they waited for the bus. A dash of lime juice and sugar in each Collins glass, a couple of crushed mint leaves, then ice cubes and white rum. He topped both up with club soda and full sprigs of mint.

He'd made a good dent in the workload to ready the house for showings, having amassed on the garage floor a huge mound of trash bags filled with junk, garden bags filled with dead plants and weeds, a pyramid of paint cans, old rugs, and appliances—all of it destined for the dump.

"It's almost four thirty," he called upstairs.

Her flip-flops smacked on the stairs and Elise came into the kitchen in a tank top and sandals, short sarong skirt knotted at her waist. She exuded strength and power, his wife. All sinewy muscle and bone. Coiled tight and ready to strike. Cass seemed so soft and overflowing in comparison. Being around her made Matt feel more masculine.

"I was thinking spaghetti tonight." He handed Elise a cold glass. "Nice comfort food for her after a big day."

"Sounds good."

Drinks in hand, hair still wet, they stepped outside into the sunshine and through a frantic swarm of gnats hovering above the walkway. Elise leaned down to pick a tiny, delicate buttercup and tuck it in her hair, just above her ear.

There was a faint rumbling in the distance and she looked down the road toward it. "Must be them."

"What do you want to bet she gets off begging for McDonald's?"

The high-pitched buzz of cicadas made a hot day hotter, Matt decided. It made the air feel like a heavy duvet you can't kick to the floor.

They stood shoulder to shoulder at the road's edge, moisture beading up on their glasses. A boat droned lazily in the distance.

A neighbor's sprinkler system sprang to life: *tick, tick, whir*. One of the sprinkler heads was broken—water gurgled up only to bend back over itself and give up. There was a lovely ordinariness to the moment.

A rumbling in the distance, then the front grille of the bus rounded the bend. Cartoonish daisies, peace signs, hearts, and birds appeared in all their nostalgic, hand-painted, hippie glory. The driver's face became discernible through the windshield next, fat-cheeked and content. Then the bouncing silhouettes of kids in sunhats and the sweet hodgepodge of little voices, singing:

I'm bringing home my baby bumblebee. Won't my mommy be so proud of me . . .

Dust billowed up from the wheels. Matt tapped Elise's shoulder, guided her back a few steps, up a weedy knoll to allow the bus room to stop.

. . . smashing up my baby bumblebee. Won't my mommy . . .

Flushed faces appeared in windows now. A girl with pigtails pulled so tight she nearly appeared bald stared at them as she passed.

I'm licking up my baby bumblebee . . .

A pale boy next, with round glasses and a mushroom cut; he had an arm out the window, his palm keeping beat atop the "P" in "Peace." Two empty seats, then a boy with an upturned nose. This one gave them the finger with both hands.

Won't my mommy be so proud of me . . .

From their little hill, Matt and Elise could see through to the other side. Ten or twelve kids on the bus, none of them with a tangled yellow bob, none of them with a freckle-faced grin so wide it pulled her eyes shut, none of them so impish and giggly and radiant that when the sun set your world didn't go dark.

It didn't make sense.

When the vehicle didn't slow, time did, every second a lifetime now. A wash of dust and stinging pebbles sprayed their bare feet, and a haze of soupy rainbow hues made them dizzy. Matt held up an arm to signal the driver to stop, but he blew past in a blur of colors, waving his hand through the open window.

Matt pushed his glass into Elise's hand and chased the bus up the road until the driver noticed him in the mirror and drew to a stop.

"She wasn't on today's list," the man said, his face stretched in horror. "I thought she was starting Monday."

"She wasn't there?" Matt turned to his wife. "Where is she? What the fuck, Elise? You were here with her this morning. What happened?"

"I . . . she wanted me to . . ." Elise was already in full panic. "She got on the bus. Gracie got on!" She looked back at the half-turned canoe. "That woman, Cass's mother, she was outside in her garden the whole time."

"Ruth?" Matt stared at her, incredulous. "You're talking about Ruth?"

"She saw Gracie get on."

"What do you mean Ruth saw Gracie get on? Where were you?"

"I went around back, but it was only for a second. And I saw the bus pull away. I know she got on. Of course she got on . . ."

"Well, she didn't fucking get on!"

Elise ran across the road and lawn to Ruth's front door and pounded on it. By the time Matt caught up, it had swung open and Ruth's face appeared.

"You saw Gracie, our daughter, right? This morning?" Elise turned and pointed at the half-canoe bus shelter. "There. You saw her getting on the flowered bus?"

"Elise!" Matt yelled.

"That little girl?" Ruth processed what Elise was saying. Her hand went up to touch her neck. "With the messy hair?"

"Elise!"

"Yes! Gracie. Did she get on the flowered bus?"

"Oh dear."

"Ruth, did she board the bus?" Yelling, Elise pointed to the camp bus. "Did you see Gracie get on the bus?" The driver was out of the vehicle now and standing in the road, looking panicked. Kids' faces plastered the windows. "Did you see her get on *that* bus?"

"Heavens. Did I do something wrong?"

"What's going on?" Cass had materialized from nowhere. She put an arm around Ruth and turned to Elise. "Why are you screaming at my mother? You're upsetting her!"

"I don't believe this," Matt kept repeating as he paced the porch. "Oh my god, oh my god."

"Gracie's gone!" said Elise. "Your mother saw her get on the bus. We need to know she got on the bus."

"She got on the bus," Ruth confirmed. "Edward and I watched her."

Elise looked at Matt, triumphant. "They *both* saw her."

"Jesus fucking Christ, Elise!" Matt said, his hands on her upper arms. He shook her. "Edward's been dead for ten years!"

"My mother has Alzheimer's," Cass said. "You can't listen to what she says."

The truth was unfurling and Elise didn't look like she'd survive it. "But she could still be right . . ."

"No, not that bus," said Ruth. "It didn't have flowers. You know, it wasn't a bus at all. It was something smaller. A truck, perhaps. Or a van."

A roar the size of a jet engine. It started in Elise's core, billowed up her spine, gathering force with every vertebrae until it escaped her. A roar so loud, so forceful, she could no longer hear what Matt was saying. Ruth started to weep uncontrollably in the doorway.

Elise couldn't breathe. The roar coiled itself around her and squeezed, binding her and bracing her. It was so ravenous, so crazed, so keening with outrage, it sucked all the oxygen from the street. The entire village. Its force lifted her off the ground, higher and higher, until she was hovering way above the scene. In the sky, some twenty, thirty, fifty thousand feet up, with puffy cumulonimbus clouds that looked so substantial and beautiful from the ground but now offered her nothing at all. Then the small bit of rock and moss that made up Ruth's lawn. The hedge. The roof. It all came rushing upward, fallen needles growing larger and sharper and more intricate as they hurtled toward her. Her only instinct: to travel back in time, tuck her knees into her belly to protect unborn Gracie from the impact. Her feet hit first, driving her knees into her chin. Just as the pine carpet came smashing into her face, Elise realized she'd dropped to her knees on Ruth's verandah.

She'd never made a sound.

CHAPTER 16

....

In a sea of uniforms, police badges, buzzing radios, and mounting panic, Matt held his forehead in his hands. There was no good reason for the camp bus driver, Ken, to be in their house instead of their child, and it took everything Matt had not to shake him until answers the man didn't have came out and Gracie appeared. He watched Elise pace the hall, pushing her hair back over and over. It had been well over eight hours since their daughter got into some other vehicle.

He and Elise had already run around searching—up the road and across the neighbors' properties and into sheds and garages. They'd run into the woods calling Gracie's name. They'd scoured the waterfront, boathouses, gazebos, and docks nearby—barely daring to breathe when looking under them.

They'd found nothing. Not a trace.

Ken's lower jaw trembled and his eyes were pink and glassy with tears. He was speaking to a police officer. "She wasn't there when I passed, but I didn't think anything of it. I thought it was Monday she was starting."

They had called the camp. The voice on the other end of the

phone had sounded twelve years old. After some shuffling of the phone, whispering, the horror was confirmed: "No, her leader says she never arrived. Her name wasn't on any of the lists yet because she wasn't signed up the usual way."

"Matt, come." Elise pushed out through the front door.

He followed. Two local police cars had joined the state police; their lights flashed with sickening authority. Matt felt weightless. Couldn't feel the ground beneath his feet. These cops climbed out of their vehicles to join the state troopers. The bright points of their metal badges caught Matt's eye. Police badges were in the shape of shields, he noticed for the first time in his life. For protection. But whose?

Still, the whole show was convincing. You had to believe these people knew what to do.

In a stupor, he watched Elise tell them what she knew—which was nothing. As they were calling 911, he'd remembered how Elise could fix things in an emergency. Like the woman who fell off her Segway. Like the night in the hotel room. He'd remembered and clung to her. Reminded her—surely she could summon up her superhero self for her own daughter. Yes?

But she stared at him with those eyes. There was no superpower behind them at all. They were just as useless as his.

Jesus . . . he'd been busy having an orgasm to the sight of his old girlfriend while Gracie was out there with no one even *starting* to look for her. He could have stayed until the bus arrived, not gone to sharpen the axe. Made a bigger deal about Gracie going to camp for her first time ever. It was his bus shelter. Why hadn't he thought to sit beside her on the bench? He felt his head swirl, and he leaned over his knees to stop himself from passing out.

Maybe he deserved this lightning bolt from hell.

A crowd had started to gather as neighbors wandered over to see what was wrong. He and Elise were the flaming wreck on the side of the highway.

One of the cops turned to him, her mouth moving. She was tiny. A child looking for a child. Her short hair was dyed deep red and she wore stud earrings. Tiny gold horseshoes, but one had tilted sideways. Matt stood. He wanted to tell her that horseshoes should be upright like the letter "U." Otherwise, the luck runs out.

"Sir, I'm asking you what other vehicles you saw."

He racked his brain for details of that morning; it was all so blurred, like looking through a rainy windshield. "The guys were on the roof," he heard himself say. "Then Paulie, the kid from the gas station, he was here to take away the raccoon. There were tourists—there are always tourists." A boat pulled up out back, police radio chatter echoing from the bay. The wail of sirens grew increasingly intense. "When I left . . . to go to the hardware store . . . I passed a small car. Dark. Dusty."

This morning, this—he looked at her badge—this Investigator Meghan Moody got up, showered, swiped on eyeliner and red lipstick to complement her hair. Pulled on the ironed gray uniform, pushed the tiny earrings into her pierced lobes, thinking they looked pretty.

"You notice anything else—the plates, the driver?"

Maybe she had a kid of her own. And when she got home that night, she'd remove those earrings and do what everyone who wasn't Matt or Elise would do. Thank the heavens their child wasn't the one who'd gone missing. He'd never been so fucking jealous in his life.

"I didn't think to look."

Cass's mother stood watching them. Ruth. The reason they'd already lost so many hours. Why hadn't he said something to Elise about Ruth's dementia?

Images of the day flashed through his mind, distorted and hazy. A black raccoon. Elise in the garden. The swinging FOR SALE sign. The camp kids singing. "I didn't know to look."

His wife, fragile and pale, stood staring at it all, weirdly detached with the buttercup drooping in her hair. Even her musculature seemed to have gone slack. Her eyes were too big for her face all of a sudden. Her cheeks had caved in. Her hands fluttered around her mouth like baby birds before they learned how to fly. "I'm so sorry. It was just a few seconds . . . "

This new Elise scared the living shit out of him.

She attached herself to him now, slid hands as fragile as dry leaves up his back. If she was going to go faint and watery at the one time he needed her to don a cape, could she not at least weep? Was it too much to want her to be soaked in grief?

"I don't know what to do." She kept repeating this to everyone and no one as she held her husband tighter. "What do we do?"

Neither did he know what to fucking do. What he did know was that before she came back, he and Gracie were fine. Until Elise decided that Gracie should go to camp, all was good.

He couldn't be in his wife's grasp, not for another second. He ducked out of her embrace and walked away.

In the kitchen, Sergeant Trenton Dorsey introduced himself as the troop commander. He stood well over six feet, and the silver in his tightly curled hair, the worn-leather-and-clean-soap scent of his cologne, the intelligence on his weathered face were calming, fatherly, even. Elise thought he appeared daunted by nothing. Certainly he would've seen everything before. He would have seen worse. He could fix this . . . he could find Gracie.

She paced the floor while Matt sat at the table with Dorsey, who explained how they worked cases of missing children. He described the initial work as a "rigorous process of elimination, beginning with the immediate family members and spanning outward."

He explained that, the next day, friends, family, and anyone in the physical periphery of the disappearance would be interviewed. The faster that could be accomplished, the faster the police would be able to move forward.

"For now, we're looking at registered sex offenders in the area." Dorsey flipped through his pad, pausing here and there to make notes. "For a pretty little ski town, we have more than our fair share. Four in and around the area, all risk levels two or three."

Elise scraped hair off her face. "What does that mean?"

"These boys are registered for life, and we keep a watch on them. They're already being checked for alibis, past movements."

"We should have sold this place from New Jersey. Made a quick phone call to an agent," Elise said. She couldn't be still. She leaned against the counter and rocked herself, then moved to the doorway. "We never should have come."

They learned that Ruth, Garth, and Cass had been deemed unlikelies, though they were not fully cleared at the moment. Andy and Lyman, too, were probably in the clear, because they'd been on the back roof when it happened.

"She wouldn't get into a strange car voluntarily. There would have been a struggle. I was gone about sixty seconds—I would have known. Gracie would have fought like hell. There'll be evidence on the road, right?"

Dorsey said, "We'd like you to look at these photos, Mrs. Sorenson."

She lowered herself into the chair beside Matt. Spread out were photos of Gracie that Cass had taken and printed. Gracie and River squealing around the campfire. Gracie, with crutches, making her way across the darkened backyard.

"These are all shot at night," said Dorsey, picking through the pile. "Your husband has shared a few photos he took this morning." Gracie grinning beside Paulie, so recent it almost seemed Elise could grab her daughter and pull her out of that moment. "Perfect in that she's wearing the outfit she went missing in, but the light's not great. Do you have any other recent photos? Taken during the day? On your phone is fine."

She pulled her phone from her pocket, opened the photo library, and scanned through it . . . they were almost all of Indie. The barn. A change room selfie at Saks in Palm Beach, where she had been trying on a sheer nightie for Matt. But the credit card hadn't gone through, so she hadn't bought it. She scrolled through the photos more quickly until she came to one of Gracie. It had been taken at Christmas in Palm Beach. Oh god. What did that say about her? She hadn't taken a single recent photo of her own daughter. "I've only been back a couple of days . . . "

"Can you give us a description? Full name, height, weight?"

"Gracie Jo Sorenson," Elise said, feeling faint. "Her birthday is October 28th, she's eight years old. She's four feet exactly and weighs . . ."

She realized she had no idea. She didn't know this simple fact about her own child. Her hand immediately went to her belly. The baby. She knew nothing about this one, either.

"Four-foot-one now, actually," Matt said. "And fifty-seven pounds. Her hair is wavy. Blond." He motioned toward the photos. "Obviously cut to the chin. Skin a bit olive in tone, freckles. Light gray eyes."

Elise said, "She has a pale brown, opal-shaped birthmark on her right arm, at the elbow."

"We have her clothing here in the photo," Dorsey said. "Denim shorts. I can see that her T-shirt is blue with white writing, but the words are obscured."

"It said something like . . . um . . . I can't think . . . " Elise said. "'No one's in control' . . . "

"'Don't worry, nothing is under control.'" Cass appeared at the table, with Garth behind her. "Hi, Trent," she said to Dorsey, before laying on the table a daytime photo of Gracie so staggeringly beautiful Elise gasped. Their daughter, sitting on the dock's edge, dangling her feet over the edge. Someone must have called to her, because she was looking back over her shoulder, sunlight behind her curved like a halo, the grin on her face so peaceful Elise nearly dropped to the floor.

"Hey, Cass." Dorsey nodded in greeting—clearly they knew each other—and picked up the photo. "Mama's little girl, eh?"

"She can't run, it's important you know that." Matt's voice was hoarse. "She's about the easiest-to-identify eight-year-old you could possibly find in this town, because her walk is uneven. She uses turquoise crutches." Matt pointed at Dorsey's notepad. "Write that down. She can't walk on her own."

"Well, she can," said Elise.

"No. She can't."

Elise looked at Dorsey. "Without her crutches, she walks with a limp."

"This is all good," said Dorsey. "Helps us enormously that she's so distinguishable."

"I still don't understand how you didn't hear a vehicle come to a stop out front," Matt said to Elise. "If you were gone that short a time? Like you said, it would have taken some effort to coax Gracie into a vehicle. She's no pushover. How the hell did you not hear anything?"

"None of this makes sense."

"May I say something?" They all turned to look at Cass, who was sitting on the counter now. "I had the joy—the privilege—of spending a few moments alone with Grace yesterday. She won't be hard to find; she glows like the sun."

Elise studied Cass, willing her out of their lives. "It's Gracie. Not Grace."

She turned to face the window. Police were everywhere, some in uniform, some in plainclothes. Lights flashed in the fading dusk. Police radios buzzed. They'd brought in teams from all over the state.

Cass walked across the room. She wrapped her arms around Elise and held her, one hand stroking the back of her head. "We're going to find her. I can feel it in my bones."

Forensics people, gloved, suited, capped, bootied, were down on hands and knees on the road and the lawn. Samples went into Ziploc bags, which were labeled in black Sharpie.

"I refuse to let you blame yourself," Cass whispered into her hair. "It's not your fault."

·········

CHAPTER 17

It was Monday. A wholly separate day from the one when his child disappeared. Matt had meant to lie down on Gracie's bed for only a moment, but had clearly passed out. He struggled to sit up now, his head weighing fifty pounds. After those first panicked searches, so stupidly hopeful his daughter would be within arm's reach after being gone all day, his body had become heavy and wooden, his joints as unyielding as timber. He was no longer flesh and blood. He was a fallen oak.

He forced himself to stand. The sun would be up soon. They'd be able to see.

The faint glow of the antler light met him as he made his way downstairs. Elise was staring at something on the hall table and looked up. Invited him over without saying a word. She had metal travel mugs waiting—coffee, he could smell it—but it was a framed photo that had her attention. He crossed the room.

It was that sweet baby picture of Gracie covered in yogurt and Cheerios, about nine months old, with dimpled hands in the air. In Elise's other hand, unframed, was the sequel. When Gracie was older. In that one, Nate's papery face smiled beside his granddaughter's and the blurry smudge of Christmas tree lights lay behind them.

It would have been 2011. The week before New Year's, and they were all at the cabin, heavy snow falling day after day. Gracie had just turned five that fall and Nate, Matt, and Elise had showered her with, among a good many toys and books for Christmas, batteries of all sizes in her stocking. You couldn't imagine a happier kid. She'd opened her gifts from Santa and left them all beneath the tree to revive toys she hadn't played with in years. A baby doll that cooed when you pushed a bottle in her mouth and cried when you took it out. A cheap plastic dog that yapped and did backflips and drove everyone crazy, especially Gunner, who would've silenced the junky imposter in one chomp in his younger days. Her old crib mobile now clipped to her headboard that played "Twinkle, Twinkle, Little Star" over and over. And over.

Battery Christmas was one of unequivocal regression. But it was Nate who said, "Go with it. In about three days, she'll be grown up, forgetting her own kid's batteries all year."

Early one morning, Gracie had gotten out of bed in her footie pajamas to wake her dad and be piggybacked downstairs. She wanted Matt to drag her old high chair out of the shed. He did so with great reluctance—it was so cold out, the windows had all but frosted over. But Elise was in bed with the flu and Nate was ninety-five. Both had earned a little quiet. As Matt dragged the chair through the snow and inside, Gunner trudged dutifully behind, his movements stiff and arthritic, his black face grizzled with white hairs.

Wrangling a long-limbed child into the high chair had been a challenge, as the tray's metal sliders were lodged stuck with food and grime. Once in, Gracie banged her feet noisily against the lower rungs while Gunner looked on, invigorated by the fuss but too tired to get involved. Above the dog, as ever, the vintage Ski New York poster and Matt's grandmother's crisscrossed skis.

"Now I need baby food," Gracie the imp said.

"Shh. Mom's sleeping. How about some eggs? Or toast?"

Gracie rattled the tray in its grimy tracks and whined, "*Real* baby food."

Gunner woofed his support.

"Okay, guys. We're going to seriously take it down a notch."

Footsteps in the living room, then Nate appeared, shaved and shod and dressed in button-down shirt and sweater and crisply ironed trousers. Gunner, of course, swept across the room to greet his master. "Take it down a notch?" Nate swatted Matt out of the way. "Don't listen to your father, sweetheart. He's turning into an old man."

"He said I can't have baby food."

Now a red-nosed Elise shuffled into the room, slippered and robed and clutching a wad of tissue, spinning away from Gunner as he went to greet her. "No, no. Go see . . . anybody else."

Matt took the dog by the collar so Elise could sit at the table. "Sorry, babe. I wanted you to sleep in."

"Don't worry." She motioned to her puffy face and coughed into the nook of her arm. "Sleep wasn't happening."

Nate observed from across the room, a half grin on his lined face. "But contagion might be."

Elise's gaze snapped to Matt, as usual, wanting confirmation that Nate had insulted, accused, or otherwise maligned her. She took the man so seriously when clearly he was joking.

Matt tried to lighten the moment. "I took a bullet for all of us, absorbing the virus all night long."

"Mommy, we have a baby food problem," said Gracie, flopping on her tray.

Elise smiled. "I'll bet, Little Miss Bigger-than-Her-High-Chair."

"Baby food problem?" Nate said, leaving the room. "Baby food emergency, is more like it." He returned to set a framed photo on his great-granddaughter's tray. Infant Gracie in the same high chair. Yogurt and Cheerio madness. "You see that kid in the picture?"

Matt handed Elise a cup of coffee. Kissed her forehead and slid a hand over her shoulders as they both looked on.

"Yes."

"That kid a baby?"

Gracie nodded.

"That stuff all over her hands and face. Is that food?"

"Duh."

"Gracie," Elise warned. "Don't be saucy."

Nate didn't react. He glanced at Matt a moment, then back to his great-granddaughter. "'Duh' means yes?"

A dramatic nod.

"I give you . . ." The old man made his way to fridge and cupboard and came back with a tub of yogurt and a box of Cheerios. He poured about a cup of Cheerios onto the tray, then spooned three dollops of yogurt onto it. ". . . baby food. Go to town, sweetheart. Eat it, roll in it. Throw it in the air if that works for you."

Gracie's eyes doubled in size and she glanced at her parents in silent question. Was it really okay to make a mess? Matt and Elise laughed, told her to respect her great-grandfather's wishes.

The rest—who snapped the photo when Nate leaned down to kiss her yogurt-slathered cheek, how they got Gracie's slimy limbs out of the chair, how much of the slop Gunner ate, who cleaned it all up—none of it mattered.

He turned away from the photo. "That was such a beautiful morning." His voice was a hoarse whisper. "She could do no wrong in Nate's eyes." He took a mug and shuffled to the front door, logs for feet, barely able to see through his tears.

At the door, Elise handed Matt a jacket and baseball cap. "Put these on. It's supposed to rain." As he pulled them on, she added, "Dorsey texted. They want us in for polygraphs."

"What the fuck?" He squinted at his wife. "We're suspects too?"

She pulled on her coat. "It's standard. Booked for seven o'clock."

"And what if we refuse?"

"Why would we refuse?"

He looked at her as if she'd lost her mind. "How about because we had nothing to do with whatever the fuck has happened to her and don't want them wasting their time?"

"The quicker they clear away wrong directions, the quicker they move in the right ones."

"But what if we don't pass? What if, say, it registers our panic? We're under the worst fucking stress imaginable . . ."

"They know that. And don't forget, the search party is gathering at six. Starting from the fire station—"

"I know about the search party." He couldn't help being gruff. Search and rescue dogs were being brought in to work off-leash. What they were trained to find, Matt couldn't contemplate. He'd overheard one cop on the driveway tell someone on his radio to bring cadaver dogs. "Jesus Christ. I was there when they said it."

She zipped her coat in silence and took a cap from the hooks by the door.

His laces were undone and he kneeled down stiffly to tie them, double-knotting hard like Nate had taught him. He stood to find his wife staring at him.

He kept waiting for this to turn out to have been a terrible mistake. A prank. His wife would laugh, tease him, and there Gracie would be. None of this was really happening.

But it was.

In between those moments, rage and shock and blame and fear sloshed up against him in waves. One minute he wanted to kill his wife. The next he needed to hold her. The woman had left her child alone on a road frequently traveled by tourists. A road featured in Lake Placid travel brochures, for fuck's sake. Then again, it was only for a minute or two. He studied Elise. "What did you run out back for?"

She held up a cut thumb. "Gloves."

He stared at the jagged laceration, his own words coming back to him. *Go get the leather pair from the shed.* That was all she had done: listened to her husband's advice.

"I'm her mother," Elise said quietly. "I need my daughter back just like you do."

Matt reached out and, more abruptly than intended, pulled his wife into his chest. Elise seemed even smaller than last night. As if she herself were turning into a child. "I know you need her back." He rested his cheek on her head. "We both do."

They stepped into a cool mist that would soon turn to drizzle. Dawn was only just beginning to break apart the blackness, giving shape to the trees, the cars on the driveway, the police tape fluttering eerily around the trees and split rail fence along the front edge of the property. Only the lapping waves and their own footsteps broke the early morning silence as they walked toward the lake.

Cass's place was lit up. There she was, in the back room with Garth—both in robes. They were huddled close and it was clear Cass was weeping. Garth stood, ran both hands over his head, and left the room, while Cass collapsed onto her knees and stayed there.

"How well do you know her, really?" Elise asked, her cap pulled low over her eyes. "I mean now. It's been decades, right?"

"Last person on earth."

"You don't think it's weird? Taking all those photos of Gracie? She's known her for what—two days? And the way she was at the barbecue—calling our daughter her little angel? And now she's crying? I don't trust her."

It was more weird that Elise *wasn't* crying. Matt chose his words carefully. "Just because someone is loving and maternal, that doesn't mean they're capable of abducting a child."

Elise turned toward the waterfront and strode on. Matt lagged behind, under the pretense of checking the shed, though the door was wide open and it was clear the building was empty of life. He watched his wife search the brush on both sides of the beach, around the back of the boathouse, then inside. They'd checked all this yesterday. As had the police. "What are you doing?"

"She could have come back. Or we could have missed something."

He listened while she climbed up the wooden ladder to search Nate's antique boat, suspended from the rafters. He refused to even look as Elise checked beneath the dock. If there was anything new and ominous, he wasn't sure he'd be able to survive it.

Gracie's first word, at six months, had been "Da-da." Then she started saying "dog," and "ba-ba" for bottle, "wa-wa" for water. At thirteen months, to his mortification, she shouted "Jesus" when she saw puppies in a pet store window. By eighteen months, she was speaking in short sentences and could count. Cognitively, she was way ahead of her peers. When she was just over two, watching the video of a baby dancing to Beyoncé's "Single Ladies" on YouTube, Gracie tried to imitate what she saw and, holding on to the coffee table, started bopping up and down. Only Gracie, much older than the baby in the video, kept falling down. Until then, they'd convinced themselves it was her age, the fact that she was clumsy and walked on her toes. He'd told himself her motor development was normal. It was Beyoncé's song that prompted them to take Gracie to the pediatrician. In came the diagnosis. And the utter helplessness that came with it.

There was nothing worse than feeling helpless when it came to your child.

Finally, Elise was done. The waterfront was clear. Matt dropped to the ground to throw up in relief, his knees deep in the dead leaves and sticks and weeds. Elise rushed back, worked a knee beneath him to lean on—the sticks were jagged, piercing his palms—then produced a napkin from her pocket to wipe bile from his lips. When he was able, she helped him stand again. "I don't think you're up to this, babe. Why don't you rest?"

"I'm fine."

"There are a lot of people looking. We can take shifts—"

"I'm fine." It was more than he could take that his wife was stronger than him. What kind of father fell apart like this? His stomach heaved again. "Maybe I need some food or something."

"I can make you some eggs real quick—"

Food was a lie. It was space he needed. "You go ahead. I'll meet you . . . I don't know where. The police or fire station."

The only way to rid himself of his own uselessness was to move to a higher elevation. Allow himself the illusion that a bird's-eye view would offer up an answer—no matter how many hundreds of stairs he had to haul his faltering body up to get there.

It had been their place when they were teens. The top of the K120 at the Olympic Ski Jumping Complex might as well have been, for Matt and Cass, the highest point on earth. It had been erected shortly before the 1980 Olympics, and because the structure didn't conform to the slope of any mountain but thrust straight up from the ground to soar 120 meters in the sky, to be anywhere near the top was a heady experience at first.

Over time, however, it had become a place of comfort. Of nostalgia.

On a weathered plank bench at the top of the towering monolith, where jumpers squatted to step into their skis before pointing their tips downhill and letting themselves fly, they sat now as they had dozens of times before, looking down at the mist that lay over the horse showgrounds and airport immediately below and the base of the mountains beyond, to the northeast.

The beginnings of morning drizzle spat against his cheeks, and

Matt reached up to pull the brim of his cap lower. Cass, hooded, opened the small umbrella she'd brought along.

"This was a bad idea," he said. His thighs ached from the steep climb up the ramp's endless staircase and, before that, the ladder at the base of the jump. "World looks too big from here."

The wind picked up and they both reached for an edge of the umbrella. Her free hand found his shoulder as the drizzle morphed into an audible patter.

"But it isn't, Matt. Technology has shrunk the world down. Already her picture, the details have been blasted all around the world, right? All the border guards know. We will get her back."

He looked at Cass, wet curls dancing around her face. "How well do you know Dorsey?"

"Well enough. See him around the village. His daughter goes to school with River. Carly Jane. A real sweetheart."

"You think he's any good?"

"For sure. And hugely respected around here. Plus, he knows who you are, which helps. You're a Sorenson. You're not just any-one, and neither is your child."

That was a good point. Most people in the area would go a little further to help in the face of Nate's legacy. He let out a long, mea-sured breath, vaguely comforted by the goodwill his grandfather had created. "We shouldn't have come here this summer."

"Don't say that."

"I'm serious. I never should have contemplated selling the cabin. I should have waited for Elise to come home the night of Gracie's play. Stayed in Montclair. Carried on as we always had until we had to file for bankruptcy. The creditors could have forced the sale of this place from afar, and it all would've worked itself out fine. Gracie would be lying on the carpet in her room right now, lining up her animals for the firing squad."

"Stop it." She handed him the umbrella and lit a cigarette. "This is not in any way your fault."

He watched a pair of birds fly by in the dreariness. "Gracie has two parents. I'm one of them. The math's pretty simple."

"Not from where I sit."

He turned to her, searched her face. "I told Elise to go get leather gloves."

"You didn't tell her to leave your eight-year-old at the side of the road, Matt. Especially that road. Your place is heavily treed out front, set way back. My place, I could sort of see. But yours? No chance. Whatever she needed to get, she should have waited. Like you or I would have." Cass took a long drag and exhaled, knocking ash to the slick wood at their feet. A heavy gust of wind nearly sucked the umbrella inside out, and she patted his wet knee and stood. "Come. Let's get down before this gets any worse."

CHAPTER 18

....

Elise drove along Old Military Road toward the fire station, thinking about the matching photos of their daughter in her high chair. She'd studied them for a good few minutes before Matt came downstairs. He was wrong about that morning being beautiful. It had been anything but.

Once Gracie had been freed from her high chair, stripped of her sopping pajamas, and ushered up to the bath by her father—while Elise was down on hands and knees in her robe, wiping the floor lest the old man slip and break a bone—Nate came back into the room in Sorels and a puffy Canada Goose parka. He was about to walk Gunner down to the lake, his morning ritual.

Elise sat back on her heels. "Thank you, Nate, for being so unbelievably sweet with her."

Leash in hand, the old man allowed his gaze to light upon Elise for a half second. "I don't know how you live with yourself. She would've been born perfect," he said before following his dog out into the snow.

Emptied of all strength, Elise had lowered herself over her knees until her forehead rested on the wet floor. Here, in child's pose, she remained, listening to the clock tick, listening to the splashing upstairs in the bathtub, until, what felt like days later, Nate's boots stomped up the back steps with hollow, menacing thuds.

The command station had been set up in the local fire hall out where Mill Pond Drive met Old Military Road. It was where the searchers were congregating before setting out, and where representatives from all the different agencies met, and the streets around it were narrowed by parked vehicles. Elise pulled into the parking lot and cut the engine.

Hundreds of people, it seemed, had descended upon the area, even a few locals on horseback. Members of the state police canine unit were there with German shepherds, a bloodhound, another shaggy black dog of indeterminate breed. There were local cops. State troopers. Firefighters. In the engine bay, there was a table holding stacks and stacks of plastic-wrapped ponchos. All this for Gracie.

All this because of Elise.

She climbed out of the car to the crackling buzz of police radios and just stood there. She could have been anybody in the parking lot: a waitress from the village who wanted to help, a frustrated neighbor who couldn't get out of his driveway, a curious jogger who'd been off-line for the past fourteen hours. For a moment, she could almost imagine it was all happening to somebody else.

She couldn't help herself; her eyes searched for blond heads in the crowd, in cars passing by. She looked at the parents in the search party, ambling alongside their children as if they had a lifetime together. Which they most likely did.

They all had to be thankful it wasn't them. They'd be feeding their sons and daughters chicken fingers or hamburgers or, yes, spaghetti come evening. And later, after a bonfire on the beach or a quiet night at home watching a family movie, they'd be tucking those warm little bodies into bed, running their fingers through the strands of silk that are the tousled heads of freshly bathed children.

As she started toward the station, a ponytailed woman in hiking boots and a flannel shirt who was headed the same way offered her a sad smile. "Terrible occasion to be out early on a Monday morning."

Elise didn't know what to say.

"Says a lot about human nature," the woman said. "To see how many people turned up."

From the lack of curiosity in the woman's eyes, Elise realized she didn't know she was walking alongside the missing girl's mother. "You're right," Elise replied. "There is so much kindness."

A resigned frown. "And so much evil." The woman held up a hand in parting and jogged into the station, to where a bearded man who looked like Gracie's old kindergarten teacher was organizing people into groups.

Elise tripped and fell. Arms appeared to help her to her feet— a firefighter in a clear plastic poncho. He recognized in an instant that he had in his hands the tragedy's ground zero, the mother of the missing girl. Right away came the Mrs. Sorenson this, Mrs. Sorenson that. She'd never been called Mrs. Sorenson more in her life. There were offers of coffee, water. A granola bar. A chair. But not before his face flickered with judgment: *You're the one who left that little angel out on the road.*

Elise hurried inside to find the restroom, feeling sicker still as she passed people rolling out maps and huddled over laptops and talking on cellphones at a small city of collapsible tables. After two wrong turns, someone led her to the ladies' room. There, Elise's middle twisted into hard cramping, followed by a gush of warmth between her legs. She burst into a stall and tugged down her jeans in a panic. Almost violent against bleached white briefs, more blood. Too much blood.

Her heart started to pound. This was no longer like what she had experienced with Gracie. She squatted and her palms found the cold tile floor as she squeezed her eyes shut. This wasn't the usual spotting during pregnancy. This had to be a miscarriage.

She folded toilet tissue into her underwear and fought to get her pants zipped and buttoned. A flash of the high chair photos. The BIG SISTER T-shirt Gracie so desperately wanted. Elise got up to run the cold water, held her wrists under the icy flow, if only for a distraction.

Orders shouted through a megaphone echoed through the fire hall. The volunteers were about to mobilize. Elise dried her arms and marched past the bedlam, fully aware of the stares that followed her to her car.

There was too much bleeding. She had no choice but to get medical help.

McKenzie Mountain Urgent Care sat on Highway 86 just past Whiteface and Carolyn Road, where the buildings grew fewer and farther between, eventually giving way to forest. As Elise rolled into the parking lot, wipers working hard now against driving rain, she made the mistake of looking farther up the road to where traffic had stopped. Beyond, a flash of troopers holding rifles or what Dorsey had said would be AR-15s, standing wide-legged behind neon orange pylons. Some were bent over open windows, peering into back seats.

Others were looking into trunks.

Dorsey had described the roadblock. It was another thing entirely to see it.

Coming up the knoll from behind the clinic, seven or eight heads, then rain jackets and booted feet, along with an older cop who had a bloodhound on a leash. They used sticks to part the bushes and weeds in the rain. As they approached a copse of young trees, the group split, some entering the forest, ducking under branches, the others continuing through the long grasses at the edge of the road. Two men waved over the cop and dog, headed for the Dumpster.

Elise fumbled, in a panic, to turn the car around and park on the other side of the building. She failed to get the vehicle into reverse as, in her peripheral vision, more searchers gathered around the Dumpster. She forced her gaze into her lap, fingers digging into her jeans.

The flash of a red jacket—someone had climbed up and into the big blue bin. Elise cut the wipers and allowed the rain to blur out the brutal reality before turning off the engine.

When the search party had become a smudge of color in an otherwise gray landscape, she ran for the cover of the clinic.

The waiting room held about eight or ten patients flipping through magazines or dozing in vinyl chairs when Elise burst in to find no one at the receptionist desk. Seat by seat, the room came alive with nudges and stares as Elise was identified. Her palm found the silver bell.

A youngish female in denim shirtdress and runners came out from the back, glasses pushed back on her head, open file in hand. Elise all but grabbed hold of her. The woman looked up to see Elise's stricken face, waved her into an examining room that smelled of rubbing alcohol, and closed the door, tucked stray blond hair behind one ear. "I'm Dr. Jennifer Upton." Her voice was so kind and safe. Elise wanted to put her in charge of everything. "And you're Mrs. Sorenson."

Elise paced the room like a caged tiger. "I shouldn't be here. But I'm bleeding." Her hands shook and she sat. "A lot."

"It started when?"

Elise tried to think. Stood again. "A bit lately, but mostly just now."

"Are you pregnant?"

"I took a test."

"So there is a chance?"

"I might be, yes . . . I can't really think."

Dr. Upton frowned kindly. "Of course you can't think. You don't know which way is up, and you don't know which way to turn. I understand." Cool fingers on Elise's wrist, then a paper gown in her hands. "Let's give you all the answers we can as quickly as we can. Bring your focus right back to where it needs it be. Does that sound good?"

Elise nodded wildly. This woman was straight from God.

"Strip down to bra and panties. Put on the gown, ties to the front. When you've done that, open the door. I'll be waiting on the other side. And I'll take you down the hall to Oliver in ultrasound. We'll know very quickly what's what."

The room was so tiny it was a closet. A womb. Oliver rolled fresh paper over the examining table and helped Elise lie down on her back. Flannel blankets covered her pelvis and chest as he parted the gown to bare her belly. He was an overgrown puppy in the sliver of space between exam table and monitor, all big knees and folded limbs and hair that flopped like spaniel ears.

He shook a plastic bottle of gel in one hand and smiled. "I'm not going to lie, this is going to be cold."

She gasped as he squirted the goo over her lower abdomen and spread it around with the Doppler. The exam was a blur of bright lights and gel and the plastic fist driving into her stomach. The memory of her first ultrasound with Gracie made it hard to breathe—in the clinic back in Montclair, Matt holding her hand as the female technician probed her belly, searching, searching, searching. Then the Doppler stopped moving and the tech's face broke into a smile. The sound of Gracie's wicked little heartbeat filled the room.

Oliver put down the Doppler and excused himself. Said he'd be right back.

....

Every choice, big or small, that she'd made over the past day. Week. Month. Eight years. No—eight years plus a pregnancy that didn't go all the way to term. Every crook of a finger. Every pause at a stop sign. Every weed pulled. Word uttered. Breath inhaled. Horse mounted. How far back could you look, really, for why things worked out the way they had?

Many times she'd wondered what would have happened if she hadn't woken up late that night, sick and feverish, with aching joints and chills, her pajama top stuck to her back. It was her parents' bridge evening, the summer between ninth and tenth grades, but everyone had long gone home and the house was quiet. Elise had gotten up to get a drink of water and noticed a light on downstairs. Her father wouldn't like it. He'd wonder aloud, in the morning, why he had to pay for them to light up the entire neighborhood.

As Elise tiptoed down the steps, she heard a rhythmic thump, the rustle of fabric, and the scrape of furniture feet against hard floor. At the entry to the family room she stopped. There, beneath Big-Mouth Billy, was her father. His pants were off and his bottom rose and fell as he thrusted between Briony's open legs. On the sofa back were her feet, still in sandals: beige cloth with a rope wedge and crepey soles. Expensive-looking gold buckles on the ankle strap.

Elise ran upstairs, waited before knocking on her mother's door. Telling her mother could lead to divorce. But the thought of Rosamunde's face the next morning, earnest as she soft-boiled an egg for her husband, served it with half a grapefruit and whole wheat toast and absolutely no knowledge that one of Briony's crepe soles had been pressed into the sofa in the next room? Elise couldn't stand to watch that, knowing her beloved mother was being deceived. It was wrong.

It may have been minutes that Elise stood at her parents' bedroom door. It may have been hours. But eventually she pressed her face to the door crack and whispered, "Mom?"

And what if she hadn't?

Oliver didn't return. Dr. Upton came in instead, to lay Elise's clothes at the foot of the exam table, to sit on Oliver's stool and take Elise's hands in hers. There wasn't a chance the news would be good. "You are pregnant. About seven weeks. But I'm afraid the gestational sac is empty. There is no embryo, no yolk sac. We call this a blighted ovum. A phantom pregnancy. I'm sorry."

Elise struggled for a place to put this information in her brain. All she knew was she had to get dressed and go. Find her daughter.

"We can book an appointment for you at the hospital in case you don't miscarry on your own and need a D&C."

This pregnancy was zero to sixty in three seconds, it seemed. Motherhood was instant like that. The prospect of losing your baby, even at the worst moment of your life, was devastating.

"I can't book anything."

"I hear you. So I'm going to let you get dressed and step back outside to face what to any mother is the pits of hell. You're not going to be giving yourself and your health a single thought, and that's just fine. It's the way it has to be until you get your daughter back. But I want you to promise me this, Mrs. Sorenson—if you develop a fever, or if the bleeding gets too intense, you'll get yourself back here or to the ER. Are you okay with that?"

Elise nodded. She started to sit up, pulled the blankets over her belly. "Can I ask you a favor?"

"Of course."

"Can you use my name—Elise?"

The doctor came around the other side of the table to set the stack of clothes on Elise's lap. She placed her hands on Elise's shoulders. "You are in the worst of this. Your heart is broken, you're afraid for your daughter's life, and you're questioning every decision you've ever made. I expect every day until you find your daughter will be infinitely worse. And you may not have even reached bottom. When you do, you will stumble. You will fall. But after that, you'll climb. It's what we do as mothers. Because no matter how vicious that inner voice can be—and, holy hell, what a heartless bitch it is—we are made to survive. And you will survive this." She removed her hands. "Elise."

The door clicked behind Jennifer Upton when she left.

Chapter 19

....

Expecting to find Elise inside, Matt had walked into a police station abuzz with muted voices, shouted orders, ringing phones, buzzing radios, and the zigzag energy of search dogs in yellow vests being led in or out of the building. And, every few minutes, the authoritative and promising squeak and rattle of cops marching past, vests loaded with pistols, Tasers, handcuffs, and mobile phones.

He tried his wife's phone twice, but she didn't pick up. Incredulity turned to fury, which turned to alarm. Had she found something? Was she hurt?

Inside the bare bones office that was the polygraph suite, the din was a faraway bustle that Matt could almost convince himself was happening because of someone else's tragedy. Elise had been booked to go first. When she didn't show, they brought Matt in to be attached to a blood pressure cuff, rubber tubing on abdomen and chest to record breathing, and metal plates strapped to two fingers to measure perspiration.

From the moment the examiner—a gawky young male with razor burn on his neck—hooked him up, Matt couldn't get his lungs to fill, not completely. He felt he was sucking every breath through a furnace filter. Gracie was gone—could he be in a bigger panic to begin with? The control questions made him panic more: Are you wearing a green shirt? Are you in New York State? Is your name Matthew Sorenson? Then his panic created still more panic. What if his upset read as lies on the machine? The combination of shallow breathing and racing heart surely must've shot his blood pressure skyward. The examiner kid was poker-faced, let out a muffled sigh as he unstrapped Matt's fingers and chest, wound up the cords, and slid them into a drawer. "That's it. You're done."

Matt didn't dare ask if he'd passed. It seemed like a question only a guilty person would think of.

Elise ran in, pale and breathless, as Matt came out. "Hey."

"Where've you been?"

"Is there any news? Have you seen Dorsey?"

"There's nothing."

"Ronnie called on my way here. He'd heard on CNN."

"Please tell me you're not going to Toronto."

She closed her eyes and breathed deeply. "Of course I'm not going to Toronto, Matt. Our daughter is missing."

Before he could reply, the examiner was at the door, ushering her inside. "Mrs. Sorenson? We're ready for you now."

Matt stepped outside to wait for Elise. The air beneath the doors' overhang was a curious mix of cedar and old cigarettes. The former because most of the building was covered in cedar shakes, the latter because of all the crushed butts tossed into the grass. He looked down at them. In a place like this, a good many of those smokes would have a story—most of them better than his.

The moment he sat on the stone bench, his phone vibrated within his pocket. He pulled it out to tap open a text from Cass. It was a photo he hadn't seen in decades. Cass and him, about thirteen years old, lying on the grass, heads touching, amber sunlight making them squint. He remembered the day like it was yesterday. That she was hanging out with him at all was a miracle. By that age, every boy in town was after her.

Billy Joel's "Only the Good Die Young" had been playing from a little radio on the grass, and they both knew all the words. Matt had just gotten his braces off. Cass had a single daisy in her hair and Matt was plucking the petals off another, wondering aloud if she loved him. Or loved him not. Cass had stood up, saying she didn't want to be there for the last petal because "You have to leave some shit in life unknown" and sauntered inside to get ready to go to a movie with Adam Lerner—a sophomore jock at Lake Placid High. After her screen door slammed, Matt had pulled off the last petal to "she loves me," rolled onto his back, and grinned.

These other guys were just a phase, he'd thought. She'd come back to Matt one day.

To marry Cass had always been his dream. Their juvenile plan at one point had been to build a little place up at the lake. He'd be a lawyer in town. She'd take pictures. They'd spend their summers canoeing and their winters skiing. It had always slayed him how she was so kind. Once, she found three newborn squirrels after a storm, and when their mother never returned, raised them in her bedroom, taking them outside every day to grow accustomed to the forest. They lived out their lives in her yard—or so Cass charmingly believed. He used to tease her—who the hell could tell one squirrel from the next?

They would've had a slew of giggling kids running around underfoot—all growing up with German shepherds and rock collections and the ability to point out the Little Dipper in the night sky. Cass's goals would have aligned with Matt's. Family first.

If Cass were Gracie's mother, not only would she be around every day, but Gracie would grow up with room to shine. She would take center stage, as every child should.

As it was in the Sorenson family, there was only room for Elise to shine. Gracie and Matt hovered around like devoted fans. They waited for Elise. They swelled with rare sightings of her. They clapped. They held their breath with anticipation. They stood up and cheered. It had always been clear that the stage belonged to Elise and there was no understudy.

Now, a male voice called out from the parking lot. "Matt?"

Alan Dionne, an old friend from camp, had morphed from wiry soccer player with black hair and sunburned skin into a stocky man with a silver crew cut and a face that had toughened into leather. But the thick black brows were the same, as was the nose bent from Alan's end of the canoe crashing down onto his face while they were portaging one summer. Clearly a cop now, he was in full uniform. When Matt rose, Alan slammed him with a hug, held him close. He still smelled of the same Polo cologne that had attracted mosquitoes all those summers ago. "Buddy. I couldn't believe when I heard. I can't imagine how you're coping."

God, to be able to step back into those simple days. "You know."

In Alan's hand was a crumpled white bag—a takeout breakfast he was bringing to work. "Yeah. I've got three boys."

"They brought us in for polygraphs."

"That's just to be by-the-book on this. It's a good thing, trust me. Every name that gets cleared narrows the search."

"Will the neighbors be cleared today? What about Cass and her boyfriend? I'd like to know they don't have this looming over their heads."

"They all have appointments later this morning." The breeze kicked up and the lake behind them churned gray, dotted with whitecaps. Alan fished around in a pocket and pulled out a card. "My cell's on the back. When I say use it anytime, I mean it. Middle of the night, you need a shoulder? I'm there for you, man."

Matt took the card, nodded.

"Hell of a thing you did. Quitting law to stay home and raise your little girl. Admirable."

"I didn't quit law."

"Huh. I thought you were doing the stay-at-home-husband thing while your wife is riding."

"No. I'm . . . no. I work. Every day."

"Ah. Well. Rumors, right?" He motioned toward the doors. "I'd better head in. But I mean it about my cell. Stay in touch."

As Alan started inside, Matt called out, "Hey, Al. That forty-eight-hours thing. Is that true? If you don't solve a crime within the first forty-eight hours, it's pretty much over?"

"Shoot, no. It's bullshit conjured up to sell papers. All you need is a viable lead in that time."

Matt felt his stomach drop. They didn't have anything close to a viable lead and they were barreling toward the twenty-four-hour mark. "And if you don't have one?"

"Sure doesn't mean you aren't going to find her. Don't be filling your head with that."

"But what are the odds?"

"Seriously, Matt. Every case is unique."

"Just level with me. If we have no lead, what happens to our chances? Do they go to nil?"

Alan waited a minute, his collar fluttering in the breeze. A low buzz came from the radio slung from his vest.

"Please. Alan. I need your honesty here."

"You're still looking at a fifty percent chance of success. Which is a lot. It means your chances of finding her are every bit as strong as . . ." Alan's voice trailed off. There was an awkward moment in which he raised his breakfast in goodbye and marched through the metal doors.

Matt dropped back down onto the bench. As the doors swept shut, he set his gaze somewhere over the treetops.

Every bit as strong as . . .

"Babe?" He looked up to find Elise staring down at him, hair blowing in the wind. He had no idea how long she'd been standing there. She sat on the bench beside him and pulled on her jacket and baseball cap.

"How'd it go?"

His wife pushed her hands into her pockets. "Can we talk?"

"Of course."

Her eyes followed his, hovering over the tree line. "It feels like . . . we're so far apart right now, and it's making this doubly painful. If we're broken at the same time as her being gone . . . I mean, how are we going to do this?"

He didn't answer.

"We need to be together. On the same side."

"We're her parents. Of course we're on the same side."

A strand of hair caught in her mouth and she tucked it behind her ears. "I need to know you love me."

"I will *always* love you."

She mulled this over, saying nothing. A pair of police cruisers pulled out of the driveway and sped toward 86. She zipped her jacket to the chin and turned to him. "You know I'm sorry, right? You know I'd never have left if I'd thought there was even a one percent chance of anything—"

As Elise went on, what Cass had said on the ski jump that morning came back to him. That he wouldn't have made the choice Elise had made. Not in a million years, with all the trees and the cabin set so far back from the road.

Nor would Cass.

CHAPTER 20

....

After Warren left them for Briony and her expensive blouses, the hangers that had held his clothes never hung still again. There must have been a vent in his closet that kept them huddled together, softly shivering. Or else they, too, were saddened and needed the comfort of bumping shoulders. It drove Rosamunde out of her bed. She began to sleep in the spare bedroom.

Warren's financial support was steady but meager. Elise's part-time pay from working at a local tack shop on weekends helped. And Rosamunde continued to work her Tuesday and Thursday shifts. But she gradually stopped driving. She walked to work and back, and Elise now got herself home from school and the barn on the bus.

Rosamunde's old Tercel sat in the garage, green paint filmy with dust.

Seeing Briony at school had become an issue for Elise. The woman made painful attempts to befriend her. Elise had taken to arriving late and bolting at the last bell. When weather permitted, she ate her lunch in a nearby park. Warren's suggestions that she come over for pizza and tone-deaf assurances that she'd "really like"

Briony if she gave her a chance were flatly ignored. Eventually, in some sort of gift from the gods, Briony left the school.

All this came at a time when Elise's competitions took her away most weekends, often funded by Ronnie, as Elise was showing his horse. Breaking the news to her mother every time she was set to go had become worrisome. Rosamunde would arrange her face into a smile. Tell her daughter she was happy for her.

But as the edges of Rosamunde's world began to fray, as holes grew where her husband's fishing trophies used to be, as Elise's ribbons piled up, she stopped coming to her daughter's room to stare at the sky. She began spending more and more evenings on the back porch, drinking Sanka on her own.

Then the divorce papers arrived; Warren wanted to get remarried. And everything about Rosamunde began to shrink back. Elise couldn't tell if her mother was losing weight from not eating or if her skeletal structure was getting smaller, but one thing seemed certain. Her mother was vanishing.

Elise skipped horse shows. She took over the shopping, the bill paying. She cooked the meals and cleaned the floors. Eventually, Elise began to lie in bed next to her mother. Rosamunde had become the child. Elise would smooth the hair off her gaunt face and point to the stars out the window. For months, Rosamunde refused to look. Then, one Thursday night, her gaze lifted to the garage roof, its outline illuminated by a streetlamp. "I can't go back. Not ever."

"Back where?" Elise asked.

"I can never go back."

Nothing she said made sense. Elise shushed her. Held her mother close until she calmed, eventually fell asleep.

Later, as she was tidying the foyer, Elise gathered up the things her mother had left on the hall table: house keys, wallet, sunglasses, and a manila folder. Curious, Elise opened the file. It was a patient's test results: HCG levels of 118,082. Even at sixteen, Elise knew she was looking at a positive pregnancy test.

The name at the top of the report was Briony Lagasse.

Elise took the file outside and dropped it into the trash can, now able to see that it wasn't a streetlamp illuminating the fence and the trees and the roof of the garage. It was the moon—big and white and unabashedly full. She marched inside and yanked all the curtains in the house shut.

With a slam of the screen door, splattered with the rain that had just started to fall again, Elise stepped into the Sorenson back porch with a hammer from the shed. Methodically, she unrolled a huge world map and, holding nails between her teeth, hammered the map into the log wall that was the exterior of the original house. She reached for a tiny container of pins with colored heads and scanned a printed email on the table.

Sightings had begun to pour in to the police hotline, and Elise had decided she'd keep track herself. It gave her something to keep busy with.

She divided the pins by color. Navy was a credible sighting. Purple was a "way-out-there" sighting. Pink was a psychic vision.

A couple in a Savannah flea market had seen a girl with crutches with a swarthy man who didn't speak English. She was overheard asking him when she could see "Mommy." Into Savannah went a navy pin. On a bleak, windswept road outside of Wichita, a girl who "had to be Gracie" was spotted hanging her head out the window of a Hyundai while a nervous couple changed a tire. Another navy. At Disneyland in California, a freckled girl started to cry as she waited in line for *Pirates of the Caribbean* and the woman with her smacked her hand. This one had a photo, and the child looked nothing like Gracie. Purple pin. A spiritual counselor in Chicago had a vision of a canal, of Gracie on a long, low barge in what she swore was Amsterdam. Pink.

That there were so many sightings was good. Through social

media, the story had already spread around the country, along with Cass's photo of Gracie—freckle-faced and grinning, her scrunched nose giving her smile a mischievous look. Gracie in on her own secret joke.

There was one bright green pin on the map. This one Elise put slightly to the right of Lake Ontario, south of Montreal. Partway up the east side of Lake Placid. On this spot, she'd written 217 Seldom Seen Road, Lake Placid, NY.

Little Green, back in the cabin where she belonged.

She looked around for her phone to take a picture of the pin. It should be the home screen on both her phone and Matt's.

Her search brought Elise through the kitchen, where fruit and food baskets and cards of well wishes were beginning to pile up. She'd already opened a cheese and cracker box sent from the parents at Summerhill Prep, from Deborah, Melanie, and Jackie, who proclaimed, "We just adore your little girl, Matt." And a tin of store-bought cookies from Andy Kostick that his note boasted were homemade.

Matt's phone was lying on the counter, so Elise grabbed it and walked back to the map, quickly typing in his password as she stood in front of the colored pins. The phone unlocked to a text exchange between Matt and Cass. It had started at 5:17 that morning.

Matt: Hey, saw you're up. I need to get out of here
Cass: Come over
Matt: K120
Cass: Seriously? Weather will suck up there
Matt: I just need lift-off
Cass: Meet out front in five. Dress warm

Elise stared at the phone, stunned. That's what Matt had done when he hung back, claiming to need food? He'd climbed the big ski jump all the way over by the horse showgrounds—with his ex-girlfriend? When their daughter was missing, it was Cass he needed? His ex-neighbor was who the man turned to when their daughter was missing? She continued to scroll through the messages to a sunny photo of Matt and Cass as tweens, lying in the grass, heads touching, him plucking petals from a daisy.

There was way more to this relationship than Matt was letting on.

....

CHAPTER 21

I n an act of cruelty, the rain and fog had lifted and now everything beyond the screened porch windows—the birch trees, the boathouse and shed, the rocks, and the calm water—was bathed in the softest, most golden light imaginable. The mountains beyond glowed red, and a robin warbled a tranquil evening song.

Matt wanted to go outside and throttle it.

"I know no one feels like eating. I'm sorry, but I'm going to force it," said Cass, backing into the porch from outside with a foil-covered salad bowl and a bag of dinner rolls. Matt lurched forward to help her through, while Elise continued working on her map of the world by the fireplace.

River came in behind his mother, so fully absorbed in his gaming device that he dropped down onto the rug without looking up. When he did, he seemed surprised to find he was no longer at home.

To see him sitting there—with the drawings he and Gracie had been working on just two days ago—Matt didn't think he could take it.

Cass looked over to where Elise was stationed at her map. "What's this?"

"Sightings," Elise said, her face drawn. "The navy ones are more reliable. Purple less likely." She stuck a pink pin somewhere in the Greek islands.

"What are pink?" asked Cass.

"Psychic visions. Less credible."

"I don't know about that." Cass set her offerings on the long picnic table on the other side of the fireplace. "I think loads of cases have been solved that way."

The news droned softly from the small TV Matt had brought down from the bedroom. He couldn't look at River, who'd stretched out now on the rug, bare toes bumping against each other as if he hadn't a care in the world. The memory of Gracie giggling with him at the picnic table was debilitating.

Matt debated sending him up to play in Gracie's room. But, no. That might be worse.

Cass pulled the foil from the food. "Here's a big salad, and it's better than my usual because you two need your energy. We've got arugula, sunflower seeds, beets . . . what else? A little goat cheese and cucumber. Be good and healthy for you. And I've ordered a party-sized pizza just the way Matty likes it: slathered in meat."

He watched her move easily around the room, warming when she went into the kitchen to help herself to dinner plates and glasses. She knew what was what and what was where in this house. Somehow there was comfort in that. He caught her eye as she came back into the room to set out the cups, the stack of plates. Mouthed, "Thank you."

Her fingertips grazed his forearm in reply.

"Hey, all. Excuse the work attire." Garth banged his way through the back door in khakis and a pink dress shirt, leather portfolio in hand. "Think I had my first appointment over on Saranac at seven thirty this morning. Insanity." He dropped the portfolio onto a chair. "I brought over some comparables. Help you get a sense of what's been happening out there."

"Garth!" Cass said, a hand on her hip. "Is this really the time?"

"No, hey, sorry." Garth's embarrassment was genuine. He looked from Matt to Elise. "Guys. I'm only thinking the sale could help you financially during this, is all. You know, in case you need . . . whatever. To hire a private investigator. Anything."

Elise turned to Matt. "We should discuss that."

"The police are being amazing. Plus, the FBI is going to get involved."

"Yes, but we're not in the city. We're dealing with small-town cops."

From the floor, River started to make wet shooting sounds as his thumbs attacked his game device. Then the pings and pongs and electric explosions. Matt couldn't take it and was pretty sure Elise was faring no better. But he couldn't tell Cass to take her son away—the kid was certainly traumatized as well. She couldn't leave him alone at home.

Without taking his gaze from his screen, River rolled onto his back and stomped a foot. "When's Gracie coming back?"

Everything went silent, all conversation, all birds chittering in the trees, all lake water lapping against the dock. Cass's embarrassment was clear as she looked at Matt and Elise. She knelt down next to her son, pushed the hair off his forehead, and pressed a kiss to his cheek. Softly, she said, "That's what we're trying to figure out, toad. We are on it."

Suddenly, Matt was ashamed of his irritation.

Cass got up again to arrange plates around the table and the room came to life again. Cass began to hum, her sweater slipping off her shoulder. When she asked Matt for help locating salad tongs, he led her into the kitchen.

"You were amazing with River just then."

"He's unsettled, is all. Worried about his friend."

"Yeah, but you knew exactly what to say."

Cass jumped up to sit on the counter and watched Matt root

through drawers packed tight with a lifetime's worth of wooden spoons, stamps, potato mashers, rubber bands. Tangled spools of string. "You ever throw anything away?"

Her teasing expression was so familiar. Pulled him back to the days when life was beautifully ordinary up here. You had time to watch a wet dog shake out his fur in the sun. To clear a skating rink on the frozen lake. To take a girl to the movies and feel a thrill when you both reached into the popcorn at the same time.

He almost smiled as he handed Cass a pair of large forks. "What good would that do me?"

A knock at the front window. Matt opened the door to the Casa Italia delivery man, a wiry sixty or so, with the crooked nose of someone who'd entertained a few blows to the face. He held out a huge pizza box, looking like he'd rather be anyplace else. His car sat running in the driveway. "Thirty-one ninety-eight."

Cass set the pizza on the hall table as Matt dug through his pocket for bills.

"I couldn't believe it when I heard." The driver motioned toward the crest on the face of the house. "Nate Sorenson was the best. Gave my brother a loan back in the seventies when my sister-in-law was having a tough time, their kid needed surgery."

As Matt handed over four tens, he felt Cass's hand slide up his shoulder. "Those stories are wonderful to hear," she said. "So heartwarming."

The man started to count out change and Matt waved it away. "Keep it."

"We're praying for you with your daughter. My whole street, we did a little candle thing last night. A vigil." He nodded his respects. "I don't listen when folks talk trash. People just like to knock anyone who's better off than themselves. You gotta just keep your head down and focused. 'Night, Mr. Sorenson, Mrs. Sorenson."

Cass held up a hand to wave.

"Good night." Elise's reply was crisp behind them. She gave her husband a long, level look and carried the pizza onto the back porch.

The air held a chill now and Garth was bent over the hearth trying to get a fire going. He was using the old-fashioned tent technique and Matt couldn't stand watching it. He crossed the room and nudged Garth out of the way. To busy himself with something—anything—helped. Matt stacked five thick logs across the fireplace grille, four slightly smaller split logs atop those, on the perpendicular, another layer of kindling, then a layer of crumpled newspaper and broken twigs.

"Upside-down fires," Matt said to no one in particular. "My family swore by them."

Cass opened the pizza box Elise had left on the table and started slapping square slices onto plates. "Every layer burns and then ignites the one below. So the heat builds until the lower logs finally ignite. Burns longer, hotter. Very low maintenance. You don't have to stoke it. When we were kids, Matty told me he'd invented it. I was stupid enough to believe him."

"You've never built one for me," said Garth.

"I forgot about them till now," said Cass. "Come. Everybody eats. This Mama Bear doesn't take no for an answer. Elise, that includes you."

Matt's cell started to ring on the coffee table. Elise looked at the screen. "Barrans."

He reached for the phone, only to turn off the ringer and set it down again. "I'm sure he just wants to say he's heard what's happened." He sat at the table and eventually the buzzing on the coffee table was replaced by the sound of silverware scraping against china.

"You could've taken it," Cass said.

He hadn't gotten back to Barrans about the partnership. Not

that the man would've asked under the circumstances, but Matt's ability to shoulder anyone else's horror over his daughter's disappearance was nonexistent. "He'll call back."

"You're eating two slices, Elise," said Cass, putting salad on everyone's plates. "We can't have you wasting away. You need your strength. Matty, did I tell you that preorders of the book have already begun? Kind of crazy."

"Cass," said Garth. "No one can think about book orders right now."

"I'm just trying to keep up the chatter."

"It's okay," said Matt. "Appreciated."

River, who hadn't joined them at the table, turned the TV volume up. CNN broke the silence with a story on a small plane crash in a farmer's field on the west coast of Scotland. Five dead, including the pilot. Three survivors, one of them a dog.

Garth said, "Poor thing."

They all watched in silence as the owner of the dog—who hadn't been on the flight—talked about the dog's state of mind. Scared of any loud noise, but otherwise okay. The screen showed the remains of the travel crate. It was charred beyond recognition, but Lucky was found wandering the side of a motorway.

"He's going to be completely traumatized," Elise said, staring at the screen, mesmerized. "He'll need someone who knows what they're doing."

The screen filled with Gracie's face. The photo on the dock that Cass took—Gracie beaming with that sunburst of a smile. They all froze as Gracie was replaced with a shot of a journalist with perfectly layered auburn hair standing on their driveway back home in New Jersey. Cass jumped forward to turn it off.

The room was silent but for bleeps and pings coming from River's electronic game.

Matt couldn't fill his lungs. He pushed back his chair with a scrape. Stood. "Got to get some air." He stuffed his feet into sandals, strode through the kitchen, and opened the front door to find

Dorsey about to knock, the two officers behind him shadowed by the dusk sky.

"We've had a sighting here in town. Wanted to show you this before we go." He handed Matt a blurred photograph of a child on a rusted swing. The girl's face wasn't visible thanks to leafy branches in the way, but the messy ponytail—her hair was the right length, streaky blond.

"Oh my god." Elise appeared at Matt's shoulder to stare at the photo. She grabbed her small purse and struggled to stay balanced while pulling on sneakers. To Dorsey, she said, "Do we come in your car or drive ourselves?"

Matt answered first. "I'm sure the parents don't get to come along."

"Actually, I prefer if you do," Dorsey said. "If it is your daughter, she's young and she'll feel a whole lot safer if at least one of you is waiting in the car." He started for his cruiser, waving for them to follow.

Elise stared out the window in the back of Dorsey's car as they traveled from the southernmost point of the village up Old Military Road, where density gave way to larger, more rural lots. The airport. The ski jump where Matt had his tête-à-tête with Cass.

The police debated over the radio whether to turn on John Brown Road or Old John Brown Road—both of which ran west and converged about a half mile in. Didn't seem to matter: both were heavily clogged with traffic. The car slowed to a crawl as they neared the bronze statue of Brown himself walking with a young slave boy. Tiny bugs swarmed in what little remained of the daylight.

"Sorry about this." Dorsey swerved around traffic, his forearm bumping the heavy-duty laptop mounted on the center console. "Not the best timing. Big award ceremony here tonight." Elise watched families walking by with older children, toddlers in pajamas, and infants in strollers. One mother carried her young daughter on her hip. Elise looked away fast. "We're better off passing all this and doubling back on Old John Brown Road up at the wishbone," Dorsey continued. "The trees on the property we're approaching are nice and dense if we approach that way. Don't want to tip anybody off before we're ready."

When Rosamunde made turkey, she always saved the wishbone. Let it dry overnight so that, the next day, they could hold opposite ends and pull. Whoever got the Y of the bone could make a wish. That Dorsey had chosen this route, where they would traverse the Y, had to be a good sign, thought Elise. They had the big piece of bone. Their wish would come true.

Two other state police officers were in the car ahead of them, and as they drew nearer to the gates of the modest farmhouse, they swirled their lights to signal any cars or pedestrians blocking the road to move aside. Matt did a double take as they passed a sign, and Elise followed his gaze—was that Lyman the roofer's picture on it? A balloon escaped from the crowd and she watched it drift up into the sky, its string bucking and twisting in the breeze.

"I hope all this activity doesn't scare them off," Matt said.

"It's not a bad thing for us that the area's a bit congested. Three police cars creeping up an otherwise quiet street would wave a pretty big flag."

Elise leaned forward. "How long ago was the child seen?"

"Reports came in from several neighbors earlier this evening. Older woman's lived here forever. All of a sudden she has a little blond girl living with her that no one's ever met before."

"Using crutches?" Elise asked.

"No one thought to look. We're not going to get ahead of ourselves. Could mean nothing."

Elise sat back in her seat. *Could mean everything.*

Dorsey held up a finger. He turned onto Old John Brown Road, where the woods grew tighter to the road. The homes here were sprawling chalets made of stone and timber, boasting Range Rovers and Jaguars and a perfect blend of manicured grounds and untamed shrubs and copses of trees.

Nonsensically, the affluence gave Elise hope. As if finer china and Amex Centurion cards would spell Gracie having been misguidedly "borrowed" by entitled but good-hearted weekenders for the sole purpose of pampering her, feeding her good food, and putting her up in a bedroom filled with expensive toys. She was their treasured guest, to be cossetted and revered until her hosts grew bored and decided to drop her back at the upended canoe.

Elise allowed herself the vision of Gracie, freshly bathed and dressed in fluffy pajamas, surrounded by oversized versions of her tiny animals, all of them lined up and hopeful for hugs. Gracie staring at them, arms crossed, patiently explaining, "There is a rule."

She glanced at Matt to see if he shared her vision. But this area was nothing special to him. This wealth was normal.

The car stopped at a screen of ragged spruce trees that only partially hid them from a dilapidated house. Torn blinds lined the upper windows. The garage roof—corrugated metal fuzzy with rust—sagged in the middle and the faded yellow siding was filthy. In no way did this cottage fit in with the multimillion-dollar homes nearby. Beneath an exposed electrical meter, a tired Big Wheel. Everything about it felt tragic.

Elise's eyes bored into the metal siding as if she might be able to see through to the interior.

Dorsey typed something into the computer and an aerial view of the street popped up.

"Why are we just sitting here?" Elise asked.

"Few more officers about to arrive."

"Shouldn't we wait someplace less visible?" she said.

Matt's leg jiggled up and down with nerves. "Elise . . ."

"Here they come."

A local police cruiser pulled up and parked just ahead of them. The two cops from the first night nodded to Dorsey and got out, walked around the side of the house.

Dorsey started out of the car. "You folks sit tight here."

"But I want to see her," said Elise.

"If it's her, you'll see her."

An undercover car pulled up and Dorsey walked over to lean in the window. There was too much action on the street. Anyone inside only had to glance outside.

"I don't like this," said Elise, fingers on the door handle. "Why are they all just hanging around?"

"Let them do their thing," said Matt.

An explosion of barking came from behind the solid wooden fence. A voice from inside, a woman's, shouted at the dog.

"Great. Now she knows her property's crawling with cops."

"They know what they're doing, Elise."

"They're small town, Matt. An abduction would happen, like, never."

Elise opened her door and Matt grabbed her arm. "Stay here like he said!"

Dorsey and one of the undercover cops started up the driveway. Elise shook Matt off and bolted across the grass to join them. The sound of a television grew louder and louder. Cartoon voices.

Dorsey, halfway up the sagging steps, turned. "Elise. Get into the car. Please."

"I can't." She ran past him to the door. Through a dirty diamond-shaped window, Elise could see the backs of two heads. An old woman and a young girl sat there watching cartoons. Only the very top of the girl's head was visible. Elise couldn't breathe. The light was dim in the room, to be sure, but the child's hair—that beigey undertone with streaks of white. "I think it's Gracie," she whispered.

Elise realized Matt was out of the car too, standing beside her. He took her hand, balled it into a tiny fist, and wrapped his around it in the way she adored. She pointed. "Look . . ."

He peered inside and nodded, less certain.

Elise could have put her fingers around his neck and squeezed the last breath out of him for not being as sure. If they both didn't believe it in equal measure, if they both weren't dead certain, it wouldn't be their daughter.

One of the younger cops silently nudged them both to escort them down to the grass, but Dorsey held up a hand, gave Matt and Elise a look that said "Stay cool," and knocked.

The television went silent. The floor creaked as the woman got up, but they could only see her in silhouette. Short hair, stiff as a brush. Hunched body, thickest in the middle. They heard a series of fumbled clicks. Then a chain lock.

Dorsey's fingers tapped against his holster. His other hand rested on the doorframe. In the periphery, the other police officers waited.

The door swung open, revealing a dark, paneled room with a tartan armchair, gold carpeting, and an old TV. A naked doll on the floor. The woman, gray with loose, fleshy skin, squinted at them, the whites of her eyes yellowed toward a stub nose. "Can I help you?"

Elise strained to see past her. The hair. The girl started to stand on the sofa. Swung her hair around until she was fully facing them. A sound escaped Matt. A groan, like an animal trapped beneath a car. He broke away and lurched toward the road. She heard the pound of his fist on the hood of the police car.

Dorsey nodded to the woman. "Wrong house. Sorry to bother you folks."

CHAPTER 22

·········

They hadn't spoken much to each other since Dorsey dropped them off at the cabin. Matt couldn't think of anything to say. Nor, it seemed, could his wife. Coming so close—in their minds—to having their daughter back and having it not be Gracie had all but flattened them. They'd spent the rest of the evening uselessly driving up and down every street in and around the village, up 86 to the northeast and back down River Road. They got out and walked in a few spots—a sleepy cul-de-sac, the low-lying airport buildings, an abandoned real estate office with a wraparound deck. They gave a miss to the recycle center. Let the police handle that one.

Matt had dropped onto the sofa on the back porch and pulled an old quilt over himself. He must have slept deeply—the last time he'd looked at his phone, it had been before five, and now the sun was fairly high in the sky.

Cass tapped on the back screen door and came inside—a welcome haze of tanned skin, wild curls, and fresh soap—when she saw him lying there. She knelt on the braided rug and covered his hands with hers. "Hey. How are you doing?"

The ticking clock from the kitchen caught his attention and he rose up onto an elbow. "It's Tuesday, right?

"It is."

"What's the time?"

She plucked something off his chest. He looked down to see he was still in the same white T-shirt he'd had on for days. "Time for you to change your clothes. Listen, I'm making fresh coffee and muffins for you over at my place. I want you and Elise—"

"Where's my phone? I need to know the time."

She reached for it atop the magazines on the painted end table. "It is . . . eight eleven."

Tuesday morning. He dropped back onto the cushion and did the calculation. In about twenty minutes, they'd pass the forty-eight-hour mark with no credible leads at all. "Fifty percent."

"What are you talking about?"

He shook his head, unable to speak.

Cass stood up and took the quilt off his body, pulled him up to sitting. "Go splash some water on your face. Change that crusty shirt. Get your wife and meet me out front. I have an idea."

"The thing is, sometimes she does remember." Cass led the way up and onto her mother's stone verandah and waved them over to the wicker love seat and chairs, where coffee and fresh muffins waited with slices of banana and oranges on a low table. "I thought, if we recreate Sunday morning from her vantage point, there's a slight chance something twigs, you know? Sometimes that's how it works with her these days. Wait here and I'll get her. We want her to see the bus go past, because you never know."

Matt sat down and looked around the porch: red geraniums dying in one pot, spiky grasses thriving in another. An old ceramic gnome beneath them, his face faded away to almost nothing. He remembered that gnome from the days when he still had features. Elise dropped onto the crushed floral cushions beside him. They had little choice but to stare at the police tape unraveling from the split rail fence and the canoe bus shelter across the road.

What struck him from this vantage was how truly seques-tered the canoe was from the cabin. From the end of the driveway, you could see the Sorenson house, but the bus shelter was a good fifty feet to the right, with a thick wall of cedars dividing the two. If a person wanted to nab a child sitting there, it would be nearly impossible to see from the front door, the garage. The spot where Elise had been gardening had a partial view. But to go out back at a time when there'd been a fair bit of activity out front? Cass was bang on about that.

Was Elise thinking the same thing?

His wife pulled her cardigan closer around herself. "A couple from San Francisco emailed me this morning. Mary Anesko, I think was the woman's name. Their newborn son was taken from the maternity ward in Minneapolis and they got him back. Eight days later. She said if it happened for her, it can happen for us."

"How on earth did they find you?"

"Online, she said. Some blog post where I was interviewed once."

"I guess this is what we do now."

"What?"

"Before your child goes missing, you hear about a baby going mis-sing in Minneapolis and you tell yourselves it's faraway and rare. The odds are overwhelming that it will never happen to you. Now, we look at the even more unlikely event that these parents got their child back from a stranger with no good intentions, and we soothe ourselves with it. This time, if it can happen to them, it *can* happen to us."

Elise shifted away from him and reached for a slice of banana. Her bare legs were a constellation of blackfly and mosquito bites. She glanced at the door. "This is a ridiculous exercise. Alzheimer's hits the short-term memory."

"Not a hundred percent. Ruth might actually remember some weird detail that will turn out to matter."

Elise looked at him, brows raised. "I guess this is what we do now."

Touché, he didn't say.

The door opened and Cass led her frail mother out in her pale blue housecoat. When Ruth saw Matt and Elise, she stopped, smoothed her collar, hands ribboned with veins. An inch or so of white roots haloed her scalp before the abrupt edge of dyed black hair. "Oh dear. I didn't know we had guests out here." She turned to go back inside. "I'd better go put my face on."

"Not guests, Mom. That's Matty. Nate Sorenson's son."

Her head wobbled. "Who?"

"Nate from across the street."

A rumble from up the road announced the Camp Imagine bus. The vehicle's grille appeared in the shadows, then the smiley faces and rainbows and cartoon flowers burst cruelly into the bright sunlight. Cass said, over the din, "Does it make you remember anything, Mom—about the other morning? Do you remember a blond girl sitting across the street waiting for that bus? Inside the canoe shelter?" The vehicle bounced along, windows dotted with morose faces, and roared on past. "Did you see anything happen that day, Mom? Did you see anyone approach that little girl?"

Ruth stood taller, a flash of recognition in eyes yellowed with glaucoma. She seemed to be thinking hard and, slowly, began to nod. "You know, I did see something. There was someone." A shaky hand pointed across the road, but she went silent.

Matt and Elise's need for her to continue nearly lifted the stone cottage from the ground. Elise couldn't hold back. "Did you see a car or . . . or a truck?"

Matt touched his wife's arm. "Don't rush her."

"It was a man." Ruth turned to Cass's verandah—a classic, covered log porch complete with porch swings on either side of the screen door. "He was sitting just there on the left. Keeping to himself, I thought. Something about him made me curious, and so I went across to see. Wasn't till I got up close I could see his chin was slumped onto his chest. The man was dead."

A slow sigh escaped Cass. "Mom, that wasn't this week. That happened ten years ago. You're talking about Dad. Your husband. Edward."

Disappointment stretched across the entire streetscape, beyond the lake, to cover the sharp peaks of the mountains like plastic wrap. From the underside, it was difficult to breathe. Matt leaned over the porch rail. Elise ran down the steps.

Cass led her mother back inside. "I'm so sorry, guys. I thought maybe there was a chance . . . "

It was 2012. *Darkness always falls sooner than anyone is ready for on the day the clocks turn back*, Elise thought as she arranged a pile of clean laundry in her daughter's dresser at the cabin. It wasn't even five o'clock and the pines edging the lake had formed a jagged black line against the sky.

Nate, still unbelievably able-bodied in his advanced years, was out on the lawn, raking before the snow fell. Gracie, wearing a knit hat, a jacket, and thick tights that sagged around the knees, was playing in the leaves. She looked up at her mother in the window and waved, her cheeks chafed and red, her nose scrunched up enough to show a perfect row of tiny Chiclet teeth. She'd just turned six five days before.

Elise waved back.

Gunner watched from the dock, tail thwacking contentedly against the old wood as he watched Gracie play.

As usual, the child's drawers were sticking. The dresser was a junky piece Elise had picked up at a thrift shop in Keene years before and painted pink. She'd been eyeing Matt's childhood bedroom set for their daughter's room for years. It was medium-toned mahogany with dove-tailed corners and a gorgeous patina. More to the point, there was a roomy armoire that would be a godsend for a girl with no closet. Keeping Matt's room as a shrine to his twelve-year-old self wasn't practical in any way. In fact, it bordered on creepy.

The idea had cleared the Gracie test. She'd been bouncing with excitement. Matt was fine with the prospect as well. And, because the Giants were playing the Steelers, Matt was fine with Elise doing the asking.

She pulled on a coat and gloves and stepped outside. The sharp, metallic essence of snow charged the air with promise, though not a single flake had fallen yet. It had been a terribly hot summer—the sun incessant, the air gooey and thick. It had clogged the transition from day to night. Dusk had an easier time now that the seasons had changed.

"Mom, look what I can do." Gracie's red woolen hat tipped drunkenly to one side, shaggy with oak leaves. With crutches and a rake to contend with, she'd had far more success free-falling into leaf piles than raking them up. Elise laughed.

In his ancient wool jacket, Nate squinted up at the sky, his face thick and creased like a dried-up riverbed, then looked at Elise. "It's going to come down any minute."

"I'll help."

Elise grabbed a rake and started filling a thick brown paper bag. A gust of wind skimmed the leaves off the top and back onto the grass. From the tree above, a crow shrieked its indignation. Gracie cawed back. She grabbed a handful of leaves and half-heartedly threw them at her mother, laughing when they drifted back to her feet.

"You heard your great-grandpa. We've got to get serious. Stop fooling around," Elise said.

"I'm too tired to stop fooling around." Gracie went wild, thrashing her arms and legs. The closest bag split at the seam, tipped over, and dumped its contents.

"Now look what you've done," said Nate.

"I'll get a new one from the shed," said Elise. When she returned, she went straight to Nate. "I was wondering, now that Gracie's older, what would you think of letting her use Matt's old bedroom set? It's so beautiful and I'd so love to see her grow up with nice pieces that really have a history. And she could use the armoire space to hang her dresses. We could just swap out dressers, nightstand, and cupboard. Wouldn't take long."

Nate took the bag from Elise and examined it. The paper was rotten along one edge—moldy and torn. "We can't use this."

"It was the last one."

He trudged up the side of the cabin and disappeared. From the back could be heard sounds of boxes being dragged about in the garage. Cupboard doors opening and closing. The clash of a metal lid falling onto the concrete floor and spinning to a stop. He returned with a newer bag and shook it open. Together he and Elise started filling it with leaves.

She checked to make sure Gracie wasn't within earshot. "So did you give it any thought—the furniture swap?"

He leaned down for an armful of leaves and didn't look up as he pushed it to the bottom of the deep paper bag. "I did."

"And . . . ?"

"I think you want for your daughter what you never had."

Elise was confused. "Of course. As parents, we all want the best for our children."

"Sure. And the rest of us earn it."

Elise paused. "It's just sitting there. Gracie would be using it in her room; that's the only difference."

"It doesn't work like that—getting something for nothing."

This was about money? "We'll pay for it, then. I just really want her to grow up with her dad's furniture."

Her grandfather-in-law glared at her in the near dark. His words came out in a hiss. "You, Elise, can't pay me what that set's worth." He dragged the overflowing leaf bag away and headed for the garage. From the backyard, she heard the thump of the front door.

"Mommy." Gracie's eyes were huge. "Do I get the furniture?"

Elise ruffled her leafy hat. "You know what? I think we'll have more fun hunting around for more pieces—you and me. We can paint them any way you want."

Matt came out the back door just then in sweater and wool cap, big work boots. "My grandfather's making spaghetti in there. Head down and chopping like a madman."

Madman is right. Elise said nothing.

"Look," Gracie said, pointing to the sky.

It was always magic, the silent earthward spiral of the season's first snowflakes. Faster and faster they fell, the ground quickly vanishing beneath the sugary whiteness.

With hardly a dusting of snow on the grass, Gracie dropped down to make a barely there snow angel. They watched as their daughter's arms and legs swiped up and down like sticky windshield wipers.

Matt nudged his wife. "How'd it go—the big ask? You get what you want?"

She looked at him, hat covered with snow, grin on his face because here they were—the four of them plus Gunner—at his favorite place on earth. She reached up to squeeze his ruddy cheek. "I already have what I want."

Elise was staring at the very spot where Gracie had made her invisible snow angel that night when an unmarked police car pulled into the driveway. It wasn't a scheduled visit. In fact, she'd texted Dorsey when she woke and hadn't received a reply. She couldn't help it—she broke into a run, with the vision of Gracie bouncing her feet in the back seat. Matt came through the front door just as Dorsey climbed out of the car, a plastic file folder in his hand.

Cass sauntered over from her driveway. Were they never to have another important moment without this woman slipping herself in their lives?

"These were found at the side of Highway Seventy-Three, just before Upper Cascade Lake, this morning. So, not far off. " Dorsey held out an eight-by-ten photograph of Gracie's sticker-covered crutches against a white backdrop, tiny notes pointing to various markings. "I can't give them to you physically, not just yet. Just want to confirm they're your daughter's."

The sight of them struck Elise with joy, horror, hope, dread, and everything in between. She was terrified to ask what finding them might mean.

"They're hers," was all Matt said.

"The area is taped off. It's being heavily combed right now by forensics," Dorsey told them.

Elise's hand slipped beneath Matt's arm. She needed support as she dared to ask, "Is this good or bad?"

Before Dorsey could answer, Cass—astonishingly—spoke for him. "I'd say it means nothing more than someone didn't want to carry around eye-catching evidence."

Elise looked at her, shocked by this know-it-all insertion into their moment. Then she turned to Dorsey. "What can we read into this?"

"I'm afraid Cass is right. Right now we're at neutral. Turquoise crutches are going to attract a lot of attention with all the buzz in the media."

"And the testing?" asked Matt, staring at the photo.

"From our initial findings, it looks like they were wiped clean." Dorsey frowned. "But they're being disassembled. If there's anything there, it'll be found. We're hopeful."

Matt's mind raced. "But it means she's still in the area. If these were just found today, that could only mean good things."

"They'd likely been there since Sunday."

"And what about tire marks?" asked Elise. "Footprints? There must be some markings in and around the spot they were found."

"You're talking two days in peak season," Cass said, releasing a long breath. "And a whole lot of rain."

Elise wanted to shove the woman back to her side of the property line.

"Exactly," said Dorsey. "But whatever traces remain, we'll get them."

"But, I'm sorry. If you could explain," Elise said. "Why did it take two days for these to be found?"

"There's a lot of wild land to cover." Dorsey shrugged. "We're doing our best. This line of work, you find what you find when you find it."

Matt checked his watch. "It's nine twenty." He started to pace, walking in a circle, hands stretching in the air with helplessness. "Our forty-eight hours has officially come and gone, and then some. And as it stands, we've got fuck-all to go on." He stopped next to Cass, who, for a fleeting second, reached out to cup the back of Matt's head, then seemed to think better of it and slid her hand into her pocket.

CHAPTER 23

....

It was Wednesday now—what would have been the start of two full days of mommy-and-me time before Elise needed to leave to prepare for Toronto. Instead, she and Matt had driven to nearby towns to distribute flyers with their missing daughter's face on them.

The day had brought with it nothing good. A sighting in the Disney World parking lot in Orlando that turned out to be a boy. A Twitter rant by some schoolteacher in Manchester who believed Elise should be charged with negligence. A psychic who saw Gracie sitting at a picnic table just outside a small-town Dairy Queen. Which small town eluded her. That Gracie had dropped her chocolate-dipped cone did not.

Elise had spent the evening running in and around the two big resorts on the west side of the lake, through drizzle that eventually eased up but left behind a dense mist. By the time she made her way back, it was well after eight p.m. and darkness was settling in. Here and there, porch lights flicked on. But not at the Sorenson cabin. In the fog, the cabin was visible only in outline and, beyond the fringe of dripping trees, the lake had vanished completely. Then again, with all testing complete on the crutches and the police having found no evidence from the surrounding area, it felt to Elise as if the entire world had vanished.

Including the pregnancy. The bleeding had run its course. The miscarriage was complete.

As she walked toward the cabin in sodden running shoes, the yellow police tape on the fence now twisted and torn and bucking in the wind, a large vehicle started to take shape at the roadside. Not until she drew nearer could she make out the rear end of a double horse trailer. Hitched to a filthy black Range Rover.

Ronnie.

Both vehicles were empty. Elise continued around the cedars and stopped for the greatest gift imaginable, short of finding her daughter standing there in the fog—the familiar shapes of the sleek and majestic Indie and the shaggy and ridiculous Poppins, with Ronnie Goodrich between them, lead shanks in hand.

In two seconds, Elise was in her coach's arms, her neck being nuzzled by her horse, her pockets being searched by her donkey. She wasn't sure if the sound she uttered qualified as a laugh if born from such a pit of sadness, but the moment was a faint reminder that, beyond the agony she and Matt and Gracie were enduring, as painful as it was to fathom, there was life.

Horse and companion clomped into the double stall and immediately dropped to roll in the deep bed of dry shavings at the North Elba Show Grounds. Indie struggled back to his feet first and, with a mighty shake, all but cleared his mane of cedar bits, while Poppins continued to scratch her back, hooves flailing. Elise stood over the bale of hay on the gravel and waited for Ronnie to pull out his Swiss Army knife.

The horse show was well under way, but with most classes having wrapped up by early evening, the grounds were now fairly quiet. Still, with so many competitors on the property, the air was alive with the shuffling, munching, and snorting of horses and with the squeak of stall doors being opened or shut as tired grooms and with riders performed night check: doling out hay flakes and topping up water buckets as needed. Every now and then a faraway horse whinnied, a golf cart whirred by, or a group of riders—often arm in arm—walked past laughing or complaining about their performances.

For Elise, the familiarity of the world was both comforting and sickening. "I can't believe you did this for me, Ronnie."

"Equine therapy," he said, slicing the twine and loosening the bale. "Could put the entire psychiatric community out of business."

Elise separated three flakes of hay and dropped them over the stall door.

"Timing worked out well to board these bozos here," said Ronnie. "Show organizer's an old student of mine—Pammy Stanton. She had a small barn pull out of the show last minute and had a couple of extra stalls. Said she was happy to help. Course, she knows what's going on."

Indie swung his great head over the stall door, striking hoof to wood when Elise didn't stroke his muzzle quickly enough.

"Such a goofball." She held her forehead to his for a moment, until the horse tossed his head with impatience and returned to his hay.

Ronnie sat on the hay bale and pulled her down next to him. "All right. Tell me what's happening."

She gave him what they knew so far. The hotline the police had set up had resulted in not a single solid lead, though many psychics and palm readers and clairvoyants had had visions or hallucinations or tea leaf readings that proved Gracie was alive or in another country or had been sold on the black market.

"And Matt, how's he doing?"

"As expected," said a male voice.

Out of nowhere, Matt came walking along the breezeway in sweatshirt and shorts.

"There he is now," Ronnie said, getting up. "Man of the hour." The two embraced self-consciously. "I don't know what to say, buddy. I love that kid like she's my own."

"Appreciate it." Matt rubbed both noses that appeared over the stall door to greet him. When Ronnie handed him two apples, Matt offered them up with flat palms, juggling the juicy chunks that dropped from their mouths. Nanny Poppins, as was her way, turned her nose away at the last bite, saving it for her charge.

"Thanks for doing this." Matt put a hand on his wife's shoulder and dropped down to the hay beside her. "I know they're a lifeline for Elise."

It was impossible to keep track of what Matt was feeling from one minute to the next. She would have thought he'd be angry about the animals arriving. In Ronnie's SUV on the way over from the cabin, she'd actually been in a panic about how to tell Matt. He hadn't wanted the horses there to train for Toronto. She sure as hell hadn't thought he'd want them now. Elise reached over to squeeze her husband's arm in thanks.

"Without Elise as reserve, will you go up to Toronto?" Matt said to Ronnie.

"Hey, I'm not going anywhere. As long as you need me, I'm here."

"No, no." Elise leaned back against the stall. "Please, Ronnie, don't pass on Toronto. Seriously. You brought me Indie. That's the biggest gift imaginable."

Ronnie studied her, hands on his hips. "I don't feel good about going without you."

"It's nonnegotiable," Matt said.

"I just can't imagine what you two are going through, and I'm not even a parent."

"I feel so unbelievably helpless," said Matt.

Elise took a long blade of hay and pulled it apart with her fingernails. "I want to turn the world upside down. Shake it and shake it until our daughter falls into our arms."

"You're driven," Ronnie said. "Used to getting the hell on with things. That's your style."

"That only works if you know which way to point yourself. Not much use to me now."

"Bullshit. You won't accept anything less than bringing your daughter home. You and I both know you can handle anything."

No, she didn't say back. *I can't.*

"And you've got each other. You've got to hold tight there. This is tough as all hell, and don't you dare let it destroy what you've got in each other."

Elise looked at Matt, who didn't seem to have heard what Ronnie said.

"And if you need money . . ."

"No." Matt waved that away. "We're good. Well . . ." He stopped. "You know what I'm saying."

"Does your father know?" Ronnie asked Elise.

She leveled him with a stare. "I don't know. Does he?"

"Smartass." Ronnie pulled her to standing. Wrapped her in a hug, then did the same with Matt. Just before he trudged through the fog to his truck, he added, "You don't think this makes for the right time to stop running from the guy?"

"Nothing will ever make it the right time."

CHAPTER 24

....

Matt and Garth sat at the window of the bustling Starbucks on Saturday morning. Manfred Wolfe wore no jewelry, no fancy watch. His jeans were dated. He wore the wrong kind of white sneakers and had tucked in his Polo shirt too snugly. Yet his haircut was expensive, and the interested but faraway look in his eyes gave him the air of a man used to getting what he wants in life. Matt and Garth sat across from him and listened as he explained Wolfe Resorts' plans for the Sorenson land.

Competing for Matt's attention, however, was a corkboard on the wall. Beside yet another black bear warning that encouraged tourists and residents to seal up trash, to refrain from taking pictures or videos, and to wear bells on their shoes when hiking in forested areas, was a picture of Gracie with big block letters: MISSING. The poster flapped in the breeze from the open door. It had been six days since she'd gone missing, with zero credible leads. How far the odds had fallen now Matt couldn't begin to contemplate.

Elise had set out early with a group of volunteers to tack up flyers farther down the highway and was to meet him across from the movie theater once Wolfe had gone on his way.

The rest of the week had passed in much the same way as the first couple of days. On the 800 hotline, calls from parents whose children had been found alive, calls from parents whose children had been found, sadly, dead. A letter from an Australian man whose grandchild had disappeared only a month prior: he wondered if there could be a connection, because his boy had also had crutches. Calls, letters, emails—even a knock on the door—from psychics.

Early in the week, Matt and Elise had both spent time on the hotline, only to realize how many well-meaning souls clogged the line with messages of sympathy, suggestions as to how they might have better protected their daughter, and sightings in Melbourne or Punta Cana or Reykjavik that didn't even come close to sounding like Gracie. And when a lead did seem promising, the photo invariably showed a face that looked nothing like her. The map on the back porch was heavily pinned with leads now. They no longer looked at the pins with the same optimism. People meant well, but thousands upon thousands of false leads, it was becoming clear, could make finding their daughter impossible. The little green pin? It was almost impossible to see now in the sea of pinks, navies, and purples.

Elise had suggested they move the map into Nate's office. The sight of it now was near debilitating.

Cass had been wonderful, appointing herself responsible for all meals. And Garth had produced, right here, a serious buyer.

"Löyly is what we want to call it—complete with umlaut. The Finnish word for 'sauna steam.' *Sowna* steam, as they pronounce it. We're talking about total relaxation," said Manfred. "The Finns do it better than anyone, and that's what we're looking to recreate. And then some. Wood-burning saunas, eucalyptus steam baths, and outdoor saltwater and freshwater baths. Thermal and Nordic waterfalls. Go from a hot bath into an arctic plunge. Massage, Himalayan salt cave. Every guest has their own cabin with sauna, a private outdoor mini pool, heated in winter. Yoga, massage, hot stones. The works. Four-season facilities that would fit in perfectly with the natural beauty of the area."

"No worries about filling the lake with hot-dogging wake boarders." Garth looked at Matt. "That ought to alleviate a bit of guilt for you."

Nothing will alleviate guilt for me, thought Matt.

"We'd have boats, but canoes and kayaks. A few old Chris-Crafts for tours. Actually, I'd like to talk about the one in your boathouse. If you've a mind to sell it."

"I appreciate what you're saying. I do." Matt reached into his pocket for a couple of Tylenols and washed them back with his lukewarm latte. "I just can't give you an answer today."

"Understandably. The only reason I asked to meet was to let you know we're happy to advance whatever you need to help fund the search. Finding your daughter is bigger than another Adirondacks resort."

Garth explained, "Obviously, Manfred knows what's going on."

"Hey, I've got two grown kids of my own, and now five grand-children." Wolfe sat back in his chair and shook his head as if trying to comprehend the enormity of the situation. "I know that the longer this continues, the more money it's going to take. Eventually, it becomes a mountain only the parents keep trying to move."

The tactless statement hung in the air between them.

Gracie's crutches, now leaning against the wall of her bedroom, flashed in Matt's mind. He'd spent an entire night holding them. They'd been such a strong identifier. A blond girl with turquoise crutches. Though, likely, whoever took her would change her appearance. But knowing that, even if she had an opportunity to flee, she couldn't. It was a thought Matt worked hard to bounce from his mind.

"I remember your grandfather," continued Wolfe. "We used to run a small ski lodge over by Whiteface when we were just getting started. First two winters were terrible—too warm, any snow that fell melted within days—no one wanted to spend a weekend in a rain-soaked, muddy mess. And then Nate Sorenson lent us enough money to squeak out one more year. Did you know that?"

"I didn't."

"Could've gone either way. Could've been another crap winter. But the snow fell early and didn't stop till April. That was enough for us to thrive, and repay your grandfather."

"Nate believed in helping people," Matt said. "And he believed in this town."

"But no pussycat, I'll tell you." Manfred laughed softly. "You were one month late in your payments and, man. Down came the hatchet."

Matt stared at him. So this was what people had been talking about—Nate's insistence upon making good. But that was just the way he was. He didn't help you as an act of charity. He actually wanted to educate. To teach people how to be.

His grandmother Sarah died when Matt was Gracie's age and that summer, Nate had taken to waking his grandson early and heading down to the boathouse. The 1947 Chris-Craft runabout, in gleaming mahogany, was christened *Elsa*, after the German shepherd bitch at their heels, swollen teats swinging as she trotted, only too willing to escape the outrage of her ravenous pups in the kitchen. The old engine had boomed and glug-glugged with importance as they pulled out of their bay and cruised along the shoreline, fingers of sunlight stretching out just enough to set the treetops aglow.

Matt, as always, would sit next to his grandfather on the leather bench, heavy orange lifejacket over his shoulders. Elsa would pant contentedly between them, her fur already wet and quilled and dripping from a quick plunge. They traveled up the east side of the lake, just past Pulpit Rock, where Nate cut the engine and pointed to a metal stake where sand met water. The stake was painted orange and marked where Sorenson land ended. "I'm the wealthiest man in the world not because of this. Because of my family." Matt rested an arm across Elsa's shoulders, swelling at the sentiment.

Nate allowed his only grandson to stand on the seat, one hand on the windshield to steady himself, to watch a family of four loons they'd spotted on Blueberry Island—a small landmass Nate had recently acquired that groaned with berries in late July, early August. They'd been watching this loon couple for years, certain the pair had nested on the island. Nate pulled the boat up to a flattened patch of grasses and pointed out how the land dropped right off into the water on one side, so the loons and their two youngsters could reach it underwater. Loons do not move well on land. But the male rose up to flap his wings vigorously in warning, while mama and babies dove deep to surface about a hundred feet away.

"We've got a few more weeks till the berries ripen," Nate said. "We'll come back. Figure out how to make a pie."

"How many blueberries will there be?"

"Thousands, I'd say."

It struck Matt—these were *his* thousands of blueberries. How many kids back home could boast such a thing? He might not be the coolest boy in school or the most athletic, but this, what Nate had done for him, made him special. People would pay attention to him. He would matter. He'd turned to his grandfather, bare feet squeaking on wet leather. "I have my very own island now!"

Nate had stared at him for a moment. He narrowed his eyes and said nothing. Fired up the boat and raced it back to the dock, the hull slamming over waves from a nearby cruiser.

The next week, he called Matt into his office. The slanted light of a summer evening glinted with dust motes behind his big leather chair. "There are two things that will ruin a man: runaway ambition and unearned conceit." Nate pushed a sheet of paper across the desk. It was a deed. Signed. "Don't ever get cocksure again, kid. Or I'll get rid of all of it."

He'd given Blueberry Island away to a local land trust.

Extreme? Yes. But an invaluable lesson. The summers Matt spent with Nate shaped him. Made him the person he was today. And for that Matt would be eternally in his debt.

Matt looked at Manfred. "That was just how Nate was. Never let an opportunity pass when he could teach you how to be a better person."

"So. Consider my offer to have a dual purpose." Manfred's eyes smiled at Matt. "To secure our dream locale and to repay a kindness for which I'm forever grateful." He stood, drained his coffee. "Either of you have any questions, I'll be around another day or so." He reached out to shake Matt's hand. "Good luck. I hope you find your daughter."

He ducked through the lineup at the door. Matt and Garth watched as he crossed the street and climbed into a navy blue Tesla.

"This is the best deal you're going to see." Garth sat hunched over his venti cup as if preparing to fight for it. "And it's a deal everyone can feel good about."

Two college-age girls walked to the exit, cups in hand, both dressed in tight jeans and T-shirts. Garth's gaze followed their asses out the door. He turned back, smiling, eyebrows raised, and downed the rest of his coffee.

Matt studied him.

"Hey." Garth tossed his empty cup in the trash as they got up to leave. "I look, I but *never* touch."

By the time Garth had climbed into his Porsche and roared off to meet a pair of young newlyweds whose parents were funding an eight-thousand-square-foot ski chalet, the morning air had cooled. The sky had gone steely gray and thunder rumbled in the distance.

....

He shouldn't have picked this spot to meet Elise, Matt realized right away. They'd passed it once with Gracie the summer before Nate died. She'd been enchanted by the lichen-covered stone rabbit peeking out from beneath the bushes near an old gate and dropped to the sidewalk to pet it. She wanted to go through the gate and into the bunny's secret garden. It was such a small request, but they'd been late for a movie and he'd said no. Matt stared at the rabbit. This was what life was like now. Every little thing Gracie had noticed, touched, treasured—even for a moment—made it impossible to breathe. There was a sign on the gate that hadn't been there before.

FOR LEASE. OFFICE SPACE WITH LAKE VIEW.
AVAILABLE IMMEDIATELY. INQUIRE AT 555-9223.

The gate squawked when he pushed it open. A wobbly brick path led him through ferns and hostas along an ivy-covered wall. The trellis on the right did double duty, disguising a tiny parking lot and directing the eye out to the real view: the fingers of mist forming over Mirror Lake in the dropping temperature. At the back of the building, a metal staircase led to the second story. Matt climbed up to a locked door, a sign upon which said:

DR. JANET DUENES, MD
PLEASE REMOVE BOOTS IN INCLEMENT WEATHER.

Through the window he could see a large paneled space with a back wall of glass, lake and mountains beyond. Dr. Duenes had already moved out. The space was empty.

Matt's phone rang. Elise. He could see her down on the sidewalk, the bag full of flyers slung from her shoulder. After one last look at the office, he jogged back down to meet his wife. In the mounting wind, her face was lined. Sharply angled. Gone was her usual tidy hair. It was greasy. Darker, somehow, in her pain.

A shot of rage surged through him. Her agony struck him as intolerable today. If you drove across a bridge with no hands on the wheel, did you really have a right to be shocked when you landed in the river?

She looked toward the office staircase and pulled her hair back, twisting the ends and tucking it down the back of her cotton sweater. "What were you doing up there?"

He noticed her irises for the first time in ages. The kaleidoscope of glassy shards that pulled you in forever. God, how he used to love those eyes. Now they seemed more like an omen he hadn't recognized until it was too late.

"Nothing." Before following her to where they'd left the car, he turned to snap a photo of the agent's phone number.

As they navigated through the crowds of tourists on the sidewalk, the bookstore's window display caught his eye and they both stopped. Another bear poster. And a sign that said MEET THE AUTHOR, with a gorgeous photo of Cass in a white tank, her hair flipped over and wild on one side. Next to that, a poster of her book cover with her dancing Woodstock photo. Just beneath the title, *American Dreamer*, was a quote from Cass: *I dream of a world in which every little child is safe.*

Elise stared, openmouthed. "I do *not* believe it."

"Wow. Beautiful," Matt said.

"'Every little child is safe?' Matt. She's using our daughter's disappearance to sell books."

"That's not what she's doing. It's a nod to Gracie."

"Yeah. With bestseller lists in mind."

"Seriously? That is so fucking beneath you, Elise."

An overburdened couple with a dog on a leash and kids balanced on their hips came bumping awkwardly out of the bookstore and Elise stepped aside to let them pass. "You don't see how she's been . . . inserting herself into our problem in a way that is . . . self-serving?"

"Cass is like family. She's done nothing but try to help us."

"Well, she's creeping me out."

"She's a good soul. A single parent. River's father is a total dead-beat. Her boyfriend is a noncommittal asshole, and she watches her buyers get rich from reselling her work. She helps other people because she knows what it's like to struggle. She's had *no one* to make life easy for her . . ." His voice trailed off.

Elise looked at him sideways. "Unlike me? Is that where you were headed?"

Two kids raced away from their father to yank open the book-store door as Matt pushed a hand through his hair and turned away. "Jesus Christ. Can we not go there?"

"I always had horses to ride. I wasn't as desperate as your grandfather thought I was."

A crowd of tourists in baggy pastel clothing nudged them farther from the store. Matt took Elise's elbow, led her along the sidewalk to a garden overlooking the water, and spun her around. "Believe me when I say this is *really* not the time to insult my grandfather."

She nodded slowly. "And believe *me* when I say this is really not the time to side with everyone but the mother of your child."

The wind whipped up for a moment, sending collars flapping and bits of stinging dust and trash skittering up their legs like tiny electrical shocks. They each turned away from the swirl. By the time Matt cleared his eyes of dust, Elise was marching back to the sidewalk, to vanish into the crowd.

The year before she and Matt married, Elise was riding and show-ing a jet-black Dutch Warmblood gelding named Jordie, who belonged to a wealthy couple from Boston. Jordie was flighty and distractible, and Elise worried the DeWitts would take him away to have someone more advanced in their career train their expen-sive horse.

One afternoon, still in breeches and boots, Elise had been cleaning her saddle in the tack room and looked up to see Nate standing in the doorway, out of place in every way, from his navy blazer and gray trousers, his crisp shirt and tie, to his presence there at all.

"Nice stable. Your coach must have money," Nate said.

"Is there something I can do for you?"

"There might be." He walked in, pulled out a linen handkerchief, wiped a chair seat, and sat. "So, you compete nationally, do you?"

"I do."

"And next is CDI; I looked it up. Concours de Dressage International. The big shows. World Games, the Olympics."

"Correct."

"To get to the Olympics, you need a very expensive horse, true?"

"Of course."

"And you don't currently own such a horse."

Tattoo, one of the barn dogs, a fat Jack Russell terrier, waddled in. Elise pulled a horse treat from her pocket and let him stand on hind legs to take it from her hand.

"No."

"I'd like to make that happen."

Sue, Ronnie's stable manager at the time, a short and sturdy brunette with an Australian shepherd always at her heels, passed by with a saddle and shot Elise a curious look, then mouthed, "Alcatraz?" Elise widened her eyes in confirmation.

"You're saying you want to buy me a horse?"

He nodded, noticed dust on the arm of his blazer, and wiped at it with a thumb. "That's right."

The man couldn't stand her. There was no way this offer came without conditions. "Why would you do that?"

"My grandson means everything to me. And you're not what he needs."

Elise pulled her boots off at the wooden boot jack in the corner and stuffed her feet into clogs, aware how ridiculous she would look to Nate, breeches tucked into striped knee socks. "I'm what he wants."

He stood and motioned toward the parking lot. "Two very different things. Come with me."

She followed him out into the blinding sunshine to a black horse trailer she'd never seen before. Nate motioned to someone inside and, in a clatter of hooves, two men carefully backed out a dappled gray stallion with a black mane and tail. Black socks and muzzle. Nearly eighteen hands of supple, well-toned muscle. "His name is December. Bavarian Warmblood stallion of impeccable lineage. Nearly six years old, and if you do a good job with him, he'll make sure you reach your goals and provide you with a steady income from stud fees."

Elise touched the horse's warm and velvety-soft muzzle. He was the most majestic horse she'd ever seen up close. With kind eyes, he was calm for a stallion, already nudging her pockets, looking for treats. Groomed to perfection with a glossy tail that dusted the ground. She squinted at Nate. "You're taking an awfully big risk, aren't you? That I won't tell your grandson?"

"Not in my opinion." A knowing smile spread across his lips. "I think I understand your type."

December had a low-set hip joint perfect for the highly collected movements. The angles of his croup and pelvis were parallel, which would allow for the pelvis to tilt forward and engage the hind limbs. All the power in dressage comes from the hind. She would love to see this horse move, see if he had big movements and balance. Gauge his ability to collect. He was exactly the sort of animal she'd dreamed of.

But not at this price. Never at this price.

"Your grandson adores you. Truly. Worships you."

"As I do him."

"I think he'd be pretty interested to know about your offer." Elise pulled her cellphone out of her pocket and tapped Matt's

242 | Tish Cohen

name. She smiled at Nate as she put the call on speaker and waited. Matt picked up on the first ring.

"Hey, babe," Matt said. "I was just going to call you. I was thinking Indian for dinner. But let's do takeout. I want to watch the Mets game."

Nate crossed his arms in front of his chest, widened his stance as if about to stop a moving train. His stare never left Elise's.

"Sounds good," Elise said.

"Great. Listen, I'm about to go into a meeting. Was that what you called about—dinner?"

Elise watched a lazy wasp drop down to inspect Nate's gold watch, land on the face, and crawl around looking for sweetness. It found none and flew away.

"E?"

She smiled. Let her eyes close for a moment. She loved when Matt called her "E." Tattoo returned to put his paws on her leg. Somewhere in a faraway paddock a horse squealed. "Yes, babe. That was it."

She slid the phone back into her pocket and looked at Nate. "You don't deserve what I just did for your grandson. Get the horse off the property before I change my mind."

She'd called ahead to let Pammy Stanton know she was coming to the showgrounds that afternoon, with no further plan than to get onto her horse's back and walk around the perimeter of the action—just to allow Indie a bit of a stretch after being cooped up in the stall for so long and give herself a cooling-off period before she saw her husband again.

There is more to being atop a horse than loving the sport or cherishing the animal. Every horse person knows it. Once you achieve a secure seat, horse and rider move as one. The horse becomes an extension of your body. You're conjoined. It was similar to the experience of being pregnant, she thought now. She wondered if that was why women and girls loved horses so much.

She'd arrived in the midst of a busy show day, the grounds alive with snapping flags and scores being announced over the PA system. Spectators, riders, and barn staff with dogs and children gathered around the jumping rings and milled about the outdoor exhibitors peddling books, food, breeches, jewelry, and saddles. Moving through the crowds were horses in various stages of preparedness, from show-ready horses taking practice jumps in warm-up rings, to sleek wet equines being led from the wash area back to their stalls, where sweet flakes of hay awaited, to those with a hoof between the farrier's knees waiting for a shoe to be adjusted.

Elise found Indie already clipped into the crossties and partially tacked up in a dressage saddle, with a bright white pad underneath. He tossed his head and snorted when he saw her, the vaguely wild look in his eyes saying he wasn't quite sure what was going on.

A shiny pink face appeared from around his hind, tail comb in her grasp. "You must be Elise. Pammy Stanton." Pillowy and not much taller than five feet, Pammy came forward with a big smile and an outstretched hand. "I wish we'd have met under different circumstances, but let me just say I am honored to meet such a talented lady. I've seen you in all the online interviews and in the magazines. People have no idea how tough dressage is. You, especially, make it look completely effortless."

"You're kind."

Poppins, just slightly too short for the stall door, rested her whiskered muzzle on the edge. As Elise gave her the stub of a carrot, her long ears flicked with outrage. She was clearly not being brought along on this outing. Was she not part of the family?

"I'd seen you around town over the years, but I'm not one to just walk straight up to someone I don't know. Seems a bit presumptuous. Especially you—such a big rider and then, wasn't Nate Sorenson your . . . what would it be? Grandfather-in-law, I suppose."

Elise took Indie's bridle from a hook on the wall, unclipped the crossties to remove his halter, and wiggled a thumb in the corner of his mouth. After pulling away to stretch his neck down toward the ground and yawn, he nudged Elise in the shins and consented to the bridle.

"You knew him?"

"Everyone knew him—he was larger than life. Sometimes I wondered what it would've been like to marry into his world."

Somewhere outside, a motorcycle roared by.

"Wasn't easy, that much I'll say."

"Anyway, none of my business." A Siamese cat wandered along the aisle and wound around Pammy's legs before leaping onto a stack of hay bales to have her ears scratched. Pammy picked up the cat. "You know, I have a second cousin living in Nevada whose son went missing. Very different situation—this was a divorce and it was the father who took the boy. Christian was only eight months old. The story has a happy ending: Karen did get her boy back. But it took thirteen months. Just, you know, being so close to her that year, I saw how the case gets so much attention for a while, but then things just go quiet." The cat saw something down the aisle and struggled out of Pammy's arms to stalk it. "The most important bit of advice I can offer you is this: don't give up hope. Because the moment the parents do, the public loses hope and the media loses hope. Then the police lose hope. And the worst that can happen is that the coverage stops and the headlines disappear."

The advice was good. And well-intentioned. But the thought of thirteen months without Gracie nearly took away Elise's ability to stand upright. She thanked Pammy, relieved when the woman hurried down the aisle to get back to her chores.

....

CHAPTER 25

Matt woke up sweaty and disoriented from a late afternoon nap, expecting to find that Elise had come back. He called out to her from upstairs, but the place was silent. In the bathroom, he pulled off his shorts and T-shirt and stepped into the shower without waiting for the water to heat up. Rinsed himself off and turned off the taps so emphatically the whole house shuddered.

Cass was home, he could see through the window as he reached for a towel and stepped onto the bathmat. Out in her yard, picking up River's various action figures and balls and beach towels. Still on the line, the same River socks and T-shirts, little boy briefs, Cass's suede bikini. It all hung limp and heavy now, mildewed from the rain.

The towel slipped from his grasp and, in his lunge to catch it, Matt knocked over the wastebasket and sent the contents skittering across the room.

Swearing, he wrapped the towel around his waist and began stuffing trash back into the receptacle, pausing when what looked like a digital thermometer dropped from a wad of tissue and clattered to the floor. He reached for it, realizing as he turned it over that this little wand was no thermometer.

Elise was pregnant.

Fate must have intervened the day Gracie was born, because not only was Nate up at the cabin, but he had a sinus infection and wasn't allowed anywhere near Mountain View Hospital in New Jersey.

After the bedlam had died down and Elise was sleeping off the anesthetic, Matt had visited Gracie's Isolette in the NICU. At thirty-one weeks and two days, she was deemed to be moderately premature, with nasal cannulas offering respiratory support and a peripheral IV providing nutrition her digestive system might be too immature to handle. The equipment was more intimidating than the preemie herself. Gracie wasn't thin-skinned or sharp-featured, as a very premature baby would've been. She wasn't expected to face long-term consequences from the earliness of the birth; the concern lay solely in its traumatic nature. In her pink cotton hat and matching oversized sleeper, his daughter already had the same plucky, long-suffering look on her elfin face that she would have years later when he picked her up from Funducational.

Gracie had been a force from the start.

He'd called Nate to give him the news. Elise had gone into early labor. It was a scary birth, but mother and baby were doing fine. Nate asked where Elise had been when she went into labor. Matt hadn't prepared himself for that question. His mind raced with possibilities: knitting caps for preemies (too close for comfort), wallpapering the nursery (toxic adhesive), getting her nails done (again with the carcinogens). Ultimately, he settled on a nap. But even that set off alarms. "Was she lying on her back?" Nate asked. "They show it on the TV, but it's not safe to lie flat on your back that far into term. Puts the baby at risk. The doctors don't always talk about it. You have to lie on your side . . . "

Matt hadn't been able to shoulder the guilt. Eventually, he told his grandfather the truth. Nate handled the news with dignity. Class. In spite of his early reservations about Elise as a mother, he never once said, "I told you so." He went silent on the topic of the accident.

Matt stepped out onto the back porch and looked toward the lake, completely baffled as to why his wife would keep this new pregnancy from him. Was she unwilling to add another bit of drama in the midst of their devastation? He thought back to her mounting neediness with a modicum of guilt. No wonder she wanted reassurance: they were barely surviving Gracie being gone . . . and now to add a new baby to it all.

He went back into the house and slid into a kitchen chair, the vinyl cold against his legs. Grabbed his phone to call his wife, but she didn't pick up.

At the far end of the table was a note. He slid it closer and stared at it, incredulous: *Gone riding.*

Knowing she was pregnant, with *his* second child as well as hers, after all they'd been through—were going through—his wife had gotten onto a horse. Matt buzzed with outrage. Did he have no rights at all as a father? He reached for a pen, scrawled across her note: *Meet me at the Village Diner at 5.*

Elise wrapped Indie's legs with fluffy white polo bandages, more for the need to fuss over her horse than out of any need to protect him. He was curious, ears forward and head up, as she led him out into the busyness of the show, but instead of taking him toward the warm-up ring as she would if they were showing, she led him toward a large patch of lawn beyond the parking lot. The air smelled like fresh-cut grass, the dust of the sand rings all around them, and water. The sprinkler system had kicked to life over near the road.

She lowered the stirrups and was about to mount when she noticed a small car cruising along the road on the other side of the white rail fence. She'd seen that car before. That black Honda Civic with a dull, red hood and green Vermont plates had passed by her on Seldom Seen Road the day before Gracie went missing.

And again the morning of.

There was no jumping that fence on Indie—not with sprinklers soaking the grass. Pammy appeared at the mouth of another breezeway and Elise waved her over. Tossed Pammy the reins and sprinted after the car, which was making a left onto Park Preserve Road.

She tore across the wet lawn, slipping and hitting the ground twice in the spray of the sprinklers, and somehow got over the equally drenched fence to hit pavement and flat-out run toward the car, which stopped at the intersection with Highway 73, waited for a break in traffic, and turned left. Toward the Cascade Lakes.

Where Gracie's crutches had been found.

Elise ran so hard it felt like her lungs were on fire, but the car disappeared from sight as it worked its way into traffic. All she caught of the license plate was "GL."

Chapter 26

....

He knocked. When no one came to the back door, Matt did what he'd always done—stepped inside and announced himself. The thumping and wailing of a good old-fashioned tantrum from upstairs almost certainly drowned out his voice—and made it clear River wasn't always the gentle creature he'd seemed. The kitchen revealed the epicenter of the upset: milk and cereal and shards of a broken bowl splattered across the linoleum floor.

Matt found a broom and swept up the sopping mess, dropped the worst of it into the trash, and rinsed broom and floor. He heard bare feet padding down the stairs as he wiped up the last of it with a dish rag.

"You didn't have to do that." Cass stood a moment in the doorway, in panties and a milk-stained tank top, then took the soggy cloth from him. "My jeans were a mess. Riv saw a bear through the window and lost his shit."

"An actual bear?"

"Exactly what I thought, but yes. Big old Papa Bear on the driveway. I called Garth, but of course he didn't answer. Nothing new." Without doing a thing about her state of dress, she motioned for him to sit and poured two cups of coffee. "Never seen a year like this. Everyone's gone nuts with these sightings. I made my mom stay over—she could easily go for a walk and not even notice a bear." She handed Matt a mug of coffee and settled by the window to light a smoke. "I'm glad you still take it black. Matty Sorenson drinking coffee any other way would be blasphemous." She took a drag and blew smoke through the screen. "Plus, we're out of milk."

In another lifetime, he'd have laughed. "I was napping. Came downstairs to a little note from my wife. *Gone riding*."

If Cass felt any sort of judgment toward Elise, her face didn't show it. "Maybe it's calming. You know? Her happy place."

He rubbed his beard. "She's pregnant, Cass."

The gravity of it nudged Cass back in her chair. "Holy shit. How far along?"

"Would it matter after Gracie?" He stood, paced the room. "I found a test in the garbage just now. She didn't even tell me. And now she's on a fucking horse. You know, Nate warned me off her. And I didn't listen. I'm honestly going insane. I don't sleep. I feel like I'm going to have a heart attack. I see families everywhere and I actually find myself wishing it had happened to them." He closed his eyes. "Which makes me feel like shit. And then I think—Elise is going through this too. And I feel even more like shit." He hoisted himself up onto the counter and found himself nose-to-nose with a photograph tacked on the fridge: Garth asleep on the Adirondack chair out back.

Matt leaned over his thighs and scrubbed his head with his fingertips. Cass crossed the room to push him upright and stand between his legs. She rested her hands on his thighs, just above the knees. "Hey. I'm going to help you get through this. You'll get Gracie back, and then you'll know what to do."

"About?"

"About your marriage. Doesn't matter if it's obvious to me; you have to come to this on your own."

"You think I should leave her."

"It's not for me to say."

"But that's what you think." He studied her. "You were right—what you said about the gloves. I told her to go get them, but never did I imagine she'd leave Gracie at the road to do it."

"Shh-shh-shh." His boyhood sweetheart wrapped her arms around his shoulders and pulled him close. He lost himself in the maternal stroke of her hand on the back of his head. As she pressed herself into him, her breasts flattened against his chest. His hands found her shoulders, her spine, the curve of her hip.

"You ever wonder what would have happened between us if I hadn't taken off?"

How to answer this? He'd wondered many, many times.

Soft footsteps pattered down the stairs and suddenly a bare-chested River was in the room. Cass backed away from Matt, immediately busied herself at the sink. The boy looked from his mother to Matt to his mother. "I want Gracie to come back so I can show her the frozen rats at the pet store. She would think it's so cool."

Cass and Matt locked eyes, released the same breath between them. Cass cupped her son's chin. "I know, bugaboo. We all want her back."

Matt looked homeless and he knew it. Elise, he noted, had taken the time to shower and comb her wet hair into a knot before coming to meet him at the diner. She'd slipped into a pretty gray sweatshirt and white jeans. Her manicured feet were in sandals. Her face may have been gaunt, but damned if she didn't look fashionable. There, beside her, was the big red handbag she refused to let anyone touch—even her own daughter.

The clash and clatter of dishes and voices from the kitchen were an assault. Matt and Elise sat on torn green vinyl and studied each other over club sandwiches barely touched. Around them, people stared, whispered, clearly aware of who they were: the couple no one wanted to be.

The pregnancy stick flashed in his mind. The pink lines. Two kids and he couldn't fucking protect either of them.

"I've had such a feeling about it, you know? Like, why would that car stand out for me? It's just some dirty Honda Civic, just like any car you see dozens of times every day." Elise leaned closer, elbows on the table, eyes so full of hope his anger nearly softened. Nearly. "It has to mean something, right?"

"I don't know."

"Well, Dorsey has people looking for it. He definitely thinks it's of interest. That's what he said—'of interest.'"

Matt looked around for the waitress. They were going to need wine—or stronger—for this talk.

"The first time I saw it was the day before. Saturday. It was sort of creeping along our road. Even with the bends, it was going weirdly slow, you know? And Vermont plates."

Matt scrubbed scratchy eyes with his palms, then let his hands drop to the table's edge. "Seldom Seen Road is in all the tourist blogs and articles. There are always sightseers, and they all move slow. It's been filled with lookie-loos my entire life."

She watched him silently a moment. "Allow me a little hope, Matt. It costs us nothing to hope."

"Hey, guys." The waitress, a tall, beaky but attractive redhead somewhere in her thirties, stopped at the table, pen and pad in hand. Her name tag, Matt noticed now, said KIM. "Is everything okay with your food? I'm happy to get you something else . . ."

"Sorry, it's not the food," Elise said.

"I know, darlin'." Kim patted Elise's hand. "We're all praying so damned hard for you and your little girl."

"Can I get a whisky—neat?" Matt said, leaning closer, voice low. "Only . . . could you put it in a coffee mug?" He nodded toward the other diners, who were pretending not to be watching. "I don't want to read about this on the Internet."

"Of course. No need to explain." Kim looked to Elise. "For you too?"

"Thanks. No."

Kim strode away, energized by the ability to help in even this small way.

A mother and father with their young son slid into the next booth. Matt tried not to watch as the mother pulled off the child's cardigan and kissed his rosy cheek. The little boy turned around to face Matt, wide-eyed the way only a toddler can be.

It could be a boy, this next baby, he thought. *A son.*

"I've been thinking," Elise said as a Village Diner mug appeared in front of Matt. "I know it makes sense that we're doing this divide-and-conquer thing. But I just—I feel like I'm cracking up. I think we need to spend these hours . . . these days . . ." Her voice caught and she rocked forward to sip from her water glass. "I need us to be side by side. This tension between us is just getting bigger and bigger. And I don't think it's helping . . ."

"Of course there's tension. What the hell do you think—we're going to bond over this?"

"There's been some kind of seismic shift between us that is, yes, of course, brought on by Gracie's disappearance. But it's weakening us and our ability to—"

Her words drifted into the pings and clangs and called-out orders from the kitchen.

He swirled the scotch around in the mug, mesmerized by the reflections in the amber liquid. It hit him as Elise spoke that the seismic shift wasn't new at all. It had been there since the day Gracie was pulled from his wife's body with monitors bleeping alarm and doctors and nurses and anesthesiologist and a chaplain—yes, they'd assigned Matt a chaplain—filling the emergency room from wall to wall.

The shift that had occurred when his baby girl came out blue was a silent scream that had never abated. He'd pushed it down to his core in an effort to be present for his infant daughter and the woman he'd married. As if, over the years that followed, keeping it below the surface would allow time to rub against it and smooth out the roughness. But, he realized now, time had done the opposite. It had made his anger grow sharp and craggy. And now, with Gracie gone, it scraped against the inside of his skin.

"Do you realize . . ." He looked at his wife, rocking to soothe herself, hands hugging her mug for dear life. "You've never, ever said you're sorry."

"What are you talking about? Of course I have. Over and over. You know I would change every single thing that led to that moment if I could. God, Matt. Tell me you know that."

He reached into his wallet. Pulled out a folded photograph and opened it on the table. It was the picture taken that day inside Ronnie's arena. A younger Elise sitting atop Indie, smile wide, one hand on her belly, on Gracie, the other holding the reins.

Elise looked at him. "Where . . . how did you get this?"

"In the hospital. That girl, Amy, the one who took it, she handed it to me when she came to visit you. I was going to throw it away, but I realized . . ." His voice caught and he downed his scotch. "I realized this was the last moment Gracie was as she should have been. She was whole."

Elise sat taller and, slowly, started to shake her head from side to side. "That's what this is about? That's why we're sitting here . . . you drinking scotch from a mug?"

"This is about everything. You haven't even cried. I mean, what the fuck? Our daughter could be dead."

"Don't say that!" Her chest rose and fell. "I can't cry, Matt. You think that's from lack of pain? It's a million times worse not being able to release what I'm going through. A *million times* worse."

Heads snapped in their direction and he leaned over the table so he could speak softly. "Is there anything, Elise . . . anything at all I need to know?"

She slumped back in the booth and gawked at him. "What are you talking about?"

This baby, he didn't say. *My unborn child—who doesn't seem to matter enough to mention.* He waited, then said, "I can't do this anymore."

Her eyes searched his face as if answers might seep out of his pores. "Can't do what?"

He motioned back and forth between them. "This. Us. Not with Gracie . . . Not now."

"What does that even mean?"

"I just . . . I feel . . . I'm going to snap."

"What does that *mean*?"

"I need space."

She gazed steadily at him. "This isn't the time to be apart, Matt. In the middle of the worst nightmare any parent can imagine."

Matt signaled to the waitress to bring the bill and handed her his Visa. As Kim pulled out the machine and inserted his card, Matt watched a family dressed in matching purple T-shirts file out. There was only one reason a family on a vacation would wear matching T-shirts: so that one of their children wouldn't get separated from the pack. It dawned on Matt that Gracie's disappearance had likely precipitated this family's caution.

The waitress pulled a receipt from the machine, frowned at it. "I'm sorry. That transaction was declined. Sometimes these machines act up . . ."

It wasn't the machine. Matt pulled out his Amex card and tried to appear casual, as if there was no chance in hell this card would give her trouble.

"Modern technology . . ." The waitress handed him back his Amex as well.

When Matt went to dig up another card from his wallet, mumbling something about needing to move money around, Kim pressed two fingers to his forearm and leaned over them. "Guys, this one's on me. It's the least I can do."

The bill was for twenty-four dollars. He was being declined for less than the price of a tank of gas. He stood abruptly and pulled a few tens from his pocket—he did have some pride left. Enough, at least, that he wasn't going to take charity from a small-town waitress who probably needed every cent. He pushed the bills into her hand.

Aware of how many eyes were on him, he leaned over Elise as if giving her a casual hug goodbye. In her ear, he whispered, "I'm moving to a motel for a few days."

Chapter 27

·········

Elise looked up at the stag's head above the stone fireplace. She'd always hated that Nate had found this poor animal in a ditch and brought it home to mount the head on his wall like a trophy. It made her sick to look at it. She couldn't stand it one more minute.

She marched out to the shed and returned with a ladder. Leaned it against the fireplace and climbed up to dislodge the shockingly heavy creature's neck from its anchor on the wall and drop the head with a thud onto the sofa below. She then hoisted it by the antlers and dragged it out back, through the mossy dirt and into the woods.

The deer deserved the dignified burial that Nate's entitlement hadn't allowed.

With a shovel from the shed, she dug furiously until, arms and white jeans covered in dirt, the sun having disappeared over the roof of the house, the hole was big enough to fully bury the stag. No way was Elise going to snap the antlers off to make her job easier.

After lowering the head into the earth, she gazed into the huge eyes—the black glass orbs shining in the fading daylight. The poor animal seemed even more vulnerable now.

She widened the hole, then returned to the house in search of Gunner, eventually finding him behind a chair in the living room. She carried the stuffed dog outside and laid him next to the stag. A companion for eternity.

Satisfied, Elise dropped to her knees and bulldozed the dirt back into the hole with her hands, pushing faster and faster, until her father's face appeared in her mind's eye. As he walked out the door with his suitcase. His bullshit line about loving her mother forever. She saw him standing there at the funeral. Head bowed like it wasn't his fault, Briony at his side. Elise packed the dirt down hard, slapping it open-handed until her palms numbed.

Did Matt really believe she was able to cope with even a second of not knowing where her daughter was or whether she was suffering? Did he realize that every time Elise fell asleep she heard Gracie's croaking voice calling for her mother—only there was no way to know if the child was across the road or across the world? Elise stood and stomped on the earth, kicked it down.

She'd give her life to turn back the clock for every parent who'd ever had a child go missing.

By the time she finished, the sun had long set. Exhausted, sweaty, filthy, she let her legs carry her down to the dock, where she sat and stared into the deep purple shadows. The lake was inky and flat. No movement at all and total silence. She would have preferred a big wind. Lightning slashed the heavens as if commanded by a god she had never believed in but was now ready to accept as, if not the reason for all that had happened, at least someone at whom to direct her wrath.

There was just enough brightness left to make her feel small, lost among the trees, the mountains, the sky. The first stars had begun to flicker. Tiny pinpricks of gold from camps and cabins spread up and into the hills beyond. Gracie could be bathed in one of those lights right now. Then again, Elise thought as she watched the red lights of a faraway plane cross the sky, Gracie could be anywhere.

On the dock beside her, her phone lit up and rang. Elise grabbed it, pressed it to her ear. "You found it?"

Dorsey's voice was too flat for the news to be good. "We did locate the Civic. License plate was GLR 271. We caught up with the driver filling up at Eagle Gas."

She fought to stay calm. "And . . . ?"

"Elise, his name is Warren Bleeker. He says he's your father."

....

CHAPTER 28

Matt had checked himself into the Swiss Miss Motel at the southernmost tip of town for two reasons: he'd always loved the nostalgic brown sign and the rooms were relatively cheap. He'd called his bank. Had the credit limit increased on his Visa. It bought him a few more weeks. Elise, too. The card was shared.

What he hadn't considered was how utterly devoid of creature comforts the place would be. Shampoo came in individual tear-open packets that were impossible to tear open, and forget a stocked minibar—there wasn't even a mini fridge. So, with heavy rain on Main Street creating a nearly impenetrable mist, Matt drove north again to pick up the necessities. Very few people were out and about in this weather, especially at this end of town, where the shops and restaurants gave way to board-and-batten or stone-and-beam plazas that housed veterinarians' offices, a walk-in clinic, and independent pharmacies. The miniature golf course where Elise had taken Gracie when she was younger was closed. Only the McDonald's drive-through and Grocery Mart had any sort of traffic.

As he pulled into the parking lot, a shiny black pickup truck pulled out. Matt did a double take: on the side it said KOSTICK & SONS FISHING LODGE. He nearly smiled. Look at Andy, keeping his marketing going.

At the grocery store's entry, beneath the dripping overhang, was a long table displaying American flags, Fourth of July T-shirts, and beach towels—limp and tragic in the rain. The banner that hung above them read: 4TH OF JULY SAVINGS STOREWIDE!

Matt checked his watch. The Fourth was next Saturday. The thought of even more tourists descending upon the village made him nauseous.

He pushed a wet shopping cart up and down the aisles to what sounded like music from *The Price Is Right*. Tossed in a bottle of Dove for Men shampoo. He paused in front of the Aveeno body wash he always bought for Gracie. It was lavender-scented and calming. He always dumped it into the water to use as bubble bath because she said it made her sleep better.

He dropped the body wash into the cart. Then, fuck it. He walked over to the candy aisle and picked out everything Gracie adored. Raisinets, Reese's Pieces, the arrowroot cookies she called "baby cookies." He grabbed some chicken noodle soup—two pop-top cans he could slurp down cold. A bottle of cheap red wine.

The girl at the register was somewhere in her twenties with soft mocha-toned skin, pale eyes, and fuzzy brown hair pulled back in a messy chignon. Like a ballet dancer who'd just spent a week on a beach somewhere exotic. Long, lanky limbs, exposed collarbones in her wide-necked top. She grinned when he set all the candy on the counter and started ringing it through.

"You don't look like a guy with such a sweet tooth."

"Well. Appearances."

She held up the arrowroot cookies. "I *love* these dunked into tea. My grandmother taught me that. You wait for them to get real soft, then let them fall apart on your tongue." She held his gaze while she rang through the shampoo and body wash. "I'd forgotten about them. So . . ." Her smile was coy now. "Thank you for the reminder."

A couple of college-age boys fell into line behind Matt. One pulled a copy of *People* from the display and started spouting off facts about the Kardashians.

"What can I say?" Matt shrugged. "I bring back memories of a kinder, gentler time." He hated himself for what he was doing. Attempting to sound normal. Hated himself even more when he realized the boys behind him were listening.

She laughed and set the last of his purchases into a brown paper bag. "That will be nineteen seventy-eight, Captain Cookie."

Muffled snorts behind him. Matt reached into an empty pocket. Where was his wallet?

"You're not from around here, are you?"

"New Jersey, actually." He patted the rest of his pockets.

"I wish I was not from around here." Her laugh was weary for a girl her age.

He'd left it on the desk at the motel when he'd called the bank. For a moment, he considered grabbing the grocery bag and dashing. As if possessing these treats would ensure that Gracie would come back to him. Feeling his face flush hot, Matt said, "I forgot my wallet. Can you do me a huge favor and keep all this aside for me? I'll be back in twenty minutes."

"I'll put it all back in the cart and you can push it out of the way . . ."

Someone from the lineup behind him handed forward a twenty. Matt looked past the sniggering college boys to see Lyman Williams holding a shopping basket in front of his thighs. Lyman nodded his insistence that Matt accept the money.

The girl put it in the till and pretended Matt wasn't the most pathetic excuse for a man ever.

He carried his purchases out into the rain and, in his struggle to get into his car before being soaked to the skin, he dropped the keys, accidentally kicking them beneath the vehicle. By the time he'd gotten down on his knees and managed to grab them and get the door open, Lyman had emerged from the store, holding a grocery bag on one hip. He sprang open his umbrella and marched to his own car.

Matt called out, "Hey, man, thanks. A bit embarrassing back there. If you can tell me where to send it, I'll mail you a check."

Lyman pointed his keys at his car. The lights flashed twice as the doors unlocked. Lyman shook his head and climbed in. He started the car, then opened the window to say, "No need."

"Seriously. I'd feel much better. I pay my debts. Eventually."

Lyman looked up at Matt. "Is that some kind of joke?"

A joke? "What do you mean?"

Lyman took his hands off the wheel and stared straight ahead as if debating how much to say. "Our families, is what I mean," he said at last.

Matt searched his memory for anything that connected him to Lyman's family. He drew a blank. "Our families? Do we have a connection?"

Lyman looked up at Matt. "My father went to your grandfather for a loan after we had a few lean years. The farm that we lost, as well as a property on the lake, had been in our family for five generations."

"I don't understand."

"Why would you? It was nothing to your family. Nate Sorenson lent him thirteen thousand dollars to get him through the winter."

"He did that for all sorts of people. It's why the town revered him."

Lyman's laughter was angry. He sighed and tipped his head back. "Revered by some, but despised by the rest."

"Despised? Look, I've heard that Nate could be tough about repayment, but he was fair. He—"

"When Nate Sorenson lent out money, it was secured by the debtors' properties. If someone couldn't repay him on time, Nate didn't extend their terms. He helped himself to the property. Didn't matter to him if the land value was higher than the loan. He took it."

"That is not true."

"My parents and my little sister and I lived in a van for an entire winter after we lost our farm. Athena lost part of her leg to frostbite. Nate Sorenson knew who couldn't afford to fight him. And he grabbed their land, then hired them to work their own farms. He humiliated them."

"No," Matt said. "My grandfather bought those farms fair and square. He bought them from people who'd had enough of the risk. And not only did he let them stay on, he paid them to do what they'd always done. They thanked him for it. I was there!"

"You weren't there when the deals went down. And you most certainly weren't there when the deals went south. He was a greedy, grasping—"

"This is bullshit."

"Do a little research. That land you're selling? Not one acre of it beyond your original tree line was legitimately bought."

"That's all lakefront and forest. There's no farmland there—"

"My grandfather bought his piece of lakeside figuring his kids and grandkids and great-grandkids beyond that could enjoy a bit of leisure time up in this northern country. Your 'revered' grandfather took everything. The farmland and the waterfront. Then he turned my father and mother out on the street. With two young children." Lyman grabbed a scrap of paper and scribbled down an address. "If you want to square things up for your purchases today, mail the check here."

Matt was speechless.

"I'm sorry for your troubles, Sorensen. But it doesn't change the past. Best I can say about your grandfather is he was an equal-opportunity thief. Stole from anyone he figured he could swindle." Lyman put the car in drive and lifted his foot off the brake. "I sincerely hope they find your little girl. Wouldn't wish that on anyone, no matter what's gone on in the past."

Matt stood in the rain, collar flipped up, shoulders hunched to his ears, and watched Lyman's car disappear. Then he walked the few blocks down to the village, to the bench he'd commissioned when Nate died.

In Memory of Nate Sorenson
1918–2013
Who Gave So Much

He squinted and bent over for a closer look. Wiped the rain from it. Had someone gone at it with a nail? He sat down, his jeans soaked through in a second. From the mullioned windows of the Black Dog Grill, people had turned to stare at him. He got up. Stomped back to his car. What the hell was happening?

....

CHAPTER 29

It wasn't enough to run, to jog. She needed to sprint, to flee nothing and chase everything. She ran so hard through the rain, every muddy footfall jammed thigh into hip. The trees blurred, swam, like a fever, a hallucination. She'd taken off along the lake's edge, up and over wet docks and stone patios, and through prickled hedges and tidy gardens. Then into the woods, ducking and bobbing to avoid branches, tripping and slipping over fallen logs and rocks. Her jeans had torn at the knee—blood now stained the already filthy white denim. Wet hair stuck to her cheeks. Rainwater streamed into her eyes. Then out onto the road again. Past massive homes until a sidewalk appeared, then squat brown buildings and the lights of town.

By the time Elise got to Main Street, every breath was a sharp gasp. Passing restaurants and stores, she slowed, catching her hunched and sodden reflection in the window of the bookstore, sliding across Cass's poster like an apparition. It was late. The shops were closed. She pushed open the first door that wasn't locked and stepped into the glaringly overlit ice cream shop, with its yellow walls and checkerboard floor.

An employee in a yellow striped shirt was cleaning up behind the counter, clearly preparing to close. It was just a kid, his hair like beige steel wool beneath a silly paper hat. He turned to stare at Elise. Her cheeks were hot and wet—her hands went up to wipe away the water. Or sweat? It wasn't until her body started heaving with gulps and sobs that she realized she was crying. For the first time in her memory. She stood in front of this adolescent, who looked terrified and embarrassed for her, and sobbed uncontrollably. She dropped and squatted on the floor. The teenager came to lean over her, bless his perplexed soul. Likely all he wanted was to get the hell out of there and go meet his friends to drink in a farmer's field. He asked if she was okay, if he could help.

Elise stood up again and sobbed. "She's gone. No one can find her." She paused to gulp in air. "She's out there somewhere."

He looked like he wanted to be swallowed up by the mop in his hand. She was pathetic in his eyes. ZACHARY, said his plastic name tag.

Poor Zachary.

"I don't know what to do. What do I do? How do I do this all alone? How do I find her?" Her face felt red and ugly and swollen with pain. "What do I do . . . ? No one can help me. No one knows any better than I do." She wiped at hot mucus running down her upper lip.

Zachary vanished into the back. Maybe to climb out a window, maybe to call his manager or the police. Elise bent over, crying to the glass display now. How was this possible? What was wrong with her? Shouldn't the first time she sobbed be somewhere more dignified?

Looking equally horrified and brave, Zachary was back with a paper cup filled with water. He came around the counter again and gave it to her, spilling on himself in the handoff. It was the last thing she wanted, but she didn't have the strength to disappoint him. It dawned on her that he was some other mother's child, and she cried harder. Poor Zachary. Anything could happen to him.

She drank what was left of the water. Thanked him, still sobbing. Why did anyone say you need a good cry? It was terrible. She grabbed a handful of napkins to blow her nose, surprised by how gratifying it felt. She headed for the door. Only then did she notice a rumpled old man at the corner table, his untied dress shoes and dirty tie unsettling evidence of a mentally ill vagrant or an unkempt genius. He dropped his pink plastic spoon into his empty ice cream cup and wiped his lips.

Elise moved past him, hunched over her sobs, slowing only because she had to navigate a couple of concrete steps in the rain. The old man stepped outside behind her, his pockets jangling with keys or change. He pulled on a baseball cap and started across the street. Halfway across, he turned. His eyes narrowed, neither kindly nor unkindly. "Welcome the grief, no matter how ugly," he said. "Doesn't matter if it takes you to the rooftop screaming or has you balled up under the bed in silence. It's yours to feel however you damned well see fit."

....

CHAPTER 30

Heavy pine boughs overhung the long driveway, scratching and thunking against the roof of Matt's car. He wasn't really expecting Jeannie to be at Camp Imagine at ten p.m., but there she was. She'd seen the headlights slide across the face of the main lodge and come out to the covered porch to wave him in, throw a towel over his wet shoulders, make him a coffee.

"Between the bears and the rain, we've got all our sleepover campers in the dining hall for yet another movie night." Jeannie sat down behind her desk, pale gray hair falling out of a haphazard ponytail, her face bare of any makeup. The honey pine walls behind her boasted a series of whiteboards with names of cabins and checklists for leaders and leaders-in-training. There was a CPR poster and an eye wash station. A defibrillator on the wall. A Rubbermaid garbage can labeled LOST & FOUND. "Noise level can get pretty intense on a day like this. We actually created a mud race— before the heavens opened up—just so they could burn off a little energy." She straightened a pile of flyers on her desk. "The extra laundry for us tomorrow will be more than worth it."

"I didn't mean to barge in unannounced. I know you must be ready to pack it in."

"Nonsense. I'm thrilled to see you. I've been worried sick."

"I'm sure this was the last thing you needed." He noticed a chalkboard on the far wall. "Cancelations" was written neatly at the top, with dozens of names below. "I'm sorry."

"Please don't be." She pulled her polar fleece over her shoulders. "You don't owe me—or this camp—an apology, Matt. If your daughter's name had been on our list like it should have been, we would have known she was missing a whole hell of a lot earlier. Garbage happens in this world. No matter how hard we try to prevent it."

He leaned back in the wooden chair and exhaled.

"Now. What can I help you with?"

He wanted to hear the truth about his grandfather. He needed to talk about something—anything—other than a life without Gracie. Or maybe this *was* about Gracie. Because if what Lyman said was true, maybe there were many families out there who wouldn't mind seeing the Sorenson family taken down.

"You knew my grandfather pretty well?"

If she was surprised it was Nate he wanted to discuss, she didn't let on. "We worked together on more community projects than I care to count. He was a real doer, Nate was. Don't think I ever saw him idle."

"The thing is, I'm hearing some things now. A pizza delivery guy, our roofer, Lyman . . . As far as I knew, a good many people relied on him when banks rejected their loan applications."

"Yes. He was in the business of lending for decades."

Matt shifted closer. "Did you ever hear about . . . any instances where my grandfather's dealings were less than fair?"

She reached for a bottle of orange juice on her desk and took a slow drink. Replaced the lid carefully and swirled the pulpy liquid. "You're talking about the ones who couldn't make good."

It wasn't a question.

He didn't know what he'd been expecting. A look of confusion, perhaps. Maybe a slight squint to reassure him that what he'd suggested was too bizarre to contemplate. Or laughter. That would have been good. But Jeannie knew exactly what he meant.

"I'd heard a few things about those mortgages, if that's what you're asking," she said.

"Such as?"

"Matt, I'm not sure this is the time, with your daughter missing and—"

"Please." He sat back in his chair. "I need to know."

What she told him then was so foreign to him, it was like she was describing a character in a movie—the cold-hearted antagonist. Everything he thought he knew about Nate was false. He wasn't kind or benevolent. He was a calculating man, a patriarch who used his power to prey upon people on the edge of financial desperation. Worse, he would target folks to go after.

Matt shook his head. "What do you mean 'target'? Wouldn't they come to him?"

"It's a small town. You knew who was in trouble and who could weather a dry summer or a recession. He went to those who were desperate, offered them money on his terms. But only if he wanted their properties. The farms were one thing—if the land had appeal for future development, he was in. If it was arid or too far off the beaten path, not so much. Your grandfather always wanted more shoreline. That was his drug."

"So he loaned these people money."

"He made them offers they couldn't refuse and sat back to wait for them to default."

Matt felt his stomach drop. How could he have been so stupid? How could he not have known? All those years. He reached up and wiped his nose with the back of his hand. "How many people know?"

She shrugged. "Again, it's a small town."

Matt stood, disoriented. He'd always believed that, by the time a person reaches midlife, there was a clear "You are here" pointer dot you could count on. His dot had just been erased. He no longer had any idea who he was. His life was built on conceit and lies.

....

CHAPTER 31

Elise heard a thump and sat up in bed. Pulled on sweatpants and stepped softly into the hall. She hurried downstairs, forcing herself not to hope it was Gracie. Not to imagine the improbability that her daughter had made her way up the porch steps, pulled a stool to the door, and swept the key off the doorjamb to let herself in. And that now she was sitting on the sofa bursting with questions about coyotes who steal gold medals and what the deductible would be on an insurance-covered wheelchair.

The letdown would be too painful.

The front door was open to the porch and light glowed from Nate's office. Outside, Elise saw the outline of a cream BMW. Matt was here. She debated what to do, but Matt had already spotted her from Nate's sofa, where he'd clearly been riffling through the Rubbermaid containers full of files. "I need some of my grandfather's papers," was all he said.

"For what?"

He didn't answer. Picked up an ancient manila file folder and thumbed through it. Pulled out old documents, small scraps of paper. She watched him lay them all out on the desk and move them around like puzzle pieces. As if, in a different order, they'd make more sense. "Unbelievable."

She moved closer to see rudimentary sketches of property lines and hastily scrawled contracts—one on the back of an envelope. All dated, signed, witnessed. "What are they? Properties he bought?"

"Mortgages." Matt held one up and leaned back in the chair. The name on it was Williams. "He didn't buy the properties. He took them. Screwed people out of their land. Turned them out of their homes." He twisted side to side in his grandfather's chair, stopping when he faced the wall of framed newspaper clippings. Then turned to Elise again. "And for what? If you think about it." Matt shrugged a shoulder, motioned around the room. "So he could cruise up the shoreline and feel like he was winning at life somehow?"

She thought about all the Nate moments she'd endured. Would this have been easier on Matt if she'd shared with him what she knew: that Nate put on something of a teeth-gritted display of fairness for his grandson? Had Elise's kindness been self-serving in the long run—or, worse, an act of cowardice?

She went around the other side of the desk and leaned down to rest her arms around her husband's shoulders and chest. "I'm sorry. He raised you and you loved him."

Instead of softening into her touch, Matt stiffened. Turned away from her. She let go and his focus returned immediately to the deeds.

"But," he said. "It's not like any of this can't be undone. I can make good on every single thing. Starting tomorrow. Or tonight. I just need to make a plan of action . . ."

He had deep smudges beneath his eyes and his beard had grown in nearly white. The man wasn't sleeping. He'd lost maybe ten pounds in less than a week.

"Matt . . ."

"What I have to do—I have to look up these people. Many of whom will be dead. But I can trace their ancestors." He stopped, glanced at the phone. "I'm going to need a lawyer."

"You are a lawyer."

"Not this kind of lawyer."

As he stuffed various files into his backpack, she could see his hands shaking. "Matt, I think you need to rest tonight. Take something to help you sleep. You have to take care of yourself. This land stuff—you can think about it later. Once we find Gracie. But to take on this enormous task—which has to be emotional—right now . . . it isn't healthy. You don't have to deal with it right this minute."

"Gotta go." He packed up his bag and strode through the office doorway. Started out onto the porch.

"Matt."

He stopped, one hand on the knob. Behind him in the misty gloom, the chirrup of crickets was almost deafening.

"Please stay."

He left with no more to comfort her than a quick "I'll be at the motel," and made his way to the car as quickly as he could.

He didn't need to rush his escape. He was gone before he even backed out of the driveway.

....

CHAPTER 32

Just after one in the morning, Elise jumped out of bed. She threw on rubber boots and went out back to dig up first Gunner, then the stag. It went against everything they'd taught Gracie about keeping buried creatures buried—a lesson badly needed when, three months after its funeral, the child dug up a blue jay who'd broken its neck flying into their sliding glass door. Her reason had made plenty of sense to her: she was making a headstone out of a brick and needed to confirm whether the bird was male or female. There wasn't much left but dessicated bones and claws and an unholy stench.

The guilt of having buried the two animals had been haunting Elise. Was it really such a good thing to put them in the earth to rot? Was it really any better than Gunner sitting on the hearth with a tilted head and a macabre grin, or the stag hanging over the fireplace, watching the family's every move? More importantly, by playing God with the dog and the deer, might Elise be tempting fate into assigning something equally terrible to her daughter?

What had she been thinking?

Dragging the deer head up and out of the earth was arduous. The ground was wetter now—though not nearly as sodden as it would have been without the heavy canopy of trees overhead. Back in the kitchen, she wiped and brushed both animals clean. Neither emerged unscathed. Both had bald patches. One of the stag's glass eyeballs fell out onto the floor. She dug through a drawer for a tube of Krazy Glue and reset it, but now it bulged in a way that made him look vaguely unhinged. A journeyman who'd encountered lands and storms he'd never anticipated but, man, did he come back with a story.

Please let Gracie come back with a better story . . .

Unable to still herself, her arms and abdomen aching from the effort, Elise headed out to the dock again. At the edge of the sky, a big, brilliant star shone, a tiny tear in the blackness. It was Sunday morning now and her daughter was still missing. Eight forty a.m. was rushing at her, bringing with it a brutal shift in time reference. They would officially move from days to weeks.

A sharp stinging on her ankle. Elise slapped hard, pulled her hand away to see her dirty fingers smeared with blood. Yet another in the map of bug bites.

"I heard that." Cass's voice. The swish of bushes being parted, then Cass's wild hair. She came along the dock, sandals flapping. Looked at Elise's ankle. "Blackfly bite," she said. "Come inside, hon. Let's treat it before it gets itchy."

The thought of making small talk with Cass in the middle of the night had no appeal. All Elise wanted was to curl up in bed and hide from the world. "That's okay. It's late . . ."

"A little tea tree oil. I swear by the stuff."

Cass took her forearm, and Elise's desperation for human touch obliterated any will to resist.

There was no sound but their own footsteps as they climbed up the dirt path through Cass's yard. Inside, Cass's back room was crowded with cartons of her glossy new hardcover. A stack of about thirty sat on the floor, the top opened with a black marker poised. As if she'd been signing. "I don't even want to go ahead with the launch now. But my agent and publisher are adamant. Crazy thing is, all these Woodstock bloggers have found out about the book and it's starting to sell online."

Elise had no reply. She looked at the wall, at the black-and-white photos of River. In the water, on the dock. On a high, jagged cliff overlooking the lake. In jeans, no shirt, with a Batman mask. Another, hands on hips, wearing white briefs and a cape. In the water, floating on his back in a full Spider-Man costume.

On the first step of the stairway, a battalion of green army men stood sentry. Cass climbed straight past them and motioned for Elise to follow. "Sorry about the mess. River loves his soldiers. I told him he's a little warmonger."

Elise forced herself to look away. If you're dying of thirst, the last thing you want to torture yourself with is the sight of someone guzzling water.

"The beauty of tea tree oil is that it disinfects at the same time," Cass said from the bathroom, where she riffled through a cabinet. "I think every blackfly bite creates a tiny infection, and if you clean it right away, you don't get the itch or the swelling. Just something I've noticed over the years." More sounds of bathroom items being shuffled. "I'm looking for a cotton pad or anything classier than TP . . ."

Elise peeked into River's room: his bunk bed ran straight across the window so that the other walls could house a desk and packed bookshelves that sagged under the weight of many spines. The bunks were empty. "Where's River?"

"Sleepover."

Elise paused in front of a collage of old photos in the hall. Cass as a one-year-old with hands in a chocolate birthday cake. Cass diving from a towering cliff. Cass and her parents with matching hippie headbands. And, right in the center, wrapped in a towel on the bow of a wooden boat, a deeply tanned teenage Cass, joyous and relaxed, her hair untamed in the wind. She was sitting on the lap of an equally summery and contented Matt.

"Here we are." Cass was holding a dripping cotton pad that smelled like gasoline. She moved into what was likely her room and motioned to the bed. Patted the red tartan duvet, which was folded down to expose sheets dotted with tiny pink roses. "Come. Sit."

Elise dropped to the edge of the mattress and allowed the woman to press the dripping pad to her ankle while she looked around.

The bedroom floor was strewn with kicked-off jeans, T-shirts, and tanks. A lacy black bra. But the real attention grabbers were on the walls. Black-and-white photographs again, all nudes. Of Cass. Elise stared at the rounded curve of her ass, the pinkness of her labia and the fullness of those breasts. One of Cass swollen with motherhood, her perfectly formed forest child in her womb.

A child whose whereabouts were not a question that might never be answered.

Elise stood. "Thanks. I should go."

"Are you sure? You could sleep in River's bunk bed . . ."

Not a chance. As Elise crossed the room, a cellphone pinged on the dresser. She couldn't help but glance.

At nearly three in the morning, her motel-staying husband had just texted the girl next door.

Back at the cabin, Elise sat on Gracie's bed, where her daughter's tiny stuffed animals were still arranged around the pillow. She lay down carefully and, hoping Gracie would approve, raised her arm and let her hand find the animal most in need of her love. Her fingers found a small frog, his legs stretched out long, as if running away from something scary. Or, perhaps, toward something wonderful. He had a loop of string sewn into his back so he could hang from a Christmas tree.

It was a good sign, Elise thought.

Turning onto her side, she coiled her body around the frog and inhaled what little remained of her daughter's scent on the pillow.

CHAPTER 33

·········

Matt had dodged Garth's calls all night and knew he had a slew of messages waiting. Very likely Wolfe's offer was in, and there'd been more than one local news story about real estate prices dropping as a result of Gracie going missing. Garth was probably in a panic to accept the offer while it was still on the table. There was a lot of money at stake for Garth, too.

One thing at a time.

Matt cracked open the twist top of his six-dollar bottle of wine and looked around the motel room for a glass. The Saran-wrapped plastic cup would do. He poured. Sipped and grimaced. Engine oil would taste better.

The clarity he'd had since moving to the motel was remarkable. It was as if the fog had lifted and he'd sprung into action, knowing exactly what he needed to do. It was after three a.m. and he didn't have the slightest inclination to sleep.

Music thumped quietly from his iPhone—Queen's "Bohemian Rhapsody." He turned it up and poured more wine as he surveyed the notes he'd been studying for hours, spread out on the fake wood table in the corner of his room. To-dos.

First thing in the morning, he would email Barrans to say he wouldn't be accepting the partnership. Nor would he be coming back at all. At this point, all he could determine was where he *didn't* want to be.

What his future would contain would be his daughter. And this baby. He would get Gracie back, along with full custody of both kids. He'd handled enough divorce cases to know his chances were good.

Was that banging on the door? He looked through the peephole to see nothing but insects buzzing around in the eerie yellow light beneath the covered walkway. Another thump, this time clearly from the wall. Matt banged back. His music wasn't that loud.

Next on the list was to call Dorsey. Tell him to update Matt simultaneously with Elise from here on. Then there was Cass's book launch. And after that, he'd spend the day systematically researching his grandfather's former debtors. Figure out a way to make restitution with each and every one of them. Matt had never questioned his identity before. He'd had the good fortune not to need to—or so he'd thought. He was born of decent people. The First Family of the Adirondacks.

Fucking joke of a lifetime.

He had to atone; it was that simple. And fast. It would lead to his daughter. You did good shit, good shit happened.

Not until these land investigations were complete would he speak to Garth.

He refilled his plastic cup. Toasted his newfound drive.

There was one more person on his to-do list. He picked up his phone and stared at the text he'd sent twenty minutes before: "I left Elise."

Moments later, Cass was in the doorway, a bottle of wine, a flowered pillow, and a red tartan duvet in her arms. "I refuse to sleep on motel bedding," she said. She looked around at the nearly empty wine bottle, his notes, the untouched bed he should have been hunkered down in. "What's going on here, Sorenson?" She picked up his wet towel. "It's three thirty in the morning . . ."

He grabbed her and kissed her deeply, the door closing with a thump. His pelvis mashed hard into hers as he pressed her against the wall. Cass pulled away long enough to throw her duvet cover over the polyester bedspread, then tugged a shirtless Matt on top of her. "You okay, buddy boy?"

He kissed her again, then sat up to rub his jaw. "I can't lie still."

"You are way strung out," she said, leaning up on one elbow. She patted the duvet. "Lie back. Let's pull your energy earthward, wind you down. Let me give you a little massage. I'll make you sleep like a baby."

"I just need to send a quick email." He jumped up and went to the table—his master control center. He opened his laptop and started to type a Dear John letter to the man who'd offered him a piece of the company.

"Can't it wait until morning—actual morning? You need to rest."

He shook his head as he typed. "No. I have to quit my job."

"Wait, stop!" She crawled across the bed and leaned over his computer, pulled his hands away. "You're not thinking straight. Don't make a decision like that right now . . . hyper and drunk and"—she started to laugh, looking at him in his underwear—"unbelievably hot."

"I'm not drunk."

"You're still unbelievably hot. Plus, you need to sleep."

"I'll be able to sleep once I send this." He held up a finger to hush her for a moment and focused on his screen. He needed to word his resignation very carefully.

The dream was one he never wanted to wake from. He was walking along Whiteface Inn Lane, just north of 86. Gunner trotted by his side. They passed cabins that sat tight to the road and curving driveways flanked with massive stone walls and elaborate landscaping that hinted of large houses tucked just out of sight. It was late September. The summer foliage was tinged with scarlet sugar maples and sumac, orangey-red smoke bush, and pinkish-yellow katsura trees—all fragrant with hints of brown sugar. Gunner heard it first—the yipping of puppies up a long, rutted driveway lined with trees cracked and craggy from brutal winter storms. The happy barking led them to a tumbledown kennel made of particle board, two-by-fours, and peeling black paint. A corrugated metal roof had rusted gashes. Must have leaked something terrible.

Gunner rushed forward to push the busted door open. As Matt approached, he heard Gunner's tail thwacking the walls. The dog yelped excitedly. Matt burst inside to the sweetest sight possible: Gracie grinning on the concrete floor, her freckled nose scrunched up in delight as Gunner licked her face.

Matt scooped her up. With Gunner dancing around his feet, Matt held his daughter so tight they almost became one. Her soft cheek against his. Hair scented with Johnson's baby shampoo in his eyes, his mouth, nearly weightless arms around his head. Finally, Gracie pulled away to look at him. She held up a finger in mock admonishment. "What took you so long, Daddy? I waited forever . . . "

It was just past sunup and Cass was grinning at him, snapping photos as he rolled over in bed. "Someone was out like a light."

"I didn't mean to sleep." He rubbed the hollows above his eyes, checked the clock: 5:12. "I dreamed I found her. God, she was so perfect. The way she smiles big and can't keep her eyes open. Sweet freckled nose and cheeks."

"It's a sign."

Yes. It had to be. *Please let it be.*

"It's going to happen." She took his bearded chin between thumb and forefinger. "Matty, we're going to find her, you hear me? I'm witchy about these things."

"When I find her . . . I've been thinking I should stay. Gracie loves it here. And I need to start from scratch. Recreate my life. I can run my own practice. I've already seen a place I can work out of. Gracie can go to school in town." He paused. He'd need a nanny at home for the baby, but he could work from home more while the child was young. "I can do this. Get a puppy. A German shepherd."

"Is Elise just going to walk away?"

"I'll wind up with custody, without a doubt. I'm Gracie's primary caregiver. Elise can make her own choices. This is where we will be."

Cass turned onto her stomach and rested her chin on one fist. Gazed at him with those honey-colored eyes. She was truly striking—a watery spray of caramel freckles across her nose, thick copper lashes—even in the tragic light of the Swiss Miss Motel.

"Did we, uh . . . ?" he asked, wincing. "Last night?"

She laughed, slid a hand up his chest. "We did not. Believe me, if we did"—she played with the hairs on his chest—"you'd remember."

He held her fingers. "I really think I could do this. Live here."

"I could handle that." Cass moved on top of him in lacy tank top and thong, all pillowy breasts and wild hair and soft lips. Kissed his bearded jawline to his earlobe. "Right now, I could handle a lot of things."

So could he. Matt tugged off her panties, slipped her top over her head, and let his fingers explore the wonder that was Cass Urquhart's body. Then, for the first time in thirty-three years, he lost himself in the woman he'd never gotten out of his thoughts.

CHAPTER 34

·······

Elise woke up just after eight in the morning, toy frog still in her hand, to the high-pitched crystal ping of her cellphone. Bleary, she sat up in Gracie's bed to fish around in the covers, eventually finding her phone between mattress and headboard—no doubt nudged there by her daughter's tiny dejected animals. An email had come in.

It was from her father.

Lisey,

I haven't felt right about intruding, given what hell you're facing. But the police spoke to me yesterday, so I'm guessing you've heard that I'm here ... staying at some god-awful fishing lodge up the lake, have been all week. Imagine moldy walls, zero water pressure, and a stow-away beetle in my suitcase hoping to wind up anywhere but this place.

Asbestos be damned, I came here to see you. Unless you reply, I'll be at your dock—eastern shoreline with the black boathouse, big S over the door?—around 11:30.

Dad

She immediately tapped out: "No. Please don't." But didn't press send. She got up, restless, and paced the upstairs bedrooms. Her mind was awhirl. She hadn't expected this reaction—after all, it had been twenty years—but part of her wanted to see Warren.

She went downstairs and stared at her handbag on the kitchen table. Matt had always believed her sensitivity about anyone touching the purse was driven by possessiveness. But it wasn't that at all. She reached inside, dug beneath the stiff leather bottom piece to pull out a stack of unopened envelopes. The first few were addressed to Lisey Bleeker, but later he'd started addressing them to Lisey Sorenson. She spread them out and examined them, reorganizing them by date posted.

Was it time to finally open them . . . hear what her father had to say for himself?

In her mind's eye, that day had been unusually hot and muggy for September. Elise had just started eleventh grade and had stayed late after school to sort out some confusion—she and another girl had both been assigned the same locker. The other girl was a senior, so she had priority. Elise was assigned another locker down an airless hallway by the gym and had spent the better part of an hour setting it up. Aware that her mother might be starting to worry, Elise jogged the whole way home and arrived sweaty and parched.

As she drew near, Elise could see that Rosamunde had turned on the sprinkler and forgotten about it. There were deep pools of water on the driveway, even on the lawn. She followed the snaking hose to the garage and tugged hard on the metal handle.

The door wasn't halfway up before Elise smelled the exhaust. Strapped into the passenger seat, where she used to sit when she was married and her husband did most of the driving, was Rosamunde, her face calm and expressionless. Her skin translucent and—for the first time—free of makeup. She'd had her hair cut to the chin and smoothed straight. She wore a white blouse Elise had never seen and the navy skirt Warren had deemed to be "business casual." This Roxborough Rosamunde was so very compact. Smiling and composed. Sure of herself, finally, in death.

Now, Elise stared down at the envelopes from her father. Never, in all the years since Rosamunde died, had her profound grief, the agony that could bring her to her knees if she stayed still long enough, been anything less than resolute. It had been the flag she planted in the ground that day in the garage, certain it was immovable.

Until now. For the first time in her life, the image of her mother sitting in the car with the motor running brought anger. Not even anger—that was too tame. Fury.

How could she? Rosamunde was a parent. So goddamned what if her husband had walked out? She had a daughter who needed her. Who—she had to have known—would be the one who would pull up that garage door and find her. Who she was leaving so alone in the world that Elise would spend the rest of her life on the run, so filled with sorrow for all that had befallen her mother that she would harden and grow fierce with resolve and ambition and drive. Who, as Rosamunde must have realized, would misdirect her resentment and aim it squarely at her only remaining parent, a man she would have no choice but to hate.

Rosamunde didn't take away one parent from Elise; she took away both.

Elise thought back to those nights in her airless room in North Carolina. How she'd pondered all the possible reasons other aspiring Olympians might have to make such profound sacrifices in their lives. Of course, you could throw in Academy Award and Nobel Prize winners. Those who climbed Everest. Any pinnacle strived for that almost no one reaches. If you examined the childhoods of those who worked hardest, those who forfeited so much in their lives to win whatever prize they sought, would you find any who felt whole from the start? Or, like Elise, did they simply find themselves so broken one day that they would spend the rest of their lives trying to prove they had worth?

Had Elise done anything remotely as despicable with Gracie?

She'd cut her thumb. She'd run to the shed. And someone out there had capitalized on those moments she was absent. Someone out there—for whatever reason—had gone and done the unconscionable.

Elise ran a fingertip across her name on one of Warren's letters. It occurred to her, like the light of dawn peeling back the night sky, that all these years she'd been running from the wrong person.

....

CHAPTER 35

The Sunday morning crowd at the Bookworm was full of tourists, mostly baby boomers—Matt was certain everyone in attendance had grown up pondering the identity of the Woodstock Girl. Cass couldn't have looked more the part. Natural and summery in faded jeans with frayed cuffs, leather flip-flops, and a creamy, loose-knit sweater.

She was terrific in front of her audience. Held the mic to her lower lip as she admitted that day at Woodstock was the day her life really began. The photographer had been a scruffy redheaded guy, college age, with a bag of camera equipment. She followed him around and he taught her how to find the beauty shot within every frame. He let her practice with his Polaroid camera, then gifted it to her. Cass reached into her bag now and pulled it out to excited oohs and aahs. "When they stopped making these a few years back, I bought out every package of film left. Course, now they sell them everywhere." She looked through the lens at the audience, snapped a one-handed photo, pulled it out, and fanned herself with it. Her laugh was throaty. "I've always said, people look their best in Polaroids."

Matt leaned against a table in the travel section, baseball cap pulled low to avoid being recognized. With his beard, he was fairly certain no one but the staff had so much as glanced his way. Also, he could best observe the street from this vantage point. Ridiculous, of course. No one would be parading his daughter past the bookstore.

He'd sent Barrans his resignation. Caught up with Dorsey on communications—the latest was a psychic certain Gracie had been taken to the Netherlands. She'd seen a vision of her squatting in a wooden child carrier on a bicycle ridden by a blond man. There were windmills. Tulips.

A woman in a long flowered dress and drapey bead necklaces put up a hand to get Cass's attention. "Which day was the photo taken? It doesn't look as crowded as I've always imagined Woodstock to be."

"Good eye," Cass said. "This was Monday morning—because of the rain, they'd extended the schedule. The crowd had shrunk down from half a million on the weekend. The day was dismal, and in every direction you looked, the muddy, sloppy field was splotched with lumps of soaking-wet sleeping bags and backpacks. I remember thinking it looked like a field of dead dogs. Everywhere was this sort of sad aftermath. But still, it was an intimate vibe. It was, 'Look at us, the lucky ones, still here.'"

The crowd was rapt. The only movement came from the store's owner, soundlessly checking on the coffee, the tidiness of the books; she'd been careful to avoid Matt and his aura of tragedy. Now, she moved past him with a hushed "Pardon me." Her name tag caught his attention: VAL REISER. Wait, this was the source of the Annie Leibovitz comparison—the bookstore owner?

"I was goofing around until Hendrix launched into that crazy edition of 'The Star-Spangled Banner.' I mean, his amps were so freaking loud, and at first he played it sort of as is, then—I'm sure some of you guys remember it—he went mad crazy with the feedback from his amp. Used it to mimic bombs dropping, jets racing, people wailing . . . holy shit, was it something. That was the moment the picture was taken. This photographer I'd been hanging with, he went nuts snapping people's reactions. I mean, people were dropping to their knees, pulling out their *hair*. Some weren't even breathing, it was so intense.

"So everyone was strung out and way inside their own heads with what they'd just heard. Then Hendrix went into 'Purple Haze' and everybody started dancing like it was their last moment on earth. I'll never, ever forget it—or that nameless soul who snapped the photo and sparked in me a forever love of the lens." She held a hand up. "Thank you for coming, folks."

A thunder of applause. Val took the mic to thank Cass, thank the crowd for coming. She invited all in attendance to help themselves to refreshments and be sure to bring their books to the table where Cass would soon be signing.

Her face flushed, Cass sauntered over to Matt and stood, flipping her hair off her face. "I survived."

"You were *so* natural. Like you've been doing this all your life." He glanced at his watch. "Listen, I've got to head—"

"Wait." She reached up to touch his jaw. "I was thinking before I went on . . . I love today. Waking up with you. Looking across the room just now to see you there waiting. Feels . . . like the way things should be."

Maybe it was time for them to rewrite history, he thought. River and Gracie adored each other. Cass could sell her place, he'd sell his, and they'd start fresh. He'd *always* wanted a son. And there'd be no more perfect little girl for Cass than Gracie.

Then there was the baby. Cass would be wonderful with an infant.

It would be an idyllic life—probably the one he was meant to lead.

So why was his heart thumping?

Cass laughed and looked toward the back of the store, shaking her head. "Okay. Heard you loud and clear."

"Don't say that. It's just so soon."

"I wasn't proposing. We shared a very romantic morning. Passionate."

"I know. It's just . . . I don't even have my daughter back yet. I'm not ready to think about romance or passion, if that makes sense."

Val waved to Cass from across the room. There was a lineup of people clutching books at the signing table, excited to chat with the Woodstock Girl in person.

Before Cass walked away, she said, "That's the thing about romance and passion, Matty. The last thing either should do is make sense."

·········

CHAPTER 36

Her arms had long since stopped aching from burying and unburying the dead animals, but the cramping in her belly had steadily grown worse. Now, Elise was hit with enough heavy nausea that she put Warren's letters away and made her way back to the medical clinic on Highway 86. This time, a receptionist was there—a huge-eyed girl with a pointed face all but hidden by two sheets of glossy hair. A mouse in the curtains. When Elise asked for Dr. Jennifer Upton, the mouse shook her tiny nose. "I'm so sorry, Mrs. Sorenson. Dr. Upton's not working today."

No. Elise needed Jennifer Upton, with her gentle authority and her cool hands and her life-giving advice. "Is she on call? Can she drop in?"

"I'm afraid she's incommunicado on Sundays. Family time."

The girl's face morphed into a rat's now. How dare she say "family time" to Elise, when she clearly knew who she was? And how dare this Dr. Upton make Elise need her and love her, tell her to return with any problem and then, when there *was* a problem, have taken off to mother someone else?

"But she did leave instructions, if you did come back, to send you straight to Oliver."

Elise forced calmness into her voice. "That would be good."

In minutes, she was paper-gowned and lying on her back, bare abdomen slathered in cold gel, the lights overhead permanently singeing her retinas, and Oliver once again jammed into the tight place between exam table and wall.

"Not to worry," he said, digging the Doppler down around her left ovaries. "Whatever's going on, we can deal with it. Sometimes a bit of remaining tissue gets infected. The important thing is, you knew to come in."

He probed harder, toward the center now, pressing so deep she gasped.

"See anything?"

"I do." He squinted at the screen, his expression dour. Pushed hair behind his ears and, wiggling the Doppler, moved closer. "Yeah. I think I know what's going on here." The screech of his wheeled stool. "Can you excuse me a moment?"

What choice did she have?

The wait was short. Almost immediately, Oliver was back at his post and armed with his magic wand. "I'm an ultrasound tech. I'm not usually authorized to give patients any sort of diagnosis. But I got the okay just now." He turned the screen around so Elise could see, and worked the Doppler down around her lower abdomen again. He turned up the volume and the wavering, vaguely underwater swish of her body filled the room.

"You see that there?" He pointed to a black hole in the mottled gray clouds, then a ghostly keyhole shape. "That's what we're focused on." He slid the wand to the right. "Almost got what I want. There." He looked at Elise and grinned as the room filled with a speedy, rhythmic *swoosh, swoosh, swoosh*.

Elise looked up at Oliver, stunned. Could it be?

Oliver's smile spread across the entire room. "That's your baby's heartbeat, Mrs. Sorenson. You're eight weeks pregnant."

CHAPTER 37

....

With the crowd around Cass thinning out, Matt stood at the food station, trying to spread cream cheese on an everything bagel, sending seeds skittering across the tablecloth and onto the floor. The more he tried to clean it up, the more cream cheese appeared on his hands, his forearms, and his jeans.

"Cass is going to kill me for being so late. Listed a condo over at Whiteface, took forever." Garth had appeared beside him to fill a Styrofoam cup with coffee. "So, Wolfe's offer is in, if you have a minute to sit down and go over it."

Matt picked up his bagel only to have it fall apart in his hand and hit his shirt on the way to the floor. He grabbed a handful of napkins and wiped down his shirt, the carpet. Even more napkins to clean his hands. "Yeah. I think I need a bit of time."

If Garth was surprised, he didn't show it. "Expires at midnight. We don't want him to walk . . . Another piece of land's come on the market on Lower Saranac."

"Man, it's so hot with the lights on, all the people." Cass's face was flushed as she fanned her neck with the collar of her sweater. She gave Garth a look. "Were you even here?"

"You kidding? I was at the back the whole time."

"Turns out my grandfather owes all these families money . . . or land," Matt said. "I don't even know the extent of it. I have to figure it all out before I make any decisions."

Garth paused. "But wouldn't it be better to settle up from a place of security? It's a *lot* of cash. You could pay back God and still be fine."

Certainly he could take the money, then figure out who was owed what. But these people would never be able to buy back their land once it went to a resort.

"Matty, you need this money," Cass said.

"Believe me when I say, Lake Placid has become a buyer's market catastrophically lean on buyers right now," Garth said.

"I have a plan. I have to stick to it."

"You're not thinking straight," said Cass. "Whatever's up with these families, it happened a long time ago."

"When it happened isn't the issue." Jesus fucking Christ. People needed to back off. "I have to do this. Everything hinges on it. *Everything.*"

"Cassidy?" Val's arms were tucked through those of two kids with pale red hair and freckles, in or around their late twenties. "You aren't going to believe who these two are: Nicholas and Sophia Redondo. Their father took the photo. Hatch Redondo."

"We were so stunned when we saw your book cover online." Sophia appeared nervous as she took Cass's hand in her own.

"Dad would be over the moon right now if he were alive." Nicholas was flushed. "To see you doing so well—a photographer, no less."

"Wow. I don't even know what to say." Cass didn't appear nearly as excited as Matt imagined she should. She looked truly stunned. "You're sure it was him?"

"Totally," Sophia said. "That photo was on our fridge our entire lives. It was like we grew up with you."

"He never knew who sent it to *Life*. He would have had their heads." Nicholas laughed. "He hated publicity."

"How long ago did he die?" Cass asked.

"About five years ago. He and Mom were hiking in the Andes. Soph and I take care of his estate now. None of his photographs had anywhere near the success of that one. Dad was a total hippie; he didn't care. It was all about making art. Not selling it."

"We're pretty proud of him. And protective." His sister winced politely. "We'd really love it if you gave him a posthumous credit somehow."

"Well." Cass glanced at Matt and Val. "Of course, let's discuss it. I mean, I literally didn't even know your father's name. But I'm happy to do whatever it takes to make good, obviously."

"Look at this." Val beamed as they exchanged numbers. "History being made at my little bookshop. Isn't life funny."

Chapter 38

Elise returned to the cabin in a trance. Pregnant. A real, solid, healthy pregnancy—Oliver had confirmed it. She didn't have to lie down with her feet up or cross her fingers or pray to Mother Nature. She was free to be herself. The baby had been there the whole time. Maybe the embryo implanted late or maybe Elise had been wrong about her dates. Didn't matter. She was pregnant.

She sat on the back porch now and opened every envelope Warren had sent over the years. She'd expected page after page of empty platitudes about silver linings, and how much he missed her, and how much she would love her new seventeen-years-younger half-sister. But that wasn't what he'd sent at all.

Every envelope contained a single Polaroid of Elise in his banged-up aluminum fishing boat on "Lake Puddlejump," really not much bigger than a large suburban pond where he'd taught her to fish—Elise in her boxy red lifejacket, Elise piercing a worm with a hook, Elise holding a sandwich crust over the boat's side to unsuccessfully entice a loon.

The loon's call had been their shared magic. Every time you heard it, they'd decided, something wonderful was about to happen.

She stared at the photos for a while. Then put them away to fill the bath with hot water and lie still until it went cold. Finally, she soaped, shampooed, scrubbed her arms and legs pink with a loofah, and dunked. Climbed out onto the cotton mat, dripping and cool.

She combed her hair back and secured it at the base of her neck, then examined her face. Skin pulled taut. Eyes wider, somehow. Like the stag, maybe they'd taken in too much. Before pulling on a bathing suit and shorts, she looked at her belly. Was there a slight swell or was that hopeful thinking?

Gracie would have beautiful news to come home to.

The lake's surface glittered as she waited on the dock. Coming toward her in a bright red canoe was the man who had promised her the world and then walked away with it. His paddle stroke was as crisp and smooth as it had ever been. He wore a floppy gray fishing hat covered in lures, just like his old blue one. His frame seemed brittle; his shoulders narrower. He put up a hand to wave.

That same toothy grin as he reached the dock. "Lisey. All grown up."

She pulled the canoe perpendicular to the dock and reached for the rope to tie it. "Come. We can sit inside on the porch. I made coffee."

He set the paddle across his thighs. "I think better with a fishing rod in my hands. You know that. Hop in."

Somewhere south of Hawk Island, he laid his paddle down beneath the seats and they sat face-to-face. She noticed that her navy blue polish on fingers and toes was peeling from when she'd painted it on with Gracie. Warren reached into a rusted coffee tin for bait.

"You still have the same can," she said.

He waited until the lid squeaked back on and the worm he'd punctured stopped squirming. When he drew the rod back, a little red and yellow bob bounced on the line.

"This one does the job just fine."

"So did Mom."

Hesitation in the rod before he cast. The bob landed with a tiny plop. "I deserved that."

A seaplane flew low overhead with a deep hum. They both tilted their chins up to watch as it cruised toward the north shore and the mountains beyond. They waited to see if the bob moved at all, and when it didn't, Warren reeled his line back in to cast again. "You remember when you used to love baiting the hooks?"

"I hated baiting hooks."

"Not true. When you were very small, you insisted on baiting both our hooks. One day you pricked your finger and blamed it on the worm. You thought he had teeth. You were about eight."

"Gracie's age."

He shook his head sadly. "Couldn't believe it when I saw the news. I saw the picture and thought, she looks just like my Lisey." He reeled in his line very slowly, pausing to jiggle the bait. Then cast again.

"You haven't seen me in a while."

He reached into his tackle box and pulled out another envelope addressed to her, unsent, and put it in her hands. "Go ahead. Open it."

She stuck a finger in the flap and ripped it open. Glanced up at him before pulling out the photo. There she was atop Indie, her freestyle test completed, saluting the judges. It had been taken at Tryon, the day she got long-listed. "You were there?"

"I was. And then I drove up to New Jersey because I thought you might be at Ronnie's the next morning. I was going to leave this for you, but when he said you'd all come up here . . . I figured I'd stop in on my way home to Vermont instead."

"You left the flowers at the wrong house."

"I had the right house." He smiled sadly. "I just lost my nerve and left them next door. Didn't want to put you on the spot. I figured you'd maybe call when you got them, so I stayed overnight."

"And then it happened."

"And I don't plan to leave until you have your little girl back in your arms." He folded the worm onto itself and pierced it twice to better secure it on the hook. Started to cast and stopped. Looked at her. "Want to try?"

She took it from him. "So light."

"They make them better nowadays. Like most things." He watched her cast smooth and far. Smiled his approval. "Fathers included, I hope."

She didn't comment. Slowly began to reel the line back in. "Remember my old rod? Covered with pony stickers?"

He nodded. "I still have it."

"Gracie is just the same. Stickers all over her crutches." Elise cast again and slowly reeled her lure back in.

"He a good father, Matt?"

"The best."

She cast again, then shifted to a more comfortable position on the canoe seat.

"You want to catch a fish, you gotta stay still. Move around too much and you scare them off."

"Sitting still isn't my strong point. Don't think it's yours either, outside of a rowboat." Elise reeled in the line all the way. Just as she pulled it up, not twenty feet away, a pair of loons surfaced. They drifted past in their sleek, dark beauty. The male let out a long, haunting cry that bounced off the shorelines.

They looked at each other. *Something wonderful.* If only.

"Loons mate for life," he said. "I didn't know that back then."

"Probably a topic we should stay away from." When the hook was out of the water and dripping, she handed the rod back to Warren.

"Briony finally came to her senses and left me." He pointed to a scar on his cheekbone. "But not before sending Big-Mouth Billy sailing into my head."

"Mom would never have done that."

"Your mother was all elegance. She handled my big dreams and lousy follow-through in one manner, Briony handled it another. Lost my shirt in that divorce. So . . . I've decided to relieve women everywhere of my shit and live out my days as a lonely fisherman." He waited a moment. "Is this a good time to mention that your half sister wants to meet you? Chloe Diane. I drive down to stay with her every other weekend when Briony is at her boyfriend's. You'd like Chloe."

"We should get back. I didn't bring my phone."

"You're the boss." He set down the rod and grabbed his paddle, pointed them back toward civilization. "Mentioned I'm staying at a little fishing lodge up on Barrel Bay. Pretty out there, but plenty rustic. No electricity. Outhouse is a long walk through the woods. I had to drive into town just to get a cell signal. Emailed you from outside Starbucks."

He dipped his paddle into the water, pulled hard, then turned the paddle away from the canoe without a sound. The perfect J-stroke. "Kostick and Sons Fishing Lodge. Nice enough guy just opened it. Retired. Always been his dream."

"Andy just fixed our roof. We know him."

"Lives out there in the bush with his granddaughter."

Elise thought about this. Why did it sound wrong?

"Never told me what the story is, why this kid's willing to live in a place where even the toilets are—"

She interrupted her father but spoke slowly, confused. "Andy has no family. Matt told me he has no family. We joked about it because of the 'Kostick and Sons.'"

"Well, I'm only going by what he tells—"

"Have you seen the girl?"

"No. She keeps to herself in their cabin most of the time because of all the bears. Has pet rocks, he said. Draws little animal faces on them. I've heard her boss them around, though." Warren chuckled to himself. "Real character. She picks one rock at a time to hug. Teaches them discipline or some such thing."

"Dad. Dad, that's Gracie!" Elise stood, wobbling the vessel side to side. She looked up the lake as if she might be able to see her. "That's Gracie—the doled-out hugs, the fear of bears—"

"Sit back down before you sink us! I'll get us there."

"No—I don't want anyone to see me in the boat. I'll swim—you follow."

"Wait!" Warren braced the paddle across the thwart and leaned his weight over it. Elise dove off the canoe, feeling it rock beneath the balls of her feet as she plunged into the cold, heavy depth of the lake and started to swim.

Chapter 39

....

Lake Placid Public Library was tucked away between Main Street and Mirror Lake. White clapboard, with a Norman Rockwell front porch. The place was historically significant: Melvil Dewey himself had been instrumental in the library's growth, donating newspaper and magazine subscriptions.

Matt stepped into the comforting fragrance of old books and waxed floors and looked around, his head afloat from lack of sleep. He'd developed a tic in one eyelid.

At the microfiche, downing black coffees from a machine, Matt discovered five properties his grandfather had swindled from their rightful owners, and managed to come up with some sense of where these families had later settled.

He'd never been one to buy lottery tickets, but if there was a chance in hell this would bring Gracie back, he'd hunt down every person his grandfather had even bumped into in a store, short-changed in a poker game, or cut off in the fast lane of the I-87.

He rubbed at his spasming lid.

....

Lyman Williams—the first of that name—rested in North Elba Cemetery on Old Military Road. Matt had bicycled or jogged through it many times when he was younger without sparing a single thought for who might be buried within. Williams' gravestone was slender and tall. Gray stone, the edges softened by lichen. Along the bottom platform, the name WILLIAMS in block letters. On the face, both Lyman Williams' name and his wife's, Hannie Williams, whose headstone matched his. He had died in 1897, Hannie five years later.

Nate Sorenson was fifty-five when he foreclosed on the Williamses' land for an unpaid debt of $13,000. Matt tried to imagine the full narrative—what Nate told his wife, what he told Matt's father, and mostly what he told himself about throwing a hardworking family with two young children out of their home, taking their land, and leaving them without an income.

A twig snapped behind him. Matt turned to see Lyman.

"Thank you for coming," Matt said.

"He was a sheep farmer," Lyman said, looking down at the headstone. "Came here with his wife and two kids. They bushwhacked their way onto a plot given to them by New York State's wealthiest abolitionist before the Civil War, then built a cabin out of the trees they'd felled. Gerrit Smith offered land parcels to three thousand black men to so they could have the right to vote in state elections, learn how to farm, keep themselves and their families safe from slavery. The effort was called Timbuctoo. This land—it was rocky and treed, the winters were harsh. Not many of the families were able to make a go of it. But mine did. My ancestors sold off part of their original farm plot, but they went on to found a school, a church. And here we are today."

Matt recalled the sign he'd spotted as Dorsey drove them through the crowd on John Brown Road. "So that was you accepting an award last week at the John Brown place? On behalf of your ancestors?"

He nodded. "Timbuctoo was the reason Brown settled here in the first place."

The ceremony had honored the man whose descendants Nate would one day swindle. The sun suddenly grew unbearably hot. Matt rolled up his sleeves. "Your family owned thirty-seven percent of the land I'm selling. There's no way for me to immediately sever it and return to you what's rightfully yours, but I want to give you thirty-seven percent of my sale price."

Lyman said nothing.

"Your land's worth a lot of money." The stretch of wooded shoreline had a sandy inlet and an archipelago of smooth rocks that reached out into the lake; Matt used to hop from stone to stone as a child. But for his grandfather's greed, it would have been Lyman and his sister who spent their childhoods playing on those rocks. "More than half a million."

"I appreciate what you're doing, Sorenson. But what's done is done—"

"I realize it's nothing in the face of what your family lost. I can't undo what my grandfather did. Please don't walk away from this."

A crow in a tree cawed. Another answered back.

"I don't take handouts."

Long after Lyman had gone, Matt continued to stare at the Williamses' headstones.

....

CHAPTER 40

Elise lifted her head from the water a moment, heart hammering, lungs paining. For all the years of wind sprints, of cross-training, of riding until the seam of her briefs cut into her skin and made her bleed, all the mucking stalls until her hands blistered and mucking more stalls until the blisters split, the schooling when it was so cold she had to ride with no saddle, the cold-water-bath plunges Ronnie promised would sharpen her focus, the endless pushups and lunges and power yoga classes that made lying in a grave sound like relief—never had she pushed her body harder.

The canoe was gliding along behind her. Warren held a hand low in greeting.

With electric jolts firing from every cell, Elise caught her breath and looked toward the shore. The lodge appeared, from the water anyway, to be made up of a main building surrounded by cabins so small they likely didn't hold more than a bed. About eight or ten of them dotted the piney hillside, looking down at the shoreline. A couple of smaller docks ran perpendicular to the shore, along with one long central dock that had seen better days. Near the end of the long dock was a dilapidated hut. It wasn't until she swam closer that Elise caught movement beside the little structure, a flash of green dress.

Can it be?

She ducked underwater and swam nearer, coming to the surface as quietly as she could, lest she attract the wrong attention. Another flash of green. Elise made sure to stay behind the dock in case anyone was watching from land. Bits of slimy plant life curled around her feet. She dove down, propelled herself underwater, and, with a mighty thrust, reached the end of the dock. She surfaced, worked herself to the corner to see, perched on the long side of the dock, leaning against the hut, the single most beautiful sight possible—a girl with messy blond hair who bounced her bare heels as she peered down into the water.

Gracie.

Elise waved frantically to her father, following behind her in the canoe, and motioned that he should paddle to a ladder at the end of the dock, just around the corner from Gracie. Anyone could look out and see them. Anyone could try to stop them.

Elise felt herself hyperventilating as she drew closer, willing with every stroke that no one would approach, that Gracie would stay put, that this would really be true. The stones were sharp beneath her feet as she struck land for a moment. Then the lake's bottom dipped down again. She moved closer, close enough to see Gracie humming, to see her tiny toes painted in chipped navy, like her own.

The bow of the canoe drew near the ladder.

"Gracie. Honey. It's Mommy."

Gracie scrambled to her feet. To Elise's shock, she did so without crutches.

Then the girl looked over toward the ladder and saw Elise's father pulling the canoe alongside dock. She started to whimper.

"It's okay, my big girl. Sweetheart." Elise found land beneath her feet, but just barely. "That's your grandpa . . . my dad. You're safe now. We're going to take you home." Elise held open her arms. "I need you to jump. I need you to hold your breath and jump into the water, okay?"

Gracie sat and scooted to the edge of the planks. "I'm scared."

"I know. But you're going to do it anyway. Fall toward me."

"But I've never gone underwater."

"Hey!" A male voice, yelling from up on the rise. Elise looked toward a row of tiny cabins—it wasn't Andy. It was a big bruiser of a man in a bathing suit and sweatshirt, coming out of his cabin. He started down the slope toward the beachfront. "What's going on down there?"

Warren was climbing out onto the ladder.

"Gracie, jump now!" Elise shouted.

"What the hell are you doing?" the man hollered.

"This is the time, sweetness! Lean forward and let yourself fall. You must trust me, okay? Let yourself fall, and then we're going to hold each other tight, okay?"

The man was running now. Warren was halfway up the ladder, but an old man was no match for this man's heft. "Andy!" the man called toward the main building. "Andy!"

Waves from a faraway speedboat sloshed over Elise's head and she lost her footing.

"What if I go under and can't find my way up?" Gracie said.

"Baby, I won't let you out of my sight. You're going to drop down and we'll both go under. But I'll be holding you. I won't let go. I'll pull you up. I will not let anything happen to you. Ever. You can do it. I'm strong and you're my girl."

Gracie looked back to see the fishing lodge guest running toward the dock. She tipped her upper body and, gripping the edge hard, locked eyes with Elise. Sucked in a big breath and, as her grandfather slipped back into the canoe and grabbed his paddle, she pushed away from the dock and let herself fall into her mother's arms.

The force pushed them both under. Elise grabbed Gracie first around the waist. Her feet hit the sandy bottom and she spun her daughter, took her hands. Through water the color of steeped tea, they saw wonderful suggestions of each other, bubbles escaping grinning mouths. In one heartbeat, Elise kissed Gracie's face and pulled her daughter close. Gracie's limbs wrapped around her tight, and with a mighty push, Elise shot them up through the water to burst into the dazzling yellow openness, the possibilities of a perfect summer sky.

....

CHAPTER 41

Matt walked into the cabin to the smell of burned coffee. The machine had turned itself off long enough ago that the coffee had grown cold. He dumped the thick black liquid down the drain, then filled the carafe with warm, soapy water.

A flash of movement down on the dock caught his eye. Matt went through the back porch and outside, down onto the path. An old man in a hat was bent over something in a canoe. Matt was about to call out, tell the confused tourist he had the wrong dock, when he saw Elise, hair wet and slicked to her head. Elise lifted someone up and turned around. Gracie.

Elise had their daughter.

He was already running.

Grinning so hard her eyes were pulled nearly shut, a dripping-wet Gracie tentatively half-walked, half skipped toward him. He scooped her up and held her tight, spinning her around and around. He caught sight of Elise as he turned. Her face streamed with tears.

CHAPTER 42

....

Elise pressed her face into her daughter's freshly shampooed hair, arms closed tight around the lithe little body on her lap. She closed her eyes and inhaled. There was a point, she thought to herself, when you no longer tried to contain the swell of your joy. It was simply too big and no longer yours to hoard. It emanated outward, upward. In her case, through the porch roof, the tips of the trees, all the way up to the pinky-gold light in the sky.

The evening was perfect. The table littered with dishes and wine bottles, a huge pot of spaghetti sauce drying up on the stove. Joni Mitchell playing on the stereo. Warren had made a big fire. Gracie was seated on her mother's lap and holding on to her father. She was watchful, wary—she hadn't said much, and the consensus was not to push her. She'd open up when she was ready. There hadn't been a moment, however, that she wasn't touching one or both of her parents. Or that one of them wasn't touching her. Smelling her. Kissing her.

Seeing their daughter in a dress given to her by her abductor was more than Elise and Matt could take. Their daughter was fully bathed and in her own jeans and hooded sweatshirt now, with thick socks. One blessing had been Gracie saying she'd changed her clothes in the Kostick cabin bathroom.

Conversation was kept deliberately benign.

Elise had no idea how Cass and River had worked themselves into the reunion, though she supposed it was no real surprise. Cass walked around snapping photos and fussing with dishes. River had started a big puzzle on the floor by the fireplace.

"I picked you up a nice chocolate cake in town, Gracie," said Cass as she went into the kitchen with dirty plates. "River says every kid on earth loves chocolate cake. Do you think that's true?"

Gracie pulled her mother's arm tighter across her body, like a seat belt.

"I always liked onion cake when I was a boy." Warren winked at her. "I could make you one tomorrow if you'd like."

"Onion," Matt repeated. "That sounds terrific."

River, by the fire, groaned. "That's dis-gusting."

"Not if you make it with pickle icing," said Warren. "And then you lay a few anchovies across the top for decoration. How does that sound, Gracie?"

River rolled on the ground, feigning nausea.

"It looks best if you lay a few worms or snakes around the plate," Warren elaborated, topping up wineglasses. "For garnish."

"Can you have it ready for breakfast, Dad?"

"Absolutely. Breakfast is when onions really bloom."

Gracie cracked the hint of a smile.

"Cake for breakfast, huh?" said Cass, nudging Matt. "You going to help make it?"

Without waiting for her husband's response, Elise turned her gaze back to her daughter.

"I prefer chocolate," Gracie said quietly.

"Well. I am honored," Cass said, as everyone breathed a sigh of relief. Every word Gracie spoke bolstered their hopes that she was going to be okay. "I'll bring it in."

Gracie sat forward. "What's going to happen to Andy?"

Everyone went silent. Elise rubbed Gracie's knee. "We don't know, hon. He did a very bad thing."

"He's a kidnapper!" said River, triumphantly. He used puzzle pieces as imaginary guns and shot the air. "He's going to jail."

"For real?" Gracie seemed worried. "He taught me to fish with a stick."

Warren leaned over, his elbows on the table. "Did you catch anything?"

Gracie shrugged.

"Your grandpa will teach you to fish with your very own rod," Matt said. "Like your mother used to do when she was your age."

Elise glanced at him, the nod to her family catching her by surprise.

"I still have your mother's rod," Warren said. "You can use that."

Ever since Warren had placed the call to Dorsey to tell him they had Gracie, Seldom Seen Road had been crawling with police, media, and curious neighbors and tourists, some of whom came in vehicles, some on foot. Apparently, the same thing was happening at their home in Montclair.

The police had been gracious. After Gracie was checked over at the hospital—never sliding off Elise's lap for a second—and found to be physically unharmed, they'd allowed the Sorensons to go home and settle in before asking too many questions. For that, Elise was grateful. No such compassion from the press, however. The phone in the kitchen had been ringing constantly since they got home. Every media outlet in the country wanted to give their audience a long-awaited happy ending. Elise had taken the phone off the hook.

Cass brought in the cake and dessert plates. "I love you with this beachy look, kiddo. Very natural. Very Adirondack." She leaned across the table, touched the soft strands of Gracie's washed but unbrushed hair. "Don't you think, Matty?"

Yes, Matty, don't you think? Elise held her daughter tighter.

"Did you try to get away?" River came to stand close to Gracie. "Did you ever punch stupid Andy and kick him?"

A loaded pause. Gracie swung her feet back and forth. "Andy said there were so many bears in the woods, if I tried to leave I would get eaten because they're starving to death. And he said when you stop trying to sell the cabin, he would bring me home."

Matt and Elise looked at each other quickly. That was what this was about—the sale?

"Why did you get in a stranger's car? You're not supposed to." River had returned to his puzzle on the floor. "Everyone knows that."

"He wasn't a stranger!" Gracie wasn't going to stand for being made to look uninformed or naive. "Plus, he promised me a turtle with a broken leg."

Elise and Matt were dumbfounded. Matt spoke first. "That was what did it? You got into his van because you wanted a turtle?"

"I wanted Paulie's turtle. Andy said we could catch up to Paulie and he'd drive me to camp after."

Matt rubbed his jaw and processed this. "You wanted it. And I said no."

"Don't." Elise reached out to squeeze Matt's hand. "She's here with us now. Nothing else matters."

"What's wrong?" Gracie asked.

"Everything is so right, nothing can ever be wrong again." Elise kissed the top of Gracie's head. "Daddy's just unbelievably glad to have you home. Like all of us."

Gracie accepted this. Then wiggled off Elise's lap. "I want to check on my animals." On the hearth were Gracie's twenty-five tiny animals, warming their hopeful faces. Gracie hoppity-skipped across the room, using the furniture for balance. She knelt and, one by one, pressed each toy to her chest, closed her eyes, and rocked it back and forth. Set it up on the hearth again, told it to be good or else, and picked up the next.

She stopped with her brown-and-white cow. "Andy used to work at Grandpa Nate's cow farm, Daddy. He showed me the picture. He said it was the only time he had his picture in the paper. The same picture as in Grandpa Nate's office."

Matt and Elise looked at each other. Both pushed their chairs back and rushed to Nate's office. There, in the faded photograph from the *Adirondack Times*, standing slightly behind Nate and a farmer—Andy. A boy on the edge of manhood.

"Oh my god," Elise said. "It *is* him."

"He was there when it was all happening," Matt said, thinking back to Andy's last day on the roof. *An eye for an eye is usually what happens.* "All that time, he knew what Nate was doing to his borrowers."

When Matt came down from helping Elise get Gracie into bed, Cass was on the sofa, feet tucked beneath her. The puzzle box was on her lap, and she was handing River pieces that might fit. Warren was stoking the fire, trying to get it roaring once again. A cool, more insistent breeze had gathered, ruffling the pages of the old magazines on the coffee table.

Warren looked up. "Everything okay?"

Matt nodded. "What a gift to see her snuggled under the covers, those crazy animals all around her pillow. I won't ever need a single thing after tonight." He topped up all the wineglasses, including Elise's, still on the dinner table.

Cass stood. Tilted her head toward the back door as if to signal to Matt that they should make an excuse to go down to the water together. No way. Not a chance. He pretended not to notice. And when Elise's father went to take another log from the old iron log holder, Matt jumped forward. "Here, Warren. Let me help you with that."

Chapter 43

....

I t was Monday evening. The rear balcony of the store-top apartment on Main Street overlooked a strip of grassy wilderness between the back of the buildings and Mirror Lake. If one looked straight down, the view was of the alley, the trash cans and parked cars. But sitting, the view was everything anyone would want it to be. And Lyman—or his sister—had done it up nicely: lights on either side of the back door, two navy Adirondack chairs, and a planter overflowing with ivy and evergreens.

As Lyman had led Matt through the house, they'd passed a walker, an assortment of pill jars on a table. A closed bedroom door.

"So, Andy Kostick." Lyman shook his head, his glasses perched in his long hair. "Felt sick when I heard it on the news yesterday. Like I should have sensed something was off with him. Guy lived right next door until last week."

"I still can't believe it," Matt said.

"All to prevent your sale?"

"That's what the police say. To rattle us." Matt glanced at Mirror Lake. "He figured a resort so close to his own property would ruin his business. Fishing lodge wants a whole lot of quiet."

"I was on the back roof that morning. You know how your roof-line is—different sections added over time. Andy did head out for coffee, but he came back quick. That's what I told the police. If he was gone any longer than he should have been, I didn't notice."

"None of us suspected him."

"I was home when they checked his apartment." Lyman motioned to the darkened balcony next to his. "Not sure they ever went out to his fishing lodge, though."

"They did. But it was pouring rain, and since Andy wasn't high on their list . . . we'd all said he was on the roof."

"I'll tell you, though—I never saw him look twice at your daughter."

If Andy knew about Nate, he knew what Nate had done to Lyman's family. All he'd been waiting for was an opportunity. Matt had been blaming Elise when it was his own grandfather's avarice that had likely laid the seed for Andy's actions. Wreaking havoc from the grave, even.

"Anyway. Your little girl is home."

"Elise and I are eternally thankful. It could've ended much, much worse."

They sipped beer, looked up at the pine boughs waving in the breeze.

"Anyway, that's not why I'm here." Matt sat forward and pulled out his grandfather's ledger book. He flipped to the Lyman page, pointed to the original loan amount. "I don't like the deal my grandfather struck. I mean, how do I even know your land was worth thirteen thousand?"

Lyman glanced at the number and met Matt's gaze. He waited a moment before speaking. "Don't tell me you're after more money, because that's not going to happen."

"It was a bum deal. And then you've got to consider the taxes we've paid all these years."

"What's done is done."

Matt had no choice but to make some sort of peace with who his grandfather had been. Jeannie had returned a call he'd made to her that morning to ask whether she could pull strings on the land severance issue. There were few people more connected in the village than Jeannie Robbins. She was more than happy to help do anything to prevent another resort from setting up on the east side of the lake. But before Matt hung up, she'd insisted he hear her out on the topic of his grandfather. "I'm going to say one last thing, and I want you to listen. Whatever else you take from what I've told you, this is the most important. No one person is all good or all bad. What your grandfather was to others does not change what he was to you. The man lived and breathed his grandson. You were everything to him until his last breath. And nobody can take that away from you."

"Not necessarily," Matt said now. "You've been saving for a property for you and your sister. Pay me back the thirteen grand and I'm willing to eat the taxes."

Two bats swooped by and lost themselves in trees.

"And that leaves me where?"

Matt held out his hand to shake. Lyman took it and started to laugh. "What the hell am I shaking on, Sorenson?"

"Upon receiving your check, I'll have been repaid in full. Which will officially make you the owner of one twenty-acre farm off Old Military Road and half an acre of waterfront on Lake Placid, just north of our place. I am not going through with the resort sale. After you refused a percentage in lieu of land, I found a way to come at it from a better angle. I've decided to sever the land first and sell only my family's original plot on the lake. All the other plots will be returned to their rightful owners or their descendants. It will take a bit of time to officially divide the waterfront land, but feel free to use it as your own until such time. Once it is severed, you can do with it whatever you like. Live there, sell it, place it under conservancy protection. You may not know this, but there's a small yellow cottage on your lake property, sits out over the water on a jutting rock. I've never been inside, but I looked through the windows. Looks like a living/dining space and kitchen, then two small bedrooms all on one floor. Heated by woodstove. Dry and in relatively good shape; whoever built it did a great job. Roof's solid. There's a bunch of keys in my grandfather's drawer. I'll see if any of them work. But it's yours. And you might as well make use of it."

A sly smile spread across Lyman's face. He shook his head, looked down at his shoes, and crossed his legs. "You got me good, Sorenson." He reached out and took Matt's hand. "And I'm really happy you have your little girl back."

When Matt pulled into his driveway, Cass was waiting on her porch steps, sitting with arms wrapped around her knees, smoking a cigarette and flicking the ashes into a Diet Coke can. As he climbed out of the car, she waved him over. "Wow. Big couple of days."

"The biggest."

"She's a beauty. Just an absolute joy."

"She is."

They were silent for a long time. "What happened with Redondo's kids?" Matt asked. "Did you get in touch?"

She shook her head, brushed a mosquito from the back of her hand. "People sniff out opportunity. Book's doing well. I have to be careful."

He thought back to the Redondo kids' faces. He'd bet his entire career they were sincere. "Even if you don't share the royalties, their father deserves a bit of posthumous recognition, no?"

"I don't want to talk about my book."

He let silence fall between them again. "Don't be stingy with your good fortune, Cass," he said at last. "Share it with Hatch Redondo. Put his name on the book when it goes for a second printing—give the guy his due credit. His photo made your career possible. He deserves it. His children and grandchildren deserve it."

"What is this—come down on Cass day?"

He half-grinned. "Maybe."

"Did you say anything to Elise?"

"About?"

"Us."

He nodded toward her cigarette. "You got another?"

She pulled one out, lit it with her own.

He took a long, satisfying drag. "It's not the time. Gracie has barely been home for twenty-four hours."

The screen door swept open with a long creak and a flushed River leaned against the doorjamb. "When are you coming in, Mom?"

"Soon."

He turned to look inside. "I don't want to be in the house alone. What if Andy comes here?"

"Andy's been arrested, toad. Go back up to bed. I'll be there in a few minutes."

River cast Matt a disgruntled look and left.

"Now that she's back, he's hit harder. Go figure."

"Go ahead in, then. He needs you."

She glanced at Matt sideways. Wind ruffled a long curl across her mouth and she tucked it behind her ear, then flicked ashes into the soda can. "And you don't."

He didn't answer.

"Okay, okay. I get it. Not the right time."

"My whole life has been turned upside down. I'm seeing what's salvageable."

"Salvageable," she repeated. Her tongue moved around in her mouth as if trying to locate a hair. She looked toward the water. "What's to salvage? Life can suddenly be all peachy between you two? She's not going to change, Matt. A person is who she is. You said so yourself. Elise is out to please Elise." She sat directly beneath the overhead pot lights her father had installed in the soffits some thirty years earlier. The harsh light made her look cruel.

"Even the plane crash that night on the news. Five people die and all she has eyes for is the dog who lived."

He stared at Cass. How righteous he'd been in his certainty that Elise did everything wrong.

"You're lucky it worked out the way it did with Gracie," Cass said.

"I won't argue that."

He ran through it all in his mind. Nate? Elise was right about him. The crutches? Elise was right again. Even about saying yes to the turtle. And who the hell had found Gracie? Elise. She hadn't said anything about the pregnancy yet, but could he really blame her? He'd all but removed himself as her support system. And if she did ride pregnant because her horse was the only lifeline she had left? Almost all professional riders rode. This was dressage, not eventing.

And never once through the dark, dark days of Gracie being gone did Elise call Matt out for telling her to go get gloves. She fully bore his brunt.

"You've got to think about your daughter, Matt."

They watched as a raccoon crept along the fence line, crossed the road. Tiptoed toward Ruth's garage door to inspect for gaps. The deep, haunting call of a loon penetrated the darkness, a long and plaintive cry from across the lake.

"You're right." His daughter needed her father and her mother. She needed to be a big sister to her younger sibling. Matt extinguished his cigarette beneath his heel and stood. "That's exactly what I'm going to do." Without a glance in Cass's direction, he parted the bushes and walked home to his family.

In the darkness of Nate's old master bathroom, Elise stood at the window and watched her husband step through the bushes at the edge of Cass's overly lit property and across their driveway. When she heard the creak of the front door opening, she returned to where she'd been sleeping with their daughter.

....

CHAPTER 44

Matt stood in the doorway and watched his wife and child slumber, so still it was almost eerie. They faced each other, Gracie using her mother's arm as a pillow, Elise using her daughter's forehead as oxygen.

He stepped forward on the creaky floorboard and Elise stirred, sat up halfway.

"We tried to wait up for you, but she was out like a light. And then I guess I was too."

He crossed the room. Ran a hand over Elise's hair, then Gracie's. "Unbelievably beautiful."

"She really is."

"I meant the two of you curled up together." Matt pulled back the duvet and climbed into his side of the bed, wrapped himself around their daughter. He kissed Gracie's cheek and took Elise's fingers in his. "We never talk about the day she was born."

Elise picked at the duvet with her free hand. "I've been . . . afraid to." She hesitated, looked at him. "Actually, I guess my rationale was that, if I brought up the accident, I'd be shining a light on what happened and you might realize you despise me for it. And leave.

And how would I survive that? Besides, saying sorry didn't begin to cover what I was feeling, what I've felt ever since."

"Wow." He rolled his eyes. "If that wasn't lifted straight out of *O* magazine, I don't know what is. You're better than that."

Her face went slack with confusion for a moment, then the twitch of his lips gave him away. She laughed. *"Jerk."*

"Hey. Lightened the moment."

"Stunk up the moment."

"Anyway, that's not what I meant. About the day she was born. Even with all the rushing and the doctors and nurses, even with the fear, I remember thinking we had the most gorgeous baby ever born."

"I kind of felt sorry for other parents." Elise relaxed and let herself smile. "I still do."

"Me too. Losers." They both laughed.

After a few moments of silence, he said, "I was no better. In my own silence, I mean. I had no idea how I felt. I was having so many mixed emotions, I couldn't get past the tangle of it. It wasn't until she was kidnapped that I realized what was churning me up inside was rage—it had been there since she was born. I totally blamed you."

"Who wouldn't? I blamed myself."

"But you were just as excited about having a baby as I was. You'd have offered up your own life rather than put our baby in harm's way. The truth of it is that I'd have trusted Indie too. It was just so damned easy to point a finger at you in my head. It was lazy on my part. And wrong."

Coyotes yipped and barked across the lake. Elise reached over and pulled the duvet up over Gracie's chin.

"How did I miss it?" he added. "That we are everything?"

"We always were, Matt."

"I know. I do know that now." He threaded his fingers through hers. "I want back in. I mean, for real. Nothing hanging on from the past. Just us, now. And the future. She needs us whole, right?"

"It's not enough to want it for her. You need to want it for you."

"We're a little pack," he said. "I want to love you badly again."

Elise hesitated a second too long.

"What?" Matt went into a free fall, a full panic. Did she know about the motel? Did she follow him? Worse—follow Cass? Here, on the brink of having everything, he could wind up with nothing because of his own foolish conceit. "Say it."

"I need to know that nobody is a threat to us. I don't want to move forward thinking there's anyone who holds your admiration or . . . your desire more than I do." She looked at him coolly. "No matter how long you've known them."

"I was . . . honestly, there is no excuse," he said. "So much hit me when I got here. I was a prick, and I'll spend the rest of my life proving to you that it'll never happen again. No one compares to you. Not in any way." He touched her face. "It's Gracie and you for me. Please tell me you're in."

Elise paused. Then, "I'm in."

He leaned across their daughter to kiss his wife's forehead, temple, cheeks, jawline, mouth. To tell her he loved her. "We'll be amazing. I'll be behind you like never before."

Beneath him, Gracie grumbled in her sleep, reaching up to rub her eye with the back of a hand before turning onto her side to face her father. He lay back down and, together, he and Elise watched Gracie's rib cage rise and fall.

"I'm not going to try for Rio," Elise said.

"What?" Matt held her eyes. "No. Don't do this. I won't let you do this." His face spread into a sly smile. "You're pregnant and you think I'll disapprove. But I don't."

"You found the test."

"I found the test." He shaped her hand into a ball and wrapped his around it. "And we can do it all. This is your time in every way."

CHAPTER 45

....

For the old donkey, it was like being a princess for a day. She'd been the "nanny" for years, always watching Indie being fussed over. Poppins swelled with importance as Matt ran a brush along her sides and Warren sprayed her tail with Indie's silicone show spray. With Elise guarding Gracie from an accidental kick, the child squatted down and brushed thick, gummy hoof polish onto Poppins' tiny hooves. Elise then slid the borrowed saddle and pad along Poppins' withers to settle it on her swayed back.

Sunny, warm, and quiet, it was a great day for their daughter's first ride on Poppins. The horse shows and crowds were long gone and the grounds were all but empty at the end of August. They had their pick of which rings to ride in. Farther up the breezeway, Indie snorted in the crossties, already tacked up and impatient to get going.

"Why does Daddy have to lead me when I ride with you?" Gracie groaned. "It's not fair."

"You can hold the reins," said Elise. "He'll just keep a hand on her bridle."

"Then how am I going to gallop?"

"*You're not,*" Matt, Elise, and Warren said together, laughing.

Elise grabbed a child-sized helmet and set it on Gracie's head, snapping the strap under her chin.

"Mom, I don't think he meant to do something bad."

Every time her daughter mentioned Andy, Elise's breath still caught in her throat.

"He just didn't know how to give me back. He didn't want to go to jail. Every night he would tell me how bad jail is and say he just had to figure out what to do next. He was sorry. You shouldn't be mad at him."

Matt spoke first. "It's good that you're not angry. And we're very glad he was . . . decent to you. But it's a bit more complicated for your mom and dad."

"When he was in third grade, he got bullied. It's not fair. He had to go to the hospital."

"Let's just enjoy our ride today, pumpkin," said Elise. "Enough talk about Andy."

"Daddy, do you still have his fishing lodge T-shirt?" Matt and Elise looked at each other. "That sort of fell into the fire, Lil' G," Matt said.

It had been Elise's idea to stay at the cabin until summer's end. To whisk Gracie back to New Jersey too quickly could cement in her a fear of the area, of being away from home, and they all wanted her to come out of the summer strong. Besides, staying would give Matt the chance to finish the land severances and transfer the original lots back to their rightful owners before putting the place back on the market—this time with Phyllis Promislow. It was the year of making good.

The added bonus of remaining at the lake was having Warren stay on; Elise was reconnecting with her father, and Gracie was getting to know her only living grandparent.

For Matt, his small-town practitioner dream would take seed in New Jersey. He'd lease a small space in an old building and maintain the freedom to be close to both kids. Ronnie had mentioned that his next-door neighbor's place was about to go on the market: a small acreage with a charming stone house and a nice barn. It wasn't a bad idea, selling the house in Montclair and moving to a property where they could keep Indie and Poppins right there in the yard. Make horses more of a family affair.

"Okay, Lil' G." Matt went to lift Gracie up and onto the saddle, then stopped. Glanced at Elise and positioned the left stirrup for Gracie to climb up herself. She managed to get her foot in, hop a few times to give herself momentum, and hoist herself up until her stomach was over the saddle. Then Warren set a hand on her back and she swung her other leg over to sit tall and proud.

"Maybe one day your grandpa will get you a fat, shiny pony," Warren said. "A real beauty. Any color you want. How would you like that?"

"Dad," Elise said before Gracie could reply. She set a hand on Poppins' neck and arched her brows at his big, dreamy promises.

Warren nodded. Grinned sadly. "There I go again?"

"We all slip up once in a while."

Her own words sat with her. All the damning she was guilty of over the years. All that wasted time. She never would have believed she'd forgive her father. Though she wasn't entirely sure forgiveness born of freshly discovered bitterness was the best absolution.

She'd forced her mother from her thoughts since finding Gracie.

Matt started to lead Gracie and Poppins along the aisle and into the sun. Elise followed behind, leading Indie. Elise was thrilled Gracie was finally willing to ride. It would remove some mobility issues. Build her confidence, because the playing field would be leveled. And Poppins was an old pro from her Santorini days.

Out in the sunshine, Elise pulled down her stirrups and led her towering horse over to a wooden mounting block, positioning him alongside it and throwing the reins over his head.

Squinting, Matt looked back at Elise. "Which ring do you want us in?"

Elise stepped up onto the block, holding reins and the pommel of the saddle in one hand, the cantle in the rear in the other, and started to slide a booted foot into the stirrup. There, she stopped.

"Hon? Do you want the big ring or the smaller? They're both empty."

She looked at the saddle, the horse's shiny black mane. Reached over to rub his neck.

Warren came out of the aisle, banging brushes together to clean them. "You okay, Lisey? You need a leg up?"

She looked at her father, earnest and helpful, scrubbing every last bit of dust from the brushes. At her husband, helping Gracie shorten her reins. And her daughter, bouncing in her saddle, willing the old burro to take off.

"Lisey?"

She stepped off the mounting block. Handed Indie's reins to her father. "Would you mind taking off his tack? I think I'd like to help Matt." She walked over to her husband and daughter. *Let Gracie be the star of this show*, she didn't say. She tapped the girl's foot. "You know what I just realized, sweetness? You haven't been sucking your thumb."

The girl looked surprised. "Oh. Yeah!"

Elise reached into her pocket, sorted through a few bills, and handed her daughter a fifty. "A deal is a deal." She searched her daughter's clothing for a safe place to put it and settled on the used paddock boots they'd bought her in town. Elise took hold of the bridle on the other side and started to lead the donkey. "Let's go, guys."

Matt looked at her, then at Warren leading Indie back to his stall.

"What's going on?"

Another spray of bubbles fluttered in her belly. She couldn't do it. Couldn't get on a horse. Not until this baby was born—full-term and safe.

"Elise?" Matt jogged to catch up. "What are you doing?"

Her dream of going to the Rio Games was no more.

Her free hand went to her belly. "What feels right." She smiled to herself as they led donkey and rider to the small ring. Tokyo would be a glorious place to visit in summer.

CHAPTER 46

....

The sun was only a suggestion, in deep rose and tangerine and violet, growing ever more adamant above the pines. The driveway was still grainy with darkness and the definitive bite of summer's end.

Gravel crunched beneath their feet as Warren gave Elise a hearty hug, kissed the top of her head, his hands weighty and solid on her shoulders. Matt and Gracie were still asleep, having said their goodbyes the night before. Behind him, Warren's battered black Civic was packed, engine running, Gunner strapped awkwardly into the passenger seat.

"I don't even know how to thank you. Especially for the stuffed dog."

She laughed. "Anything to prevent you from buying another Big-Mouth Billy."

He gazed at her, his lashless eyes rimmed with pink, deep lines fanning out as he smiled. "And . . . for forgiving an old man his lifetime of bad choices. Keep giving me a chance to make some good memories with you and your kid. Kids."

"You're officially invited to carve the turkey this Thanksgiving in New Jersey. With Chloe."

He gave her shoulders a squeeze and set himself in motion. Climbed into the car. Started the engine and rolled down the window, leaning an elbow outside. "I'm not a man who's made a big success of his life. Not that I need to tell anyone that; it's plain to see. I was a self-centered ass who forced his family to bend to his fantasies and then punished them for not becoming what I imagined." He squinted up at her. "But I've learned a thing or two along the way, and one of them is to speak up about things that aren't so easy to talk about." He held out his hand and Elise took it. "When a person reaches that low point like your mother did— and I acknowledge my own hand in helping her get there—it's not cruelty or selfishness or lack of caring that drives them. All they have is their own pain. You can't judge them on anything else."

A crow cawed from the towering pine beside Ruth Urquhart's house, then took flight, leaving the treetop swaying in its wake.

"Why are you telling me this now?"

"Just in case you need to hear it." He squeezed her fingertips and blew his daughter a kiss, then put the car in gear.

Elise watched her father's Civic make its way down the driveway and turn onto Seldom Seen Road, snake its way around the bend and disappear. It wasn't until the sound of the engine could no longer be heard, when the birds began to stir and chirp about the day, that Elise turned to go back inside.

An hour later, the trunk and doors were open wide while Elise and a clean-shaven Matt went in and out of the cabin to cram bags and suitcases into Nate's Range Rover. Matt's old BMW had finally died and the Rover seemed more practical for their growing family. Elise's car was to be driven back to New Jersey by a vehicle-moving service.

Elise passed Matt with a bag of clean laundry. When he blocked her way, she poked him in the side. Laughed.

She caught a whiff of ash in the air from last night's bonfire by the lake, and her stomach lurched. By her second trimester with Gracie, the nausea had abated. Not this time. She'd read that prolonged nausea could mean you were carrying the opposite sex from your first child, but she and Matt wanted it be a surprise. She leaned against the porch railing a moment. Matt moved past now with luggage. "You good?"

"I'm great."

Gracie came out the front door wearing a BIG SIS T-shirt she'd made herself with a fat Sharpie. In one hand was a sand pail stuffed with her tiny animals. Using the railing, she hopped awkwardly down the stairs. She wedged the pail between packed suitcases and her old high chair in the back seat, then buckled herself in beside them.

Elise climbed into the passenger seat. Matt trudged out of the house again to load another bag into the back, jostling the car and making Elise's stomach flip. She put a hand on her belly. "The thought of a long car ride is a bit daunting." She looked back at Matt. "Are there any towels left unpacked—just in case?"

"None."

"I'll go borrow one from Cass," Elise said. She hurried through the bushes to the front of the cabin and knocked on the screen door. "Cass?"

"Come in," Cass called. "I'm just getting out of the shower. Be right down."

Inside, the kitchen smelled like baking. Sure enough, there were banana muffins on a plate by the stove. "Do you have an old towel we can borrow? In case, with the car ride, I lose my breakfast."

"I was the same way with Riv. Nonstop nausea. Try the laundry basket by the back door," Cass said. "Take any one of those. They're all old. But clean."

Elise walked across the back room, noting the half-finished puzzle on the table and a well-loved copy of Margaret Atwood's *The Blind Assassin* propped open on the big leather armchair by the window. A life being well lived was what the room felt like.

As she pulled a folded towel from the basket, a stack of photos on an end table caught her eye. Specifically, her husband's smiling face. She took the stack and flipped through it. Photo after photo of Matt in and around Cass's cabin, on their back porch. The look in Matt's eyes was one of sadness. Of a lifetime of memories. Of love.

The last photo stopped her breath.

She'd suspected, but hadn't known. Until now.

"Don't you guys leave till I come say goodbye, okay?" Cass called down. "Promise?"

Heart hammering, Elise stared down at her still-bearded husband, asleep. Matt's beautiful head was resting on a pillow covered in tiny pink florets. Pulled to his chin, a red tartan duvet.

Slowly, carefully, Elise replaced the stack of photos, but took the one of Matt sleeping and grabbed a towel and threw it over her shoulder. On the way back to the car, she folded the photo into quarters and slipped it into her pocket.

Matt was in the driver's seat, hand shielding his eyes as he watched his wife cross the driveway with a towel and get into the Rover. The engine was running. "Wasn't she there?"

"House was empty." Elise avoided his gaze, climbing in and tucking the towel down by her feet. "Let's motor, what do you guys say?"

They backed out of the driveway and onto the dirt road where the upended canoe used to sit. It now lay shattered at the dump. Matt and Gracie waved goodbye to the big Sorenson shield on the cabin's face, and the car pulled away. They passed all the gracious homes, the trees, the inns. They turned right onto Saranac, then sped by the heavy pines that bordered Old Military Road. They passed the Olympic Training Center, the Promislow house, and Old John Brown Road.

Elise pushed her hair behind her ears and studied her husband as he fiddled with the car radio. Her clean-faced, freshly devoted husband. His demeanor so relaxed now; the man was completely at peace with himself, his family. He glanced her way. On his lips, a gentle smile as he tucked her hand into a ball and wrapped his fingers around it in the way she loved best.

"You guys," Gracie said to her menagerie in a bucket, the animals' heads tilted every which way as if desperate for answers they knew better than to hope for, "are going to learn to hug each other. Because I am going back to school and will be very busy. Plus, I have a donkey named Poppins . . ."

Here they were, driving home together—a family. A growing family.

"And when my sister is born, you have to stay in my room so she doesn't choke on any of you. If it's a brother"—Gracie paused to groan—"he'll probably set you on fire and stuff."

Matt stifled a chuckle.

Elise thought back to her conversation with Laurel on the plane. About forgiveness. To forgive Andy, no matter how tough his childhood, was not only irresponsible—and impossible as Gracie's parents—but catastrophically complacent. To look at it any other way was nearly as abhorrent as the offence itself.

Elise's eyes traveled the curve of the lips Cass had kissed. The jawline she'd caressed. The thick silver hair she'd grabbed hold of while Elise's husband made her moan.

Matt had betrayed her.

"I can't be the boss of you furry little weirdos forever," Gracie mock scolded.

Elise turned to the window and let the scenery go by in a blur. Matt had raised their daughter well in Elise's absences. He'd been a good father, a patient and insanely supportive husband. And he genuinely wanted this beautiful growing family.

Matt squeezed her fist. "You good?"

Her father's words came back to her. *When a person reaches that low point . . . All they have is their own pain. You can't judge them on anything else.*

She thought of her mother's newly bare face. Rosamunde needed to get from agony to relief. And a dirty Tercel with the engine running was the only path she saw.

"E?"

As for Matt, he'd lived through a war zone this summer; they both had. Perhaps, just this once, she could suspend judgment and look to the future.

But just this once.

For herself? Whether she forgave herself for her decision that morning in Ronnie's arena, she'd realized, was and always would be immaterial. What she thought didn't matter. One day, when her daughter was old enough, Elise would tell her exactly what had happened. Explain that she would spin the world backward if it meant she could undo that moment. And hope that Gracie had it in her heart to forgive her mother's choice.

"Babe?" said Matt, a hint of concern in his voice. "Still love me badly?"

"I do." She pulled up their fists to kiss his hand. "And madly." *And, for a while*, she thought, *a little bit sadly*.

This satisfied him. He released her fingers and maneuvered into the fast lane. The car sped south on 73, toward the pretty little twists and bends of the next village and, beyond that, the long stretch home, with Gracie humming contentedly in the back seat.

Acknowledgments

....

The people of Lake Placid inspired and informed many scenes in this novel. In particular, Jennifer V. Fleishman of New York State Police Troop B, and the staffs at Lake Placid Lodge and The Bookstore Plus—the bookshop I imagined while writing Cass's book launch.

This story wouldn't have been possible without the clarity, encouragement, and advice of Daniel Lazar, my sassy and beloved literary agent at Writers House, and Jennifer Lambert, my brilliant and dedicated editor at HarperCollins in Canada. The two of you dared me to get ever more brave with this story. To the inimitable Jackie Cantor at Simon & Schuster in New York for not only giving the book a home in the U.S. but also bringing a swell of insight and clarity that truly made the novel come to life. Appreciation to the fabulous Victoria Doherty-Munro at Writers House, and, always, to the elegant and wise Iris Tupholme at HarperCollins Canada. To Allison McCabe, editor extraordinaire, for finding this story's spine. Thanks to Sue Sumeraj for sharp-eyed copyedits, and Natalie Meditsky, production editor, for keeping us all on track.

Thank you to Belinda Trussell, two-time Olympian on the Canadian Equestrian Team. That you squeezed me in between training, competing, and precious family time was incredibly generous. To Barbara Fogler for too many reasons to mention, but in particular for splaying open your life with horses. Barbara Sinclair for competition details direct from the sand ring in Wellington, Florida. Nicholas Fyffe for U.S. Olympic qualifying advice from the saddle. The Hartles of the Creemore Equestrian Centre. Marcia, you are an excellent coach. Jennifer Kolari, Harriet Goodman, Cassandra Rodgers, and Kassie Evashevski for early reads. Liliana Reyes, Deborah Jiang-Stein, Timothy Fitzpatrick, Pamela MacKinnon, Sydney Cameron, and Geta Winberg for endless patience and support. John Truby for so much story wisdom. The generous and exquisite Caroline Leavitt for the book's first endorsement. To Dr. Rory Windrim for facts about high-risk labor and brain injuries. Dr. Tony Hanbridge for referring.

The Angel Ladies, Deb and Jean, in Niagara-on-the-Lake, for kindness and counsel when life went off track. Amy MacKinnon in Boston for breathing life into me, for knowing exactly what I needed to hear. Amy's wisdom and words inspired the scene with Elise and Dr. Jennifer Upton in the medical clinic and changed my life. Gail Konop in Madison, Wisconsin for strength, grit, and laughter. You are a gift, Cowgirl.

To my mother, Patricia Gill, and my father, Lachlan Mackinnon Bleackley II, for instilling in me a love of books from day one and forever telling me I could accomplish anything. Peter Auvinen for a sharp legal eye and knowing just the right moment to knock on the door again.

Finally, most of all, to my sons, Max and Lucas. I cannot believe what incredible young men you've become and what you've both accomplished already. Go after what you want, my boys. Be brave. It's all out there waiting for you.